P9-AFW-915

History Became A Lie

History Became A Lie

ANOTHER DICK SWEPT M.D.
MEDICAL-ESPIONAGE THRILLER

David B. Rosenfield

Library of Congress Number: 2004098546
ISBN: Hardcover 1-4134-7495-0
Softcover 1-4134-8127-2

This is a work of fiction. Names, characters, places and incidents either are the product of the author's imagination or are used fictitiously, and any resemblance to any actual persons, living or dead, events, or locales is entirely coincidental.

This book was printed in the United States of America.

To order additional copies of this book, contact:
Xlibris Corporation
1-888-795-4274
www.Xlibris.com
Orders@Xlibris.com

27311

Contents

DEDICATED TO MARIA AND OUR CHILDREN

DYLAN MILTON AND LILLIAN IRIS

Joshua fought the battle of Jericho and history became a lie.

—Bob Dylan (1941-)

The following events occur within a period of three months.

Acknowledgment

This is the second *Dick Swept* novel. The first, *Dick Swept, M.D., Tomorrow the World,* has been well received and is being made into a full-length motion picture. In *History Became a Lie,* Swept continues to face the dilemmas of caring for patients, trying to discover causes of disease, and fight those who are evil. Within this context, Swept has now found Iraqi weapons of mass destruction, the existence of which continues to be questioned and is an increasingly heated topic of political debate. Swept, clever, cunning, and possessing inner resources to solve problems, seeks to save the world from those who crave power and lack concern for fellow human beings.

Joan Appel's phenomenal copyediting skills have proven invaluable. I thank Joan not only for her critical input but also for her constant smile. I thank W. Carr Burgoyne for his confidence and optimism. Ms. Dalia Angel kindly provided technical assistance. James B. Rose, M.D. permitted us to photograph his antique model of the human brain.

I extend special thanks to Ron Eisenberg, president of ETD/The News Group, and his colleague, Ken Kayes, for their unwavering support and suggestions. Ron and Ken are true friends, and I thank them very much.

There are several other individuals who have been very helpful, both with their criticisms and insights. I thank you all.

Lastly, I extend eternal gratitude to my wife, Maria, who understands the world of fiction and the fiction of the world.

David B. Rosenfield, M.D.
Houston, Texas

Chapter One

EDINBURGH, SCOTLAND

Jeremiah MacGregor was enjoying the damp, somewhat chilly weather in his native Edinburgh. Prior to this day, he was an unknown. He drove his cab, carrying passengers to sundry destinations, including the airport, train and bus stations, hotels, and, of course, the castle. But today was different. Today, he would make his statement to the world.

At six feet two inches, handsome and muscular, Jeremiah would appear to an outsider as happy and self-assured. His short hair, clear complexion, and boyish face seemed well coordinated; everything fits. His body was well proportioned; he was in good health, intelligent, and well-read. However, he had never been content. Jeremiah seldom spoke of his discontent and, for all intents and purposes, seldom spoke much about anything.

Although he never talked much, largely due to his embarrassing stutter, Jeremiah thought a lot, a whole lot.

That was why today was so important. Today, he would make his statement. Today, the world would know. Today, he would become famous in his own right. The only problem was no one would know he was the culprit.

The *Scotsman* and *Edinburgh News* openly published the name and activities of the sexual predator recently released from prison. Everyone knew who *he* was. And certainly, everyone knew about al-Qaeda. Jeremiah's activities, although less derelict, were just as predatory. Believing that his cause was noble, it bothered him that no one would know his responsibility for the acts to follow. Regardless, Jeremiah was nothing but secure in his quest.

Earlier, when Jeremiah carefully filled and stored several large containers of petrol in a local garage, he thought carefully and thoroughly about his plan. It was his first plan, his first attempt. For some reason, he kept thinking about Marcel Proust, who constantly bemoaned his asthma, bellyaching that most people never ponder the joy of breathing without difficulty, a pleasure known only to nonasthmatics. Proust wrote about how asthmatics taste that problem daily, seldom knowing the pleasure of easy breathing. MacGregor found it unfortunate that Proust was not a stutterer. Otherwise, the famous French writer would have shined a light on the fate of those who cannot speak without struggling to achieve fluent speech, unlike those who talk without effort. Stuttering had produced ridicule and pain for Jeremiah. Were it not for his stutter, he believed he would be perfect.

So today was different. Jeremiah had orchestrated his plan from a strategic and a tactical standpoint several times. Yes, today was the day.

Jeremiah arrived at work early in the morning, as he always did. He struggled in his morning salutation to the receptionist at the entrance to the taxi pool. "G-G-Good morning, I-I-Iris."

Iris, a pleasant middle-aged woman who had seen and known too much about too many men for too long, had long felt at ease with her interactions with Jeremiah. He was shy, spoke little, and bothered no one. Iris's interactions with Jeremiah were not complicated, and she liked it that way.

"Good morning, Jeremiah. Hope you have a good day." Her matronly smile was always a welcome ingredient in Jeremiah's morning. He liked Iris.

"Thhh—anks," Jeremiah stumbled and went to his cab.

Jeremiah signed his docket, entered his taxi, and rehearsed his plan. He drove a short distance, parked off Canongate Street, and then walked back to the pool, approaching Iris.

"Yes, Jeremiah. Any problems?"

"M-M-M-My cab isn't working right. I-I-I drove down C-Canongate but it kept s-s-stalling. Now, I-I c-can't get the engine to turn over. It-It st-starts but then stops. C-Can I get a new c-c-c-cab?"

Smiling, Iris reached behind her, removed a set of keys from the board, jotted down the number on the attached tag, and handed Jeremiah the keys. "What's the address of the cab?"

Jeremiah gave a halfhearted smile, leaned over, and, obviously avoiding the task of speaking, wrote the name of the cross street. Iris smiled, sympathetically acknowledging his pain, and Jeremiah entered the alternate vehicle. He then drove to the garage where he had stored the petrol, walked the two blocks back to his first taxi, still parked off Canongate, and drove that car to the garage as well. He had about thirty or forty minutes before the wrecker appeared, looking for the supposedly disabled cab.

Jeremiah was not an expert in making bombs but had acquired considerable information from articles he read about terrorists. He knew that fertilizer could be used as a makeshift weapon but that petrochemicals also had potential. Jeremiah opted for the flammable gasoline and nails.

Jeremiah loaded the first taxi with twenty-two containers of petrol, carefully placing them throughout the car, including the backseat and trunk. He inserted hundreds of small plastic bags filled with nails, any place they would fit. Yesterday, he carefully confirmed that the duct tape covered all container caps. There could be no leakage, given the flammable nature of gasoline. Then, Jeremiah rigged his waterproof fuse, stuffing it into a series of switchback PVC pipes, placed putty at one end, filled the pipe with water, and inserted putty into the other end, allowing a small fuse to exit. He put on his large hat, pulling it down to his brow, a pair of sunglasses, and placed the headphones around his neck. In short time, he was on King's Stables Road and turned left at the Esplanade.

MacGregor parked as close to the castle as he could, without disobeying traffic signs. He was not worried about the guards, since most of them were inept, spending the majority of their time trying to impress female tourists. He was, however, worried that the area might soon reek of petrol, which it did not. Jeremiah surreptitiously arranged the fuse, stood outside his cab as if waiting for an errant customer, then pretended to have a call on his cell phone, prompting him to walk a short distance, feigning difficulty hearing, searching for better reception.

Slowly, certain that he detected no fumes, Jeremiah returned and kneeled on the cobblestone opposite a cluster of loud-speaking German tourists, lit the fuse, and felt a shiver as the incendiary information entered the water-filled tubes. Then, Jeremiah went quietly on his way, walking toward the West Princess Street Gardens, listening to music on his headphones, feeling good.

Jeremiah, enjoying his feeling of power, listened to Beethoven's *The Eroica,* a symphony composed in honor of Napoleon, whom the composer believed would change Europe forever, making it a better place. Jeremiah knew how disappointed Beethoven had been that Napoleon, like all politicians, was concerned only for himself.

MacGregor loved *The Eroica,* as well as most of Beethoven's later pieces, especially the Ninth Symphony. Beethoven used loud French horns, just as Jeremiah MacGregor would soon make loud noises of his own. MacGregor liked the fact Beethoven added loud music to his later pieces, perhaps due to his increasing loss of hearing. Jeremiah was pleased Beethoven had problems with hearing. Hearing was important for speech.

Jeremiah had not given much thought to his soon-to-be victims. He had no idea who might die or become disabled. He was not even certain the explosion would occur, since this was his first bomb. All MacGregor cared about was that an explosion did occur, providing him the opportunity to send his letter to the press.

When the blast sounded, the noise was not a thunderous roar but, instead, a series of loud, irregular, almost muffled explosions, as the car burst into flames, shedding its metallic skin like the sun sheds its glow, in perfect form and dazzling yellow. Metal objects (the nails) flew short distances in all directions, breaking windows and occasionally ripping flesh. A filthy smoke permeated the air as pandemonium broke out among the small group of tourists. A young woman wearing a Canadian maple leaf T-shirt was crying, with black soot across her forehead. Another woman ran past her, screaming that people were dead.

"Wh-Wh-What happened?" Jeremiah said to some people running. "Wh-Wh-What was that noise?"

A young woman wearing a University of Michigan sweatshirt, bleeding from her right shoulder, cried, "I don't know. Something blew up. It must be terrorists."

A young man, running and out of breath, joined in, "The world's gone crazy. Someone must have tried to blow up the castle."

Several people were running, a few huddling over children. Jeremiah feigned his bewilderment and now, somehow, had lost the sense of power, the feeling of doing something of worth, something of merit. He had wanted more.

From his perspective in the gardens, he had witnessed the explosion and the fire, but he could see only little physical damage to the castle, primarily blackening of portions of an outer wall. Within a few minutes, the ambulances arrived. Jeremiah learned from the crowd that four people, two Germans and two Americans, had been killed. "They even killed a dog and burned a baby's face," he heard someone say.

The result of the whole scheme was possibly anticlimactic. Here was Jeremiah MacGregor, listening to Beethoven, smudging his beloved castle, killing four people, hurting a baby, and annihilating a dog. Jeremiah felt no shame and had no guilt but did feel disappointment. He had been prepared for death and destruction and would not have been perturbed by a greater loss of life. But now, he felt empty, wondering whether he had accomplished anything worthy of his careful planning.

No matter, he thought. The local papers, as well as the *Wall Street Journal* and the *International Herald Tribune*, would soon have his unsigned statement. He had to get back to the second cab parked in the garage.

Walking past Morrison Street and West Port Terrace, MacGregor entered the garage, changed clothes, dumped his garments into a plastic bag, opened the driver's door of the remaining taxi, drove a short distance, and discarded his debris into a trash receptacle. Then, Jeremiah scurried passengers, entering several false entries in his logbook. He knew the police would identify the burned cab near the castle as his, and he mentally rehearsed his reply that the cab had malfunctioned, as he had told the receptionist, and he had no idea what had subsequently happened.

*   *   *

Chapter Two

WASHINGTON, D.C.

Spring in Washington, D.C. has a quasi-mystic quality. Cherry blossoms beautify the parks, and although everyone in the capital knows things are pretty, most feel the beauty is counterlevered against the toughness and meanness of Washington politics. Everything in Washington is politics, and everything in Washington politics is money. For the neurologist Dick Swept, one year out of CIA training, it felt good to jog along his favorite trail in Rock Creek Park.

Swept frequently jogged, relaxing from his medical research at the CIA. Currently, he investigated the biochemistry of memory systems, focusing on Alzheimer's disease. Swept recognized, as did many of his superiors at the CIA, that understanding how brain cells process memory in normal people and patients afflicted with Alzheimer's disease supplied information on how brain cells function. Were the CIA to understand how brain cells function and what made them work better or less well, the agency could develop chemicals to obtain information from uncooperative terrorists, learn how to counteract elements of bioterrorism, and, of course, help demented patients.

Swept had frequently discussed with his CIA colleagues the importance of investigating Alzheimer's disease. "Alzheimer's affects two percent of the population in industrialized countries, and the risk of AD, as we scientists call it, dramatically increases beyond age seventy. For several reasons, the number of new cases will increase threefold over the next fifty years."

"True," many replied. "But what does that have to do with Central Intelligence, with the agency? Why not just leave the research up to the National Institutes of Health and the medical schools?"

Repeatedly, Swept's response was the same. "First, Major Cervantes, who has been at the agency forever, wanted me to come and promised I could investigate Alzheimer's disease. The reason he wanted me on board is because this work is so important. It's not only important for the patients but helps provide information on chemical agents affecting brain function, positively and negatively. This can help fight terrorists, bioterrorism, and a lot of other chemical agents. As for the medical schools and the NIH, let them do what they want. There's no harm in another lab investigating Alzheimer's, certainly one with an overlapping concern for the nation's safety."

More than once, Swept discussed the neurochemistry of the brain. He often focused on beta amyloid, a chemical that accumulates within brain cells of AD patients. "When too much beta amyloid is present, there is disruption of another chemical, glutamine, a neurotransmitter in the brain. "Glutamine," Swept explained to his seemingly sometimes bored CIA operatives and administrators, "is necessary for brain cells to communicate with one another. Further, glutamine activates certain receptors in the brain, known as NMDA receptors. By exciting these receptors, the brain engages in learning and memory. If the glutamine cannot function properly, problems with memory occur."

Time and again, when Swept discussed his neurology research at the CIA, members in the audience tried not to yawn, but their facial appearance portrayed their disinterest. Swept knew that many people in the agency had no interest in his research, yet they wanted him to pursue his scientific endeavors. Dick Swept knew the real reason.

* * *

Eighteen months ago, while at the Texas College of Medicine, in Houston, before relocating to Washington, D.C., to work for the CIA, Dr. Richard Michael Swept practiced clinical neurology and also had a wet lab, investigating a chemical similar to growth hormone. That chemical activated NMDA receptors and affected memory. It was his work with interactions of growth hormone and memory that thrust Swept into the bulwark of a plan involving Russian ex-KGB agents, including a Chechen, thwarting their attempt literally to take over the world. Swept found himself in the middle of international espionage and, somehow, survived. Now, the physician-scientist-turned-spy worked for the Central Intelligence Agency.

Swept's main goal as a neurologist was to help Alzheimer patients. The government supposedly shared his concerns, but not out of direct empathy for those stricken with Alzheimer's disease. The Central Intelligence Agency was embarrassed and concerned that the United States had briefly been outdistanced by Pi-Two, the ex-KGB organization Swept had thwarted, and the United States government did not want that to happen again. They wanted to stay current in this area and offered Swept a position allowing him to see patients and to pursue his research. Underlying all this, Swept recognized that the real issue for the government was their focus on power.

* * *

Swept's research was going well, but the hard work and late hours were stressful. Jogging was a great way to relax. Besides, it gave him time to think what to do about his girlfriend, Ricki Hardson, who wanted to get married. Swept did not.

As Swept jogged, he thought about his training at the CIA. Although he was a neurologist and his training was primarily medical, he had learned certain military skills when he had previously been in the army reserves, assigned to Special Forces. In the army, Swept's superiors discovered he was a crack shot, quick to learn, and agile on his feet.

Now, at the CIA, Swept expanded these skills. Although he was a physician-scientist who had entered the CIA through the back door, he welcomed this opportunity to test himself, which the courses all provided. He learned about shadow operations, intelligence, counterintelligence, tactical equipment and conversions. He became skilled with the Barrett M82A1 semiautomatic rifle, various machine guns, explosive devices, and pistols, ranging from the Glock to the Unertl 1911 semiautomatic, single-action pistol. Swept studied different types of U.S. military weapons, as well as weapons from other countries and various insurgent groups.

Soon, Swept could disassemble and reconstruct any gun with his eyes closed. He scored the highest grade in high explosives, munitions, and counterintelligence courses. He ran the mile under five minutes thirty seconds, performed thirty overhand and underhand pull ups, and learned how to survive in the worst of circumstances, ranging from being taken hostage to attacks from an angry mob.

Swept fit well into the CIA structure, studying his manuals with diligence, exercising hard, and learning the skills of clandestine operations.

Swept's only problem in the agency, initially, was that of jealousy. Many CIA colleagues begrudged his higher educational status as a physician and, even more, his being a brain specialist. With time, everyone appreciated that Swept was committed to everything he did, and he did everything well. He worked hard, was responsible, and, in short time, made many friends within the agency.

In all instances, Dr. Richard Michael Swept excelled in his training at the CIA. The six-foot-tall neurologist seemed sedate, his youthful and somewhat angular face and muscular body ensnaring many women, while his often taciturn demeanor and even-handed manner served as a barometer of an internal lethality that the CIA was quick to appreciate. As for women, Swept continued to remain monogamous with his current lover, Ricki Hardson. He knew that an argument about marriage was forthcoming, and he tried to remove that issue from his thoughts as he jogged through the park.

Swept ran past some people peacefully protesting research in animals. He snickered to himself, wondering what would happen to research in AIDS if animal research came to a halt or how people could take vaccines without testing them for safety in animals As he snickered to himself, he again recognized his growing cynicism.

Swept believed that all religions want their brethren to thank God each morning when they wake up, praising God they have the gift of another day. He had long cherished the joy of being alive but increasingly detected within himself this expanding cynicism. Within the matrix of these feelings, there was a part of Dick Swept that ached to be more active in the fight against evil, however it was defined.

Swept believed the American system, a constitutional republic essentially created by James Madison and promulgated to nonbelievers through the *Federalist Papers*, was a system that mediated conflict well. It was not always easy to follow the rules, making the country a "nation of laws, not of men," but Swept always tried to do his best as an individual citizen. Now, here he was, working for the Central Intelligence Agency, ready to fight the bad guys, simultaneously working in his laboratory on NMDA receptors and glutamine, and occasionally seeing patients at the National Institutes of Health. He was about as overextended as a man could be.

Swept spent most of his time in the laboratory, participated and won most of the activities at the firing range and martial arts contests, and always enjoyed jogging. Next to the water, Swept saw the man who was present daily, sitting in his wheelchair, reading the *Wall Street Journal*. Swept had read that paper earlier in the day, before his three-times-a-week three-mile run. There, next to an Op-Ed piece on the importance of finding the "Weapons of Mass Destruction," an editorial mentioned a botched-up explosion outside the Edinburgh Castle. The article commented that the United States must be winning the war on terrorism, given the inefficiency of this latest explosion. Four people were dead, but the toll could have been higher and the damage more extensive.

Swept could see that the man in the wheelchair had the *Journal* open to the editorial page. He had powerful arms, contrasting to trousers hanging loosely over surely atrophied legs.

The man was sitting in his wheelchair every time Swept ran. Swept noticed him in the mornings, when he usually ran, but also in the evenings, should he decide to run at a later hour. Whenever Swept drove past the park, the man was there. It seemed all the man did was sit in his wheelchair and watch joggers and other people playing in the park.

Swept wondered what might be the man's problem. What caused his loss of leg function? Swept could not know that years ago, as an adolescent, the man was driving his parents' sporty BMW without parental permission and, attempting to avoid hitting a dog, slammed into a fence, becoming paraplegic.

The subsequent investigation anecdotally noted the fence was erected to keep children out of a municipal pool, but the pool had not been used for years due to mechanical problems with the water circulation pump. The municipality had decided not to repair the pump, so the pool remained empty. The fence protected the pool from the children. Nothing protected the BMW from the fence.

* * *

Swept completed his jogging and drove his Bentley Continental GT coupe to his laboratory at CIA, showering in the agency's facilities to freshen himself. He politely smiled to one of the personal trainers, a beautiful woman who always tried to engage him in conversation. He returned to the office and read through several memoranda that lay atop his desk. All of the communications pertained to the possible presence of weapons of mass destruction. The reports covered what types of WMD might exist, how to construct the WMD, how to transport them and, in particular, whether Iraq had WMD prior to the American-led invasion.

* * *

Chapter Three

BUCHAREST, ROMANIA

Friends called him "Stoli," after the most famous possession Russia had to offer Romania, their famed Stolichnaya vodka. Stoli was supposedly part of a shipment of orphans to Sinaia, not far from Bucharest. Sinaia, pronounced *sih-NIE-uh,* wedged into the Prahova Valley and surrounded by the beautiful Bucegi Mountains, is a celebrated Romanian alpine resort that achieved fame in the 1880s as a retreat for the Romanian royal family. The spectacular hiking trails and beautiful palaces attracted many tourists, and until the recent Romanian moratorium on adoptions, many people had visited the local Sinaia Orphanage, hoping to take home a baby.

It was at this facility that Stoli, good-looking and quick-witted, learned to interact with people from all over the world. It was there he thought about his background, his heritage, his DNA.

Stoli was surprised, as were his peers and teachers, at the ease with which he mastered languages, learning various dialects possessed only by native speakers. He worked as a local tour guide, jokingly telling attractive females how to pronounce the name of his city, and sometimes scoring sexually with them in the evenings.

Fluent and at ease in all four Romanian dialects, especially Daco-Romanian, Stoli could converse with anyone in his country. He also spoke French and English, as did many Romanians, the popular German and Hungarian languages, and was fluent in Russian, a language most Romanians disliked due to their distaste for the former Soviet Union.

Stoli's knack for languages made him a valuable asset to the orphanage. The staff frequently needed someone to translate for foreign visitors, and these visitors had money! Many administrators at the orphanage had considerable financial needs, and with not-so-clandestine cooperation from the government, despite the recent 1991 constitution, there were many profitable under-the-table deals. Stoli's knowledge of these deals soured his views on public decency, scaffolding his belief system in doing things that benefited him.

Stoli's relationship with the orphanage was bizarre. Often, Stoli had inquired, "I want to know about my parents. Who were they? Where were they from?"

Always, the answer was the same: "We don't know. All we know is the date and time of your arrival. That's the only information we have."

On several occasions, Stoli sneaked into the files pertaining to his adoption. He was aware that his dossier was much thinner than for the other children. On one such occasion, Stoli found official orphanage correspondence dated close to the time of his arrival. The letter made reference to a child who was one of triplets, from Moscow. All the other children who arrived during the time of his arrival had parental or geographic history that failed to mention Moscow or triplets. Thus began his belief that he was originally from Moscow and one of triplets. Based upon this meager information and occasional misdirected conversation with orphanage administrators, as well as his own desire to have biological siblings, Stoli affirmed his belief that he was one of the triplets and that his family was from Moscow.

Stoli had no complaints about the orphanage. They had cared well for him, but he still wanted to know more about his birth parents. He also had a lingering suspicion that his not being adopted as an older child related to his linguistic skills, providing a financial asset for the orphanage.

Long ago, as an adolescent, Stoli had planned one day to access government documents pertaining to his adoption. However, this plan became complicated by the destruction of all Romanian orphanages' papers during the 1989 revolution, when the dreaded *Securitate*, the secret police, arrested a popular Hungarian priest, which led to a revolt. In December, clashes with Bucharest security forces erupted into rioting, resulting in the trial and public execution of the dictator Nicolas Ceasescu and his wife. While huge numbers of people watched the televised Christmas Day trial and execution, Stoli bemoaned the destruction of Russian documents, including records of the orphans' parentage.

Bit by bit, over the years, Stoli gleaned more information about himself, reinforcing his belief that he was born in Russia and that his mother gave birth to triplets, one dying during infancy, another reared in Russia, and the third, Stoli, for unknown reasons was shipped to the orphanage in Romania.

Stoli believed this, although he recognized that the scenario was unlikely. Under the former Soviet system, before the USSR dissolved, the Russian Ministry of Education processed all adoptions. Time and again, Russian and Romanian authorities told Stoli there was no possibility a Russian orphan could be shipped to Romania. Regardless, Stoli overheard too many conversations in the orphanage and had his many suspicions. He steadfastly believed he was pure Russian and, for some reason, was shipped to the Romanian orphanage.

Probably, Stoli reasoned, his family lacked money or political connections or both and the Soviet communist system forced his parents to send little Stoli to Romania. He hoped one day to meet his siblings. Until then, all he could do was work with tourists, hope for good tips, and now and then receive some of his favorite cigarettes, Sobranies.

Unlike many people in the world, but similar to others, Stoli had no desire to decrease his intake of cigarettes. Sobranies provided pleasure, and it was pleasure that kept him going. If he died or became ill, so be it. All life ended in death. Now and then, he would cogitate on being a pulmonary cripple, but those thoughts were only flickers.

Inhaling his Sobranie, Stoli brushed back his hair and went to join his tour group at the *Castelul Peleş*, the Peles Castle. Built in 1883, under the demanding eye of Carol I, king of the newly independent Romania, the castle boasts opulence and exquisite detail. Each room has its own unique décor, whether German Baroque, Italian, Moorish, or Turkish. Stoli knew all the styles and gladly conversed with attractive female tourists who loitered after the tour ended. Stoli was a very knowledgeable man.

* * *

Chapter Four

ESCAPE FROM MOLDOVA

Russia imprisoned Jokhar Gantemirov following what few could call a fair or open trial. He had no idea where he was incarcerated. There were no fellow inmates, visitors were not permitted, and Gantemirov received no newspapers. Were it not for his heart pumping and his pulmonary tissue exchanging oxygen, he had no life. He ate by himself, slept by himself, and lived by himself. Twice daily, a guard delivered food to his cell. Every three days, he was allowed to walk within a small courtyard, where he saw no one except guards in elevated kiosks. Gantemirov became impressed, over time, that he maintained his sanity.

Gantemirov stayed sane by attending to his emotional and physical needs. Daily, he mentally recalled Chechen and Russian underground contacts, including addresses, telephone numbers, and drop-off points—information that Russian authorities had repeatedly been trying to obtain from him.

"Who leads the Chechen cells?" the interrogators inquired.

"I have no idea. I do not work with terrorist cells," Gantemirov responded.

"Why were you, a Chechen, living in Moscow?"

"I had several different jobs. We've discussed that. Besides, I like Moscow. You have culture. Why does anyone live anywhere?"

"Do you know about weapons of mass destruction?"

"You must be kidding."

"Where are the weapons?"

"I have no idea."

"What is your name? What is your height? What color are your eyes?" All day, all night, sometimes with pain (it was difficult for Gantemirov to remember), the questions continued. Gantemirov tried to appear cooperative, poorly informed and naïve, and always providing only minimal information. The Russian authorities, certainly no fools, could not tell whether he was a repository of information to which they had no access, or whether he was exceptionally skilled at withholding data.

As the Russians' questions continued, days extending to weeks and months, sometimes employing medication to dull the Chechen's senses, sometimes inflicting pain with electrical prods and hot steel, it became apparent that no significant information was forthcoming.

One day, several men escorted Gantemirov, now blindfolded, into a vehicle, drove him to an airport, and took him to this place. Jokhar Gantemirov had no idea where he was. Only, that he was in prison.

Gantemirov remembered little from the interrogations, only that he was occasionally subjected to pain, which he had been able to tolerate, and many times not allowed to sleep for days. Sleep deprivation renders captives psychotic, and in their confused state, it is difficult for them to retain secret information. The process takes days and is not suitable for quickly extracting information from prisoners. However, if time is not an issue, the method of depriving a captive of sleep is highly effective.

* * *

Eighteen months previously, Jokhar Gantemirov was a free man, until his capture in Houston, Texas, after which he was turned over to Russian FSB authorities. For the Russians and Americans, time was not pressing—or was it? Regardless, Gantemirov did not know what he had revealed during his interrogation.

Concerning Gantemirov's current physical prowess, he performed one hundred push-ups, two hundred sit-ups, and ran in place for at least ninety minutes daily in his small cell. He would have preferred to do his pull-ups too, but there was no place to perform this exercise. The cell had no overhead rods, hooks, or anything from which he might hang himself. The Russians wanted him alive.

Although Gantemirov's exercise routine kept him physically fit, prison had changed him. He still stood six feet six inches, but his weight decreased from two hundred eighty pounds to slightly less than one hundred ninety. His hair was still slicked back, and his huge hands, owning thick fingers, remained strong. He was less muscular than previously, but he could still overpower most men in an instant.

Today, in the courtyard, he noticed the large metal door was ajar. He had seen that door twice a week for one year, towering in height and expansive in width. Bolts were on the edges, and there was no handle. Now, it was ajar. Why? Puzzled, Gantemirov nonchalantly walked toward the door and spotted an alley through the opening. Viewing his life at a dead end, he opened the door further, walked toward the alley, saw another open door topped with barbed wire, and, in short time, was in a field in the middle of who knows where.

Gantemirov wondered whether this too-easy escape was a ruse. Was he being tempted to escape, only to be incarcerated again? Was this an excuse to kill him? He quickly reasoned the latter unlikely, given the authorities could kill him any moment at their own choosing. After all, he had been an active participant in Pi-Two, the sponsor of the failed "Operation Hippocampus," and was a leper in the eyes of the *Federalnaya Sluvhba Besopas*, the FSB, which replaced the KGB following dissolution of the Soviet Union.

Gantemirov decided to go for it. The prisoner walked across the field and heavy brush surrounding the prison and soon found himself at a wooden fence. There was barbed wire on top. Had he a blanket, he would have used the common trick of placing the blanket over the wire, rolling across. Without the blanket, there was little chance of avoiding the sharp edges. Fortunately, there were several adjacent concrete blocks. He piled them on top of each other, removed and placed his prison jeans over the coiled wire, and was soon on the other side, grasping his jeans, now embedded in the wire, to soften his landing. He tugged a few times on his pants, unavoidably tearing them in several places, and was pleased they were still functional as a garment.

Although he was now free, Gantemirov had no idea where he was. Without money or food and highly noticeable in his prison shirt and torn trousers, he walked a short distance, pondering his next move.

Gantemirov heard the sound of an automobile. Still ignorant of his location or whether he was near friends, he walked away from the automobile sound, stooping low near the scattered brush, trying to decrease his visibility.

Several miles later, somewhat nervous and tired, Gantemirov heard laughter and the distant sound of waves hitting the shore. Gantemirov was near a beach. A beach! The beach was packed, absolutely packed, with people.

Removing his shirt and tearing at his jeans to produce cut-off shorts, he walked toward the water. The escapee was soon among average, free citizens, who spoke Russian as well as another language he recognized—Romanian.

Young girls laughed while men tried to impress women (and themselves) with their athleticism, catching inflatable balls. Gantemirov just stood there, thinking. Where was he? Was he released on purpose? Were people following him? Were people in the water watching him? Presuming the open door was not an accident, why had he been released?

Gantemirov, a Chechen who had lived in Moscow and participated in the Pi-Two group's failed mission, "Operation Hippocampus," had multiple contacts with

Islamic fundamentalist funding and was a trained killer. He eyed the beach, looking for people to leave belongings on the sand before entering the water. He soon possessed a towel, shirt, baseball cap, and sunglasses, quickly filched a pair of shorts, wrapped the towel around his waist, removed his wet cutoff jeans, and stepped into the dry shorts. Now, all he needed was food, money, and to figure out where he was.

Gantemirov saw two tourists, apparently husband and wife, with a guidebook in English. The man was tall, although not as large as Gantemirov. Despite prison, Gantemirov was still huge and a threat.

Fluent in English, the escapee shyly asked the couple where they were from. The man responded, "The States."

"Where in the States?"

"New York. New Rochelle. It's a suburb outside New York City."

"Actually," he lied, "I have been to New York City. It's much nicer than Russia, where I'm from. New York has wonderful museums and great food. And nice people."

The couple smiled and inquired where in Russia Gantemirov lived. Chancing it, he replied, "Moscow. Been there all my life."

"Wow! We're hoping to visit there. After we leave Moldova, we're traveling to the Ukraine but aren't certain we'll have time to visit Moscow."

So that is where I am, thought Gantemirov: Moldova. This must be the Black Sea, and given that Moldova had only one nice beach, this must be the popular resort town, Vadul Lui Vodã.

Gantemirov searched his memory, which had not faltered while in prison. Vadul Lui Vodã was seven and one-half miles northwest of Chişinău, the capital of Moldova. Knowing Americans pronounce the capital, *Kishinev,* he ventured another question. "I take it you've been to Kishinev?"

"You bet," replied the woman. "We're staying at the Hotel Meridian. Nice, but expensive."

The man interrupted, annoyed, "It's okay. It's not that unreasonable." Turning to Gantemirov, he inquired, "Where are you staying?"

"Oh, I'm just touring, staying in youth hostels, at times camping. I was riding my bicycle, but it broke down. The chain broke. I left it a few miles north of here. I need to find some spare parts. Right now, I have to get back to Kishinev. Some people gave me a ride to the beach, but they decided to stay in the area another few days. That's a little longer than I expected. I'll probably go back tomorrow, if I can find a ride."

"If you want, come with us. We have a car and room."

"No, I don't want to impose."

"Not a problem. Happy to do it, if you don't mind sitting in the back seat with a bunch of luggage."

Gantemirov looked around—thankful no one appeared to be watching the threesome. "Thanks," he said, extending his hand. "My name is Igor, Igor Stresnev."

"Glad to meet you, Igor. I'm Jim Alliston, and this is my wife, Mary Lou."

The newcomers shook hands, Gantemirov telling himself to remember the fabricated name. The three entered Alliston's rented Volkswagen and drove toward Kishinev. When they were in a secluded area, Jokhar Gantemirov embarrassingly asked, "Can I stop to relieve myself? It will only take a minute."

"Not a bad idea, Igor," Jim Alliston said. "Mary Lou, you wait in the car. We'll be back in a second."

"You guys sure have it easy. Just find a spot and go. Women have it tough. We can't go wherever we want, anywhere in the world, like you men." The two men smiled and entered the wooded area.

After five minutes, Mary Lou called for them, but there was no answer. She called again after another five minutes and, ten minutes later, decided to see what was going on. She left the VW, locked it to be safe, and walked into the woods, calling out her husband's name. When she was out of sight from the road, she briefly felt a powerful arm around her neck and soon lay motionless on the ground, next to her dead husband.

Gantemirov rifled the Allistons' clothing, took their car keys and money, five hundred lei in local currency, and drove the dead couple's car into town. He then boarded the Iasi-Chişinău train.

*   *   *

Chapter Five

WEAPONS OF MASS DESTRUCTION

Dick Swept sat in Conference Room A-3, on the second floor of one of the many buildings on the CIA campus. The room teemed with high technology, each attendee having a computer in front of him, but no paper or writing instruments were allowed. Everyone could make notes on their computer, and when the meetings adjourned, everyone could remove their disc. The disc was the property of the agent, but it was obvious the agency would know who had what on their disc, the nature of the notes taken, and any knowledge or data that left the room.

Swept sat in the second row, close enough to help him pay attention, behind a beautiful woman, Suzanne Miller. Ms. Miller was incredibly officious, wore jackets and ties, and seemed to be a giant ball of string, waiting to unravel for the right guy. Swept, still focused on Ricki, had not sought any personal relationship with Agent Miller, an interaction that would have been frowned upon by the agency but nonetheless occurred every day.

Swept logged on to his computer and accessed the folder with information pertinent to the talk today: weapons of mass destruction. Then, to Swept's surprise, Agent Miller stood before the small class and spoke.

"I have been asked to discuss the WMDs. Most of what I am about to tell you, you probably know. Regardless, it is on your hard drive and, if you want, copy the information to your disc." Agent Miller then pushed several buttons, and a giant screen descended from a recessed alcove within the ceiling. Swept knew that information on the screen was a large blowup of what he had on his computer.

Ms. Miller looked around the room and politely acknowledged everyone, focusing too little time on Dick Swept. The neurologist took note of this, wondering whether she had feelings she might be trying to hide, or whether Miller, for whatever reason, disliked him.

Brushing a wisp of auburn hair from eyes almost too far apart, licking her lips for some unknown reason, Ms. Miller began. Swept listened attentively.

"Many individuals in our State Department contend that the *Mukhabarat*, the Iraqi intelligence service under former president Saddam Hussein, met with al-Qaeda several times, as far back as 1993. We have documentation that in 1996, the head of the *Mukhabarat* personally met with Osama bin Laden in Khartoum, Sudan. Secretary of State Powell presented evidence to the United Nations that bin Laden met at least eight times with officers of Saddam Hussein's Special Security Organization. Therefore, regardless of what the press or anyone else says, there was some connection between al-Qaeda, bin Laden, and Iraq.

"Further, in 1998, an aide to Uday, one of Hussein's sons, defected and told journalists that Iraq was providing funds to al-Qaeda. Our satellite photos, which you can see on your computer, documented a Boeing 707 parked at a camp south of Baghdad, where terrorists trained to take over aircraft. After U.S. forces captured that camp, the commander confirmed al-Qaeda had trained there in 1997 and in subsequent years.

"Everyone is asking, 'Where are the weapons of mass destruction?' I don't know, we don't know, but they must be somewhere, and, at one time, were probably in Iraq. Think about it. If they weren't in Iraq, why would Saddam not allow the United Nations to inspect his weapons?"

Swept raised his hand, arching his right eyebrow. "May I ask a question?"

"Fire away."

"Is it possible Hussein wanted his neighbors, many of whom were enemies, to be frightened of his military capability, so he established the innuendo of having weapons of mass destruction? It would also be a method to keep the Kurds within Iraqi borders from further resisting his authority. Or perhaps, maybe his subordinates wanted to please him and falsely stated Iraq had weapons of mass destruction. Or maybe Saddam did not want to go down in history as the ruler of former Mesopotamia who gave in to the Infidel West."

Before Suzanne Miller could answer, a voice from the back of the room responded. Swept turned, as did the others in the audience, and saw Major Cervantes, Dick Swept's direct superior.

"Richard, those are good questions and, obviously, we've all thought about them. Look, the problem is simple. If there are WMDs, then it is certain they can fall into wrong hands. If that happens, the world is in for considerable violence. The Americans and British maintained that the invasion of Iraq was a good idea even if there were no WMDs. However, it would help the United States and Great Britain considerably if these weapons were found, as well as improve popularity ratings of the our president and the British prime minister. And I can assure everyone here, these weapons exist. They're in Chechnya."

"Now," Cervantes continued, his voice strong, clear, and crisp, "download the remainder of the lecture and review it later. Some of you have a lot of work to do."

Suzanne Miller seemed miffed that she had been cut off from the remainder of her talk. She approached Swept as he was leaving his desk. "You always have questions, don't you, Dr. Swept?"

"Actually, Agent Miller, I am always without answers. I still have yet to learn why you insist on calling me 'doctor'."

"Isn't that what you are, some kind of a doctor?"

"Some of the time, not all the time."

"Also, *Doctor* Swept, why are you here? People are only supposed to be allowed in clandestine operations if they are thirty-five or younger, I understand you're a few years older."

Swept smiled. "Well, again, some of the time, not all the time."

Agent Miller turned on her heel and walked out. Swept approached Major Cervantes, who offered a strong handshake. "Don't mind her, Richard," Cervantes commented. "Miller's a bit stuffy, but real smart."

Swept acknowledged the remark, and the two walked to Cervantes's office.

* * *

Swept's main contact in the Central Intelligence Agency was Major Cervantes. Ever since Swept met him, more than eighteen months earlier, he had not accustomed himself to Cervantes's first name—Major. The nomenclature possibly had significance for Cervantes, witnessed by his military demeanor, despite the fact that Cervantes had never served in the military.

Major Cervantes looked exactly the same as when Swept first met him. His hair was closely cropped; he was almost too clean-shaven, making Swept wonder whether Cervantes shaved during midday. The man spoke too rapidly, but always in clear, crisp tones. Cervantes's features were sharp, his demeanor formal, and his office walls boasted pictures of James Madison, Thomas Jefferson, Ronald Reagan, William Jefferson Clinton, and the current president.

Cervantes presented the CIA's first overture to bring Swept into their organization. Now, his home was in the CIA. Major Cervantes remained Dick Swept's primary contact.

* * *

After they arrived in Cervantes's office, Swept's mentor asked him to sit. "Richard, our president and allies have no idea how correct they were. Three weeks before the American-led invasion, Iraqi weapons of mass destruction were loaded onto trucks and driven out of the country, heading toward Chechnya."

Swept was dumbfounded. "Why haven't we made that clear to the media, which keeps hammering away at this? Why—"

Cervantes cut Swept off. "We can talk about that later. We have another problem."

"What's that?"

"You remember Jokhar Gantemirov?"

"Sure. He was the Chechen who participated in Pi-Two, the renegade FSB outfit from Russia."

"Correct. We previously captured him in Houston. We wanted to hold him, not turn him over to the Russians. However, the bureaucracy has a way, and he was incarcerated in Russia. The FSB did permit us to ask some questions, but we got nowhere. Then, they took him. Now, evidently, he escaped. We informed the Department of Homeland Security, and they blame the CIA as well as the FSB for his escape. Homeland intends to complain to the congressional committee overseeing their department that they should be the ones coordinating all antiterrorist activities, whether in our country or outside our borders. If they were in charge, they argue, Gantemirov would be here, in the States, and still in prison. Now, and we all agree on this, there's no telling what damage he might cause, especially if he's involved in the WMDs."

"Does Homeland Security know there are weapons of mass destruction?"

"No, they do not."

"Then they don't know that Gantemirov might be in a position to access them, given his Chechen background and connections."

"Correct again."

"And, may I ask, why are we not telling them?"

"We have our reasons."

Swept inhaled deeply, allowing air to exit in a slow and steady manner, contemplating his response. Before Swept could say anything, Cervantes reached over and handed Swept a manila folder.

"Open the folder. Read about the Allistons. Regarding the bureaucracies and competition among the different agencies, that's a talk for another day."

Swept took out some sheets and began reading.

* * *

When the Allistons' bodies were found, the local police did not know their identity or who might be the culprit. Due to the influence of the pro-Russia Communist Party of Moldova (PRCM), coupled with lack of progress in the local police investigation, the Moldova police soon contacted the FSB. The FSB, after discovering a Volkswagen rented in Romania had not been returned, obtained the names and drivers' license photos of the renters and matched their pictures to the dead bodies. Since the victims were Americans, the FSB contacted the U.S. State Department, but only after they were satisfied with their own investigation.

* * *

Gantemirov was amazed to learn he had been imprisoned in Moldova. During his days at the KGB, he was aware of many prisons scattered throughout the USSR but did not know about the one in Vadul Lui Vodã, Moldova. The more he thought about it, the more sense it made.

Earlier attempts to impose Russian culture on the region antagonized the largely illiterate peasants, who felt culturally aligned with Romania. After a formal Romanian state was established in 1881, there emerged a nationalist surge for a Moldovan country, an extremely popular cause. In 1917, Moldova renounced Russian rule and declared independence. The Bolsheviks then invaded Moldova but were driven out by Romanian support. In 1918, the grateful Moldovans joined Romania.

Following World War II, during which the Romanians were allied with the Nazis, Russia integrated Romania and Moldova into the USSR, labeling the former as the Moldovan Soviet Socialist Republic.

In 1991, the Republic of Moldova formally declared independence, following the dissolution of the USSR, several years earlier. A civil war ensued, resulting in a sliver of eastern Moldova, Transdniester, becoming a separate country, closely allied with Russia. The remainder of Moldova was loyal to Romania, the country on their western border, because Romania had assisted them during their previous struggles.

In 2001, the Communist Party of Moldova took control of both the parliament and presidency. It was within this setting, thought Gantemirov, that the Russians thought it a good idea to incarcerate him in Moldova. And why not? Who would think of finding a terrorist in an out-of-the-way place like Moldova, making any escape difficult? This way, the Russians could rest assured their captive was securely behind bars. So, Gantemirov wondered, why was it relatively easy to escape? Again, thought the Chechen Muscovite, was he let out intentionally, or was it an accident? Who, if anyone, was behind this?

Gantemirov viewed his murdering the American couple as a matter of necessity. Killing a man while he is urinating is easy, and the woman proved no problem. Jim Alliston's clothes were loose fitting, inconspicuous, and would serve him well.

Reasoning the authorities would soon connect the murders to him, he wanted to submerge himself in Moscow as soon as possible. Moscow was his favorite city and one where he had many friends. Maybe that was what the FSB bureaucrats wanted and expected. Maybe they figured he would have to do something to help himself, such as find support among his colleagues. Then, all the FSB had to do was to wait until Gantemirov contacted his underground associates, enabling the FSB to identify a Chechen terrorist network.

Gantemirov thought carefully about these possibilities as he rode the Iasi-Chişinau train, noting its incredible inefficiencies, traveling toward the Ukraine. On the train, Gantemirov saw a copy of the *International Herald Tribune.* There were several articles about the Americans and British in Iraq and their failed attempt to find the alleged weapons of mass destruction, but a different subject caught his eye:

Explosion Rocks Scotland

> The recent explosion, more akin to a loud barrage of dangerous firecrackers, outside the Edinburgh Castle is not thought to be the work of organized terrorists. Despite the loss of four lives and minor damage to the castle, the authorities find no evidence of Islamic terrorists. A spokesperson for the Edinburgh police acknowledged a letter from an alleged assailant, but they dismiss it as juvenile and without purpose.

Hardly, thought Gantemirov. Nobody tries to blow up a national monument unless they have a purpose. And, he thought, if the letter was truly juvenile and without purpose, perhaps the perpetrators were incompetent or unskilled. However, they must feel strongly about why they did what they did. They had to have a purpose.

* * *

Chapter Six

BOTULINUM TOXIN Q

Major Cervantes provided Dick Swept with volumes of reading material about the WMD. Swept inquired why he was assigned to this task and was continually told that, as a neurologist, he would be more adept in ferreting out information pertaining to the WMD, especially if they involved neurotoxins.

* * *

Swept sat in his office, reading about Iraq. He learned that 650,000 tons of ammunition lay dormant at thousands of sites used by former Iraqi security forces that fled or disappeared following the American invasion. For at least six months following U.S. troop arrival in Baghdad, these ammunition dumps were neither secured nor heavily guarded. The *New York Times* argued it would take years to destroy these dumps.

Although the Pentagon initially stated these ammunition supplies were secured, journalists reported otherwise. On September 30, 2003, an American official provided an infrared videotape to the *Times*, identifying several huge hangars stripped bare of roofing and siding, containing hundreds of warheads or bombs. None of these were guarded. Matters became even more unsettled when General John P. Abizaid, the senior American commander in the Persian Gulf region, told the Senate Appropriations Committee there was more ammunition in Iraq than any place he had seen in his entire military career, and this would be very difficult to secure.

Subsequent to this disclosure, American forces uncovered two large stockpiles of weapons, one in Tikrit, Saddam Hussein's hometown, with 23 surface-to-air missiles, over 400 grenades, a mortar, and over 1,000 pounds of high explosives. A separate raid near Kirkuk, in northern Iraq, had uncovered 8 surface-to-air missiles, 190 helicopter rockets, and several electrical devices suitable for homemade bombs.

Within this setting, the search for weapons of mass destruction seemed increasingly futile. The American president emphasized WMD when he sought world support for his country's military efforts in Iraq, citing the demonic nature of Iraqi president Saddam Hussein's regime and his fear of Saddam using WMD against his neighbors, as he had done earlier against Iraq's own Kurdish citizens.

Major Cervantes knew what most American officials did not know: The weapons of mass destruction were in Chechnya. The agency was not certain exactly what the WMD were, but they suspected neurotoxins. Were this incorrect, the WMDs could be biological weapons, nuclear devices, or something else equally as sinister

* * *

. What no one knew, except for a few Chechen friends of Jokhar Gantemirov, was that the WMD consisted of almost two thousand canisters of a form of botulinum toxin, called botulinum toxin-Q. This chemical, known as B-Q, was designed by a man known only as "the Chemist."

* * *

The Chemist previously worked for a pharmaceutical firm that manufactured botulinum toxin. He was supposedly a Sunni Muslim and contended that Jews in the firm kept him from appropriate advancement. He never thought his cocaine addiction played a role in his outbursts of bad temper or a disposition that thwarted any semblance of appropriate interaction with co-workers. He did not leave quietly, promising everyone that, one day, he would destroy the firm and, hopefully, every person in it. Being of Iraqi ancestry, the Chemist soon found himself in Baghdad, where he offered his services to develop lethal drugs.

* * *

Botulinum toxin is used for treating many neurological disorders, as well as having cosmetic applications, such as lessening facial wrinkles. The toxin binds to a chemical receptor on muscle, resulting in weakening and decreased tone of that muscle.

When a nerve instructs a muscle to contract, it does so through a release of certain chemicals known as neurotransmitters. Botulinum toxin blocks this interaction, weakening or even paralyzing the muscle. Usually, botulinum toxin is injected into a muscle with a small hypodermic needle. Botulinum toxin-Q, however, was different. It was readily absorbed through the skin or by inhalation. Since B-Q was so volatile and highly absorbent, it was deadly.

Botulinum toxin-Q rapidly evaporated at room temperature. One drop in a room would kill anyone who inhaled it within two hundred feet. The B-Q paralyzed all muscles in the body, including respiratory muscles, making it impossible for the victim to breathe. Exposure to B-Q meant certain death.

Saddam Hussein had 1,944 canisters of botulinum toxin-Q. If someone opened one of these canisters, which were the size of an average thermos, and poured a few drops of the contents onto the floor, the B-Q evaporated within several seconds, and any living creature inhaling these vapors died from respiratory paralysis.

One of Hussein's sons, Uday, obtained five milliliters of this agent, put on a white polyester gown, gloves, shoe coverings, and a gas mask, and spilled some B-Q on the floor of a room filled with prisoners. He had his guards videotape the suffocation that ensued, while over two hundred men died. He subsequently viewed the videotape, later that evening, alone in his bedroom.

* * *

Transportation to Grozny, Chechnya, had proven simple. Saddam Hussein may have been the evil ruler of Iraq, but he was cunning, smart, and had many loyal supporters in his Baathist Party. A band of Saddam loyalists had no problem moving the WMDs. All they needed were two trucks for the transport and eighteen more for distraction.

Three weeks prior to the invasion of Iraq, Saddam loyalists placed their cargo in two large black Ford trucks. The botulinum was distributed in 1,944 canisters, 28 to a box. Thus, there were 69 boxes of the lethal agent, divided between the two trucks. An additional box carrying twelve canisters was up front with the driver. The driver was the Chemist.

The number 3 road, the main artery out of Baghdad, goes north, to Ba'Qua bah. That was where the caravan of trucks switched to road number 4. From there, the caravan traveled through western Iran, Azerbaijan, Tbilisi in Georgia, north to Bladikavkaz, then directly east to Grozny, entering the Chechnya capital through Route M29, traveling through Nazran, forty miles west of Grozny. The total distance from Baghdad to Grozny, is less than four hundred miles. The trip took two weeks.

The drive was not simple. Kurds in northern Iraq were not friendly to itinerant travelers, especially Sunni Iraqis. But the plan was simple, and it worked.

The fleet of trucks was filthy, slow moving, and had conventional weapons and financial resources, as well as the WMD. Three or four trucks routinely drove ahead, reconnoitering the area, reporting foreseeable problems. Bandits could often be bribed. The same was true at military checkpoints. Always, the drivers said they were carrying medical supplies for the suffering Chechens, who were being mauled by Russians or succumbing to their own internal strife.

Truly, the trucks were also loaded with medical supplies. In instances when people could not be bribed and violence seemed probable, the drivers in the scouting mission became irate at the guards interfering with their passage, began violent action, and then drove away, allowing themselves to be pursued. While the bandits or military guards engaged in the chase, the rest of the caravan drove ahead. If the trucks being pursued could not escape, they usually were able to kill the aggressors with conventional weapons, such as grenade launchers and surface-to-surface missiles, weapons the bandits could seldom counteract.

The bandits and the military, often identical, never suspected anyone in the caravan had missiles capable of blowing up any vehicle within a twenty-mile radius. By the time the vehicles arrived in Grozny, twelve of the original twenty trucks were still operational, including the two black Ford trucks with their cargo intact.

After the boxes, with large red crosses emblazoned on all six sides, were safely stored in a hospital administered by the International Red Cross, the Chemist thanked everyone for their help, including the Hussein loyalists, most of whom had no idea what they were transporting, and the Red Cross personnel, who were grateful for the medical supplies. He clandestinely put on a white suit totally covering his body, installed his gas mask, and poured a small aliquot from one of the canisters. Then, the Chemist left the building. Those remaining inside became acutely weak, unable to breathe, move muscles, or dial a phone. After a few minutes, they were dead.

Within a short time, with help from the Chechen underground, the canisters were moved to another medical facility, and the entire Red Cross hospital was set ablaze, including the doctors, patients, and nurses within. The Chechen rebels blamed the Russians.

Many Chechen rebels wanted to use the WMD against Russia in an attempt to secure liberation from the overpowering Russian government. However, if some of the weapons could be had for a price, they would sell them. Their price was 250 million dollars.

* * *

Jokhar Gantemirov sat in a bar in Tbilisi, the capital of Georgia. The rule of law was not strong, and Gantemirov felt secure as he drank vodka with some friends. Aslambek, who had known Jokhar for all their lives, made it clear, "I can put you in touch with our people. Two hundred-fifty million buys the weapons and they're yours. The Americans, the British, hell, the entire world is looking for these."

Aslambek continued as Gantemirov listened intently, "The Americans and their allies will never find the weapons in Iraq or Pakistan or Syria."

God, I love my people, thought Gantemirov. *We have them!* "Make certain no one in Chechnya sells anything. I'll find a way to make the purchase."

"It will be difficult, my friend. The figure of two hundred fifty is fixed."

"I shall find a way."

Chapter Seven

LUPUS LADY OF LONDON

The Crillon Hotel in Paris and the Kempinski in Berlin have long been outstanding hotels. Indeed, the Nazis headquartered in both during World War II. To this day, the Bristol Kempinski Hotel remains one of the finest hotels in Berlin, Germany.

The lobby of the Kempinski has been remodeled several times since the failed Nazi racist enterprise, making it currently remarkable for the number of blacks, Arabs, Jews, Persians, Asians, and just about everyone from every walk of life who stay there. The staff is splendid and the atmosphere international.

No one is shocked at how different a hotel guest may appear. The hotel personnel are accustomed to the unusual, whether in attire or demeanor. The guests, able to afford the steep prices, are often better tolerated than in their own countries.

It was with surprise, therefore, that everyone stared at the young woman in the Bristol Kempinski Hotel lobby as she sat for afternoon tea. The woman placed her hands across her eyes, shielding them from the light. Sitting with the European edition of the *Wall Street Journal* and the *International Herald Tribune*, one could not help notice her beautiful blond hair and skin-tight buckskin garb, with silver rivets bordering the lateral part of her legs, while the inner border of her pants ended tightly on her crotch. Above her loins, one-quarter of her breasts strained against the tight fabric, creating a picture of beauty and enticement.

The men in the room gaped at her stunning figure, attempting to see her face. When she placed her hands down, as she frequently did while reading the papers or trying to enjoy her tea and scones, most of the men snickered, feeling a fortunate release they need not ogle further over the heretofore thought-to-be beautiful creature. The woman's face was incredibly unattractive, with scarring, a huge rash, and seemingly random fluctuations in pigment and swelling.

Constantly squinting, with a facial rash appearing like a large butterfly, frequently placing her hands over her eyes, the woman tried elegantly to endure the onlookers. She was angry she had forgotten her sunglasses and would have to buy more today. Hiding her face at times with her scarf, the woman bemoaned her lack of facial coverage. Maybe she should go to her room, but why should she have to do anything? This is what she was—facially disfigured, all from her disease, systemic lupus erythematosis, or SLE.

No, she would not use her scarf! If the photophobia were not severe, if she did not have such incredible discomfort from lights, she would keep her hands down and shove her face into all of them. This is what she was, and that was that!

The woman heard one of the men, with a British accent, comment, "I'd keep my hands over my face too if I were that ugly. What a shame, with such a beautiful body."

That was it! Jennifer Pettigrew picked up her *Journal,* turned toward the man, and smashed the paper hard against his face. "And it's a shame you have such a small penis. You should cover that!" she exclaimed, stifling her cry and poking the paper as hard as she could against his groin, forcing him to double over. The Brit, mumbling about crazy women these days, slowly straightened, grimaced, and rubbed his now-reddened face, watching the well-figured woman disappear into the elevator, while men in the lobby now looked at him disapprovingly.

In the elevator, fighting back her tears, Jennifer Pettigrew looked at her newspaper, trying to forget the problems of her life. Her eye caught the brief editorial on the botched bombing at the Edinburgh Castle. The editors commented they and other papers believed the West was winning the war on terrorism. After all, all one had to do was look at the failed bombing attempt. However, they noted, it was striking there was a rambling letter addressed to several major newspapers, something about the rights of people who stutter.

Jennifer Pettigrew did not spend much time thinking about the rights of people who stutter. Her main concern was herself, her feelings, and her humiliation at being belittled by those jerks downstairs.

She could not help it if she was not attractive. Jennifer did everything to make her figure more appealing, to make her mind more fertile, but what could she possibly do about the ravages disease left upon her face? Her disease! She hated having lupus. She hated systemic lupus erythematosis.

Between the skin changes and the steroid side effects, her face became what it was—bloated and disfigured.

Jennifer had seen dermatologists, plastic surgeons, a slew of them. All the doctors said the same thing: "There is nothing we can do. Don't worry about it. Focus on the rest of you. Looks aren't everything." Besides, they inferred, your face, even without SLE, is still not without its problems.

No, Jennifer would not hear of it. There was nothing wrong with her face aside from the lupus. Were it not for her lupus and the necessary steroid medication, she would be so much more of whatever she wanted to be.

Jennifer had many friends, most of whom were idealists and enjoyed having a friend like Jennifer—someone intelligent and who seemed to wear her disease almost as a weapon against the world. Most of her friends had pent-up anger of their own. Either they had problems with a parent, a sibling, a lover, or a concept. None was happy with herself, and each liked being seen next to a woman who, were it not for her face, reeked of sex.

Years ago, in college, Jennifer Pettigrew primarily befriended students who were left of center. They seemed to have a kinder set of social values than those right-wingers and were more tolerant of her disfigured face. Or so she believed, which was why she was so often sexually promiscuous with them.

Then, as now, her friends were loyal to her. And Jennifer was loyal to them.

* * *

Chapter Eight

STILL A NEUROLOGIST

Dick Swept felt good. He was pleased with his day. His research on cellular dysfunction following cholinesterase exposure was going well. His earlier work at the Texas College of Medicine, in Houston, focused on how animals process memory. Swept's development of Compound 1040 proved effective in allowing animals to learn a simple task, but because of opposition by his chairman, Dr. Harold Ranger, he had not been allowed to try the medication on humans. The series of events that subsequently transpired, which now whizzed through his mind in a flash, resulted in the discovery of a small group of renegades within the FSB, as well as the fact that the medication had many side effects.

Back in Houston, Swept had had no idea Russian ex-KGB renegades were investigating a chemical similar to his, scheming to alter how people think, from those in the media to politicians, and achieve control of the world. They actually planned world domination! Swept soon found himself in the middle of international intrigue and was able to stop them, fighting the likes of Aleksander Kostokov and Jokhar Gantemirov, foiling their plans.

Swept had personally killed Kostokov. Gantemirov had been incarcerated by the Russians, allegedly against the CIA's wishes, the agency supposedly having lost the battle. Besides, some thought the Russians, being less constrained by a sense of morality or human rights activists, might be more successful at extricating information from the Chechen.

Jokhar Gantemirov, a Chechen who had lived in Russia a long time, was involved in siphoning money from Islamic fundamentalists into the Pi-Two project. Gantemirov worked with Aleksander Kostokov and others to attain world domination. Perhaps, thought some in the agency, if Russia (or the United States) could ascertain these sources, their efforts against terrorism would be more productive. However, Gantemirov was tough and yielded little information to his Russian interrogators, steadfastly denying any terrorist connections.

* * *

Swept enjoyed jogging in Rock Creek Park, especially enjoyed this time of year, spring, when the cherry blossom aroma wafted through the air and the city seemed electrically alive. Swept was thinking about his research at the CIA and his relationship with Ricki Hardson, who moved from Houston with him. Ricki wanted to get married, but Swept was not interested. He was just not the marrying type.

As Swept thought about Ricki and his research, again he noticed the man in the wheelchair, his *Washington Post* neatly folded. The man stared blankly at the joggers, deeply immersed in thought.

Swept continued to wonder who this man was. He was there, in the wheelchair, virtually every time Swept was in the park. He always had a newspaper and always stared at the joggers. His upper torso was muscular and thick, almost robust, and his facial lines were etched with contempt. The man's legs, covered by pants, seemed thin and weak. He never smiled, sometimes smoked a pipe, and interacted with no one.

Many people had commented to Swept that he was a caring neurologist, perhaps more sensitive than he wanted to be. However, he increasingly felt a hardening, a cynicism, entering his thought processes. He was aware that he was not only a physician-scientist working at the CIA but was also trained as an operative, one who might be called upon to engage in clandestine operations.

These thoughts and perspectives swirled in his mind as he looked at the man in the wheelchair, wondering how their lives overlapped. Both lives pertained to the sphere of neurology, Swept a researcher and provider of health care, the other a recipient, and both knew all too well the repercussions of neurological disease.

Swept no longer listened to music as he ran, primarily because of his CIA training: always be familiar and at ease with your environment. Listening to and being energized by Bob Dylan's music, which had been his pattern when he ran in Houston, was no longer an option. Now, he heard only the sounds of nature and, except for cogitation about whatever plans he mulled over, let his mind relax, yet always paying attention to his surroundings.

It came as a surprise that Swept found himself thinking about Regina Bruxton, his former Texas lover. Regina, ever ensconced in the financial matrices of her plastic-surgery medical practice, corresponded briefly with Swept in a polite but distant vein after Swept moved to Washington, D.C. Swept held some good memories of their relationship, primarily their lovemaking, but felt a gelid chill whenever he thought about Regina Bruxton as a person. As beautiful as she was, the woman was cold and thought only about the dollar. Ricki Hardson, who was intimate with Swept in Houston and moved with him to Washington, D.C., was a marked and welcomed contrast to Regina.

Ricki usually wore loose-fitting blouses, tight black jeans, Greek sandals, and possessed a fresh, almost virginal look. Her long brown hair flowed lightly across her shoulders. The woman moved with a physical prowess coupled with femininity. Her speech had dulcet tones, and her face was soft, beautiful, and without makeup. Ricki was intelligent, well-read, and earnest in everything she attempted. Swept loved her very much and especially respected her values. Aside from all that, she was great in bed.

Ricki was aware Swept worked for the CIA. Indeed, she was the person who inveigled Swept into medical issues that, unanticipated by both, brought Swept into the morass of espionage that eventuated in his joining the agency. And now, here they were, the two of them, sharing their worlds.

Richard Michael Swept's world was no longer that of a physician-scientist at the Texas College of Medicine. His world still consisted of research in Alzheimer's disease, especially neurochemical aspects of Alzheimer's, but his work now also overlapped with neurobiological forms of terrorism.

Concurrently, Ricki was no longer a nurse specializing in infectious diseases. She continued to practice her proficient skills as a nurse but was no longer hospital based, opting instead to work in a large neurology clinic in Georgetown.

Swept and Ricki both had a strong interest in medicine and shared many interests. Swept thought about their disagreement over marriage as he drove home in his Bentley Continental GT, a sports coupe that recently entered the American market. When he moved to Washington, D.C., Swept sold his Ferrari 456 because it was too low to drive in snow and he wanted all-wheel drive. His new Bentley had a twin turbo-charged 6.0 liter engine, boasting 550 horsepower at 6,100 rpm, 479 foot-pounds of torque at 1600 rpm, and blasted from 0 to 60 miles per hour in less than five seconds. The automobile was the world's fastest four-seat production car, blending British flair and craftsmanship with German technology and thoroughness.

Swept arrived at his building, said hello to the doorman, who gleefully smiled as he drove the Bentley around the corner to the garage, and took the elevator to his apartment. His answering machine informed him of messages.

Swept was impressed to hear from two women. Valerie VanDance, his chairman's former nurse, a long-time employee of the CIA and currently stationed at Langley, was leaving tomorrow for Kenya and wanted to say goodbye. Valerie VanDance knew enough not to discuss more than that, just that she was off to Kenya.

But it was the other woman whose message struck a chord in Swept's brain: Louise Konos. Louise, the woman he almost married so many years ago, the woman about whom he long wondered whether he could have made the relationship last a lifetime. The woman who moved off somewhere and he had not put forth the effort to find out where.

"Richard, Louise. I want you to know I am getting married. I'm not certain why I'm calling. I just wanted you to know. He is a wonderful man and we love each other very much. I called the Texas College of Medicine and they told me you moved to Washington, D.C. I then called Dr. Harold Ranger and he gave me your number. I hope that was okay. Anyway, I wanted to say hello and tell you the good news."

No, it was not all right that Harold Ranger had given Louise his number. Ranger, his former chairman of the Department of Neurology at the Texas College of Medicine, at one time was Swept's mentor at Harvard, when Swept was a research fellow studying the scientific basis of memory, following his neurology residency at Vanderbilt. It was Ranger who thwarted Swept's attempts to test Compound 1040 in humans, which may or may not have been a wise move but did result in the string of events that led to Swept's working for the CIA and being with Ricki. Ranger had no right to provide personal information about Swept to anyone, especially Louise.

* * *

Jokhar Gantemirov read his copy of the *International Herald Tribune.* Again, there were numerous articles on the weapons of mass destruction. The Americans feared they might fall into the wrong hands. The media increasingly reported there were no WMDs and that the United States and Britain had used this concern as fodder to enter the Middle East.

As he read the paper, he came across a brief report:

> To date, no person or group has been identified as the perpetrator of the failed attempt to destroy the Edinburgh Castle. The police earlier commented

> on a rambling letter to the *Scotsman* and several other newspapers, including this publication, but no new information has been released.

Gantemirov found this interesting. Perhaps it was a failed attempt or, perhaps, the damage was more than the perpetrator anticipated. What was the content of the letter? Was there really a letter? Why was there so little publicity and, when he thought further, why was there any publicity? Gantemirov decided to keep a wary eye out for future similar activity: attempts to blow up a structure but done so poorly that the newspapers mocked the attempt.

Gantemirov continued to wonder about something else: Why was his "escape" mentioned only briefly in the papers? Several newspapers ran a picture of him and Aleksander Kostokov, one of his accomplices. The coverage was intense but very brief, and Gantemirov had little difficulty avoiding capture.

Was no one out to find him? Was the lack of more expansive news coverage intentional? Were the authorities subtly tracking him? Why was there so little attention to the dead tourists? Surely, someone cared about them.

*   *   *

Chapter Nine

ALLENDORF REX

The local Scottish papers, as well as the *International Herald Tribune* and *Wall Street Journal*, paid Jeremiah MacGregor little mind. "No one cares about people who stutter," he muttered to himself. "Not even when they try to destroy a national monument or discuss their cause, my cause, the cause of those unable to talk."

MacGregor held little esteem for organizations concerned with literacy in young children, imploring people to help those unable to read. Sure, those organizations empathized with the illiterate, but what about those unable to produce normal speech? Why did no one care about them?

As Jeremiah MacGregor planned his next deed to focus attention to his "cause," he opened his mail. There was correspondence from the International Speech Forum, an organization to which he belonged, announcing their forthcoming meeting in Paris. Dr. Rex Allendorf, the famous neuroscientist at Cornell, was going to speak on the role of the brain in causing stuttering.

Allendorf, a world-famous investigator who focused his energies on understanding how the brain produces speech, had proven to the neurological and neuroscience communities that stuttering was an organic disturbance. Stuttering, he argued, was a disruption of speech, not language. Speech reflected motor processing, the lips and tongue and jaw moving in particular ways so as to alter sound waves produced by the throat and mouth. Stutterers' brains lacked normal control over this speech-motor apparatus.

Stutterers, he further contended, have abnormal speech, although they have normal language: People who stutter know what they want to say but cannot do so. Their problem is the inability to move their articulators and vocal apparatus to produce normal sounds. Yet, these same muscles function normally when chewing and swallowing and, especially, when singing.

No stutterer is dysfluent when singing. Why? Allendorf queried. Why might a ten-year-old child who stutters be terrified to give a book report in front of his class, due to fear of being ridiculed, yet that same child, suffering embarrassment when singing, is fluent?

Allendorf promulgated a theory that stutterers have problems in the motor-control systems within their brains. He maintained that the processing of the hearing signal, the auditory input, is erroneously transcribed within the thalamus, a deep part of the brain, and this signaling error causes problems in the output of speech.

Many colleagues kidded Allendorf, director of the Institute for Research in Stuttering, regarding the acronym of his laboratory, the IRS. He frequently wondered whether the other IRS would cause him grief. This had not happened, but it, more than occasionally, crossed Allendorf's mind that the government was watching him.

Jeremiah looked forward to hearing Allendorf speak. He had read a great deal about his research, which focused on neuroscience models of stuttering, including brain-imaging abnormalities, problems with speech-motor control, and why speech therapy for stutterers was often only transiently effective.

The mailing also mentioned CNN and FOX would interview Dr. Rex Allendorf. MacGregor, a news junkie and an avid fan of CNN, noticed Allendorf's television interview was tomorrow and made a mental note not to miss it.

* * *

The following day was misty and boring to Jeremiah. He drove his taxi, interacting as little as possible with passengers, most of whom were locals and gave lousy tips. He made it a point to be home early to watch the interview on CNN and arrived with an hour to spare.

MacGregor was better versed in international affairs than his co-workers might suspect. This was the result, in no small part, of his access to a satellite dish, affording daily opportunities to watch documentaries about historical issues and events.

When the network aired the interview with Dr. Allendorf, MacGregor was disappointed. He had hoped the famed investigator was a stutterer, but now, he was painfully aware he was not. Allendorf, sporting a comma of hair that hung across his right eyebrow, an embroidered smile on his face, and a supercilious, haughty air, was incredibly articulate and fluent.

MacGregor enjoyed hearing what the expert had to say about stuttering: "Stuttering has a prevalence among adults of slightly over one percent. Four times that number of children stutter, but many outgrow it. A person destined to stutter as an adult enters the world every thirty seconds. The occurence of stuttering dysfluencies is not random, which is why stutterers never say 'hospital-l-l' but, rather, 'h-h-hospital.' Why? What is the cause of stuttering?"

MacGregor's spirits improved during the interview, and he decided definitely to attend the International Speech Forum meeting in Paris. However, as the interview further proceeded, he became livid. The interviewer, a hyper-nasal woman with spaces between her teeth, asked a question for which Jeremiah MacGregor was poorly prepared.

"Dr. Allendorf, are you aware that the attempt to destroy the Edinburgh Castle was allegedly done by someone trying to call attention to stuttering?"

Allendorf, his smile still stitched to his handsome face, replied, "No, I was not, until just before this interview. I don't keep up much with the news. You informed me someone sent a letter, which you said was confirmed by the authorities, and that whoever the person was who tried to destroy the castle sent a statement on behalf of people afflicted with speech problems, especially stuttering. If so, it makes no sense to me."

"Doctor," she continued, "do you see any connection between an ancient castle and the problems of those afflicted with speech disruption?"

"None," Allendorf replied, sort of chuckling. "It makes no sense."

"Well, thank you for joining us, Dr. Allendorf. This is Christine Willoughby for CNN saying, 'Thank you.'"

Jeremiah MacGregor turned off the set.

Jeremiah wanted publicity in the papers, local as well as international, but was angry he had been mocked on CNN. And that Allendorf commented against him. Did the multiconglomerate news media have a thing for him, Jeremiah MacGregor? Why was this now on CNN?

MacGregor decided to write another letter. This time, he would take more time, carefully outline his thoughts and write as well as possible. This time, people would see he was serious.

MacGregor hastened his plans to have more bombings, more terror on behalf of his speech-afflicted comrades. This time, he would achieve more attention. After all, he reasoned, every day, he read about more people killed in Iraq, as the conflict between American forces and sectors of the indigenous population continued. Why shouldn't there be attention to issues important to him?

* * *

Somewhere deep within the Russian Federation, in the Republic of Georgia, another person was watching CNN, in a local bar. The place was disheveled and a dump for human debris, but the beer-drinking and vodka-swilling men liked hearing CNN in the background. Besides, CNN enabled them to practice their English.

One of these men, the one with big hands and coarse features, listened carefully. Again, he thought, the castle. There was more to this than met the eye. He turned to a man at the table, poured vodka for them both, and each simultaneously said, "Nasdarovye!"

"Jokhar, you are a good man," said Taus. "You know, my brother has always liked and respected you."

"Your brother is a good man and a good friend," Gantemirov replied.

Taus elevated his glass of vodka and emptied the vessel with one huge swallow. "We Chechens go back a long way. Wherever we are, we are always connected. Hopefully, one day, my brother will be president of Chechnya and we will kick out the Russian dogs."

"I hope so," Gantemirov answered, pouring them both another drink. "That is why you have to help me get the weapons."

"It is not without danger. Also, you must get the money. Two hundred fifty million American dollars is not easy to come by."

"I'll find a way." Picking up his glass, studying the small amount of vodka at the bottom, Gantemirov smiled and said, "Nasdarovye."

Chapter Ten

ROSETTA STONED

It was relatively easy for Jeremiah MacGregor to enter the British Museum. Wearing sunglasses and a large baseball cap, he simply purchased his ticket, passed through the piecemeal security system, turned right, and there it was, close to the entrance, in room 4, the Rosetta Stone.

The Rosetta Stone, an archeological phenomenon discovered in 1799 by one of Napoleon's French officers during an expedition in Egypt, was engraved with identical text in three different languages—Greek, Demotic, and Egyptian hieroglyphics. The stone was carved in 196 BC at the decree of Ptolemy V. It was the discovery of this multilingual transcription that enabled the French Egyptologist Jean-Francois Champollion to translate hieroglyphics, deciphering the lost language of ancient Egypt.

These translations led to the decoding of volumes of ancient historical text, with implications for archeologists, historians, and religious scholars. And now, Jeremiah would bring the stone to a new chapter—his chapter.

Carefully removing his plastic bag of glass marbles, he walked down the hall toward the Rosetta Stone. In one quick motion, he released the marbles onto the floor. They clattered noisily as they spread—their vivid colors a contrast against the cold boring floor. Then, just as Jeremiah had planned, people started falling all over the marbles. Most of the people, especially the older ones, were increasingly unsteady, doing their best to remain upright. The loud commotion, as well as the falls, necessitated the guards' attention.

Taking advantage of this distraction, MacGregor, the self-anointed defender of those afflicted with speech problems, emptied a glass container of muriatic acid on the Rosetta Stone. He emptied an entire pint of acid, gleefully appreciating the hissing sound as his liquid weapon soaked into the granite, bleaching it as it performed its duty, and then dripped to the floor, where it produced more damage than it caused on the stone.

Meanwhile, attention remained on the people falling, as an increasing number cursed the marbles, looking for a child to blame, while Jeremiah, careful not to look up at video surveillance cameras, walked away, a seemingly puzzled look on his face. In short time, he was outside, in the middle of London, contemplating future plans.

* * *

Jeremiah flew British Airways back to his native Scotland. He would never tire looking over his beloved Edinburgh. Edinburgh, like Rome, was built on seven hills. Although weather prohibited MacGregor viewing his city with total clarity, he could make out delineations he so loved: the Edinburgh Castle, looming from the ancient volcano crags, the Royal Mile, stretching from the castle to the Palace of Hollyroodhouse, and the multiple slopes and spectacular surrounding views.

Arriving at Edinburgh Airport full of energy, conviction, and passion, Jeremiah took a train and then a bus to his home. He reported to work immediately, making certain to fill his logbook and substantiate his work activity. He was pleased not to have aroused any significant suspicion from the incident at the castle. Each night, he sat at his computer and worked on his letter to the media, finally completing his masterpiece, his *raison d' être.*

Within a few days, the *International Herald Tribune,* the European edition of the *Wall Street Journal,* the politically moderate *Glasgow Herald,* the tabloid *Daily Record,* the conservative *Scotsman,* and the popular Aberdeen-based *Press and Journal* received copies of Jeremiah's unsigned statement, his "Stutterers' Manifesto."

The *Scotsman, Press and Journal,* and the *Wall Street Journal* had editorial pieces discussing MacGregor's letter. They all shared a sarcastic filter of his comments. Were it not for threats of terrorism, they might have paid no heed at all.

Regardless, MacGregor was delighted with the attention. On first sight, he was pleased the *Wall Street Journal* summarized his letter, although dryly, which no one had heretofore printed in full:

> Terrorism is about to reach cliché status. No longer do we have Islamic fundamentalists as our problem. No, we do not even need be concerned about the

> weapons of mass destruction. Now, we have idiotic attacks perpetrated by the writer of a "Stutterers' Manifesto," a concoction dreamed up by some poor clod bemoaning the plight of those unable to talk, bragging at taking aim at a famed castle in Scotland and, now, a failed attempt to destroy the Rosetta Stone.
>
> And all this for publicity. The writer of the Manifesto wants 10 percent of all countries' budgets for medical research. Never mind that our health-care costs far exceed that. This joker wants at least 10 percent of every nation's budget to be applied to medical research.
>
> It stretches this newspaper's sensibilities to think this is how to fix problems in the world—by destroying national symbols. On the other hand, perhaps, maybe, we should all think about where we are going, as well as where we have been, such that societies allow so few to disrupt so many. We guess this is the price of freedom.

After he read the article, the stuttering Scotsman was disappointed. There was nothing about the goal of many stutterer self-help groups, to have people refer to stutterers not as "stutterers" but "people who stutter." He raised the issue of stutterers being their own clan, and that clans had tartans for issues far less important. Further, the *Journal* made no comment about his ingenious insignia, signing the letter with a stick figure of a man with an *X* in his mouth and a snake in each hand.

MacGregor transiently noted an adjacent article criticizing the American president and British prime minister, noting the two countries banked on finding weapons of mass destruction in Iraq following their essentially unilateral invasion but came up with nothing. Why should he care about Iraq? Why should he care about the Sunni and Shiite Muslims or the Palestinians or the Jews? Those groups all had stutterers among them, they all had "people who stutter." Why not focus on something afflicting all of them, at least 1 percent of the adults? Why not focus on stuttering, his stuttering?

* * *

In another part of the world, in Asia, another man was reading a paper, as he tried to do every day. Jokhar Gantemirov, still a fugitive from justice but seemingly not yet hunted, had several newspapers before him. One story, in particular, was not lost on Gantemirov.

The Chechen-turned-Muscovite understood terrorism, having manipulated Islamic fundamentalist monies into his own pocket, channeling terrorists toward his own interests, as when he had worked with Kostokov and others in the failed Pi-Two mission, to achieve control of the world.

What was more, however, was Gantemirov's own understanding of passion. No one would engage in such a hare-brained attempt at blowing up a castle with an unsophisticated bomb, a medieval castle at that, one designed to withstand cannonballs, unless one had passion. It was passion that pushed the perpetrator into this bomb making, unsophisticated though it must have been. Professionals, those from the training camps, would have had better explosive systems and avoided making caricatures of themselves.

As Gantemirov read the paper, always checking his environment, he continued to think. It was a good feeling, this kind of thinking. No, he would not contact more old friends, at least not now. He would wait to hear from Taus or Taus' brother, but he would make no new contacts. Also, he would wait and see what happened with these new terrorists. Later, he would try to contact them, whoever they were.

* * *

Gantemirov did not have to wait too long for more information on the castle explosion. Neither did Jeremiah MacGregor. Within one week, *Newsweek* featured an article, focusing not so much on the explosion but on the alleged motivation behind it—the problem of stutterers. Evidently, MacGregor's recent correspondence following his vandalism of the Rosetta Stone had drawn more attention.

Newsweek, as did the major networks, interviewed Dr. Allendorf, who was now becoming increasingly popular for interviews on stuttering. As director of the Institute for Research in Stuttering, Allendorf was delighted to discuss his hypothesis that stuttering resulted from instability in the auditory feedback system within the brain. Also, Allendorf had discovered stuttering in Zebra finch songbirds, publishing his results in the prestigious scientific journals, *Science* and *Nature*.

Allendorf explained how abnormal sound iterations in 5 percent of Zebra finches were similar to stuttering in humans. He also discussed the chemical abnormalities in avian brains of these stuttering finches and how he hoped to apply this information toward helping people who stutter.

Allendorf was trying to find the genetic code responsible for stuttering. He had screened over five thousand people who stuttered, had completed linkage analysis, and was now directly seeking the DNA responsible for stuttering.

The *Newsweek* reporter asked Allendorf his opinion on the "Stutterers' Manifesto" and what he thought about destroying prominent national property in an attempt to promote medical research or make the world focus on stuttering. Allendorf shared his views earlier expressed, that it was ridiculous.

"Stuttering is a major problem for many people," stated Allendorf. "However, the fact that a screwball thinks it is the only problem or the most important problem or that blowing up a bomb will accomplish anything is nonsense. Whoever did this should spend his or her energies trying to raise money in a productive way for research in stuttering instead of all this. These kinds of actions won't help anything."

Allendorf continued, "Science goes where the money is. Like it or not, that is true. No one cared about Alzheimer's disease when I was younger, because those patients were not in nursing homes, but now they are, paid for by Medicare. Those patients, the Alzheimer's patients, create a financial drain, so funding agencies, like the National Institutes of Health, care about them. We need more support in stuttering, not more bombs. I suggest to whoever did this to learn about the real problems of stuttering, the neuroscience of stuttering. They ought to attend the International Speech Forum next month in Paris. Then, they might find a more useful outlet for their warped energy."

* * *

Jeremiah MacGregor also read the article, which drew nothing but hatred in the mind of the man who had authored the "Stutterers' Manifesto." Standing outside Aitken and Niven, the upscale small Edinburgh department store on George Street, he made more plans. This time, he would travel to America.

* * *

Gantemirov read the *Newsweek* article as he stood near a kiosk in Moscow. He decided to meet with one more of his Chechen friends.

* * *

Chapter Eleven

SKIN, STUTTERERS, AND SILENCE

Jennifer Pettigrew sat in her dermatologist's office at Queen Square Hospital in London. After waiting three hours to see him, all Dr. Montgomery Krafterhole could do was shake his head. "Miss Pettigrew, you do not have a real problem, at least not aside from your skin. You have no problems from lupus affecting your brain, your muscle, or any internal organ. Your problem is only on the skin of your face, and I don't dismiss that. However, your skin is intact and—"

"My skin stinks," said the scantily clad, well-figured woman. "My skin stinks and you stupid doctors don't do a thing about it! Not a damn thing!"

"Miss Pettigrew . . . ," but it was too late. Jennifer Pettigrew stormed out the office, crying, in her mind feeling similar to Anne Frank, hating being locked in her

Amsterdam hiding quarters, blaming her parents for bringing her into a religion that the world persecuted. Similarly, Jennifer Pettigrew hated her parents for bringing her into the world that gave her lupus. Actually, she hated more than her parents for this deed—she hated everybody and everything.

* * *

In Washington, D.C., near Parkside Drive, the man in the wheelchair saw an article about stuttering but read first an article about Iraq. Over one million tons of weapons still remained in Iraq, and three thousand shoulder-fired missiles had not been found. The world was not a safe place.

The man now glanced at the article about stuttering and decided to read it. Something about stuttering now intrigued him. He sat there in the park, staring at the joggers, people who did not have to run because of needing to go from one place to another, but people who ran for pleasure or to keep fit. People who jogged took it for granted they could run, whether fast or slow, but it was something they took for granted. It was something they *could* do. He could never again run, never.

None of the joggers or even the nonjoggers, just people who walked around on their own two feet, ever stopped to ponder about those who could not take simple walking for granted. Walking and running were activities that seemed so natural to so many, but no longer to him.

Perhaps it was so with stuttering. He certainly took his fluent speech for granted. It was not difficult for him to speak. Yet he chose to remain as silent as possible.

As he looked at the refreshment stand far off, up the hill, he was reminded how difficult it was for him to go from one place to another. The man had never been able to find a release for this anger. Why him? Why him?

* * *

Stoli enjoyed the peaceful tree-lined side streets near Dealui Mitropollei, an area spared by former Romanian president Ceausescu's architectural renovations, and bought some magazines from a peddler on the sidewalk. Stoli devoured magazines in many languages—it was how he maintained his wide expertise in so many languages.

There it was—the article in *Newsweek.*

* * *

The editors at *Newsweek* were surprised, to say the least, at the volume of mail they received on the Allendorf piece. They were especially surprised how many people had stutterers in their family and had strong feelings about the fact stuttering must be caused by *something,* given so many people who stuttered still had their stutter despite speech therapy.

Mothers throughout the United States howled frustration at the dilemma they faced trying to get their child who stuttered to go to school and not hide at home from the taunting or go to school and present an oral report in front of a class filled with smirking students. Through it all, the parents complained bitterly of inadequate speech therapy in the public school system for children who stutter.

Word spread, as it often does among those in power in the media. Soon, *Time* and other magazines and newspapers had articles on the castle bombing, the Rosetta Stone acid attack, Rex Allendorf, and the forthcoming International Speech Forum meeting in Paris, France.

* * *

Chapter Twelve

NOUVEAU THOREAU

Larry Leventine sat in his wheelchair, staring at the grass near the pond, hearing the wind whisper, thinking about how Henry Thoreau was mesmerized by the shadow from a blade of wheat, formed from the noonday sun. Thoreau was dumbfounded that one could never say, "This is the moment at which the shadow does not move. This is a moment in time, during which time stands still," because as soon as someone made that statement, time had passed. Thoreau could never catch the time when a shadow of the blade of wheat stopped moving. He could see it move, see it change, and he could recognize time, but he could never capture time. Henry Thoreau could not freeze-frame movement.

Leventine thought what a glory and pleasure it must be to have nothing better to do than stare at a shadow from vegetation. Leventine, stuck in his wheelchair since his automobile accident, could not get free from his wheeled prison. In an ironical vein, he was similar to Thoreau. Both had the time to stare at vegetation. Unlike Thoreau, he could not get up and walk away, although it had not escaped his thinking he was still mobile, albeit in a wheelchair.

Larry Leventine hated being infirm. How could the accident have happened to him, to *him*? He had belittled bad athletes in high school. He was one of the cool guys. Now, he did nothing. And the reality of his life was he had all the time in the world to look at shadows of anything. He received money after his parents' lawsuit, disability insurance paid his bills, but all the money would stop if he became employed. He could work, but he did not. Whereas Henry David Thoreau lived in his Walden and intellectualized the universe, Larry Leventine lived near Rock Creek Park, obsessing over his misfortune, and *de facto* de-intellectualized his life.

Leventine sat there, worn-out brakes on his worn-out wheels, reading newspapers and magazines. He was a voracious reader. He had little else to do now, given how he chose to live his life. He picked up *Time* and noticed an article on Rex Allendorf.

*   *   *

In London, Jennifer Pettigrew read in *The Economist* about the Edinburgh bombing, the acid attack on the Rosetta Stone, and interviews with experts in stuttering. The plight of people who stuttered reminded her of the greater problems among those with systemic lupus erythematosis.

Jennifer Pettigrew had been an avid protestor in college, disliked the rich, and prided herself on being nonbourgeois. She hated the wealthy, the well-dressed, and all elites, believing deep within that her facial-countenance abnormalities, present since early adolescence, kept her from accessing these stations in life. Now, she wondered whether she might have new brethren—people who were also ostracized, people who could not talk.

Jennifer took the article to her lupus self-help meeting, held every month in a restaurant a few blocks off Trafalgar Square. The meetings provided opportunity for social exchange and a chance to associate with those afflicted with her disease. Further, the seminars were educational. This month, a local speaker, Dr. Seymour Burstein, was lecturing on skin problems in lupus patients.

Jennifer Pettigrew sat there, sort of listening to Dr. Seymour Burstein's lecture on lupus and associated problems of the integument, as the doctor complained about difficulty treating disease adequately in a socialized health-care system. As she sat there, Jennifer Pettigrew realized she was a part of a system, a subgroup, a portion of the country, the nation, the world. There were people from all walks of life, whether congenitally blind or deaf or both, those infirm in any way or shape, in wheelchairs or on crutches, suffering a myriad of different diseases, who shared one thing, one variable: They were different because something happened to their body that they could not change.

Jennifer Pettigrew, for the first time in her life, understood something: she truly had a family. And they were all over the world. She politely waited for Dr. Burstein to finish his talk, to which most of the audience was listening intensely, and then started to make a plan.

* * *

Chapter Thirteen

CERVANTES AND THE CIA

Previously, it had been unusual for Major Cervantes to invite Swept to his office since Swept spent most of his time in the laboratory, engaged in neurochemical research. Recently, however, Swept was often in Cervantes's office, discussing not only his research but also Gantemirov and the WMDs. This day, it came as no surprise when Cervantes's secretary telephoned Swept and asked him to come over right away.

Swept walked from his laboratory, still wearing his white lab coat, to CIA Compound Central, a large white building. He provided identification to two guards, went through two metal detectors, and turned left down the tiled hallway, stopping at Cervantes's office. He knocked firmly at the secretary's door, and a voice told him to enter.

Cervantes's secretary was not at her desk. The CIA operative met Swept at the door as he was coming in.

"Sir," reaching out to shake Major Cervantes's hand, "I understand you want to see me."

"Yes. Please come in." Cervantes ushered Swept through the anteroom, where Cervantes's secretary would normally be, and the two men proceeded into the office. Swept looked at the pictures of the presidents, all lacking signatures. He wondered whether Major Cervantes had any kind of special connection with the current president, but he dismissed the possibility.

"What exactly do you remember about Jokhar Gantemirov?"

"Not a lot. You guys picked him up in the neurology clinic, at the Texas College of Medicine, after Valerie VanDance recognized him. He was coming in to see my former chairman, Dr. Harold Ranger, probably to kill him. Then, the Russians imprisoned him. He's a Chechen who lived in Moscow. You recently told me he escaped."

"Yes, he escaped. And he's still on the run. As we discussed a while ago, the Russians wanted him in their prison, to interrogate him their own way. For what it's worth, we didn't get too far with him either."

Swept nodded politely and heard a slight drizzle of rain scratch against the window, making him wonder whether the windows were bullet proof. "Are we certain the Russians didn't obtain valuable information from him?"

"We have no idea. The Russians told us no, but who knows? We certainly understand their wanting information about the Chechen underground, but we don't know if they were successful. They say they were not, but I don't know whether they'd give us the information if they had it. Further, we don't know if he escaped on his own or the authorities let him escape. You would think a Chechen underground derelict like Gantemirov would be important enough to guard closely, but who knows, maybe not. Maybe they didn't think he was that important to guard."

Walking to the front of his desk, Cervantes continued, "From my perspective, I thought it was real important. Here, they had the son of a bitch and should have done whatever they needed to get the information. Certainly, he was a part of the Chechen underground. They needed to know what he knew—who his contacts were, how he got in touch them, and so on. If you ask me, they screwed up."

Swept decided not to argue the rights of prisoners, especially convicted terrorists, because he had mixed feelings. He was aware it is easy to become like the enemies we pursue. He focused intensely as Cervantes presented him a file containing pictures of Aleksander Kostokov, the Russian spy whom Swept killed, Jokhar Gantemirov, and a summary of Compound 1040, the growth hormone chemical analogue Swept investigated that altered memory processing.

Cervantes continued, "The thought crossed our minds that the Russians let him out on purpose, in order to track him and see whom he contacts. That might provide more information to Moscow on the underpinnings of the Islamic movement in Chechnya, as well as other parts of the former Soviet empire. However, there is another issue."

"What is that?" Swept inquired.

"The two tourists killed in Moldova, outside Romania. I showed you the report."

"Right, I remember."

"The Russians kept most of this out of the papers and got the Moldovans to do likewise. The two tourists were Americans. We did a DNA test, or rather, they did. There was evidence of Gantemirov's DNA. That's when the Russians told us Gantemirov had been imprisoned in Moldova, of all places. Evidently, they were afraid to keep him in Moscow, so they had him in this out-of-the-way place."

Cervantes went on, "Maybe they don't want to find him. Maybe they do. All we know is they told us he escaped, and I figured we should somehow get you involved in this, since you were involved in his capture and have seen him close up."

"What am I supposed to do?"

"Not much. Just be aware a man whose operation you destroyed escaped prison and probably recently killed two people. Keep an eye open."

Swept thought for a moment. "That's it?"

"That's it."

Swept, somewhat perturbed that he had left his laboratory for this interlude, frowned. "Well, I guess I should say, 'Thanks for the heads up.' So, thanks for the heads up," and walked out, being careful not to trip on the curled edges of the four-by-six-foot antique Oriental rug.

Major Cervantes, returning to his chair, eyed Swept as he left the office. Cervantes still was not certain whether he liked Dick Swept.

What a bunch of nonsense, Swept thought as he left the office. *Why is Cervantes telling me this? I'm mainly a researcher.*

When Swept was about to enter the elevator, down the hall and to the right of Cervantes's office, Cervantes called his name.

"One more thing!"

"Sure!"

"Have you read about the 'Stutterers' Manifesto'? Do you know anything about stuttering?"

"Not much. Only that a small percentage of children stutter, less so for adults, and they never stutter when they sing. There's some hotshot at Cornell, Dr. Rex Allendorf, who is a real expert in stuttering. Why?"

"I don't know. There's recent press coverage about an attempt to blow up the Edinburgh Castle, pouring acid on British archeological treasures, and a lot of screwiness around this. We may find ourselves involved. I would appreciate your brushing up on stuttering."

"My main area of neurological expertise is neurochemical mechanisms in Alzheimer's disease, not speech. I can review Allendorf's papers, but it might not be a bad idea for you or me to meet him if you really want hard stuff."

"I would appreciate your doing that, Dr. Swept. I've got a feeling. It's strange Gantemirov escapes and these stuttering events are going on at the same time."

"I thought the CIA operated on data, not feelings."

"You thought correctly. But sometimes, so do I." Cervantes smiled. "I shall expect you to look into stuttering and, next week, give me a full report."

"Done," Swept nodded and entered the elevator. *What a bunch of nonsense.*

Swept returned to his lab and went home. He decided to jog and again saw the man in the wheelchair, reading a newspaper. Swept politely nodded to the disabled man, who merely looked at him and said nothing, staring at Swept, who was engaged in a task he could not perform, and resumed reading.

Dick Swept finished his run and returned to his apartment. After showering, he prepared a light dinner and logged onto the Internet, pulling up Rex Allendorf's numerous articles. Swept devoured them until late at night. He went to bed alone, without Ricki Hardson, who lived nearby but was still out of town, visiting a sick friend in Oregon.

* * *

The following morning, Swept read the *Washington Post,* a paper whose editorial perspectives he did not share but whose investigative journalism he admired. There it was, on the front page:

Chechen Spy Escapes

> Jokhar Gantemirov, a Chechen who spent most of his life in Moscow, escaped from jail. Gantemirov, along with Aleksander Kostokov, were credited with a bizarre attempt on behalf of Russian ex-KGB fanatics to take over the world. A neurologist at the

> Texas College of Medicine, investigating a drug similar to the one being used by the Russians, thwarted their plans, killing Kostokov.
>
> Authorities are concerned Gantemirov has numerous connections to Islamic fanatics in the former Soviet empire, especially in Chechnya, and are worried he might catalyze a new wave of terrorist attacks. It is not known whether Gantemirov is involved with al-Qaeda. It is suspected he is involved with the recent murder of two American tourists in Moldova.

Swept was not surprised at his not feeling regret or remorse for killing Kostokov. He was relieved the *Post* did not mention his name and wondered whether they even knew his name. Earlier, in Houston, where he killed Aleksander Kostokov, the papers had mentioned his name. That was before Swept joined the CIA. It crossed Swept's mind the CIA was now keeping his name out of the papers.

Swept's attention turned to the photographs at the bottom of the article, one of Jokhar Gantemirov, the other of Aleksander Kostokov. Both were clear, and the features were evident for all to see.

Next, Swept turned to his copy of the *New York Times*, which had a similar article and photographs on their front page. *They must really want this guy*, he thought. Gantemirov's escape, coupled with Swept's increasing suspicion as to how or why his name was not mentioned in the article, gave him cause to ponder.

* * *

Chapter Fourteen

THE NEW MANIFESTO

Jokhar Gantemirov, living in the outskirts of Moscow, looked at the *International Herald Tribune.* Gantemirov liked this paper. It made clear what was internationally important and was not as biased as Russian newspapers.

There it was—the same article Swept just read. The Associated Press and Reuters had picked up the story. Gantemirov had not seen much reference to himself in the Russian papers, so maybe the Russian authorities did not want him found. Maybe, they wanted him to seek old friends so they could learn who had been his contacts. But how did the wire services find out, if not through the Russians? Maybe the Moldova authorities were actually competent, knew there was a local prison escape, sent agents to examine the dead tourists' car, and sent material for DNA analysis, possibly to Russia. Maybe that was how they knew Gantemirov was the murderer. Or maybe they had no DNA evidence and the Moldovans simply presumed the escaped Gantemirov was the culprit. But again, why was it so easy to escape from the jail? All he had to do, essentially, was walk out. Why?

Earlier, Gantemirov had contacted only a few friends. He had known a handful of people since childhood, and aside from drinking vodka and his brief exchanges, nothing currently was suspicious, except for his discussion with Taus.

If the Russians picked up any of Gantemirov's Chechen friends, including Taus, he would have heard about it. Maybe the Russians were waiting for something later, or maybe they were not waiting at all.

* * *

In Bucharest, Romania, at Optopeni International Airport, Stoli waited for his assigned group of incoming tourists from Vienna. Stoli preferred they come by train since he had not adapted to the bureaucratic incompetents at the airport. The only good thing about the airport was watching the new Romanian Airlines 747s TAROM jets as they landed and departed the tarmac.

While waiting, Stoli picked up copies of several foreign papers, always wanting to practice and improve his multilingual skills. There it was, right in front of him. Stoli actually felt tightness in his throat when he looked at the picture.

The article was written by staff at Reuters. They reported Jokhar Gantemirov's escape from jail and his possibly killing two American tourists. But the pictures, the pictures! There they were—one of Gantemirov, showing coarse features, with a slight scowl. But the other picture was one Stoli would have recognized anywhere. It was him! Yet the paper said it was Aleksander Kostokov, a Russian ex-KGB agent, Gantemirov's former colleague.

My God! Stoli thought to himself. *This is my brother! I am one of the twins, possibly triplets. I was correct. I'm from Moscow. This man was my brother, my blood! Everything I thought was correct.*

Stoli grabbed the other papers. There were the articles again, and the photographs. They all had the photograph. He looked at them carefully. There was no doubt. Aleksander Kostokov was Stoli's DNA mirror image.

Stoli had to learn more. All he had to do now to learn more about Kostokov, his dead twin brother, was to contact the police or go to the library or search the Internet. But he realized in an instant, he needed to find Gantemirov. If his DNA clone had worked with Gantemirov, then maybe he should too. All he would learn from the police were negative details. He wanted to know more about his brother. Why did he work for the KGB? What did he do for them? Was he really a killer? If so, was it in self-defense? Did he have a family? What kind of man was he? Did his brother die to protect Gantemirov? Stoli owed it to his dead brother to find Gantemirov.

Stoli hailed a taxi and left behind the airport, tour bus and tourists, not to mention his job. He left all of it. Stoli felt like a new man. Whatever transition he was going through, he knew it was happening now. He felt a change, a process, somehow reaching into the depth of whatever he was or would become. He felt great!

Folding several copies of different newspapers under his left arm, sitting in the taxi, Stoli did not know precisely what he was going to do but realized one thing: His brother had been in the KGB, was involved in an attempt to achieve world domination, and must have been pretty damn good at what he did. He needed to find the man who worked with his brother. That man was Jokhar Gantemirov, and Stoli had to find him before anyone else did.

The taxi driver took Stoli, without toiletries or clothes, to the closest international train ticket office, the CFR. He purchased a ticket and then went to the station. There, he boarded a train for Moscow. He had never felt so good in his life.

* * *

Jeremiah MacGregor was pleased magazines and newspapers around the world at least acknowledged his efforts. He was displeased many of these articles viewed his activities as derelict or silly. However, at least he had their attention.

Jeremiah MacGregor, a taxicab driver in Edinburgh, Scotland, had the attention of the world. The world! He felt increasing passion and focus on his task. Yes, he would make the world understand the problems of stutterers.

Jeremiah signed his taxi docket and said goodby to Iris, sitting at her desk.

"Jeremiah," Iris smiled. "Have a good evening."

"Th-Th-Thanks, Iris. You too."

"You might be interested to know that the police stopped asking us about the taxi and the bombing of the castle. Have they stopped talking to you?"

"Th-They spoke to m-me a little, a-and then once more. I-I-I told them what I told you—the cab broke down and, I-I g-g-guess, someone must have picked it up."

"Well, I hope they find whoever did that. Not to be too personal, but did they make a connection between your stutter and that Stutterers' Manifesto?"

"Th-Th-They asked me a little about it, but not again. They know I have a clean record and think maybe I was set up." Jeremiah suddenly realized the authorities could trace his flying from England to Scotland around the time of the damage to the Rosetta Stone. He did not care if he were caught but did care that he accomplish his mission, to make the world aware of the problems of those afflicted with speech problems. He instantly appreciated that he had to expand the scope of his manifesto, not only to accomplish his purpose but also to lead the authorities away from him.

He said goodby to Iris and returned home to complete a new manifesto.

Iris smiled and half-waved goodbye. "Personally, Jeremiah, I don't think they paid too much attention to the bombing. On second thought, maybe they did and turned it over to the British. The whole thing seemed a bit bizarre."

Jeremiah nodded his head and walked toward the exit.

* * *

Jeremiah spent the next several evenings thinking about his new manifesto. He wanted nothing in writing until the manifesto was completed in his mind. He was clearheaded and incredibly energized. Soon, he was done, and newspapers throughout the world received his correspondence:

The Stutterers' New Manifesto

> I am the person who tried to destroy the Edinburgh Castle and the Rosetta Stone. I speak for a large organization of people, people from cultures throughout the world and all societies. I speak for

people who cannot speak. I speak for those afflicted, not in hearing or in vision or poverty. I speak for stutterers.

We represent 1 percent of the world population. We always hear about the Jews. They are one-tenth of 1 percent of the world population. We, people who stutter, are ten times that number. Why does no one talk about us?

Recently, Dr. Rex Allendorf, a famous scientist at Cornell University, has been in magazines and on television all over the world. His research reveals stutterers have problems with how their brains control speech. Why is it only recently the media is interviewing Dr. Allendorf? I shall tell you why. It is because of me. Had I not done these things, trying to blow up the castle and destroy the Rosetta Stone, no one would be talking about stuttering. Well, everyone is talking about stuttering now.

Protect your precious panda bears in Washington D.C., your Westminster Abbey in London, protect the Eiffel Tower in Paris, museums in St. Petersburg, mosques, churches, and synagogues. Beware, because I speak for a lot of us, and we are growing in numbers by the minute.

We have demands, and I am not kidding. Governments throughout the world must make a commitment to place 10 percent of their national budgets into medical research. This need not be only for stuttering, but it must be for medical research. I want to see press statements they are doing this. I know even if governments release these

> statements they may not adhere to their promise. But if they do not do this, then I shall know they do not take me seriously, that they do not take us seriously.
>
> Again, I am not kidding. We shall wreak havoc on the world if governments do not cooperate with our demands.

Once again, the signature was a small stick-man, with an *X* for a mouth and a snake in each hand.

Jeremiah MacGregor was delighted with his letter, his manifesto. Although he had minimal formal education, he thought his writing was good. He sent the article to every paper he could think of, to every paper he knew about in Scotland, to leading international papers, to American, French, English papers. He sent over one hundred copies. He printed them on his home computer, mailed them in several different postal boxes in Edinburgh, and then erased the letter from his computer and emptied the "trash bin."

He thought about the bombing of the castle and the few people who died. He truly felt no remorse, no guilt—he felt nothing. It seemed as though the Edinburgh police were paying only minimal attention to the event, and he was fairly certain he was not being followed. Even if the police kept tabs on his leaving the country, so what? he mused. No one would be able to blame anything on him. Regardless, in case they could, he needed to work fast.

Jeremiah felt so good he decided to exercise, something he seldom did. He went to the local public gym and exercised until he could barely move. Then, he went home and decided to eat out, treating himself to a great Scottish meal. He chose a restaurant he could barely afford, the Tower Restaurant, housed in the Museum of Scotland.

Jeremiah knew little about the culinary arts but appreciated good food. He seldom ate out because of expense and lack of friends. Jeremiah had read Edinburgh eateries were increasingly improving, most restaurants sporting the Scottish-French style, founded on a shared disdain for the English. The Scots' element was plain and fresh food, whereas the French supplied the sauces, often poured on after the cooking.

The Tower Restaurant usually accommodated the locals on short notice, and they accommodated Jeremiah. Besides, they were not fully booked. The modern architecture of this rooftop restaurant offers one of the finest views of Edinburgh. Jeremiah ordered lamb stew, roast-pigeon salad with raspberry, vinaigrette dressing, and a local wine of the waiter's choosing.

During the meal, Jeremiah thought about future plans to make the world more aware of the problems of the sick. Afterwards, he went home, treated himself to a single malt scotch that a tourist had mistakenly left in his cab months ago, and went to bed, thinking.

Over the next several days, Jeremiah MacGregor was increasingly content. Many newspapers mentioned his new letter, but the article in *The Economist* really focused his attention.

> We have a new form of terrorism, one that claims a noble purpose with which we are all supposed to agree. Many terrorists feign self-righteousness, and some truly believe it. However, now we have a

> "Stutterers' Manifesto," signed with a stick figure man holding snakes in his hands and an *X* for a mouth. This stickman wants governments throughout the world to commit to medical research, placing 10 percent of their budgets into that endeavor.
>
> Well, we have done some homework. Over 12 percent of the GDP in each country in Europe, and a far higher percentage of the United States GDP, currently is directed toward health care. It may not all be for research, but the monies are directed nonetheless. Taking care of the sick is immediately more important than doing research for them, or on them. What would you prefer your doctor do when you have a cold? Place you on medicine or go home and investigate how a germ makes you ill?
>
> However, although we hate to say it, maybe the guy has a point. We do not support blowing up monuments or people, but it strikes us that armies killing people, whether for defensive or offensive purposes, unfortunately is often more popular than physicians saving lives or increasing knowledge.

Jeremiah and his self-initiated movement were making progress. He confirmed his decision to travel to America. Several inexpensive fares were available through the Internet were he to leave now. Jeremiah telephoned the taxi pool and said that he was not coming in for a few days. He provided no reason, and no one asked for one. Substitute drivers were readily available.

Jeremiah was able to afford the fare to the United States since he had saved a small amount of money, given he lived alone and seldom went out. Jeremiah booked a British

Airways flight from Edinburgh Airport to Gatwick and then to Dulles International Airport in Washington, D.C.

* * *

Everything seemed to be happening so fast. Twenty-four hours earlier, Jeremiah was in Scotland. Now, he sat in a jet headed for America. Packing, airport security, all of it seemed so easy. Jeremiah slept well on the plane and woke, just as the plane landed in Dulles.

MacGregor checked in at the Hotel Harrington, one of Washington's oldest continually operating hotels, offering few inexpensive frills, and right in the center of everything.

After taking a brief nap, accommodating to jet lag, Jeremiah took a tour bus to see the sights. Jeremiah spent the next two days visiting the Smithsonian Institution, the Washington Monument, toured the White House and . . . exercised.

Ever since Jeremiah sent his latest manifesto, he enjoyed exercising. MacGregor took the Metro to Rock Creek Park and jogged, wearing the new Nike shoes he purchased on sale at one of the shopping malls. After a three-mile run, he stopped and stretched his tight hamstring muscles. Near one of the bridges, he noticed a man in a wheelchair. What struck him was that he could see an article entitled "Stutterers' Manifesto."

Walking over to the man in the wheelchair and string at the article, the man put down the paper and gruffly said, "What do you want?"

"N-N-Nothing. J-J-Just looking." Both men looked at each other, one an invalid from the waist down, the other an invalid in his mouth.

Larry Leventine, the man in the wheelchair, turned his newspaper over and saw the full headline, "Stutterers' Manifesto: Are Their Demands Silly?"

For a few moments, Leventine put aside his self-absorbing self-pity, nodded his head, and picked up the paper, returning to the article he was reading. After MacGregor walked away, Leventine turned to the article on stuttering and read it. He liked what he read. Governments should increase their spending on medical research. He also read the interview with Rex Allendorf, who referred to stuttering as a handicapping condition. Leventine liked that too.

Leventine pondered other forms of handicaps in the world, some involving dysfunction in the legs, some involving dysfunction in the mouth, and, he mused, perhaps some involving dysfunction in how people think.

* * *

MacGregor jogged in Rock Creek Park the following day, but several hours earlier. Leventine was there again. At the end of his jog, Jeremiah stretched his legs, nodding to Leventine not far away. Leventine called out, "How're you doing?"

"Okay, I guess. C-C-Could be better." Walking over to Leventine, MacGregor was surprised at his own social forwardness. Extending his sweaty hand, Jeremiah announced, "M-M-M-My name's J-J-J-Jeremiah, Jeremiah MacGregor."

Leventine reciprocated, introducing himself, adding, "Is that a Scottish accent? Are you from Scotland?"

"A-A-Actually, I am. I'm here visiting, sort of on vacation."

“Good for you,” and Leventine wheeled away, extending a half-smile. Leventine looked at his paper and noticed an article about Milton Resnick, an abstract expressionist painter. What caught his attention was a statement from Resnick years ago, which said that creativity resulted from combining panic with faith. For some reason, this statement rang true in Larry Leventine’s mind, and he looked behind him to see the man with the handicap in his mouth walking away.

At the same time, Jeremiah, pleased he was relatively fluent when he spoke to Leventine, thought about how to kill panda bears at the Washington Zoo.

* * *

Chapter Fifteen

NOT THE MARRYING TYPE

Ricki Hardson lay in Dick Swept's arms. She had returned from a week in Oregon only yesterday. Seldom had Swept's lovemaking seemed so mechanical, so devoid of emotion. Ricki, sensing this, quit trying to cuddle with Swept, propped herself on his chest, removed a wisp of hair from her pensive eyes, and smiled.

"Richard, you really do not want to marry me, right?"

Inhaling deeply, Swept replied, "No. I do not. I truly love you but just don't want to get married, at least not now. I'm busy in the lab, busy with the CIA, and I occasionally wonder whether I should move back to Texas. I don't know, I just don't want to get married. It has nothing to do with you. It has to do with how I feel."

"Am I ever going to make you change your mind?" Ricki said, toying with his chin.

Swept sat up. "Ricki, I have no interest in any other woman. I'm just not in a marrying state. I told you, the other day, Gantemirov escaped, I met with that jerk Cervantes, I need to hone my skills in martial arts, I've got things to do at the agency, and I'm just not ready to settle down. Does that bother you a lot?"

"Only in that I want to spend my life with you, have your babies, and share our worlds." With that, Ricki Hardson flipped her legs over the side of the bed, put on her clothes, and looked down at her lover. "You aren't even going to try to stop me from leaving, are you?"

"I don't want you to leave, but I don't try to keep anyone from doing what they want to do."

"Baloney!" the now partially dressed woman responded. "I'll talk to you later," she mumbled as she finished dressing and walked out the door. Swept sighed, placed his folded arms behind his head, stared at the ceiling, and anticipated feeling grief. Instead, he felt a quasiform of relief yet did not feel good.

This was Ricki's decision. Swept wanted to see Ricki, did not want to be without her, but did not want to marry her. If the relationship ended, that was Ricki's doing, not his. If she wanted to leave, that was her doing, not his. But if Ricki Hardson left him, then he would not be with the person whose company he most enjoyed.

Swept loved Ricki's values. He appreciated her interest in various sports, her love of motorcycles, her love of food, and especially enjoyed her well-proportioned lithe body. But he did not want to marry.

Swept remained in bed as Ricki ushered herself out of his apartment. Resting his head on folded arms, Swept stared at the ceiling. For some reason, he thought about Louise.

Outside, on the sidewalk, Ricki removed her cell phone from the lightweight Versace coat Swept had bought for her birthday and telephoned a man with whom she recently had dinner twice. Ricki reached only his answering machine, to which she spoke, holding back tears. "Reginald, you wanted to know why I didn't want to get serious. Well, now I can tell you. I was seeing someone else and just decided I no longer am. Call me on this number whenever you get in. I am totally available." Ricki Hardson gave him her phone number, which rang ten minutes later, and she walked to a local café, with a determined look on her face to redo her world.

* * *

Dick Swept showered, planning his day. He would jog and then visit the panda bears. The combination of sensitivity and power in the animals always helped clear his thinking.

* * *

Jeremiah MacGregor took a taxi to the National Zoo. He always felt like a member of some unnamed club whenever he took a cab. The first thing he did was to inform the cabbie that he, too, was a cabbie. Deep within, MacGregor hoped this would deter the transporter from taking more expensive, circuitous routes, something he had heard American taxi drivers sometimes did but drivers in Scotland would never do.

The driver left him off at the Connecticut Avenue entrance, one of three main entrances to the zoo. Jeremiah walked toward the pandas and sat on the bench where he could see Mei Xiang and Tian Tian, the two famous giant pandas. A child standing next to her mother bubbled with joy. "Look, Mommy. Bear. Panda bear. Look, look!"

MacGregor found it odd they both looked at the animal with joy, each finding its beauty compelling. However, MacGregor studied how easy it would be to kill the animals—just toss a grenade or a Molotov cocktail or shoot them from the park bench outside the fencing. The little girl, on the other hand, harbored no such hopes of ill achievement, just the joy of seeing the cuddly bears.

The child's mother looked at MacGregor, briefly smiled, and walked away with her daughter. Jeremiah sat on the bench, thinking.

* * *

Dick Swept, having returned from his run, sat in his large leather chair, drinking a cup of Vienna Roast coffee, admiring the Washington Monument through his apartment window. Swept liked his coffee strong and black, as he believed all men should. It blew his mind that a coffee industry in America was booming, fostering gimmicks in what should be only boiled water percolated through coffee beans. He drank his black coffee and read the *Washington Post.*

Swept frequently went to the National Zoo since moving to the Washington area. Swept had a friend who attended the University of Illinois Medical School in Chicago, and every Saturday morning, his friend visited Monet's Haystacks at the Chicago Art Institute. His friend said it was therapeutic, providing emotional respite from the intensity of medical studies. So it was with the pandas for Dick Swept.

Swept drove to the zoo, sat on the green bench positioned above the giant pandas' habitat, and thought. He thought about his research in Alzheimer's disease, Major Cervantes, Ricki, Louise, the Edinburgh Castle, and all the complicated elements in his life. Mei Xiang looked at the neurologist, and Swept believed he saw the animal wink.

Swept winked back and drove to his laboratory.

* * *

A young man wearing the uniform and insignia of the National Zoo was addressing a group of semi-interested preadolescent students. "Approximately one thousand giant pandas survive in the mountain forests of central China. One hundred twenty are in Chinese breeding facilities and zoos, and twenty live in zoos outside China. Two giant pandas, Mei Xiang and Tian Tian, live in the National Zoo, in Washington, D.C., and are on loan from the People's Republic of China."

Jeremiah was in earshot of the lecture. He listened intently, semi-amused at the flirtatious interchanges among the students.

"During the warm months of the year, visitors to our zoo can view the pandas outside, playing and scrunching bamboo shoots. During winter months, visitors have better views inside, viewing the bears through a glass enclosure."

The weather was warm. Jeremiah studied the animals. He returned to his hotel and searched "giant pandas" and "National Zoo" on the computer in the lobby of the Hotel Harrington. Pandacam, available at no Internet charge, provided multiple live views of the animals, enabling MacGregor to study them and their surroundings.

The following day, MacGregor donned his large sunglasses, a long-sleeved shirt, baseball cap, and his bag of marbles. A taxi drove him to the zoo, where he walked directly to the giant pandas. Just as he had in London, Jeremiah quickly let loose the marbles on the ground. During the ensuing commotion, several people fell, including a grandmother and her young grandchild. Meanwhile, MacGregor threw several bamboo shoots into the area where the bears were playing. Some shoots were stuffed with peanut butter, others with foxglove plants. A few shoots were sprinkled with sugar. The pandas immediately grabbed the bamboo morsels, struggling for possession.

Jeremiah disappeared in the midst of the commotion.

* * *

Chapter Sixteen

PANDA DEATH

That evening, Swept was finishing an experiment on NMDA receptors, working late in his laboratory, when he heard a news item on the local NPR station: Someone had poisoned Mei Xiang and Tian Tian. The newsman announced that the pandas were apparently poisoned with large amounts of digitalis, a medicine affecting the heart even in small doses. There was speculation that the pandas had somehow ingested the drug during the commotion caused by people falling on a large number of marbles on the ground. Both pandas died from digitalis overdose. Evidently, someone had thrown plants laced with the deadly drug into the area where the animals played.

In another part of town, a taxicab driver from Edinburgh, Scotland, was proud of his slingshot aim and his ability to smuggle foxglove into America. It was not uncommon knowledge that foxglove contains digitalis, and alternative medicine stores abound in Scotland, where it was quite easy for Jeremiah to obtain foxglove leaves.

Jeremiah had no remorse at taking the lives of the two panda bears. His focus was on the greater good and on now sending another letter to various newspapers, outlining and emphasizing that no monuments or attestations to anything cultural or national were safe until governments earmarked 10 percent of their national budgets to medical research.

Newspapers throughout the country declared the panda crime heinous. Who in their right mind would kill—could kill—two innocent giant pandas? The answer lay in correspondence signed with a stickman displaying an *X* for a mouth and a snake in each hand. The answer lay in Jeremiah MacGregor.

* * *

On the other side of the globe, in England, Jennifer Pettigrew read about killings in Iraq, as America and its allies attempted to maintain peace until the Iraqi people were organized and strong enough to govern themselves. She also read about the killing of the giant pandas. Jennifer paid little attention, if any, to the People's Republic of China formally complaining to the United States that they should be able to protect the pandas. Jennifer did find it surprising and emotionally encouraging that an organization had emerged that desecrated the Edinburgh Castle, vandalized the Rosetta Stone, and now killed panda bears. And the idea of the stickman with the *X* and the snakes, coupled with the demand for more research dollars for medical issues, warmed her heart.

Jennifer Pettigrew typed out a manifesto of her own and sent it to the local papers, the *International Herald Tribune,* the *London Financial Times*, and the *Wall Street Journal.* Her message was simple:

> We are together. We are one. The "Stutterers' Manifesto" is our manifesto. It is everyone's manifesto. People with lupus, hypertension, kidney disease, diabetes, multiple sclerosis, Parkinson's disease, all of us, we are one. We shall tear down your monuments, which are nothing more than concrete and metal effigies of an old, crumbling order. We shall destroy you, as you have destroyed us.
>
> You destroy us, not by what you do but by what you do not do. You do not care. There is one solution, and only one: place 10 percent of national government budgets into medical research or you will die, as we die.

Jennifer Pettigrew signed her letter with a stickman holding a snake in each hand, and an *X* for a mouth, just as she had read about being the signature for the "Stutterers' Manifesto." Jennifer then drove to Oxford and mailed a similar letter, and then to Newcastle upon Tyne and sent still another. She sent another from Dover and twenty more from various parts of England.

Major newspapers throughout Great Britain received identical letters, all printed on the same laser printer and the same font. Several editors wondered whether there was a movement at hand, a movement for the sick, or whether this was the work of a singular weirdo.

Later that evening, Jennifer Pettigrew confided to her female friends what she had done. All of them had issues with physicians or parents or authority of one nature or another and hailed her actions as fantastic. They smoked marijuana until the early hours of the morning and developed a strategy.

They would go to the United States, where transportation was simple, especially if you drove or took a bus, and was not even that difficult by air. Many believed they had lupus or some other chronic disease, had seen physicians in the United States for their various medical problems, and were familiar with travel in the America.

Most of the women had muscle aches and pains for which physicians had found no cause or cure. Many had some tests positive for lupus, with many other tests being negative. Physicians explained some tests for lupus were often falsely positive, but the women latched on to the positive test results, insisting lupus was their disease.

Some of the women had other medical problems. One friend had retinitis pigmentosa, a degenerative disease of the eye that can cause blindness. Another had diabetes, one had epilepsy due to a vascular abnormality in the brain, and another had constant itching in different places at different times, symptoms for which no physician could find a cause and all tests were negative.

All these people, and some others with assorted ailments, hailed Jennifer's actions as heroic, instructive, having great purpose and possibly able to achieve grand results.

Yes, they would go to the United States. They would visit major medical centers, medical schools, and medical establishments throughout the nation, and then, this group of women would wreak pandemonium within the medical establishment. They would make their voices heard! The excitement was infectious and exhilarating. They were the embryo of a movement and, in honor of Jennifer, decided to call themselves the "Lupus Ladies of London."

The movement was spontaneous, coming from nowhere, all catalyzed by a stutterer from Scotland. Regardless, it was still a movement, posed a danger, and the public needed to be informed. Within this setting, some of the papers wrote brief stories on the manifestos, and some editorials seemed almost laudatory. After all, these people were not asking for land for statehood or money for themselves. Rather, they wanted a commitment from nations to support medical research.

* * *

Jokhar Gantemirov read the article in *Pravda* about people with disease holding nations hostage. Gantemirov was smart enough to recognize a nascent movement when he saw one. When he also read about the forthcoming International Speech Forum meeting in Paris, which focused on stuttering, he quickly decided there would be people there who felt strongly about this topic. And he wanted to get in on the ground floor.

Gantemirov felt that he no longer had to be as careful in interacting with the Chechen underground. If the Russian authorities wanted to find him, why had no one inquired his whereabouts from any of his Chechen brethren? If the authorities were watching him, why were there no suspicious characters anywhere? Besides, he wanted to join his colleagues. He wanted to be as active as possible with his people. Gantemirov was proud of his people and proud of their goals—independence from Russia regardless of the cost.

* * *

Larry Levintine read about the manifestos in the *Wall Street Journal.* He chuckled. *Sure,* he thought to himself, *these guys want to help us. But how? How could any of them help me?*

Leventine's injury would not kill him. He did not have progressive disease, only the remnants of his horrible accident that, although physically damaging only his spinal cord, rendering him paraplegic, *de facto* caused more damage to his mind and thinking. Deep within, Larry Leventine had to know he was able and fit to work, but then he would lose his disability payments. The easiest thing to do was to sit in his wheelchair, view the pond in the park, and bemoan the joggers.

On a few occasions, Leventine attended a local multiple-sclerosis meeting, where patients tried to learn more about their disease and complained about physicians, hospitals, and insurance companies. Leventine did not reveal that his being in a wheelchair related to an automobile accident, not multiple sclerosis. Rather, he let them believe what they wanted to believe. Leventine felt superior to these people. Most had progressive disease; he did not. But he was still very unhappy.

* * *

In the middle of Central Park, in New York City, on several large rocks, stick men with an *X* for a mouth and a snake in each fist were drawn in bright orange paint. The *New York Post* jokingly called it the "Day of the Stutter," while the *New York Times* had a more serious perspective. They noted that just as al-Qaeda's subtle beginning exploded into death and destruction, so, too, a new organization was appearing. The editors wondered whether some pranksters with nothing better to do had scribbled the graffiti, or whether the drawings were part of an expanding terrorist movement. The editors admonished that everyone should take this new development very seriously.

* * *

Jennifer Pettigrew read more about the movement, her movement. Jennifer and her friends were making a difference, a real difference. Jennifer was going to make certain they did not lose their momentum.

* * *

Stoli also read about the movement. He still wanted to find Jokhar Gantemirov. When Stoli read about the forthcoming International Speech Forum meeting in Paris, he realized this meeting might attract speech-afflicted terrorists. If Gantemirov really were a terrorist, perhaps he would be there. Stoli planned to attend.

Stoli continued his reading, noting the continuation of bombings in Iraq, killings among Israelis and Palestinians, and the buildup of nuclear weapons in North Korea and Iran.

* * *

In another corner of the world, at the Langley, Virginia, headquarters of the CIA, Dick Swept was enjoying a brief respite from his day, reading the *Washington Post,* when his telephone rang. It was Major Cervantes.

"Richard, are you keeping up with the Stickman X nonsense?"

"I've read about it in our daily reports and the newspapers. I understand the International Speech Forum is going to meet outside Paris, something I presume never would have made the papers prior to these recent events."

"I agree," replied Cervantes. "I think you should attend the Paris meeting and check it out. Report any suspicious activity."

After a period of dead silence, Swept commented, "I'm not an expert on stuttering. I'm a neurologist who investigates memory disorders."

"That might be," rebuked Cervantes. "But you're a scientist nonetheless. Besides, you're probably the best person we have for something like this. You should go. And one more thing."

"Yes?" responded Swept.

"What are your thoughts on Gantemirov?"

"I don't have any brilliant thoughts on that either. Going back to your last request, it may be that whoever perpetrated the incidents against national monuments might attend the Paris meeting. I can contact Dr. Rex Allendorf about the conference and stuttering."

"When do you leave for the meeting?"

"I need to check on the dates. By the way, let me remind you of one of the CIA's promises when I came on board."

"Which is?"

"I can attend as many meetings as I feel necessary and stay at any hotel I choose, all expenses paid."

"So?"

"So, I'm just letting you know that when I'm in Paris, I always stay at the Crillon."

"See that your time there is productive."

"I'll do my best," said Swept, a smile crossing his face.

"Report to me when you return. Have a good meeting and a good stay." Cervantes put down the receiver.

* * *

Later that day, after cascading through a series of telephone numbers and secretaries, Swept finally reached Dr. Allendorf, who briefly discussed the International Speech Forum organization, noting that it sponsored research and provided clinical assistance to people afflicted with speech disorders, especially stuttering. Allendorf provided Swept with the appropriate web mail addresses and Swept registered for the meeting, booked a jet to Paris, and made arrangements at the Crillon Hotel.

Swept left his lab that afternoon, making certain the reagents to activate the glutamate receptors had been injected into appropriate brain slices, in anticipation of subsequent single-cell recordings, and went to the library to obtain more articles on stuttering. Following this, he went to the park to jog.

Jogging near the Potomac River, Swept saw the man in the wheelchair, stone-faced, staring at the joggers.

* * *

Chapter Seventeen

HELP THE SELF-HELP

In Houston, Texas, at a self-help meeting for people with stress, Suzie Whitehead complained about her plastic surgery gone amok. Dr. Regina Bruxton, a superb plastic surgeon, had removed a small premalignant lesion from Suzie's face. Following the operation, the patient complained of incessant burning. She called Dr. Bruxton several times, and each time, Dr. Bruxton returned her call. Three times following the operation, at no additional remuneration to Dr. Bruxton, the plastic surgeon examined Suzie Whitehead.

"There is just nothing here," Dr. Bruxton exclaimed. "The wound is clean, healing well, and there is no inflammation."

"Then, why does it hurt so much? It burns, all the time."

"I don't know," said Dr. Bruxton. "Do you think, possibly, this relates to stress?"

"I'm not stressed. My problem is the burning, not my life. My life is fine."

"I thought you're recently divorced. I'm not familiar with too many vanilla divorces. Look," Regina Bruxton explained, "I'm not trying to be inappropriate. I'm just trying to figure out why you hurt when I find nothing wrong."

"I'm in a self-help group, and we all agree I'm fine. I am totally in touch with my feelings. The problem is your lousy surgery, not me."

"The surgery was successful."

"No, it wasn't! It didn't help me. I hurt and hurt a lot. You don't care, none of you doctors care."

"I do care. I'm trying to help you."

It was too late. Crying, Suzie Whitehead stormed out of the surgeon's examining room. Turning around, she screamed, "Just because you're pretty, you think everyone else is inadequate."

"That is not true," replied an exasperated Regina Bruxton. "I'm trying to help you."

"Then help yourself," and the angry patient stormed out of the office, tears flooding her face.

Regina, exasperated, dictated a brief note on Suzie Whitehead's medical condition, commenting on their interaction, and prepared for her next patient.

* * *

When Suzie Whitehead explained her frustration to the members of the self-help group, the story was different. "There I was," the patient said. "I had to fight cancer of my skin. I only saw this horrible woman because she was in my health plan and had a name I could pronounce. She removed the cancer, at least she said she did, but for all I know, she missed some of it, got paid, and then kicked me out of her office when I told her the surgery site hurt, and she told me it didn't. Someone should teach these doctors a lesson. They all think they're so smart. Well, I am too, and I just hired an attorney, from Fatswath and Fatswath, to look into the case. Meanwhile, I'm still in pain."

Suzie went on. "I'm telling you, people aren't going to tolerate lousy doctors much longer. The whole medical establishment, all of them, is rotten. The government doesn't care either, all because of the powerful drug companies and doctor organizations. That's why, I was just reading, there are terrorist attacks in which people want governments to put ten percent of their budgets into medical research. I think it's a great idea."

One of the members responded, "I thought the amount the United States spends on health care is higher than that."

"Sure," said Suzie Whitehead. "But the terrorists aren't talking about money spent on health care. They're talking about money spent on medical research."

Enjoying the group's attention, Suzie Whitehead continued, "Look at us." Turning to two young men in wheelchairs, she continued, "Isn't there a world of difference between the government paying for a wheelchair versus spending money on research to make people walk?" The two young men were silent, nodding politely. "I tell you," Suzie continued, "things are going to change. This organization of terrorists leaves a stickman figure, with an *X* for his mouth and a snake in each hand, whenever they do their stuff. I don't support terrorism, but I'm not so sure this is a bad idea."

"A stickman?" one of the two wheelchair victims asked. "They draw a man made of sticks, like the ones kids draw?"

"Yes, and with an *X* for a mouth and a snake in each hand. They started off being interested in stuttering, but now they care about more people."

One of the two men in wheelchairs, somewhat melancholy, remembered when, as an adolescent, he drew stickmen and four-letter epithets on the bathroom wall of a hunting lodge and how angry he had made his father. He and his dad hunted a lot, but now, his father was dead, and the man never hunted.

Both men in wheelchairs, Donald Keyman and Buster Williamson, suffered leg paralysis in late adolescence after imbibing too much bourbon and simultaneously diving into a shallow part of the Brazos River, resulting in neck fracture and permanent spinal-cord damage. Each listened intently to Suzie Whitehead. They both found her physically attractive, and each one genuinely liked her.

Neither of these men dated. They both had significant problems with sexual function, although physicians expressed to Buster much of his problems were psychological, possibly relating to the embarrassment of having a catheter in his penis collecting urine from his neurologically damaged bladder.

Donald was skinny and looked like a pastel of Ichabod Crane from the *Legend of Sleepy Hollow,* blended with Johnny

Appleseed. His neck had a huge Adam's apple, an external laryngeal protuberance sticking out at the world, and his brow and masseter lines were too well-defined. His matted hair was dirty and brown, and his eyes bore a constant twinkle.

Buster was another matter. Not a square centimeter on any part of either arm lacked a tattoo. He had tattoos of women, snakes, guns, knives, and a large fish. Buster's hair was red, his face abounded with freckles, and yellow teeth completed the picture of a derelict.

Neither spoke often of being infirm. Both had been in trouble with school authorities when young, and both had been described as sociopaths. Neither had been a good student. Each continued to consume too much alcohol, smoke marijuana, and both were confined to metallic modes of transportation.

Each had problems with bladder and bowel control due to spinal-cord damage. Each had breakdown of skin on their buttocks and sacral areas, due to prolonged sedentary positions. Proper hygiene would have helped this immensely, as witnessed by the large number of patients confined to wheelchairs who do not have skin breakdown. However, Donald and Buster were not known for discipline. Each had a host of medical ailments, ranging from bedsores to bowel and bladder problems, and sexual difficulties, but most of all, their main problem was their attitude.

These two men, each in his twenties, spent most of their considerable spare time at Carr's, the local icehouse in Channelview, east of Houston. Both felt a bond with Suzie Whitehead, especially since she was so attractive, with her page-boy haircut, supple skin, and engaging smile.

Donald and Buster, who fit anyone's definition of "rednecks," immediately took to her. In their van, following the meeting, still parked in the handicapped slot adjacent to the building where the self-help group met, they lit a joint and began talking.

"I hate these doctors," Buster said. "All of them can kiss my ass. They don't do anything and think they're big stuff."

"Right on," Donald said, taking a hit. "I've seen 'em, the plastic surgeons, for a couple of things, especially for sores down under, where the sun don't shine. I hear Dr. Bruxton is a real piece of work."

"Yeah," replied his friend. "Well, screw her." Reaching over for a toke, inhaling to the full, he picked up a beer and looked menacingly at his friend.

"You know, we should have some fun with her. What are they going to do to a couple of stiffs like us, anyway?" Smiling, he said, "What d'you say?"

"Hell, I'll try anything once," repressing the memory appended to those exact words he uttered when he dove head first into the shallow Brazos River. "Let's do her."

"Yeah, man. It'll be fun. I'll think of something," and the two misfits drank more beer and chuckled.

* * *

The following day, slightly hung over, Donald called Dr. Bruxton's office, complaining bitterly about skin sores. Dr. Bruxton's secretary scheduled an appointment in several weeks.

"See," said Donald. "The bitch is too important to see me earlier. What if I was real sick, I mean real sick? I hate these doctors."

Williamson honestly replied," Yeah, but if you were real sick, you could always go the Emergency Room."

"What are you doing, chickening out?"

"No, just talking."

Donald smiled at Williamson and said," Let's make this a real event. We'll take her in the van." Donald Keyman explained his plan to Buster as they drove off to Carr's, anticipating some cold Corona's.

* * *

It was not difficult for Donald Keyman to arrange an appointment with one of the medical complex's most prestigious physicians. Regina Bruxton's office was efficient and competent. Keyman provided a false name, Abraham Zimmerman, and a fake address and telephone number. He made clear he had no insurance coverage and was happy to pay for services at the time of his visit.

Keyman, alias Abraham Zimmerman, was polite and gave no indication of displeasure having to wait several weeks for an appointment, although he did stress the urgency of his fabricated condition. He requested an appointment toward the end of the day, stating he had to pick up his mother and a late appointment would be most welcome.

Keyman stressed the urgency of his condition and asked if he could be worked in if someone should cancel. Dr. Bruxton's office told him to feel free to call again, which he did. He was worked in a few days later, toward the end of the day, as he had requested.

When the appointment came, Donald Keyman, a.k.a. Zimmerman, arrived promptly, with Buster Williamson. Both were aghast at the opulence of the waiting room, filled with pictures of famous movie stars who had frequented Regina Bruxton's office. Keyman, nodding his head, looked at Williamson as the two sat in the waiting area. Williamson was somewhat nervous, but held his feelings inside. Deep within, he knew nothing good was going to happen from their actions, whatever they might be. However, Donald Keyman was his friend, his companion in the accident, and each without the other was not whole.

Regina Bruxton's nurse called for Mr. Zimmerman to come in. "Is it okay if my friend comes too?" he said, pointing to Buster.

"Not a problem. Bring as many as you like."

The nurse ushered the two men, each in a wheelchair, through a door and down a hallway, to the left, into a spacious examination room. Turning to Zimmerman, she said, "Dr. Bruxton will need you to slip into a gown." Handing him a well-constructed paper gown, she added, "Do you need any help?"

"No, I'm fine."

The nurse exited the room, and Donald, not without some effort, undressed and put on the gown. Fifteen minutes later, there was a brief, officious knock on the door and Dr. Regina Bruxton entered. Both men were stunned by her beauty and, especially, by her figure.

Dr. Bruxton wore a loose-fitting white laboratory coat, open at the front, providing an ample view of a stunningly proportioned body. Regina's movements were brisk, assured and confident. Saying, "Hello, I'm Dr. Bruxton," it was apparent the surgeon had femininity and style. As the men looked at her, she moved a chair to a comfortable location.

Regina Bruxton's head seemed delicately balanced on a beautifully thin neck. Her supple, creamy skin and her lips, although somewhat crooked, were inviting. Dr. Bruxton's brown eyes coordinated their beauty with her beautifully natural dark chocolate hair. The two rednecks appreciated Dr. Bruxton's perfume, not knowing it was specially prepared at Jean-Michel's of Paris. Regina Bruxton was a class act.

The interchange was brief, but thorough and to the point. Dr. Bruxton introduced herself to Mr. Zimmerman's friend, Mr. Williamson, and asked to look at the skin breakdown in the saddle area, near the genitals. Mr. Zimmerman truly was nervous, but Dr. Bruxton's professional demeanor helped him relax. She prescribed an antibiotic ointment and told him to apply it carefully to the tender areas, commenting it would toughen his friable skin.

"I appreciate your time, Dr. Bruxton. I'm glad I don't need surgery."

"No, of course not. Did you think you would?"

"No, I just wasn't sure."

"By the way," Dr. Bruxton inquired, "how did you obtain my name?"

"Oh, you're famous. Everyone knows about you."

"Thank you, but not quite. How did you obtain my name? I understand you don't have insurance, so I'm not in any book to which you have access. Who told you about me?

"Oh, I don't know. I just knew about you."

Finding this response strange, Regina smiled briefly, shook both men's hands, and ushered them to the billing secretary, near the exit. Zimmerman paid his bill and, together with his friend, left the clinic. Regina Bruxton dictated her medical note, documenting the examination and interaction, and returned to her other patients.

Alone in the elevator to the parking lot, where they parked their minivan in a handicapped slot in full view of the physicians' parking lot, Keyman turned to Williamson. "This is going to be good. All we have to do is wait."

The two entered the minivan, poured themselves some bourbon from their thermos, and lit up a joint. In the front of the van was a bag containing a few cans of cola drinks and several cans of red spray paint.

A few hours later, around dusk, Donald saw Dr. Bruxton leave the hospital, exiting through the Emergency Room entrance, walking toward the nearby physicians' parking lot. He opened the door of his van and called out to her.

"Dr. Bruxton. I saw you earlier today. Can I ask a question?"

Regina Bruxton, a Chanel raincoat draped over her arm in anticipation of possible rain, looked at the alleged Mr. Zimmerman, forty or so feet to her left. "Well, I'm on my way out. Is there a problem?"

"Just a question about my medicine. I had to wait a long time in the pharmacy and they wanted me to take a medicine different from yours."

Still at a distance but stopping her stride, Dr. Bruxton replied, "They probably gave you the generic. I specifically noted on the prescription to give you the name brand. Pharmacists do this all the time. They make a higher profit on generics. It's probably okay. Call them tomorrow and insist on the name brand."

"I don't think that's it," replied the patient. "Can you just take a look at this?" unfolding a paper bag with a supposed prescription inside.

Regina walked toward the minivan, noting how high the patient was, sitting in his vehicle equipped for the infirm. Approaching the van, she extended her arm, asking for the medicine. In a moment, the firm grip of the man who had exceptionally strong arms from propelling his wheelchair, held the plastic surgeon in a wristlock, and reaching across with his other arm, his body belted tightly into the van, hoisted the doctor inside, as Buster Williamson, sitting behind him, reached over and pulled at her torso, then pulling her legs, simultaneously sliding shut the van door.

Regina, terror on her face, extended her neck, looking over her shoulder at the now-excited Donald Keyman. "What are you doing, are you out of—" but she did not finish her sentence, as Keyman's powerful right hand grabbed her throat, nearly breaking her windpipe.

"You listen to me, you scum. You do what we say or you'll never do anything again." With that, Buster handed him a black cloth bag, which he placed over her head, overcoming her fierce resistance with his powerful arms. Regina tried to scream, but an incessant barrage of punches to her bagged face stopped her. Only when blood began oozing through the cloth and her muffled screams stopped did the phony Mr. Zimmerman stop punching.

In short time, the two men had torn off most of Regina's clothes and tied her legs apart, inside the van. Donald Keyman, whose considerable difficulty in manipulating his own body within the vehicle only served to increase his rage, penetrated Regina Bruxton with brutality and sadistic delight. As for many paraplegics, his orgasm was mental and he did not ejaculate. All the better, he reasoned—there would be no DNA samples. It was then Buster's turn.

Buster, excited but nervous and with some hesitation, positioned himself on top of the near-limp, sobbing woman, but was sexually dysfunctional. Donald could not see that his friend was unable to achieve penile tumescence, as he sat, smirking and smoking marijuana. All of a sudden, Buster became furious, screaming, "You doctors! You doctors! You dirty, filthy doctors! It's all because of you! All you!" He began pummeling Regina's bag-covered face, and while she moaned, her cries muffled by the sack as she feared for her life in a semiconscious state, he hit harder and harder.

The bag was incredibly bloodied when Regina Bruxton totally ceased moving. Buster removed the bag, threw it on the van carpet, felt pleasure at witnessing the physician's raw face, and managed to turn over the limp surgeon. As he moved her, he could feel with his hand that his penis was now rigid, a sensation his spinal-cord damage had not permitted his brain to realize.

Buster Williamson took the spare metal armrest that belonged to his wheelchair and, with all his might, began striking the middle of the plastic surgeon's back as hard as he could. He continued to do this, while Donald Keyman, thoroughly stoned, watched. "You ought to be careful. You might kill the bitch."

"I'll do worse than that," and he continued to strike the unresponsive woman until she spontaneously urinated and defecated. "Shit! Now, you've got her crap in here," Donald said.

"Don't worry about it. We'll clean up later."

Buster, energized by the sheer exercise of fighting another human being, despite that person being helpless, mortified by his sexual inadequacies but pleased his stoned friend probably did not know of his failed sexual exploit, sneered, "Open the door. Let's roll her out. Then we can clean up the car."

Opening the door, Donald replied," Here, give her to me," and he pushed the limp body onto the parking lot. "I'm too out of it to clean up. We can do it tomorrow."

Buster reached into the bag in the front of the seat, which had fallen to the floor during Regina's vain struggles, and said, "First things first." He then removed the cap from the can of paint and sprayed the unconscious woman with red paint.

Buster sprayed a caricature of a stickman with an *X* for his mouth and added two wiggly lines, one at each end of the hastily drawn arms.

"Not bad," mumbled Donald. "Too bad we don't have black paint for her crotch."

"Yeah. It would have been pretty. Listen, let's go to the carwash on Kirby. They're open late. I can drive. We should also throw away the can and wipe off any prints."

The two men drove away, leaving their handicapped-marked parking slot and a partially clad woman, possibly dead, on the parking lot ground, covered by a stickman with an *X* for a mouth and a snake in each hand. The two felons maintained the speed limit as they drove to the car wash. Once there, they washed the van thoroughly. The following day, Buster purchased some bleach at the Rice Epicurian grocery and soaked the bloodstained carpet, chemically removing all stains that the liquid encountered.

That same day, the Houston Medical Complex was numb.

News quickly spread through the Houston Medical Complex that Dr.Regina Bruxton had been raped and beaten within a fraction of her life. The *Houston Chronicle* published a lengthy article about the attack, speculating on the significance of the stickman figure. There were several paragraphs on previous rapes and attacks within the medical complex and the inefficiency of the hospital to protect its employees, staff, and patients.

Regina Bruxton lay unconscious in the hospital. Her physician, Dr. Michael Drake, consulted the best neurosurgeon he knew, Dr. Robbie Johnson. Both anticipated Regina would awaken from her coma, but both were extremely concerned that she suffered severe spinal-cord damage and her legs might be permanently paralyzed.

* * *

Chapter Eighteen

THE LADIES ATTACK

Jennifer Pettigrew had always enjoyed being on trains. Many times during the past several years, she had taken train rides with her women friends. More than once, during the ride, at least one of them commented, "The hills are so beautiful, speckled with the little farmhouses, bales of hay so perfectly squared, and those cute sheep. I love being on trains."

Others entered the conversation. "So many of these towns go back to medieval times, yet they seem pretty much intact. The train ride is almost a prism for British history and the world." Jennifer enjoyed the rides too but silently compared the disfigurement of her face to the beautiful countryside.

Jennifer often studied the many tourists in London who rode trains to the many destinations, including Cambridge, Stratford-upon-Avon, Windsor Castle, Bath, Canterbury,

Oxford, Brighton, and elsewhere. They seemed so excited and cheerful as they scurried through the train stations, whether Paddington or King's Cross Station, boarding the cars for their different destinations. The tourists appeared so happy, and she felt so miserable.

* * *

This particular day, a small group of women, all friends of Jennifer Pettigrew's, descended on Paddington Station and King's Cross Station. The Lupus Ladies all believed it was high time the normal, supposedly healthy world, especially governments, acknowledged problems that they and those similar to them endured. Each of the Lupus Ladies loved Jennifer's plan. All of them knew about Stickman X.

Since it was Thursday and therefore not too crowded with tourists, the women enacted their scheme. One let a glass flask of sulfuric acid spill in the beautiful, eighteenth-century Pump Room in Bath. The Pump Room, described in Jane Austen's works, contains interesting quirky objects found during excavations dating back over two thousand years. They also set a fire in Brighton Pier, as well as in libraries in Cambridge and Oxford, where large containers of acid splattered old books, spilling freely across library floors. The women vandalized St. George's Church, where Christopher Marlowe was baptized in 1564, a major attraction in Canterbury. They vandalized Canterbury Cathedral, poured more acid and vandalized Shakespeare's Birthplace Museum in Stratford-upon-Avon, and spray-painted state apartments in Windsor Castle.

The damage to these attractions was not major, although it resulted in closing portions of these establishments for one week. That the attacks were on the heart and history of Great Britain was appalling. What was more frightening were the leaflets distributed throughout the damaged areas and letters sent to the local papers. Again, the demands were that governments commit 10 percent of their budgets to medical research. All the printings boasted the now-familiar Stickman X.

* * *

Chapter Nineteen

RANGER REDOUX

Dick Swept became extremely upset when Harold Ranger, chairman of the Department of Neurology at the Texas College of Medicine, telephoned him. Dr. Ranger, Swept's former boss and the man responsible for not allowing Swept to try his memory-affecting medication in humans, called his former faculty member as soon as Dr. Drake informed him what had happened to Regina Bruxton.

Drake and the entire medical complex were aware that Swept and Regina had been romantically involved. The relationship faltered, just about the time Swept moved to Washington, D.C., with Ricki Hardson. Regina and Swept remained on good terms; Regina following her quest for excellence in medical care and making as much money as possible, Swept opting for medical research and some clinical activity, all coordinated through the CIA.

Swept thought often about Regina, especially their romantic interludes, but always had the reverie shaken by disappointment regarding Regina's constant pecuniary needs. Earlier, Valerie VanDance, a CIA agent who had worked undercover as Dr.Ranger's nurse, unraveled medical information about Dr. Bruxton that made her possibly understand why Dr. Bruxton had never married. Valerie had not shared that information with Swept.

Swept was very upset when he heard Regina had been beaten and raped. He was more upset when Ranger told him the neurosurgeon, Dr. Robbie Johnson, thought she might never again walk. Immediately, Swept knew he had to be at Regina's side.

Swept arrived at Bush Intercontinental Airport and took a cab to the Houston Medical Complex, having previously explained to his friends, Drs. Drake and Johnson, it was too long a drive to the airport for anyone to pick him up. Swept checked in at the Medical Complex Marriott and walked to room 1236 at the Houston Community Hospital to see Regina. He stopped at the nursing station and exchanged pleasantries with the staff, most of whom were there when he was employed in the medical complex. Swept formerly had a romantic relationship with one of the nurses, now married, who treated him with polite giggles. Swept asked how Dr. Bruxton was doing.

"She's doing okay," a Filipino nursing supervisor intervened. "But her spirits and thinking are not good."

"I can understand why," responded the neurologist. Swept went down the hall, briefly knocked at room 1236, and went in.

Regina had recently been moved from the Intensive Care Unit to the hospital floor. Swept was aware she had a contused spinal cord in her midthoracic area and very weak legs. Also, Regina had bowel and bladder incontinence.

Dick Swept had seen many patients with various injuries, including the spinal cord. It took a lot to shock him. After all, he had killed people, including Russian spies. Nonetheless, he was not prepared to see the damage done to Regina.

Regina was sleeping, while large amounts of steroids flowed into her veins, coupled with a solution of electrolytes to sustain body function. The room was quiet, filled with greeting cards from fellow physicians. Regina's once-beautiful face was bruised, swollen beyond recognition, and looked like raw meat.

Swept recalled that Regina's lips were always slightly parted, even when sleeping. Early in their relationship, he often marveled at her perfect features during sleep. Now, here she was, with swelling and bruising on her face that prohibited routine facial expression. Her lips were swollen shut. There was not a hint of her former beauty.

Suddenly, the surgeon woke. She looked at Swept and uttered a sigh. If Regina Bruxton had tried to smile or frown, no one could know, because the severe facial swelling prohibited such movements.

Swept approached the patient, his former lover. Regina's sheets were immaculate and had the "hospital smell" patients and their families know too well. Regina's hair was caked with adhesives and crusts of blood. Swept leaned over and placed his hand on her shoulder. "Regina, it's Dick, Dick Swept."

Regina nodded her head slightly. Swept could tell the movement caused pain. "I flew down here to say hello. I just wanted you to know I was thinking of you."

Regina briefly nodded her head again and went back to sleep. Swept sat in a large green reclining chair, thinking about their past, how their lives had diverged, and glanced down at the *Houston Chronicle.* There, on the front page, was an article about the brutal attack on one of Houston's finest physicians, Dr. Regina Bruxton. What Swept had not known was the perpetrators painted Stickman X on Regina's chest.

Feeling angry and wanting to visit his old stomping grounds, Swept let Regina rest and walked through the halls, where he encountered a Houston policeman making notes and reviewing data from the crime. Remembering the ineptness of the Houston police when he had been attacked while jogging, back during his ordeal with the Russians, Swept spoke with the officer but did not mention his affiliation with the CIA. The officer acknowledged that the Houston Police Department took the stick figure seriously and wondered whether there were operational groups developing in a manner similar to al-Qaeda. Swept briefly considered the possibility and then turned and saw Dr. Harold Ranger.

"Dr. Ranger, it's good to see you." Ranger seemed tired and disheveled, as he carried an old briefcase, flowers, and stumbled along, with coffee stains on his baggy khaki pants.

"Good to see you. Are they taking care of you up north, in that fancy spy place?"

Still a grumpy old gomer, thought Swept. "Yes, the CIA provides me with a good laboratory. I appreciate your telling me yesterday about Regina. I flew down on the first available flight."

"It's horrible. Incompetent hospital administrators! They should have better security in the parking lot, certainly after hours."

Swept nodded. "I understand Robbie Johnson is her neurosurgeon. Does he think her legs will recover?"

"I don't know what he thinks, but I've examined her and I think so."

"You examined her? Are you her neurologist?"

"No, but I am the chairman and made myself her neurologist. Besides, neurologists know more than neurosurgeons."

Swept inhaled deeply, smiled, and walked away, wondering why Harold Ranger was bringing flowers to the obtunded Regina Bruxton. Walking down the hallway, he ran into Dr. Michael Drake, his friend and former internist.

"Well, look what the wind blew in, our famous neurologist from the Central Intelligence Agency. Is the CIA that secret? Everyone here knows you went there," Drake said, chuckling and reaching out to embrace Swept.

"I don't do anything secret. I've got a laboratory and see a few patients. That's it."

"Well, this place isn't the same without you. No one else here has achieved spydom."

"Boy," said Swept, "what a pleasure to be back. First, Ranger. Now, you. How's Regina?"

"She lost most of her bowel and bladder control and has only minimal leg movement. Spinal shock doesn't seem to be much of an issue now, and her reflexes are brisk. Hopefully, the steroids, which we're using in massive doses, will help her. She needs a tincture of time, and maybe, all will go well."

Looking down the hall at Dr. Harold Ranger, carrying flowers as he entered Dr. Bruxton's room, Dr. Drake added, "Can you imagine that? Harold Ranger carrying flowers! I bet he didn't carry flowers to his mother's grave, presuming that old goat had a mother."

"He's not so bad," replied Swept. "Just different."

"Since when did Harold Ranger care about a plastic surgeon in private practice? He only cares about full-time physicians in the medical school, not the likes of me or Regina working our butts off in private practice."

"I don't know," said Swept, recalling Harold Ranger's personal misfortunes, losing his only son in an automobile accident caused by a drunk driver, and a wife to suicide. Ranger spent his entire life investigating mitochondria, small structures within cells. Mitochondria supply energy through a system involving an enzyme, cytochrome oxidase. Ranger cared little about patients or administrative matters, unless they directly affected him, his science, or his department. Swept momentarily began to query whether Regina's tragedy was triggering hidden emotions and feelings within Harold Ranger.

Pushing these thoughts aside, Swept turned to Michael Drake. "Have time for a bite to eat? Is Ninfa's still open?"

"Sure. I have nothing to go home to. My wife and I recently separated and now I'm in an apartment on Brompton, not far from here."

"Well," not knowing Michael's perspective about the divorce, Swept replied, "I hope you're doing okay."

"Sure. We can talk about it over a drink. You still drink Ketel One, chilled, straight up with a twist and a hint of Highland Park single malt scotch?"

"Okay, Michael," Swept smiled, "you pass the memory test. You don't have Alzheimer's disease."

"I'm not sure about that, but thanks."

Swept waited for Drake to finish his hospital rounds and the two men drove to Ninfa's, a Tex-Mex restaurant on Kirby Drive. Drake told Swept about his pending divorce, problems in his practice with health-insurance companies, problems with the medical school, and problems with hospital administrators. Swept listened intently, empathizing with his friend and colleague. Swept offered some practical advice, and the two were soon enjoying a good time, laughing and joking about their many experiences together.

Later, after Swept had returned to the Marriott, he lay down and again thought about how his own life had changed. He no longer was involved with Regina, Ricki, or Louise and was now spending his nights alone. Swept turned on an action movie, planned to call Regina's neurosurgeon in the morning, and packed his belongings, including a small medical emergency kit he always carried with him.

Feeling empty, Swept decided to telephone Ricki. No one answered.

* * *

The following morning, Dick Swept visited Regina. She was slightly more alert and offered a smile. Swept decided there was no need for him to examine Regina. She was in good, competent hands. Her physicians were excellent.

Swept took notice of Ranger's flowers, arranged in a vase probably provided by a nurse, in the corner of the room. Regina's face was still considerably swollen, and portions of her cheeks were exceedingly raw. Swept soon left the room, allowing Regina to rest, and discussed with the nurses how she was doing. He then returned to her room.

Swept's plane left for Reagan National Airport, in Washington, D.C., in a few hours. Swept noticed the hospital delivered the current *Houston Chronicle,* and he was thankful he had brought his *Wall Street Journal,* which he purchased at the Marriott gift shop that morning. Swept focused on columns of information on the front page.

Graffiti containing Stickman X had appeared throughout London, Oxford, Bath, Windsor Castle, and other places in England, all in association with vandalism of national monuments.

The *Journal* had an editorial that stressed the appearance of new terrorist organizations. Who would have thought, they sardonically mused, that a cause relating to the problems of stutterers would escalate into a series of interactions across the globe, witnessed by this stickman?

The *Journal*'s concern was development of a new organization, with independent local cells and various groups identifying with the central theme, having governments provide 10 percent of their budgets for medical research. These groups of bandits might feel connected to this ethos and, through criminal deeds of seemingly noble intent, destroy property and cause havoc.

As Swept read this, looking at Regina, sleeping comfortably after her medication, he looked up to see Harold Ranger. Ranger was again carrying flowers.

Swept stood. "Good morning, Dr. Ranger. More flowers?"

"None of your damn business. I like flowers."

"Why are you doing this?" asked Swept. "You weren't close to Regina."

"Has the CIA affected your brain? If I like flowers, I like flowers. And if I want to take them to a patient, I can do that. Is that okay with you and the government?"

"Sorry, my mistake. I should have remembered what a charming, sweet, sentimental sourpuss you are," and Swept jokingly put up his hands, as though fending an anticipated punch. "Anyway, I've got to go. I'm due back today."

Ranger briefly nodded, sitting in Swept's chair. "Damn pity security at this hospital stinks. No woman should have to go through this."

"Well put." Swept shook Ranger's hand, returned to the Marriott, and took a cab to the airport. Somehow, Swept kept thinking how bizarre it was for Harold Ranger to carry flowers. He also hoped Regina would be able to walk. Only time would tell.

Swept wondered whether Regina's severe beating would cause brain damage, possibly causing her to have no recollection of the attack. At issue would be whether she endured motor or cognitive impairment affecting her surgical and other medical skills. Swept also thought about Harold Ranger.

After Ranger's son was killed, the chairman increasingly embedded himself in his research, almost as a narcotic. He was seldom home and continually stayed late at the office. His wife, also despondent over the loss, had few friends and little support from her self-absorbed husband. When she killed herself, Ranger became even more self-absorbed and gradually lost the ability to feel. He was still an outstanding scientist, but whereas he had also been a superb clinician, he no longer cared to interact with patients.

Now, here was Harold Ranger, chairman of the Department of Neurology at the Texas College of Medicine, seeing a sick woman, a physician who possibly was also losing everything. Dr. Regina Bruxton might never walk again, operate again, or even be her former self. Swept reasoned that this must be touching his former chairman.

Dick Swept arrived at the airport and took a cab to his apartment, where he poured himself a Ketel One and added a drop of scotch. He then sat down to read the *New Yorker* and *Harper's.*

* * *

Back in room 1236 at Houston Community Hospital, Harold Ranger sat in the chair where Dick Swept had sat, looking at two bouquets of flowers and a beautiful woman who had been raped and had the daylights beaten out of her. For reasons he could not understand, Ranger could not stop thinking about his dead son and wife and found himself feeling mellow. He sat there for hours, watching nurses come and go, and thought he saw Regina smile when she groaned and looked at him. He then fell asleep in the chair. When Ranger awoke, at approximately two in the morning, he knew he was undergoing a change.

Harold Ranger did not know how he was changing, only that he was. He thought about his frequent dream—that of a man walking around in a long dark coat, taking names. Ranger again thought about his dead family. He recalled Dick Swept formerly had a relationship with Regina Bruxton, and there were rumors Regina was incredibly financially driven. He thought about multiple rumors pertaining to himself, that he was a grouch, did not care about anyone, and he remembered how much he missed Swept when Swept left the department to pursue neurological research at the CIA.

Yes, Ranger cogitated. He was changing.

* * *

Chapter Twenty

REGINA

Dick Swept telephoned Ricki Hardson. Ricki was seeing another man—now that Swept had made it clear he had no interest in marrying her. Ricki listened politely to Swept and his report about Regina. Ricki knew Swept was romantically involved with Regina when she met him and harbored no jealousy or ill will toward the plastic surgeon. Ricki felt genuinely sorry for Regina and hated to hear about any woman being attacked.

"Richard," Ricki politely said, "we haven't spoken for days, not since I left your bedroom. Now, you're calling to tell me your former girlfriend was raped and attacked. Look, I'm really sorry, and I feel for her, but why are you calling me? Don't we have other things to talk about?"

"Actually," Swept replied, "perhaps not. You knew her, it happened in the hospital where you worked, and for all you know, it could have happened to you, if you had stayed in Houston. I just thought I'd let you know."

"Maybe, that's true. But guess what? I didn't stay in Houston. And why not? Because I came here with you. You say you love me but what good is that if you can't commit to stay with me?"

"What does staying with you and being so-called 'committed' have to do with anything? Look, I think it's a bad idea I called. I thought you might want to know about Regina. I was wrong."

"I'm sorry she was attacked. And trust me, I'm sorry you're upset. Give Dr. Bruxton my best wishes, and I mean it. Now, what about you and me?"

"What about us?"

"Guess! You still don't want to get married?"

"We can discuss this all you want, but no, I do not. I told you I love you, but I don't want to get married."

"We have nothing to discuss. My best to you and Regina and anyone else in your life, but this boat is out of your water!"

"I believe the phrase is 'out of your harbor.'"

"Whatever! The boat is gone," and Ricki Hardson slammed the phone into the receiver.

Swept was surprised that he felt no remorse thinking about the two women with whom he recently had intense romantic relationships. He poured another Ketel One, iced it, added his twist and a drop of scotch, picked up some copies of *Nature* and *Science*, and began to read.

Swept could not get his mind off Regina. He wanted to know who did this to her. His anger at Regina's attack interfered with his thinking about Ricki. He decided to return to Houston and see whether he could learn more. First, he would contact the investigating Houston police officer, and if the police failed to produce results, he would try on his own. Failing that, he would work through the FBI and CIA.

* * *

The next day, Harold Ranger read his copies of *Nature* and *Science* and kept thinking of Regina. Ranger walked to her room at noontime and found her propped up in bed, half-staring at some television program. Regina turned to the chairman.

"Nice to see you. Why am I here? They tell me I was beaten? Why is the chairman of neurology here?"

"Well," Ranger politely replied, "we're off to a good start. The fact you recognize me means something. At least you remember the important people." Smiling but receiving no similar response, he added, "And whatever happened, happened. I'm very sorry it did."

"The nurses say you brought me these flowers. They're nice, well, whatever . . ." and Regina began to doze.

"Whatever to you, Dr. Bruxton," Ranger replied, more to himself than to the victim. "You seem to feel better."

"True," Regina replied, becoming more alert. "I can't move my legs, at least not well. Am I going to be all right? Robbie Johnson told me this morning he isn't sure."

"Well, I don't know what Dr. Johnson told you, but he's just an East Texas hick and doesn't know anything."

"You are something," Regina said, trying to position herself so the chairman was more in view. "You complained about Dick Swept, complain about Dr. Johnson, and seem to complain about everything. You must have a lot on your mind. I'm the one who's supposed to have a lot on her mind—not you."

"Well," Ranger answered, "I'm not complaining about you," and then rose from his chair, smiled, and walked out the door. As he walked away, down the hall to the elevator, he was fairly certain Regina Bruxton did not have significant brain damage. The fact that she could be quasisarcastic, in addition to her speaking fully normal sentences, all so early following her ordeal, indicated her brain understood duality of meaning. From a strictly organic cerebral standpoint, Ranger believed she would do well. As to how Regina's emotions might fare following her attack, no one could tell.

It was good, thought Ranger, that Regina Bruxton had no recollection of what happened. In a moment, a flash, Ranger recalled his own ordeals, the deaths of his son and wife, which he recalled daily.

Ranger realized, consciously and subliminally, that he and Regina Bruxton shared something. Regina's brutal attack now gave her a damaging past, from which she might escape, although she could have weakness in her legs and possible loss of dexterity in her hands. However, her brain seemed essentially intact.

Harold Ranger also had a damaging past, but from which he could never escape. Ranger could not get out of his head that had his day been orchestrated differently, his son would not have been where he was when the drunk driver killed him. And had he not been where he was, away from home so often, perhaps his wife would not have taken her own life. All of this, all the death, was due to him—to him! True, Ranger did not directly cause his son's or wife's loss of life, but had he been different, perhaps they would be alive today.

Now, for certain, he had to stay the way he was, even become more of what he was, become a caricature in hyperbole of what he was—purely academic, knowledge-driven, a curmudgeon. To belie these characteristics within him meant admitting earlier character transgressions. He was a flop as a man, and he knew it.

But now, for whatever reason, Harold Ranger felt good. If not good, at least he felt better. Harold Ranger, M.D., had not felt like this for a long time.

* * *

Regina drifted back to sleep, a smile beginning to appear.

* * *

Chapter Twenty-one

JOHN DEERE GREEN

Dick Swept had a knack for understanding women. Swept knew women liked men who were sensitive and trustworthy, with whom they could share their confidence. Never mind he personally knew too many who spilled the beans on their love affairs, gossiped about people at work and in their social circles, and failed to keep the confidence or secrets others entrusted to them.

Swept was different. He never discussed his romantic interactions and never broke a promise, especially if it involved sexual secrets. He might be involved with someone for two weeks, two months or longer, but intimacies shared were not available for public scrutiny. Swept had never been anything other than discreet.

Swept knew that people think what they want to think. If he were seeing a strong-willed woman, friends and colleagues often observed, "That's what Dick needs, a woman with gumption, who will stand up to him." And if he were seeing someone more subservient, the comments were, "That's what he needs, someone who allows him to walk all over her."

The truth of the matter was Dick Swept needed no particular type of woman. What he enjoyed was a woman who was intelligent, honest, and had solid values, meaning love of country and family. And it never hurt for them to believe in God or at least some type of providence. Being physically compelling, at least in some manner, was essential, given his sexual appetite. Further, Swept had been told more than once, despite *Harper's* being his favorite magazine, he was a sucker for women who read the *New Yorker.*

It was morning, and Swept went out for his run. His thoughts were not clear. He was sorry for Regina's tragedy but felt no romantic inclination toward her. He did feel romantically connected to Ricki but truly had no interest in matrimony. Trying to place thoughts about these two women aside, he began his run, relishing the invigorating air and feeling free and unencumbered. However, he could not escape a lingering sense of emptiness, a feeling that he could not explain, and wondered if it related to Ricki.

If not Ricki, maybe Louise.

Swept saw Larry Leventine, still sulking, nodded to him, completed his run, and returned to the apartment. Swept considered the day ahead. There were experiments to complete, and he made some mental notes pertaining to his data. He also reminded himself that he had an appointment with Major Cervantes this morning.

* * *

Regina Bruxton lay in bed, worrying about her weak legs. She was still hospitalized on the neurosurgery floor and received physical therapy twice daily. Regina underwent a battery of neurophysiological and neuropsychological assessments, the former designed to test the electrical responsiveness of her brain, spinal cord, and nerves, the latter to evaluate whether her cognitive ability was sufficient to care for patients.

The neurophysiological investigations, including electroencephalography and somatosensory evoked potentials, suggested improving neural function. Dr. Francisco Rivera, one of the foremost neuropsychologists in the medical complex, detected only minor cognitive damage and anticipated a full recovery.

As Regina lay in bed, watching CNN interviews of people involved in the search for weapons of mass destruction in Iraq, her thoughts wandered. If worse comes to worst, she was told, she would be confined to a wheelchair for the rest of her life. In such circumstances, she could probably use a walker, her spastic but weak legs providing some structural support. Recently, Regina's physicians said her legs would probably achieve power adequate for ambulation. Her hands, initially slightly weak and nondexterous from her injury, were also improving.

What struck the beautiful physician was not so much her infirmity but her vacuous life. Here she was, lying in bed, worth more money than most people make in a lifetime, and although several physician colleagues came to see her and to extend best wishes, there was no one who truly cared about her.

Regina Bruxton felt unloved.

*   *   *

Regina's father disappeared when she was a child, and her mother remarried to a John Deere distributor in Ottumwa, Iowa. Their entire house was painted green, on the outside as well as the interior. Her stepfather explained that the company provided free paint for the sales office, so he used it at home. It saved money, and saving money was important. All her stepfather could talk about was the importance of saving money and tractors. It drove Regina crazy, and she could not wait to leave Iowa.

Regina had a different relationship with her mother. Regina certainly knew that her mother cared about her, as did her stepfather, but not her biological father, whom she never saw. For whatever reason, her mother and she seldom talked. Regina knew the problem was hers, not her mother's.

Regina was embarrassed about her mother's lack of sophistication. Mrs. Isabelle Bruxton never read national newspapers, held few original thoughts, and had little interest in Regina's academic accolades. What Mrs. Bruxton wanted for her daughter was a husband and children. However, that was another matter.

At least Regina's mother had a nucleus, a family, thought the plastic surgeon patient. At least she had an emotional base, a den of love and caring. Regina had nothing. Regina never felt that she was an integral part of the family. To place emphasis on family values and think about being a wife, or a mother, conjured images of children. Regina knew she could not have children.

*   *   *

After Mrs. Isabelle Bruxton learned of her daughter's attack, she was genuinely concerned and flew to Houston. Mrs. Bruxton was prepared to offer emotional support for the horror of the attack, but Regina had no recollection of the physical abuse and just lay as she was, a recovering patient. The interaction between mother and daughter was pleasant but strained, and her mother left that day, returning to Ottumwa.

As Regina lay in bed, thinking about her empty shell, she decided to call the business office and request a copy of her bill. She was aware the hospital no longer waived for physicians the portion of the bill not covered by insurance. The CEO of the hospital had explained to the medical staff that to continue this courtesy violated Stark Laws, meaning that physicians were receiving special treatment if their coinsurance pay was essentially nonexistent. This violated hospital contracts with insurance companies, which mandated a charge for all patients.

Regina and the other physicians knew this was nonsense. Insurance companies and hospitals had permitted this for years. Many physicians refused to charge other physicians other than that covered by insurance, citing that the Hippocratic Oath admonished physicians from charging fellow physicians. The hospital had no such perspective.

It was all bunk. Regina knew money was tight and the hospital was not going to let any dollar slip by. She had no problem with this, having sometimes charged physicians and sometimes not. Her decision matrix was usually based upon whether the physicians referred patients to her. However, what really bothered Regina Bruxton were some of the hospital's charges.

When Dr. Bruxton requested a glass of water, there was a charge of $2. She was charged for meals she never received, half of which she never ordered. Of the meals Regina consumed, the prices were outrageous.

One morning, Regina felt well enough to try eating a soft-boiled egg. When the meal arrived, the egg was poached. Later that day, pork and beans replaced her request for a cup of vegetable soup. The hospital charged her for the soft-boiled egg, the poached egg, the pork, the beans, and the vegetable soup! The list of charges for blood tests and hospital-supplied medical services was even worse.

Taking a deep sigh, Dr. Bruxton put down the business office's printout and clicked on her television. She felt good about one thing—she must be feeling better and had no cognitive brain damage if she was harping on all this stuff. Regina chuckled, silently telling herself she was beginning to behave like Dick Swept, who paid too much attention to every detail.

Wiggling her toes under her sheet, pleased she could feel them, Regina was grateful her movements were improving. Then, she heard a brief knock, and a man in a clean, freshly starched white coat entered the room.

Harold Ranger approached the plastic surgeon, extending his hand, a smile on his face. "I was in the area, so I thought I'd say hello." Ranger handed the semisurprised patient a boxful of cookies. "I don't know if you feel like eating these, but increased caloric intake never hurt anyone recovering from anything."

"Is that so?" Regina asked wryly.

“Mind if I have a seat?” Ranger said, looking at the chair next to her bed.

“I don’t seem to be going anywhere. Be my guest.”

Ranger picked up the magazines from the chair and placed them on the adjacent bureau, briefly glancing at the *New Yorker.*

Regina stared at the ceiling and realized for the first time that the ceiling was green. She closed her eyes and thought of tractors in Iowa.

* * *

Chapter Twenty-two

BUSTER BUSTED

Dick Swept could not make Ricki change her mind about marriage. Perhaps he could, with time, but not now. Further, he could not change his own mind. Swept simply was not comfortable getting married at this point in his life.

Throughout these mental machinations, Swept kept thinking about Regina's attack. He telephoned the Houston Community Hospital Security Service, Texas College of Medicine Security Office, and the Houston Police Department. However, Swept made no headway obtaining information regarding the progress of the investigation.

There was no videotape of activity in the parking lot, nor in the elevators. There were no witnesses, and no passersby had seen anything suspicious. The investigation seemed to be at a dead end and was further thwarted by Regina having no recollection of the attack.

Swept decided to investigate the attack himself. He would not involve the CIA, whose primary focus was not local law enforcement. No federal rules were broken, so he would not contact the FBI. Instead, he would analyze the crime himself.

The following day, Swept flew to Houston and visited Regina's office, which was still operational since many patients had requests for medical records and there continued to be active billing of outstanding accounts. Without much difficulty, Swept convinced the billing secretary, who knew him well from days when he and Regina were lovers, to permit him to review medical records of her patients.

"I need to see all medical charts for the month preceding the attack and, in particular, charts from the day of the attack."

Leslie Ferguson, Regina's efficient secretary, explained Dr. Bruxton had not signed correspondence from the day of the attack or the previous day. However, the efficient office staff had typed Regina's dictation.

Within an hour, Swept had Regina's correspondence in front of him. He found it striking that the day of the attack, Abraham Zimmerman, a paraplegic confined to a wheelchair, saw Regina for consultation but had no referring physician. Regina, incredibly thorough in examination of patients as well as documentation of her examination, commented Mr. Zimmerman "just somehow" obtained her name. He had no primary-care physician and no referral. Further, he paid cash and had no medical insurance.

Swept knew that most patients sufficiently ill to be confined to a wheelchair had insurance, either privately or through Medicare or Medicaid programs. His suspicions were confirmed when he looked up the address Mr. Zimmerman wrote on the sign-in sheet—it was bogus. Further, there was no Abraham Zimmerman in the Houston telephone book, and when Swept called for directory assistance, there was no listing, published or unpublished.

Swept also began pouring over Regina's medical records several weeks prior to her attack. He did not have to go far before coming across the records of a distraught patient, Suzie Whitehead. The notation mentioned Ms. Whitehead was extremely unhappy with her medical care and was in a self-help group. Swept decided to call her.

"Ms. Whitehead, my name is Dr. Swept. I am a neurologist and was told by a colleague you can recommend a good self-help group. I have several patients with chronic pain, and I was hoping you could help me."

"Who gave you my name?"

"If you must know, I obtained it from Dr. Regina Bruxton's records. I am helping her out, taking care of some patients with neurological problems while she is recovering from an injury, and your being in a self-help group is in her records."

"I'm sorry about what happened to Dr. Bruxton. I read about it in the papers. I'm also surprised she was thorough enough to mention I'm in a self-help group, considering she never listened to me."

"Really?"

"Really! I have pain in my face where she operated on me, and she kept telling me there was nothing wrong."

"Perhaps there is some small nerve-fiber damage."

"What's that?"

"People can have mild damage to small nerves after suturing, and the pain can be quite severe."

"How come Dr. Bruxton never told me that?"

"I don't know. Maybe Dr. Bruxton did not think that diagnosis applied to you. May I make a suggestion?"

"Sure."

"I would like to attend the self-help group meeting myself, so I can know if it is good for my patients. At the same time, I'm happy to take a look at your face, where you had your operation."

"It's a deal. You're the first doctor who listens to me. Our group meets tomorrow evening." Ms. Whitehead provided Swept the address.

The following evening, after reviewing more of Regina's records and briefly visiting her, not sharing with the plastic surgeon that he was spending time in her office but being prepared in case her office staff mentioned it, Swept joined two dozen people sharing their problems. Several were in wheelchairs, several appeared depressed, and a few others complained bitterly about their various diseases or unemployment or both.

Before the meeting officially began, Swept introduced himself to several people, including Suzie Whitehead, and discussed her pain. Swept suggested Neurontin, a medication that can stop small nerve irritation, and provided a prescription, thankful he was still licensed to practice medicine in Texas.

"Thank you, Dr. Swept. Why didn't Dr. Bruxton recommend this?"

"I don't know. But why don't you give it a try?"

"I will. Thanks."

Swept, having reviewed Suzie Whitehead's records, knew Regina had recommended Neurontin, but Ms.Whitehead refused to try it because of concerns for side effects, which Regina stressed were minimal. Swept said nothing about this.

Suzie Whitehead introduced Dr. Dick Swept to the group, saying he wanted to see whether this group would be good for some of his patients.

"What kind of patients are you thinking about?" inquired one of the members.

"Oh, I don't know," replied Swept. "I have a patient, for instance, Mr. Abraham Zimmerman, who . . ."

Although government regulations forbid mentioning patients' names to those not directly connected with their health care, Swept mentioned this name. Besides, he knew it was not a name of a real person. He wanted to see what would happen. Something did.

Donald Keyman and Buster Williamson looked up, surprised. Swept continued, "Mr. Zimmerman had a problem and saw Dr. Bruxton, you know, the plastic surgeon who was attacked. He's my patient and has muscle-tension headaches. Since he was one of the people who saw her last, before she was beaten, somehow he feels responsible. Actually—," staring at Donald Keyman and Buster Williamson, "so do I."

Keyman and Williamson sat there, dumbfounded. Swept did not want to lose his pace. "Gentlemen, you look surprised."

Buster spoke first, “No, I don’t even know Dr. Bruxton.”

“Sure you do,” said Suzie Whitehead. “Remember, she was the one who operated on me and didn’t care about my pain after surgery. I discussed her here recently about how bad a doctor she was.”

Swept interjected, “I know her. I can assure you, she is a superb physician.”

“Oh yeah,” said Buster. “I remember.”

Swept looked at him. “I’m sure you do.”

After discussing many personal problems, the group took a coffee break, planning to meet again in fifteen minutes. Swept noticed Keyman and Williamson heading toward the elevator. Swept followed and watched them exit the building, moving toward their van.

Swept approached Buster and Donald as they were arranging themselves within their vehicle. “Fellas, mind if I ask a question?”

“We’re kind of busy,” Buster answered gruffly as he turned on the ignition.

“Yeah, we gotta go,” added Donald, sitting behind him.

“I’m busy too,” replied Swept. “But I want you to see something.” With that, Swept showed the two paraplegics his CIA identification card. “I need to ask a question.”

“Like he said,” replied Donald Keyman, “we’re busy.”

Swept grabbed Buster’s hand, hyperextending and removing it from the steering wheel and causing him to flinch from pain. "I need only a moment of your time, fellas. Surely, you have a moment."

Buster, grimacing, answered, "What? What the hell do you want?"

"Well, first," said Swept, still squeezing Buster's hand while he employed his other hand to open the side door of the van. Swept noticed that the rug on the floor was bleached. "Why didn't you remember hearing about Regina Bruxton? It seems to me if someone complains about a physician, and that physician is raped and beaten within a short time, bright boys like you would remember."

"Bright boys like us have other things to worry about other than a plastic surgeon in her fancy office," Keyman caustically replied.

"Who said she had a fancy office?" asked Swept, still causing Buster pain.

"Your mother," said Buster, and he floored the gas pedal, causing his arm to jerk free from Swept's grip.

What Buster had not counted on was that Dick Swept always carried his Glock semiautomatic. As the vehicle began to speed away, Swept crouched low, aimed carefully, and shot out the two back tires. The van careened into a post, and Swept ran toward the vehicle, his weapon extended, while he expected a crowd of people soon to appear.

"Get out of the van," yelled Swept, opening the doors.

"We can't," snickered Donald Keyman. "We're cripples."

"Not enough for me." Swept steadied his gun at Buster Williamson's face and tore him out of the van. "You—," pointing to Donald Keyman, "are you getting out or do I drag you out too?"

"Eat me!"

Swept leaned over then grabbed Keyman's arm, pulling him out of the van. Keyman's fat belly was exposed, hanging over a leather belt with a large buckle boasting the Texas flag. Swept, noticing a small yellow rubber tube and reasoning it was a Foley catheter tube inserted through the penis into the bladder, yanked it as hard as he could. Despite his neurological impairment, Keyman experienced considerable pain and was aghast when he saw the balloon-tipped catheter on the ground, soaked with his blood.

"You can't do this to us. You're the law."

"You have no idea what I can do," and Swept kicked each man into a spread-eagle position on the ground, with an extra measure at each one's backside. Holding his gun at both, anticipating that people would soon hear the ruckus and come to the parking lot, Swept quickly searched the van and readily found a lid of marijuana. Then, Swept slowly and softly spoke to the two men.

"You have one choice and one choice only. You tell me what happened or I'll blow your brains out."

"Fuck you and fuck that bitch doctor. She got what she deserved. Yeah, we did it. So what! It's your word against ours. I hope the bitch dies. I hope you die. What's the law going to do to a couple of stiffs like us? It's your word against ours. I hope she suffers forever and you too."

"Really?" said Swept. "You're really proud of what you did?"

"Yeah, and proud to hate jackoffs like you. You should have seen her, screaming and moaning. We could hear it all, even with the fucking bag over her face. And for all the good it's gonna do you, it was brilliant to keep busting her spine. I hope the bitch is paralyzed forever."

"Well, gentlemen, I hate to disappoint you, but two things are important."

"Screw you!"

"The first, which you may want to know, is that Dr. Bruxton will probably do well."

"Too bad. She should be like us. What's the second?—that your mother's a whore?"

"No, the second is this," and Swept removed a small recording device from his trousers. "This is you on tape."

Swept called 911, requesting assistance. Buster Williamson and Donald Keyman were silent.

While the threesome waited for the police, attendees from the self-help group began to enter the parking lot. Donald Keyman and Buster Williamson angrily turned to Swept. "That evidence is no good. It'll never hold up in court."

"Maybe not. But if it doesn't, remember you'll have me to deal with," and Dick Swept picked up the blood-soaked Foley catheter and tossed it in Donald Keyman's face.

* * *

Chapter Twenty-three

STICKMAN X MOVEMENT

When Jokhar Gantemirov learned about a suicide bomber blowing up himself and his truck outside security offices at the Russian FSB headquarters in Magas, capital of Ingushetia, a tiny Russian province bordering Chechnya, Gantemirov figured that was the place to go.

* * *

When the CIA heard about the bombing in Ingushetia, some CIA associate directors considered sending agents there to look for terrorists, possibly even Gantemirov. However, the relationship between the United States and Russia was tenuous over issues of terrorism, the United States seeking Russian President Putin's support for American activities in Iraq, and the last thing they wanted was for Russia to learn U.S. intelligence was active in Chechnya, officially Russian territory.

The CIA decided terrorism in Chechnya was a matter for Russia, not the United States. The U.S. was happy to provide support if Putin requested it. He did not.

*   *   *

Stoli also learned about the bombing in Ingushetia. Stoli, as did Gantemirov, reasoned this was the place to go. Stoli believed Gantemirov might be involved in the bombing, perhaps out of anger at his previous capture by the Russians. The reason was immaterial. A major bombing occurred in Ingushetia, Gantemirov was an escaped Chechen terrorist, and Stoli decided to travel there.

It was easy for Stoli to enter Ingushetia; the province was not well guarded, and handing a border guard $50 in U.S. currency sufficed to let Stoli through. Soon, Stoli hoped to meet the man who had worked with his dead twin brother. Stoli reasoned that his looking identical to his dead brother would serve as a satisfactory introduction to Gantemirov.

*   *   *

Swept called Regina a few times during his Houston trip and was pleased she could pick up the telephone and speak clearly. Her voice often became weary, but Regina could converse long enough to understand and appreciate that Swept wished her the best for a speedy recovery. He decided to see her one more time.

Swept did not share with Regina his capture of Donald Keyman and Buster Williamson. The newspaper mentioned that the Houston police apprehended the perpetrators. Swept was pleased the *Houston Chronicle* did not mention his name. He was also pleased that, for whatever reason, possibly because he had been so nonchalant, Regina's office personnel did not share with her that Swept visited her office.

Regina complained to Swept about problems with the nursing service, escort service, and the billing system, just as her patients had often complained. It was apparent, now that the doctor was a patient, that she had a different view of hospital and medical services.

"Richard, I never realized how truly dissatisfied patients were, and rightly so. Health care is a mess."

"You're a good doctor. I'm sure you tried to help them."

"No, I didn't. Many people had complaints, about the system and, sometimes, about me. I don't think I did my job as well as I could have."

"I'm not certain that's true. Regardless, do a better job, or a different job, next time."

"I will, if there is a 'next time.' I hope I can get back on my feet. I'll be a better doctor, certainly one who listens more."

"You're being too hard on yourself."

"I'm just beginning," and Regina turned to Harold Ranger, who was now entering the room.

Swept said hello to his former chairman and decided not to comment about the flowers Ranger was again carrying. After some small talk with Regina and Ranger, Swept returned to his hotel, showered, and put on a freshly laundered cotton shirt, dark blue slacks, and his shoes. He then took a cab to Fleming's, on Alabama off Kirby, where Michael Drake and Robbie Johnson were waiting for him

"Hey, Richard. It's good to see you," said Drake.

"Good to see you, Michael." Swept extended his hand and then turned toward Johnson. "How's everything in East Texas, Robbie? You doing all right?"

"I'm no longer in East Texas, in case you forgot that in the CIA. I moved here, where you used to live, until you left us," Robbie responded, with his pronounced Texas drawl. Swept noticed that Robbie Johnson could not stop turning his head, following the beautiful women who frequented the restaurant.

"Well, guys, it's good to be here. How've you all been?"

"Just peachy," said Michael, his boyish face almost scrunching as he engaged in conversation. "The health-care bureacracy is better, patients no longer complain, the medical school and the hospital love each other, I can barely meet my office overhead, lawyers are still ready to pounce on you any time you twitch and . . . my ex-wife is driving me nuts. Aside from all that, life's a blast."

"Okay," answered Swept, stretching out the second syllable. "What about you, Robbie? By the way, in case I forget, thanks for your help with Regina."

Turning to eye a beautiful woman, who similarly turned, only to smile at Swept, Robbie motioned for the waitress and then focused on Swept. "Richard, the attack on Regina was horrible. We all felt for her." Drake nodded his head. "But," continued Johnson, "I'll tell you something, not as sad, but almost as striking."

"Which is?" Swept inquired.

"Which is the fact that that jerk of a chairman—excuse me, former chairman—of yours sees Regina Bruxton just about every day and brings her flowers. I never knew the guy had it in him."

"Everyone can feel. It's in all of us."

"You're still a loyal guy, aren't you?" interrupted Drake. "Do you think Ranger would stick up for you?"

"Probably not, unless it was in his interest. Anyway, good for him—and good for Regina."

The other men looked at each other askance, deciding not to raise the issue of Swept's former romantic involvement with Regina. Both knew not to discuss Swept's personal relations with women, unless he brought it up.

The waitress approached the three physicians and inquired what they wanted to drink. Robbie responded first. Turning to his friends, the neurosurgeon asked, in dulcet tones, "Would you boys think ill of me if I had a bourbon and Coke?"

"Not at all," answered Drake, who ordered a J&B on the rocks. The waitress then turned toward Swept, bending over, revealing some of her cleavage. Swept ordered his signature drink: "Ketel One, straight up, chilled, with a single drop, only a drop, of Highland Park Scotch."

"You got it, sugar. If it's not done right, I'll take it back until it is." The woman then walked toward the bar, where she conversed with the bartender.

"Richard," Robbie said, "I'll leave the fact alone that you seem to attract more women in a week than I ever did in a month or a year." Swept raised his right eyebrow, beginning a prolonged inspiration. "And," the neurosurgeon continued, "I take it the CIA hasn't changed your drinking habits. You still have that same drink?"

"You bet, although sometimes I wonder why. They always put too much scotch in it. The scotch should just be enough to take out the bite, not more."

"Speaking of habits," interrupted Robison, "is that a Dunhill shirt? You still wear that English bullshit?"

"Guys, I've had these clothes forever. As for Dunhill, they closed the store in the Galleria, and besides, I moved from here. Why buy new clothes or new anything? Anything else you need to know?"

The waitress returned to the table, offering Swept his drink first. "You taste that and let me know if it's not right. I watched the bartender make it myself." She then served the other physicians their drinks, paying minimal attention to them.

"Perfect," smiled Swept.

"Good," said Monique, her name tag now showing. "I'll be back for your orders in just a few minutes," and walked away, smiling.

"Screw all this," said Robbie, wolfing down his drink and then motioning to Monique for another. "What's it like to work in Washington, for the CIA? Are you meeting women or—," wondering if he had crossed the line, "are you still seeing Ricki?"

Swept was nonplussed. "Washington is great! The museums and symphony keep me busy, my lab is fully operational and productive, I see some patients—not a lot—at the NIH, and Ricki, well, she wants to get married and I don't. So, there you go. That's that!"

"Yay, hay!" exclaimed Robbie. "I'm telling you, and you can take this to the bank or your ATM or wherever you guys go: All women want to control men! They want to dress us, tell us how to act. Hell, they want to tell us what to drink! And they all want to get married."

Robbie directed his attention toward his second beverage, looking Swept straight in the eye. "Richard, you're better off without her, listen to me!"

"Well, I miss her. I just don't want to get married. I'm not ready to settle down. I have obligations at the agency, the lab, I'm just too busy to—"

"Richard," interrupted Drake. "No need for excuses. If it doesn't work out, it doesn't work out. As my Uncle Irving used to say, 'What is, is! Kiss the broadie goodbye.'"

"You didn't have an Uncle Irving."

"So what? Everyone does, somewhere."

"Well put," said Johnson, smiling and faking a punch to Robbie's left jaw.

Monique arrived and took their order. Drake requested New York tenderloin, rare. The others ordered the large fillet, medium rare, and Swept requested a bottle of a 1990 St. Julien Ducru Beaucaillou.

"Want another Ketel?" inquired Monique.

"Not now, but thanks." Monique walked toward the kitchen.

Over dinner, Swept discussed some of his experiments. "You are still into trying to help those demented patients, aren't you, Richard?" asked Drake.

"I try," responded Swept. "It's important to me."

Just then, Robbie Johnson's cellular phone rang. It was his wife, and she wanted him home.

"Gotta go," said Robbie, smiling. "See what I mean!" pointing to the phone. "It's Daisy, and she means business."

"What about women who want to control me?" asked Drake.

"That's how I know," Johnson responded. Putting his hand on Swept's shoulder, Robbie Johnson smiled, "Richard, you are a good man and a good friend. Screw 'em all!" he announced and walked out the door.

"What does that mean?" inquired Drake, grimacing at Swept.

"I have no idea, but if you must know, at one time, he did just that," and Swept turned to his plate.

Following a long conversation about Drake's divorce and the pain of a failed marriage, Swept discussed his research, and then the two physicians' conversation turned to politics. Later, Swept made clear that he was a physician-scientist working for the government, not some super spy. Swept and Michael Drake left the restaurant together, Drake driving him to the hotel.

Soon, Swept was packing and took a taxi to the airport, taking a late-night nonstop Continental Airlines flight to Washington, D.C., where he flew first class and silently cursed the airlines' brand of vodka.

* * *

Swept arrived in Washington, D.C., feeling refreshed because he required little sleep and was able to nap on the aircraft. He briefly stopped at his apartment, showered, and drove to his laboratory on the CIA grounds. Swept checked some data on the NMDA receptor experiments and talked to the two technicians working late on their biochemical assays. Swept then returned home.

As he drove, thinking about recent events, he felt increasingly relaxed, appreciating the precision and high torque of his Bentley. He decided to stay on Interstate 95 and make a loop around the nation's capital, enjoying the nocturnal view of the city and the feel of his automobile.

* * *

While Dr. Harold Ranger sat in Regina's room, the plastic surgeon picked up the telephone and complained to someone about incompetence within the hospital. When Regina put down the telephone, seemingly oblivious that Ranger was there, the chairman commented, "That's why the medical school, the Texas College of Medicine, should run this place. All we have in this hospital is a bunch of idiot administrators and incompetent nurses."

"And you think the medical school would be better?"

"It couldn't do worse."

"Really? I wasn't aware things are so simple that all we need to do to fix a problem is change things at the top."

Ranger smiled, as he appreciated that Regina was engaged in a true conversation with him. The injured woman's language and intellectual capabilities were certainly returning. Further, it occurred to Harold Ranger that his problems were being fixed as well.

* * *

The following day, Swept worked diligently in his laboratory, pursuing brain-slice recordings and testing post-tetanic potentiation in slices of brain tissue with altered glutamate receptors. Swept's theories pertained to how these glutamate receptors were involved in memory.

Dick Swept's laboratory personnel did various things to perturb these receptors, making them more excitable in some animals, less excitable in others. Then, they tested how well animals learned, or forgot. Swept hoped to measure the importance of these receptors in the brain's memory system and ascertain whether this system was damaged in patients with Alzheimer's disease. If he could demonstrate that these receptors were compromised in Alzheimer's disease, it might be possible to develop pharmacological agents that altered these receptors and help the patients. Swept's main desire was to develop medications that cured, or at least significantly helped, patients with Alzheimer's disease.

At the end of his scientifically productive day, Swept went for a run in Rock Creek Park. Again, there was the man in the wheelchair. Swept stopped his running and decided to introduce himself.

"Hello, I'm Dick Swept. I keep seeing you here and thought I should just say hello. It seems that our schedules coalesce, since I always see you."

The man, remaining sour faced, responded but did not smile. "Larry Leventine. Nice to meet you," and Leventine did a wheelie and turned the wheelchair away, heading toward the Potomac.

As Leventine wheeled away, Swept observed that Leventine had literature on multiple sclerosis, with the local MS Society's imprint on the pamphlet. Swept called out, "Mr. Leventine, you dropped these," holding up the MS pamphlets and literature.

Leventine turned his head toward Swept, smugly nodded, wheeled back toward him, and took the literature. Swept added, "I'm a neurologist. These are pretty good."

"Yeah," said Leventine and wheeled away, remembering when he attended the MS meeting but not having MS, just wanting to be with people like himself.

As Leventine departed, he looked at the sidewalk and saw a drawing of a stickman with a snake in each hand and a large red X for a mouth. He then looked at Swept, who by now had noticed the same figure.

* * *

A flurry of articles appeared about "Stickman X," as the figure was increasingly called. Stickman X was everywhere, especially in major medical centers, including Boston, Rochester, Los Angeles, Chicago, and Houston. The figure was especially common where there were large groups of physicians and hospitals.

Stickman X logos did not only appear in urban areas. They sprang up in Fuquay Varina, North Carolina; McAllen, Texas; and Prosser, Washington. They continued to appear in Europe, outside the Louvre and in London, Prague, Budapest, and Stockholm. Stickman X was becoming a phenomenon. A movement had been born, a movement initiated by Jeremiah MacGregor, a lone participant on the planet. Apparently, Jeremiah was not alone.

* * *

Earlier, Jeremiah had queried whether, as a person who stutters, he was part of a group. Indeed, he was correct. However, his clan extended far beyond those with speech affliction. His clan, his group, included those medically disenfranchised for all sorts of ailments and seemed to be extending to the socially or economically disadvantaged.

Whatever the complexion of the group, the newspapers reported an ever-increasing occurrence of Stickman X graffiti and an increasing number of national monuments under attack throughout the world.

* * *

A rented truck dumped thirty refrigerators onto the San Francisco Bridge, with Stickman X painted on all sides, stopping traffic for most of the day. Similar incidents occurred in Dallas, Chicago, Bachelor's Gulch, Durango, New Rochelle, and Iowa City. The Stickman X vandals also attacked areas where America's ultrarich thrive, ranging from Lazy Lane in Houston and Fox Run Lane in Greenwich, Connecticut, to Park Avenue in New York City.

Newspapers and radio and television stations continued to report on Stickman X activities. For better or worse, no one knew where Stickman X advocates were headquartered, only that they seemed to have adherents everywhere.

* * *

Given the attention to stuttering, government authorities were observing Rex Allendorf. When the FBI and CIA learned that Dr. Allendorf was to be a featured speaker at the International Speech Forum in Paris, just one week away, Cervantes called Dick Swept into his office.

"First, my congratulations for apprehending the criminals who attacked Regina Bruxton, although you are an employee of the Central Intelligence Agency and are supposed to leave local criminal matters to the local police."

"Is that a compliment or complaint?"

"Neither. However, your methods, per your own report, were less than appropriate. But you did catch the bad guys."

"I hold Dr. Bruxton in high regard, and the Houston police weren't helping matters. I went through her patients' medical records and figured things out more quickly. I'm a doctor and know what physicians put in their records."

"You are also an employee of the United States government, specifically the CIA, and *you* work for me. You are not some Rambo."

"I never thought I was."

"See that you aren't. We have rules and regulations. Anyway," Cervantes, seeming to dismiss these issues as fluff, "I want to talk about something else. The International Speech Forum meets in Paris in just one week. You told me before about Dr. Allendorf. I understand you're attending the meeting. Interact with Allendort and see what's going on. If stutterers or people who support them are at the bottom of this Stickman X nonsense, he might be involved or be targeted by them. Also, it's surprising all this is happening after Gantemirov's recent escape. See what you can find out."

"I'm happy to do it. But I'd like to point out one thing."

"What's that?"

"I came here to do research on Alzheimer's disease. First, you tell me if I leave Houston and leave the Texas College of Medicine, I can have a laboratory and do what I want, right here. Then, you ask me to extend my services into bioterrorism. Then, you tell me Jokhar Gantemirov escaped, and now, in the midst of some crazies going around painting stickmen with an *X* and snakes, I'm supposed to go to Paris to learn about stuttering. Does this make a lot of sense?"

"I think so. Does it make sense that you show two Texas rednecks your CIA identification, secretly record your conversation with them, and interfere with local police work?" Cervantes leaned back in his chair and pulled out a cell phone. "The world isn't simple. You don't have to do this if you don't want to, but who's more qualified? You're a neurologist. You understand, I guess, the brain and how it works and proved yourself competent in the field. Look what you did to Kostokov and his men. We don't have anyone better to interview Allendorf or go to the meeting. You belong here. Besides, you're extremely competent. Are you on board?"

"I'm happy to help. Just remember, my major area of interest is glutamate receptors and Alzheimer's disease, not stuttering."

"Dr. Swept," continued Major Cervantes, sarcastically, "I don't say these things because I'm bored and have nothing else to do. You are the most qualified person in this underfunded agency to do this work. You are a physician, can blend in well at scientific meetings, understand neurology, and can hold your own in the field, whether against the likes of Kostokov or wheelchair rednecks. Besides, you can recognize nonsense in the scientific arena and also spot Gantemirov better than most. You know him."

With that, Major Cervantes busied himself with his cell phone and paper work. Swept thanked him and left the office.

* * *

In Edinburgh, Jeremiah read about Stickman X, his Stickman X. He was pleased, as he thought about people who had trouble talking, the pediatricians who knew so little about their problem, and other patients in the world.

* * *

Over the next two weeks, Stickman Xs tripled in their frequency of appearance. Every major hospital had Stickman X figures on the walls, in parking lots and in lavatories. Refrigerators, old sofas, various pieces of furniture were dumped on major interstate highways, boasting the Stickman X sign. In a medical school in St. Louis, family members, irate with the health-care system, wore Stickman X T-shirts and broke windows in an Alzheimer's clinic, threatening to throw demented patients to the ground, eight stories below. The patients were so demented they proved too easy to control and could not possibly provide eyewitness accounts of their ordeals.

In other occurrences, people wearing Stickman X T-shirts, in wheelchairs with Stickman X decals, waited for non-infirm people to park in handicapped parking zones, yelling and banging their cars when they did so. There were a few reports of people wearing Stickman X logos on their shirts firing small weapons at transgressors' spines, paralyzing more than a few. In one instance, a general contractor had to respond to a page, his cell phone malfunctioned, and he parked in a handicapped spot at a small convenience store, only to be surrounded by several people in wheelchairs with Stickman paraphernalia, firing at his midsection. His legs were permanently paralyzed.

Wherever these incidents occurred, and they seemed to increase daily, the Stickman figure was found, with an X for a mouth and a snake in each hand.

Major newspapers across the United States reported these events. There were countless letters to all avenues of the media, as well as comments from politicians at local, state, and national levels, addressing the demand that 10 percent of the national budget be directed toward medical research. Similarly, although less frequently, these demands were made in Europe, Russia, Turkey, and the People's Republic of China.

The Stickman movement increasingly made more headway. It seemed to be decentralized, with purpose, and progressively violent. It became especially violent in Aspen, Colorado.

* * *

Chapter Twenty-four

LIGHT OF THE IGUANA

Marjorie Sunningham, president of the American Medical Association, always enjoyed vacationing in Aspen, Colorado. Dr. Sunningham excelled in most sports. She enjoyed extreme skiing, snowshoeing, dogsledding, and in the summer, once the snow melted, she found cycling, hiking, and fly-fishing her most enjoyable outdoor activities.

Dr. Sunningham went to Aspen every chance she could, loving the small-town atmosphere, mixed with strong intellectual passion. When invited to participate in a meeting on medical ethics, sponsored at the Ritz Carlton Club at Aspen Highlands, she quickly replied in the affirmative.

Following Dr. Sunningham's lecture on medical ethics, there was a long question-and-answer period. Much to her dismay, the audience did not want to know about cloning pancreas cells to help diabetics or issues of abortion. Instead, everyone had questions about Stickman X. Dr. Sunningham's response was direct and to the point.

"This is a media-made movement. Our country, let alone half of Europe with their socialized medicine, spends a fortune on health care. True, we don't place ten percent of our budget into medical research, but we spend a larger percentage on worker's compensation claims, Medicare, Medicaid, and state-sponsored health care, when it's all combined. This Stickman nonsense is ridiculous, and you should stop giving it such attention."

Later that evening, at the Iguana Restaurant, a dimly lit establishment with arguably the most authentic and excellent Mexican cuisine, Dr. Sunningham was talking to the owners, a family transplanted from the East. The president of the AMA heard her name shouted above the crowd. She walked toward the door, looking for the person calling her. In the midst of the roar of the tourists and the locals, a man in a yellow Bogner ski suit, too warm for the current climate, wearing a red scarf, yelled her name again.

"Are you Dr. Sunningham?"

"Yes, can I help you?"

Thinking about his headaches and how good if felt to be off antipsychotic medication, the man responded, "Afraid not, lady," and imbedded a giant carving knife into her belly and then limped away, placing his scarf across the lower part of his face. Dr. Sunningham, a painful, surprised look on her face, unable to inhale, felt her legs slowly relinquish support while people around her laughed and had a good time.

The thick crowd in the dark restaurant failed to notice the dying woman, and she found herself leaning against the packed adjacent patrons, unable to breathe, experiencing incredible pain, and watching blood weep from her belly. When she finally fell, screams went out, and the manager turned up the lights, highlighting the commotion around the corpse. No one noticed the man with *talipes equinovarus,* commonly known as clubfoot, walk away with his slight limp, muttering aloud that doctors did not care about his chronic headaches and all they wanted to do was medicate him for what they called paranoid schizophrenia.

As he walked, he let float down several business-size cards, boasting a picture of Stickman X, with a printed sentence, "We want 10 percent."

* * *

Dick Swept was very concerned about Stickman X. The movement continued to expand, engulfing many people. Given the types of crimes that Stickman X advocates perpetrated and the vast geographical areas affected, it was especially frightening. Many at the FBI and CIA believed Stickman X was a potently evolving terrorist movement, one not requiring central authority, and was extremely dangerous.

* * *

On the other side of the world, Jokhar Gantemirov also paid attention to Stickman X. When Gantemirov read about the assassination of the president of the AMA, he knew an increasing corpus of people must feel strongly about the "cause" of the movement and also realized there was money to be made.

As Gantemirov thought about this nascent Stickman X movement, drinking strong black coffee in a small bar in Magas, he looked up with bewilderment. It was Aleksander Kostokov, but it could not be . . . Kostokov was dead.

Stoli reached out his hand to Gantemirov, content with the surprised look on the Chechen's face. "I am not who you think I am. I am someone else."

"And who is that?" responded a puzzled Gantemirov, mentally preparing himself for trouble.

"You knew my twin brother. I understand his name was Aleksander Kostokov."

"I know a lot of people." Gantemirov looked around the room, contemplating routes for a hasty exit, especially if he had to kill this man.

"May I sit down?" asked Stoli.

"Chairs are free. The vodka and beer are not."

Stoli quickly explained how he grew up in an orphanage in Romania. "I was a tour guide, with a knack for languages, especially grammar and dialects. I always believed I was one of triplets and that one of us died young, the other raised in Russia. I think that's when I was sent to the orphanage, in Romania."

"Is this supposed to interest me? Everyone is raised somewhere. You've got one minute before one of us runs into a real problem, and it won't be me."

"Hear me out. Your picture and the picture of my dead brother are in the papers. I recognized him. He looks like me. Look at me, for yourself. I am Aleksander Kostokov's twin." Stoli tilted his head in different postures so that Gantemirov could fully appreciate his features.

Gantemirov was no fool. “Maybe you got bored one day and underwent plastic surgery to look like someone.”

“Hardly. I am what I am.”

“Aren’t we all? What do you want?”

“Actually,” Stoli replied honestly, “I’m not sure. I just thought I should find you, and I didn’t do too bad a job of it.”

“True,” said the burly Chechen. “But you should understand something. If you can find me, and if I am some sort of prize, maybe others can find me. That would put me in a bad spot. On the other hand—” drinking from his mug, “if you are the only one who can find me, that puts you in a bad spot, as a danger to me. So, what do you think I should do about you?”

“I don’t know. But I know I should be here, with you.”

“Really?” replied Gantemirov. “Your brother was smart, and you may be too. Let’s have a little test, shall we?”

“Sure. I’m game.”

“You’re *game*?” said Gantemirov. “You’re *game*? Let me tell you something: we are about to find out how game you are or whether you’re sent here to follow me.”

Stoli nodded his head, not certain what he was getting into, but confident that what he was doing was correct. Somehow, he felt assured. Perhaps his brother was a great spy and had great courage and will. He would be the same.

Gantemirov looked around and hailed one of the cocktail waitresses. She had large breasts, full hips, dirty hair, rotting teeth, and a face that had seen hard times. Calling her over, he took out a one hundred U.S. dollar bill. "See this?" he asked the waitress, who nodded and smiled. "My friend here," pointing to Stoli, "wants to show you something outside, near the dump. I want to watch. Are you in for this?"

The waitress looked around, seeing the bar was not too crowded. "It will cost you another hundred. Then you can both have me."

"I don't want us both to have you," he said, handing her another hundred. "I want him to have you."

The waitress took the money, tucked it into her underwear, and walked outside, not looking at either man. Both followed her.

Stoli, surprised but not alarmed, still had his inner feeling of confidence. As they walked outside, several steps behind the woman, Gantemirov looked around at the men in the bar, most of whom were drunk, gulped down the rest of his vodka, and put his arm around Stoli.

"You do this!" Stoli nodded, and the two men now stood behind the building, looking at the waitress beginning to unbutton her shirt. The wind was crisp, cold, and the area stank from littered garbage.

"No," said Gantemirov to the waitress, whose cleavage was now fully exposed, as she reached to undo her brassiere. "Like this," and he grabbed her arms from behind, forcing her to arch her back forward, toward Stoli, who stood before her.

A surprised Stoli looked at Gantemirov, a quizzical look on his face. His confusion as to what he was to do soon ended.

"Kill her!" said Gantemirov. "Put your hands around her stinking neck and kill her."

The waitress tried to look behind her, amazed at these words, but the pressure from Gantemirov, thrusting his arms into her spine, obliterated her attempts at freedom and saving her life.

"If you are your brother, as you say, he would follow any order to the maximum. Kill this woman and don't think twice!"

Stoli looked at the frightened woman, realizing she must be in her early to middle thirties and had a life of her own, with her own cares, concerns, wants, and needs. She tried to scream, but Gantemirov's large right hand now covered her struggling mouth, while his left hand, still behind the poor woman's back, grabbed both arms. "Do it and do it now. End this poor wretch's life. Choke her! Kill her!"

Gantemirov then pushed his left arm further into her spine, withholding his mighty ability to snap the woman in two, keeping his other hand over her mouth. Bug-eyed, trying to shake her head as Stoli approached her, Stoli contemplated his own life, the woman's life, the world, Romania, and his dead brother. He reached out with his hands, grabbed the terrified woman's neck, looked directly into her eyes, and said, "This is not about you," and saw how easy it can be to crush a windpipe, unknowingly squeezing her carotid arteries as well, the latter prohibiting blood from entering the brain, and watched as a frightened mother of three children tried to escape the man from behind while hands around the front of her neck stole her life. She fell dead, near the garbage, behind the place where she worked. A small lizard, looking like the iguana from a continent far away, scrambled across the refuge.

"Well done," said Gantemirov, observing the motionless corpse. "You have your brother's DNA."

Stoli expected his body to shake or to feel nervous or for something to happen. Nothing happened. He felt nothing. If anything, he felt energized. It occurred to him he had just embraced the most potent experience of living—employing the opportunity to deprive someone else of their own life.

Stoli looked at Gantemirov. "Now what? Is this how you test people? Is this how you tested my brother?"

"Actually, this is how I test some people. And if you must know, I did not need to test your brother. But it is how I tested you, and you passed." Gantemirov smiled. He then ripped open the remaining unbuttoned portion of the dead woman's shirt, took back his two hundred dollars, pulled off her brassiere, removed a knife from his pants pocket, and carved a stickman on her chest, placing an *X* in the region of the mouth and wiggly lines in both hands.

"What's this about?' asked Stoli, looking around, still energized and feeling more in control of his own life and destiny than he had ever contemplated.

"You'll see. You and I are going to Paris."

"Paris? What for?"

"Be like your brother. He was a good man and never asked questions to which he did not need answers."

* * *

Chapter Twenty-five

FLY HIGH

En route to Paris, sitting in the first-class cabin of Air France, Dick Swept eyed the flight attendant, who seemed to smile longer than necessary, going beyond officious pleasantry. Given the length of the flight and the sparse number of first-class customers, the attendant had extra time on her hands. As it happened, the seat next to Dick Swept was empty.

"Mind if I sit down?" the beautiful French woman inquired, green eyes twinkling and her upper lip straining to pout.

"Be my guest," replied Swept, a cynical yet inviting grin on his face.

"It says on the clipboard you're from Washington, D.C. Is this your first time in Paris?"

"No, I've been there several times. I love Paris."

"Most Americans do."

"Well, you know the old saying: When in Rome, do as the Romans do. When in America, head for France."

Genevieve, whom Swept soon learned was the flight attendant's name, politely smiled and reached across his lap, applying mild pressure to his upper leg. "What is this? You read magazines on fly-fishing? Are you a fisherman?"

"I read different magazines, on lots of things. Right now, I'm more interested in French cuisine than fishing." The two of them, Dick Swept and Genevieve, conversed as the huge Airbus Boeing 310-300 flew across the cold Atlantic Ocean. In a short time, Swept made arrangements for dinner with Genevieve at his hotel, the Crillon, in Paris.

Genevieve thanked Swept for the invitation, rose from her chair with some mild assistance, propping herself slightly on Dick Swept's leg, and kissed him on the cheek.

As Genevieve walked away toward the front of the plane, she said, "Do you know what my favorite saying is? It's 'When in Rome, do as the Romans do. When in Paris, do as the French do.'" She continued down the aisle, looking over her shoulder, grinning at Swept.

A few hours later, after taking his melatonin to avoid jet lag, Swept and Genevieve exchanged more small talk, and the two looked forward to dinner in Paris.

After clearing customs, Swept was picked up by a driver whom the agency had hired and was taken to the Crillon.

Swept always enjoyed the Crillon Hotel. Sitting on the north side of the Place de la Concorde, the building became a hotel in 1909, prior to which it was a palace that welcomed Marie-Antoinette for singing lessons, only later to lose her life on the guillotine in the outside square.

The sheer quantity of marble in the highly praised Crillon's Les Ambassadeurs restaurant is staggering. Swept thoroughly enjoyed dining there. He also appreciated that the American embassy was next door, providing opportunity for possible assistance, given that Swept was not only an American citizen but also worked for the Central Intelligence Agency.

After being greeted by the men at the concierge desk, who knew him well, Swept checked in, admiring the efficiency of the staff. He unpacked, went for a walk down the Champs Elysees, returned to his hotel room, where he showered and shaved, and went downstairs to dine. Genevieve, dressed in a low-cut green silk chiffon dress, held on her sloping shoulders by two faint strings, greeted the neurologist with a grin.

"I love food," the trim woman said, reaching out to shake Swept's hand and kiss him on the cheek. "Well," replied Swept, "here's to food," making a toasting gesture with his right hand.

Two hours later, the couple were upstairs, on the third floor, in Swept's hotel bed. Genevieve proved herself lithesome and acrobatic, staying for the night. In the morning, she asked for breakfast in bed. After devouring her meal, the nubile flight attendant commented that the Crillon's scrambled eggs, which she had never before consumed, were the best she had ever had. Then, with a mischievous smile, she rolled over, balanced herself above a smiling Dick Swept, and arranged her breasts to fall close to

Swept's face. Taking a piece of toast, the woman licked it and placed it below, between Swept's legs, and cooed, "I'm not done with breakfast."

* * *

Dick Swept was almost bored, talking to the American embassy bureaucrat who had to log Swept into some computer array, so all U.S. agencies knew the CIA had someone working in Paris. While standing, facing the bureaucrat, Swept thought about his night and morning with Genevieve and how much he looked forward to seeing her again.

Strictly speaking, Swept's presence in France was neither "wet" nor "dark" in the parlance of espionage. He was to attend the International Speech Forum meeting in Dourdan, just outside the center of Paris. The meeting was held in a large conference center that provided multiple meeting rooms and overnight accommodations. Given Swept's predilection for the Crillon, coupled with the embassy (or the CIA) providing him a driver, he elected to stay at his hotel and drive to the conference center. That way, he reasoned, he might be able to learn what was transpiring in the speech community and still enjoy Paris.

Swept's driver, Andre, had no problem hanging out for hours and welcomed the respite. Unfortunately, Genevieve was traveling back to the United States that night and would not be able to see him. As much as Swept enjoyed Paris nightlife, he spent the night alone.

* * *

Chapter Twenty-six

MORTIS REX

Swept had done his homework regarding alleged causes and theories of stuttering. Although he had been to many neurology and neuroscience meetings, he had seldom attended lectures on speech disorders. Certainly, the brain was involved with speech and language, but most of Swept's attention focused on the memory process, not clinical and research aspects of speech compromise. Swept was amazed that almost all of the attendees were women.

For multiple reasons, the majority of speech-language pathologists are women. In Europe, where many speech-language pathologists are called phoniatricians, the prevalence of women in this profession is pronounced. Swept was also surprised at the large number of speech-related self-help organizations that were represented at the meeting. There were over twenty of them, ranging from organizations in Dachau, Germany, to speech clubs in Prague, Czech Republic.

Swept eyed the calendar of events and noted there was a symposium to which members of all speech self-help organizations were invited. The meeting was that afternoon. Swept planned to attend.

After looking at the vendors' multiple textbooks on speech and language, as well as several vendor-sponsored, computer-driven therapy programs, Swept walked toward the auditorium. He noticed a magnificent woman, at least from behind. She had a spring in her step, and like that small cadre of sensual women, her hair gently swayed from side to side as she walked, her body axis remaining stable and erect, and her tight Versace black jeans and black turtleneck sweater hugging her body.

Swept caught a better view as the two headed for the auditorium. The woman's face was scarred, swollen, and disfigured. Swept knew in an instant she had lupus and was on steroids. When the woman turned, sensing someone watching, Swept was a gentleman. "Hi, I'm Dick Swept."

"Jennifer Pettigrew," responded the well-built non-beauty, a smile on her face at Swept's response to her. "Are you enjoying the conference?"

"I'm not sure. I just arrived and was looking at the displays. The scientific and clinical conferences begin this evening. Right now, I'm looking forward to what the self-help groups have to say."

"Whatever they have to say, it can't be strong enough as far as I'm concerned."

"What do you mean?" inquired Swept.

"Simple. It's only recently that anyone cares about stuttering, or people who have trouble speaking. It's a different form of abuse, against the speech disenfranchised. People who can't talk appropriately are abused; it's just that there is no direct perpetrator of the act, just society."

"Maybe," Swept replied. "Either way, I want to hear what people have to say."

"Nice to meet you," Jennifer replied and moved to her right, saying hello to a woman she had met during registration.

Swept thought to himself, *Another person on the planet with a lot on her mind!*

* * *

Jokhar Gantemirov and Stoli checked into the Relais des Chartreux, located next to the venue of the meeting. Each had their own room, but Stoli was told to share his with four men who seemed to have known Gantemirov a long time. These four were comfortable sleeping on the floor.

* * *

Gantemirov had previously met these men in a mosque near Satoj, Chechnya. The ride to that mosque, from the restaurant where he and Stoli had murdered the waitress, was bumpy and dirty, and Gantemirov seldom spoke, except in response to direct questions. Stoli was glad to be with Gantemirov and asked many questions about his dead brother, to which Gantemirov answered truthfully but sparsely. Yes, Aleksander was intelligent and clever. At one time, he might have been handsome, but years of strain and hardship contributed un-attractive features to his countenance.

Gantemirov had no idea whether women liked Aleksander Kostokov. After Kostokov's family died in a Ukraine train accident, he never again interacted with women, except for sexual requests demanded by Liubov Usova, an unattractive but brilliant KGB and FSB superior.

Gantemirov took Stoli with him into the mosque near Satoj. A few men approached Gantemirov, at which time Gantemirov instructed Stoli to leave. Thirty minutes later, Gantemirov met Stoli outside, with these four men. The four seemed genuinely happy to see Gantemirov and appeared eager to please him. Gantemirov introduced Stoli and jokingly made it clear to everyone that if he even suspected any were working for the Russians, he would kill everyone.

* * *

In the Relais des Chartreux, the four Chechens were pleasant, polite, and never smiled. They were also aloof in their interactions with Stoli, who had little complaints, especially since he had the bed.

* * *

Stoli and Gantemirov registered for the meeting, while the other men walked around the area and read tour books in Arabic. These were abundant, given the large number of Arabs who visit France each year.

Gantemirov and Stoli entered the auditorium where the self-help groups were meeting, sitting in the back. Gantemirov, trained by Chechen and Russian authorities in his checkered career, immediately noticed Dick Swept sitting in the front of the auditorium. Gantemirov knew Swept would recognize him and probably recognize Stoli, since Stoli was the exact image of Kostokov.

While Gantemirov sat there, planning what to do, he noticed a beautiful woman, at least from behind. When she turned around, he saw the face of Jennifer Pettigrew. The woman looked at him and smiled. Gantemirov stood and approached the woman with lupus.

The meeting had not yet begun. Positioning himself so that his back was to Swept, the Chechen easily began light conversation with Jennifer, keeping Stoli in the background, out of Swept's line of vision.

As the two discussed the meeting and the beauty of nearby Paris, Jennifer let known her outspoken views about helping the disabled. Gantemirov ventured to bring up Stickman X, boldly commenting it was a great idea and a great caricature. Jennifer Pettigrew, to Gantemirov's delight, agreed and said Stickman X was long overdue.

Gantemirov introduced Stoli and provided a ruse excuse for needing to leave, but only after arranging dinner for later that evening. After whispering to Stoli, the two men left the auditorium, Dick Swept still not having noticed them. Jennifer remained, attending the ensuing lectures.

* * *

That evening, Jennifer Pettigrew and Gantemirov dined at a local restaurant near the convention center. After an excellent but inexpensive Bourdeaux and some crepes with fish, the two soon talked in tones that reflected emotional feelings. Jennifer made clear her distaste for the medical establishment and, indeed, most establishments. When Gantemirov brought up the "Stutterers' Manifesto," Jennifer repeated there should be manifestos for all diseases, for all people medically compromised.

Jennifer mentioned that there were small study sections in the morning, one especially appealing. "Which one is that?" inquired Gantemirov.

"The Rights of the Afflicted. I bet it's very interesting."

"I bet it is too. Why don't I see you there?"

"Great. I look forward to it."

Gantemirov paid the waiter and escorted Jennifer back to the conference center, thanking her for her wonderful company. Jennifer kissed him lightly on the mouth, to which Gantemirov responded in a purposefully shy way, "Thanks. I look forward to tomorrow."

Gantemirov walked away, eager to speak to Stoli, feeling nearly certain he could manipulate Jennifer Pettigrew.

The following morning, Gantemirov walked into the small auditorium where the study section met on the "Rights of the Afflicted." Fortunately, the room was crowded. Gantemirov said hello to Jennifer in the hallway, keeping a close eye out for Dick Swept, and sneaked into the back row of seats. He sat with his shoulders hunched up. He saw Swept enter the room and walk to the lower seats. Jennifer came in late, looked around the crowded room for Gantemirov as the lights dimmed, shrugged her shoulders and went down the stairs, finding a seat in the sixth row.

There was a roster of five speakers. All stuttered severely. One was hostile, stating he thought violence done in the name of the "manifesto" served a good purpose. His name was Jeremiah MacGregor.

MacGregor was treated with several denunciations and derisions. Flustered, he roamed the hallway during the coffee break, where Gantemirov was able to stop him. Gantemirov could now see Swept, who must have come out of the meeting later, talking to other speakers. A small bevy of beautiful women were near Swept, giggling and looking at their programs.

Jennifer approached Gantemirov during the coffee break. "So, there you are. I looked for you. Where were you?"

"In the back, the last row. I looked for you too."

"Well, Jokhar, thanks again for last night. Right now, please excuse me," and Jennifer left for the bathroom. At that moment, in the crowded hallway, Gantemirov saw Jeremiah MacGregor approaching and spoke to him.

"Mr. MacGregor, I enjoyed what you had to say. Too bad some people gave you a hard time. I thought you were right on target."

"S-S-S-Some thought not," MacGregor replied, forcing a smile. Jeremiah looked at Gantemirov askance and, following small conversation, during which he had multiple hesitancies in his speech, began to walk away. Just then, Jennifer Pettigrew joined the two men, at which time Gaantemirov, fearing that Swept would soon see him, again excused himself, telling Jennifer he would talk to her later.

MacGregor could not help staring at Jennifer Pettigrew. Her luscious figure, owning curves that strained her garments, soaked through to his bones. The woman felt a sense of calm in that Jeremiah did not flinch when he saw her face. Three people at this meeting had not flinched when they saw Jennifer Pettigrew's face: Dick Swept, Gantemirov, and this man.

Jeremiah felt assured when this incredibly well-bodied woman smiled at him. And she was fluent.

Smiling, Jennifer talked to the stutterer *cum* secret author of the "Stutterers' Manifesto," inquiring whether he liked the meeting. The two exchanged information on everything, ranging from the relationship between Scotland and England to scientific merits of stuttering, and the attention recently focused on the "Stutterers' Manifesto."

They both commented they looked forward to Rex Allendorf's talk in a few hours. While they spoke, Dick Swept noticed Jennifer Pettigrew and tried to pay attention to whom she spoke.

* * *

At the end of Dr. Allendorf's talk, during which Swept sat in the front row and Jennifer sat with Jeremiah, toward the back, Jennifer kept looking for Gantemirov but did not see him. She decided to relax and enjoy Dr. Allendorf's lecture, which she did. Allendorf mesmerized the entire audience.

Allendorf discussed new data regarding brain-imaging research in stuttering, as well as genetic investigations and scientific discoveries of motor-control mechanisms that explain how the brain controls the speech system. During the question-and-answer session, there were questions regarding neurphysiologic disruption in stuttering and a few questions concerning Allendorf's views on the "Stutterers' Manifesto."

"It is pure nonsense. Nothing will come of destroying property in the name of science. The problem with research in stuttering is lack of funding and, to be frank, in many instances, lack of ideas. Destroying property, killing panda bears, all in the name of obtaining more funding for research, will only bring problems, not excellence in research."

There was considerable hissing during these remarks. Allendorf continued, "I understand that people who stutter are frustrated. I am a researcher and have frustrations too. But I can assure you, violence in the arena of science only produces problems, not testable scientific hypotheses, which are what we need to drive the system."

More hisses. Allendorf felt somewhat uncomfortable, as he recognized many people with illnesses must truly feel disenfranchised. When the session ended, Allendorf left the podium and spoke to people at the refreshment table. Half the people there supported his beliefs about the manifesto. The other half thought he was a traitor.

* * *

Rex Allendorf was hungry and wanted to relax and enjoy the outside scenery. He was returning from a small crepe stand, not far from the conference center, when Jeremiah MacGregor happened to pass him and nodded briefly.

Allendorf walked to the park and saw men playing a game of dice. Being curious, he approached them. The men wore Middle Eastern clothing and were very disheveled. One turned to the academician from Cornell, asking with a thick Algerian accent, "Mister, can I have a Franc?"

Allendorf gladly reached into his pocket. It was the last time he would do so, as a chard of broken glass from behind slit his throat

* * *

Dick Swept toured the beautiful park outside the conference center. The moon was full and the breeze delightful. As he thought about Stickman X, stuttering, and Regina's attackers, he noticed movement behind a large elm tree. As he approached the tree, an arm grabbed him from behind, choking him.

"Are you Dick Swept?" a voice with a Slavic accent inquired.

"I hope not," gasped Swept, silently cursing himself for leaving his gun at the Crillon.

"You're dead," and the arm tightened around Swept's neck, as Swept noticed a man emerge from behind another tree, charging him with a huge knife. Concentrating on his predicament as he had concentrated in clinical neurological emergencies, Swept kicked his right foot backwards as hard as he could, splintering the attacker's right shin, then tucked his own chin inferiorly, throwing himself back against his assailant, and then suddenly flipping the man over. Swept picked up the distal part of the broken leg and hurled the man counterclockwise against the second assailant, the first man screaming in agony, as he knocked the knife out of the second man's hand.

The second assailant reached for the weapon, but not fast enough, as Swept propelled his right palm into the bottom part of the man's nose, aiming rostrally toward the brain, sending splinters of nasal tissue into the man's cerebrum. As the man stumbled, gasping, Swept grabbed his neck with both hands, keeping an eye on the man with the broken leg, and fractured the assailant's larynx, watching the man gasp and choke to death as Swept turned further attention to the man on the ground, writhing in pain.

Swept picked up the man by his broken leg. "Who are you? What do you want?"

A shot rang and the man fell dead, a bullet transecting his upper brainstem, as Swept ducked for cover.

Both assailants were dead, and Swept had no idea who they were or why they had attacked him.

* * *

Later that night, the entire group of people attending the conference learned about Rex Allendorf's murder, his throat slit side to side. The news services reported that a placard had been left near his body, boasting a picture of a large Stickman X, a knife going through the midsection of the stick figure.

* * *

Chapter Twenty-seven

LOVE IN A TIME OF DARKNESS

Dick Swept discussed his evening events with the French police. They were investigating the identity of the two men who attacked him, as well as the murder of Rex Allendorf. Swept also went to the American embassy and called Cervantes.

Although there was a list of attendees at the conference, there was no formal roster of attendees at Allendorf's lecture. Someone could have listened to the speaker and not registered for the conference, given the lax security at the auditorium doors, especially after the lecture began. Also, why was it not possible that Allendorf was killed for personal reasons or for money (his wallet was gone) and perhaps not for his comments about the "Stutterers' Manifesto"?

The next day, MacGregor and Jennifer had lunch in the cafeteria within the conference center. Jennifer had seen

Gantemirov briefly, made plans for dinner, but now had no idea where he was. MacGregor commented on Stickman X, stating it wasn't such a bad idea for stutterers and other people with physical disabilities to be heard. Jennifer agreed.

Jeremiah felt more sexually excited than he had in years. Jennifer was sensually compelling, had intellectual stamina, and he enjoyed her comfort level. MacGregor was too shy to ask Jennifer for dinner, but the two did agree to see each other later, during the meeting. Besides, Jennifer was still anticipating dinner with Gantemirov.

* * *

Jokhar Gantemirov possessed the same understanding of human attributes as do many successful CEOs of major corporations. As the Chechen sat with Jennifer, he could sense they were bonding.

Gantemirov and Jennifer dined in the small bistro of the conference hotel, adjacent to the meeting rooms and conveniently, thought Gantemirov, close to the guest rooms. Gantemirov looked inquisitively into Jennifer's eyes, making certain he avoided gazing, even for a moment, at her scars. "Jennifer, I feel I can trust you. Can I?"

Smiling, thankful the burly hunk of a man stared directly into her eyes, she replied honestly, "I don't know. Can you?"

"Well, we're going to find out. I think it is wonderful that people are committing acts of violence in the name of Stickman X. We should do more."

"Why are you telling me?"

"Because we are at a speech meeting, someone has been murdered, and frankly, I would be impressed if you did it. I thought Allendorf was a jerk."

"Well," she snickered, "I didn't do it, although I agree with you. I didn't see you at the lecture. Were you there?"

"I came in late and sat in the back."

"You always sit in the back. Any particular reason?" Jennifer smiled and toyed with the big man's hands.

"Not particularly. I just like to sit in the back. That way, if I'm bored and want to leave, I can."

"That only works," Jennifer giggled, "if the entrance is back there. If it's in the front, your options decrease."

"Well," replied Gantemirov, "so far, there are exits near the back. Lucky for me, I haven't had to leave early, at least not too often." Gantemirov then stood and walked around the table to Jennifer Pettigrew, motioned for her to stand, and drew her to him. Gantemirov embraced her to the full, letting her feel his erect organ as he pushed himself against her, kissing her deeply.

"We're here, in a bistro, at a speech meeting, in front of everyone," moaned Jennifer.

"Then, let's leave."

Gantemirov placed his arm around Jennifer Pettigrew, kept her close to him, and softly said, "Say nothing. Please, say nothing," as he put down some cash and escorted Jennifer Pettigrew to his room.

* * *

The next morning, Jennifer, exhausted from lovemaking, kissed Jokhar Gantemirov, who felt certain that Jennifer was now emotionally beholden to him. Room Service delivered a small breakfast to their room. Jennifer Pettigrew wondered whether she was in love with a man she hardly knew.

As the two lovers sat at a small table, eating breakfast, Gantemirov smiled, looking directly into the eyes of the beautifully bodied woman with the diseased face. “Last night was wonderful, truly wonderful.”

“Thanks,” Jennifer replied. “It was nice for me too.” Then, Jennifer thought a moment and said, “Last night, you asked me about Dr. Allendorf.”

“Yes. I said I thought he was a jerk.”

“I know. Anyway, it was as I said last night. I didn’t kill him. I’ve never killed anybody.”

“Well,” Gantemirov laughed, “you nearly killed me last night. I don’t think I could have handled any more of you.”

Jennifer grinned, feeling even more secure. “But I have to tell you something. Have you read about Stickman X?”

“Yes, I have.” Gantemirov knew he had struck oil. He delighted that his instincts were so often on target.

“I have too. There is a group of us, in London, all girls, all women. We have known each other a long time.”

Gantemirov began toying with Jennifer’s breasts, at times squeezing them hard enough to make her wince, which seemed to excite her as well as the Chechen. Pushing Gntemirov’s hand aside, Jennifer continued, “We are planning to blow up hospitals and medical schools in the States and in Europe. It should waken governments of the world to put more money into research. When governments see what's happening, they will see that what we want is good for people. We're not asking for anything for ourselves. It's for a greater good, the good of the afflicted."

Studying Gantemirov's face thoroughly, Jennifer Pettigrew continued, "These are my friends. We're loyal to one another. What do you think?"

Gantemirov, a professional to the bone and one who comprehended the human condition, smiled. "And why, may I ask, are you telling me? Or telling me now?"

"Because I think I love you and I want you to know all about me. Also, we've done some things in England."

Squeezing Jennifer under her turtleneck sweater, making her squirm in the chair, Gantemirov sadistically smiled. "Good," as he allowed Jennifer to remove his hand. "I've done some things myself. Let me tell you something about me."

"What?" Jennifer laughed, keeping his hand from her. "That you're a sadist?"

"That too," Gantemirov smiled. "But something else."

"What?" again, removing Gantemirov's hand.

"I used to be a part of the Chechen underground, fighting Russians for independence. Are you familiar with Chechnya?"

"A little bit. The Russians destroyed Chechnya. The Chechens are a tough people, sort of like the Chicago Mafia, as I understand it. Anyway, the Russians are all over them."

Jokhar Gantemirov let his hands rest on his thighs. "We are not gangsters, but you are correct about one thing: Russians have been all over us for years."

Gantemirov continued, "Listen to me. I know a lot about noble purposes. You don't want governments placing ten percent of budgets into medical research. At best, they'll say they are doing that but aren't. What you should ask for is money for yourselves. Put it in a special account and then you, you and your friends, give it to people who care about your work. You decide who gets it. If you don't know who should receive it, donate it to charities for medical research. Give it to medical schools that work in areas you care about."

Jennifer listened intently. Gantemirov interrupted her thought processes. "Listen, you get the money. I can tell you how to set up a bank account in Switzerland, a special numbered account only you know about."

Jennifer was all ears. Gantemirov pulled out a U.S. dollar bill. "Jennifer, write down the serial number of the bill. Tell no one, not even me. That's the code you want for an anonymous account in Zurich. I'll show you how to do it. And if you want, I know people who can train your friends."

Jennifer was amazed. Jokhar Gantemirov was trained in terrorism but certainly did not seem like a terrorist. "Are you one of the bad guys?" Jennifer jokingly inquired.

"Do you think I'm one of the bad guys? I am a Chechen, loyal to my country, my people, and their cause. Russia has no business being there. You have concerns about your people, your group, your clan. Well, I have the same. But my group, my people, my clan are a country. You and I are the same, Jennifer."

With a move swift and not gentle, Gantemirov stood from his chair, pulled Jennifer to him, escorted her to the bed, opened her pants and, pleased she was moist, toyed with her as his large fingers found her vaginal vault, a movement not without pain and not without causing a stinging sensation. Jennifer looked at him, digesting all that was going on—their sexual relationship the preceding evening, learning about Gantemirov's activities, which he unashamedly discussed, and, now, his vaginal intrusion. With a puzzled look on her face, focused on brief but real discomfort, Jennifer asked, "What are you doing to me? What did you do?'

"You asked if I were a sadist? I said, 'yes'. I put in a small device, sort of like an IUD. It will keep you from getting pregnant, until you and I decide we want babies. But I'll only do that after we get married. Keep it in there, so you always know I am with you."

Jennifer Pettigrew was amazed, dumbstruck! No man had ever mentioned marriage to her. Her discomfort began to subside. Jennifer welcomed Jokhar Gantemirov to her. The couple made passionate love, while the Chechen surreptitiously smirked at the ease with which he had inserted his GPS Nanoelectronic DM3382 microchip into the woman's canal.

After their lovemaking, while Jennifer was in the bathroom, Gantemirov looked at the dollar bill he gave Jennifer and softly spoke the numbers into his cell phone recording system. Later, he would transcribe them.

When Jennifer returned, Gantemirov threw his arms around her once more. "Jennifer, one more thing."

The woman wistfully looked at Jokhar Gantemirov. "What now? Are you going to tell me you run an army for Chechnya? Or that you're married?"

"Not quite. I'm going to tell you about a man I saw in the audience. He once tried to interfere with our Chechen freedom movement. He used to be a neurologist in Texas, in Houston. The fact he is here at this meeting, in the setting of Stickman X's appearing all over, and this being a speech meeting, makes me think he now works for the government."

"What do you want me to do?"

"Talk to him. Find out why he is here. Under no circumstances, tell him about our conversation regarding the medical schools and hospitals. Especially about the number. I don't even know the number. No one will, except you."

"Is he as cute as you?"

"Hardly. But he might be as dangerous, although not as much fun." They both smiled and embraced. "Just see what he wants. Please don't tell him about me. He would want me dead. If I'm right, and he's with the United States government, he is powerful enough to have me killed and get away with it."

"Don't be silly. That can't happen."

"Jennifer," the Chechen said in a low, soft, steady voice. "Listen carefully. That man, Dr. Dick Swept, is a dangerous man. Do not mention my name. Can you find out why he's here and then let me know?"

"Sure. I can go see him right now. But let me tell you something. I met him at the start of the meeting. We talked in the hallway. He seemed pretty nice."

"He isn't. Besides, he's not on our side. Find him. It shouldn't be a problem. Leave a message on the message board. Say you want to meet with Dr. Dick Swept. You can tell him you heard about his research. He used to work in memory research."

Jennifer, dismissing that Dick Swept wanted to harm Gantemirov but wondering if it were possible, looked at Gantemirov. "Not that I would do it, but how do I actually open the account in Switzerland?"

"Simple." Again, Gantemirov felt pleased. He felt he was effectively controlling Jennifer Pettigrew, ranging from her thinking to her sex life. "Fly to Zurich, go into the Zurich International Bank of Switzerland, and tell them you want to open an account with any number you choose. Choose the number on the dollar bill, or use a number they provide. Then, you or anyone else can wire the funds to them. They'll know who you are, have pictures and what not, and only you can remove the money. Give them a code so only you can do this."

"I have to fly to Switzerland for this? Can't I do it in London?"

"You can open the account anywhere they have a branch. But the best thing is to open the account in a country where banking laws favor anonymity. Do it in Zurich. Choose any Swiss bank you want. I like the one in Zurich."

"Why?"

"Because," chuckling, "they have good food in Zurich and I know all the chocolate shops. Now," grabbing her again, internally pushing at the microchip, Gantemirov produced more than a twinge of pain, "you come here for some chocolates of my own." Jennifer smiled, and the two lovers embraced.

Following their lovemaking, Jennifer looked into the deep dark eyes of the treacherous Chechen. "I don't like the idea of my name associated with any movement of any money."

"Jennifer, let me make a suggestion. Use an account I have. I can give you the number. Have anyone you like wire funds into that account. When you want to take the money out, tell me and do whatever you want."

"You're mighty cooperative, aren't you?"

"Not really. If you become unhappy with anything I do, which I personally can't conceive," playing with her body and causing her to squirm, "stop sending funds there and open your own account. It makes no difference to me."

"I'll think about it. After funds are wired in, how do I get them out or send them to charities I want to send them to?"

"Simple. Roll over in bed and tell me to do it."

Jennifer smiled, kissed Gantemirov, and offered her hand. "It's a deal. You give me your account number, I'll write it on the dollar bill, and that's the number we'll use."

"Deal it is," said Gantemirov, laughing and rolling over.

Jennifer Pettigrew mused for several minutes. She was helping the sick, helping people with lupus, and was with a man who loved her. She could imagine herself walking into fine department stores in Europe, with her husband and children, all yet to come. She was on her mission and in love.

Jokhar Gantemirov was also heavily engaged in thought. Women were so stupid and predictable. As much as he appreciated a fine body, he detested little-girl naïveté, born from neediness and insecurity. Thank goodness he had installed the GPS signaling device.

Chapter Twenty-eight

DARKNESS IN A TIME OF LOVE

Swept was busy trying to learn about people who might want Rex Allendorf dead. He had no idea who attacked himself or why someone had killed one of the attackers. Many people at the conference had taken umbrage at Allendorf's comments against Stickman X. However, who at the conference would want to kill Swept?

The French police made it clear they had little interest in the crimes near the conference center. After all, the victims were foreigners, and American! And the CIA had no business sending an undercover agent to France without permission. Swept explained that he was not in France as an undercover agent but, rather, was attending a conference as a neurologist. The French could not have cared less.

After Swept contacted the American embassy, which, in turn, contacted Cervantes, he went to dine at the Crillon Hotel alone.

*   *   *

The next morning, Swept saw his name on the board at the message booth, following which he learned Jennifer Pettigrew wanted to meet him at 1:30, near the Elsevier Publisher exhibit booth. Swept arrived promptly and had no difficulty recognizing the well-proportioned woman with whom he had earlier conversed.

"Jennifer Pettigrew?"

"Jennifer Pettigrew," said the woman infatuated with Jokhar Gantemirov. "I appreciate your seeing me, Dr. Swept."

Swept was taken in with Jennifer's figure. He looked directly into Jennifer's eyes, not in an attempt to avoid her facial scarring but because he liked women's eyes. Swept was not disgusted by any disease, which he viewed as external anchors upon patients. "How can I help?'

"Well, Dr. Swept. After we talked, I recalled reading something about you, something about memory research. Am I correct?"

"I don't know," replied Swept. "My work is pretty technical. Are you a scientist?"

"No, but I know a lot about lupus. I have it, frequently attend lectures, and I think your name came up."

"I appreciate your contacting me, but I don't know a lot about lupus. Well, in some ways I do. As a neurologist, we take care of a number of patients with lupus. There are different types, some of which affect the brain. Yours probably does not."

"Do you work in speech? Is that why you're here?"

Swept found this series of questioning strange. "Not really. I interacted with Dr. Rex Allendorf, in the past. I talked to him when he was at Cornell—and living. You may have heard he was murdered last night."

"Yes, I did. What a tragedy. I didn't agree with what he said about Stickman X and all that, but I'm sorry he's dead."

Swept silently nodded his head. "Anyway, I came here because I wanted to learn more about speech disorders."

Self-confident, Jennifer Pettigrew tested her surroundings and all people within. She also wondered about Allendorf's murder. "Do you know a man named Gantemirov? Jokhar Gantemirov?"

Swept's jaw dropped. At that moment, Swept knew that Gantemirov was implicated in the attack last evening. "He recently escaped from prison. He's a very dangerous man. Do you know him?"

"I'm not sure," replied Jennifer cautiously.

"Is he here?" inquired Swept, again thinking that his attack, Allendorf's death, the presence of Gantemirov, and this woman were probably connected. Swept did not mention the attack on himself, wondering whether she would say anything that might reveal her knowledge about this. Jennifer did not.

Jennifer Pettigrew stared at Swept, saying nothing. Swept, confident with all women, said, "Let's you and I take a walk."

Jennifer agreed, and the two walked outside, down the small walkway to the right, into the park.

* * *

Jokhar Ganemirov's GPS system, recently inserted into Jennifer's loins, enabled the Chechen to follow her movements on his screen, supplied by a satellite offering multidimensional input to within inches. He could tell she was moving, but did not know with whom or why.

* * *

Swept told Jennifer Pettigrew about Jokhar Gantemirov. He explained Pi-Two, Kostokov, the ex-KGB agents, and Gantemirov. Jennifer looked at him, smiled, and turned away. All she said was, "I have to go."

Swept let Jennifer leave, not pushing the issue. He reasoned Gantemirov could easily have left the conference by now. Swept was becoming even more convinced that Gantemirov was involved in Allendorf's death, possibly the Stickman scenarios, and certainly the attack on him. Would Gantemirov now become more desperate or pull back? Swept, carrying his Glock semiautomatic, something he always did in the United States but had not done in foreign countries, checked his weapon, making certain the clip within the gun and the spare clip both had their full allotment of eighteen bullets.

It was not clear to Swept what Gantemirov's motivations might be. Mulling this over, Swept decided to ride things out and see what happened. He returned to the conference and attended a lecture on errors in vocal-cord movements in people who stutter.

* * *

Jokhar Gantemirov was not happy when Jennifer told him she mentioned him to Dick Swept.

"I told you not to do that. Why did you?"

"I did it because I wanted to know what was going on. You said you loved me. We talked about children. You told me how to set up a numbered account in Switzerland and offered to train my friends. I wanted to know more about you. At least, I'm honest. I told you what I did. Are you honest with me? Did you tell me what you did, what you've done?"

Gantemirov understood one thing—he could only partially trust Jennifer Pettigrew. He had told her not to mention his name to Swept. Yet she did. He also recognized that if Jennifer did something that displeased him, she would probably tell him. If real problems emerged, he could always track her with the microchip device.

Jokhar Gantemirov's plan now evolved more fully. For the time being, he would be understanding and kind. Later, he would be what he was—focused, driven, and ruthless. Placing his arms around Jennifer, the Chechen replied, "Are you satisfied, now that you know? There is nothing horrible about me, only that I love my country, Chechnya, and I also love you." Gantemirov coddled Jennifer in his arms.

Jennifer responded, "I am satisfied. You shouldn't feel you can't share things with me, certainly your past. Your past is what you are. Our past is what we all are."

"Jennifer, our present, which arrived through our past, is what we are. But certainly, we don't need a discussion on philosophy. One of these days, if you and I get really bored, we can discuss Martin Heidegger's theories of being. Do you know who he was?"

"No."

"Heidegger was a German philosopher during the rise of Adolph Hitler. Initially, he was the darling of the Left, until he joined the Nazis. He was a brilliant man, and I have always enjoyed his writings. Heidegger believed language is involved in our thinking, our being, and held disdain for most of the other philosophers. Anyway, that's for another day."

"You know about philosophy?"

"You're the one who raised the issue of our past and our present. Right now, my present involves you."

"Okay," said Jennifer, tightening her physical hold around the burly Chechen. "What shall we talk about?"

"Let's talk about your efforts to make the world a better place."

"Okay," Jennifer responded, loosening her embrace, but continuing to stare deeply into her lover's eyes and, in her mind, his heart. "Go on."

"Give me your phone number in London. A friend of mine will call and tell you what to do."

"What's his name?"

Gantemirov, thinking as he spoke, smiled. "Stoli. His name is Stoli."

* * *

Later that day, Gantemirov again discussed how to set up a numbered account in a Swiss bank. Jennifer still had the dollar bill Gantemirov gave her. His account number was on it and, as he explained, all she had to do was wire money into that account. She could tell him where she wanted the money to be directed, such as charity organizations, or he could send it to an account of her choosing.

"Why can't I take it out of the account myself?"

"Because the bank won't let you. Only I can remove it. I can set it up differently if you want. You told me you don't want to be identified with the funds. The law might catch you. If it goes into my account, which is long standing, it is set up such that the bank needs my password, a special letter sequence. This was arranged before efforts to trail movement of money following the 9/11 attacks on America."

"What's your code, in case I want the money, unless you don't trust me?"

"I trust you. The code is A-Y-N-H-C-E-H-C, Chechnya backwards. But only I can take out the money. They will only wire the funds to accounts with my name, unless I tell them otherwise, in person, with my identification." Gantemirov knew the code name was a lie.

"Can you write me a check?"

"It's not the smartest thing, but I can. I can also withdraw cash and give it to you."

"What do you suggest I do?"

"I suggest you experiment and see how successful you are in your mission. Wire the funds to my account. Then, I can personally go to the bank and wire the money to wherever you want. If you want to change this one day, or one week, or one month, just do it. You can change your mind any time you want. Just stop sending the money to my account. Or if you want, and don't mind using your real name or a different name—which you can arrange if you get the right identification, which I might be able to help you with—just do it. You're in charge and can set it up any way you want. All I'm saying is that I can help you."

"But Jennifer," Gantemirov continued, "understand something: There will be a trace between your account and whatever charities receive the money. You may want to keep it under my name, at least for a while."

Jennifer was totally confused, yet it all seemed to make sense. Then, smiling his deep, loving smile, Gantemirov said, "Are you satisfied?"

"More than you know, my sweet love," and Jennifer kissed the stubble-bearded face of the dangerous Chechen. Jennifer was happy she would obtain money for medical research. Gantemirov was content for himself.

* * *

That evening, while Jennifer attended lectures, looking for Dick Swept, who was not to be found, Jokhar Gantemirov spoke to his friends. Stoli listened.

"You botched the attack on Swept, and your aim wasn't any good, considering you killed one of our own men."

The men, including Stoli, were silent.

"Listen to me," and Gantemirov spoke firmly and distinctly to his colleagues. He wanted Stoli and the remaining group to disappear and, later, train Jennifer's friends in weaponry, martial arts, reconnaissance, and military tactics. Gantemirov wrote a note to Jennifer, telling her he had to go and would contact her in London. Purposefully, he omitted mention of Swept, so as not to raise any suspicions.

* * *

Jennifer enjoyed the lectures, was mesmerized by the love and kindness in Gantemirov's note, and anxiously awaited to hear from him in London.

Dick Swept attended more lectures but did not see Jennifer. This caused little concern, given Swept had her address, which he readily found in the attendance roster. His address was also there, listing his laboratory location as his main place of contact.

* * *

Chapter Twenty-nine

TRAINING FOR TERROR

After returning to London, Jennifer related to her friends about the wonderful man she had met, the burly Chechen. She explained numbered Swiss bank accounts and the training her Chechen friend offered. All of them were excited. What could be wrong when one sought such a great purpose and noble goal?

Stoli telephoned Jennifer and relayed a message from Gantemirov. His instructions were simple: Tell the women to take a train to Tom Tower, the entrance to Christ Church College in Oxford. The Tower, designed by the famous architect, Christopher Wren, was the entrance to "The House," as modest members refer to Christ Church College. The adjacent quadrangle, named Tom Quad, is the largest in town. The nomenclature refers to the over six-ton bell that hangs in the tower.

* * *

Still in Paris, Swept telephoned Major Cervantes and told him about Jennifer Pettigrew and Gantemirov. Cervantes instructed Swept to do anything he considered appropriate. Swept flew from Paris to London, checked in at Claridge's Hotel, and telephoned Jennifer. There was no answer.

Swept took a taxi to Jennifer's apartment, knocked at her door, but no one responded. There did not appear to be scratches on the door or the outside windows that would raise suspicion of forced entry. Swept appeared in periods throughout the day, that evening, and the following morning. Still, there was no answer.

Swept was able to talk to some of the people who lived in Jennifer's building. He showed them a picture of Jennifer, stating he was a friend, asking if anyone had seen her.

"Built like a beauty, that one is," replied a young man with a briefcase. "She never talked much to me, and I haven't seen her since last week. Pretty amazing that a woman can have a body like that but not the face to match, don't you think?"

Swept was disgusted at these comments. While he was thinking of a reply, a woman came by and noticed the picture.

"Are you a friend of Jennie's?"

"I am," replied Swept. "I've been looking for her. Have you seen her?"

"Not in a while, a long while. Jennie's usually here with those hippie friends of hers, but I haven't seen any of them for a while."

Swept talked to more neighbors but made no progress on where Jennifer might be.

Swept called Jennifer's telephone number twice each

day, but still without success. Later, he was not certain when he would consider forcibly entering her apartment, enlisting the resources of the CIA, London's MI6, and Interpol to find her.

Currently, Swept knew these institutions were working incredibly hard to find members of al-Quada and disentangle similar terrorist organizations. Swept was new to the CIA and would not bother them for now. Cervantes agreed. To expend considerable manpower and money to track down a woman with no criminal history, a fact easily garnered by Swept and Cervantes, was a waste of valuable resources.

Swept believed he had limited options and decided to fly home to Washington, D.C.

* * *

There is a sense of history to Christ Church, as well as a sense of awe. Lewis Carroll taught mathematics there, near the medieval dining hall boasting pictures of former students, including fourteen prime ministers, William Penn, John Wesley, and others.

For the Lupus Ladies of London, the area also held memories of their previous vandalism. Stoli met the women nearby, opposite the meadows near St. Aldate's, the inspiration for the shop in Carroll's *Through the Looking Glass.*

Stoli explained he would drive the women to Dover in his rented van. Inside, they listened and watched videos on small weapons, methods of fighting, and, most important, how to interact as a team and communicate under fire with one another.

When the Lupus Ladies arrived in Dover, they stayed in a local hotel and went to a different park every day.

Gantemirov's friends met them there each time, and they were always with Stoli. Most of the women were fairly fit. Each ran four miles daily, performed various exercise routines, ate well, drank no alcohol, and went to sleep early. The training was rather simple: talk to no one except themselves and repeat everything so many times that the only difference between real action in the field and their training was real victims.

The women trained in their hotel room and in the van. By the end of the course, brief but intense, the Lupus Ladies were familiar with several weapons. This included various HK-USP tactical handguns, Browning Hi-Power (P-35) handguns, and assault rifles, especially the ONYX, the Polish version of the AKS-74U, incorporating a three-round burst selector, side-fold stock, and exotic sight mounts. Their sniper rifle training primarily included the Mauser M86. The grenade launcher was an HK 69A1 (MZP-1) and the shotgun was the ever-ready Remington 870. With eyes blindfolded, each one could take apart any of their weapons, including several standard Soviet-made machine guns, and reassemble them with ease.

Initially, none of their ammunition was live. One day, they drove to a gun range located in an old barn forty miles east of Dover and blew the daylights out of everything until they were comfortable with the noise, the power, and the recoil.

The training was highly focused. The important part of the training was that each woman feel secure with each weapon, her interaction with the team, and be skilled. All the women did very well. They were smart, physically fit, and committed. They were ready!

* * *

Chapter Thirty

EASY MONEY

During the next two weeks, acts of terrorism occurred throughout the world, especially in the United States. At Mount Auburn Hospital, an excellent Cambridge institution affiliated with Harvard Medical School, several women clad in black entered an Alzheimer's clinic on the third floor of the main building, quickly climbed over the counter seating secretaries who collected payments, and bound them with duct tape. The invaders then went down the hall, opening every door, and killed each person inside with a HK USP tactical handgun, silencer attached. Deaths included two neurologists, four nurses, three neuropsychologists, four technicians, and six patients.

Moving as a well-trained unit, faces blackened and wearing black garments, including black ski masks, always taking orders from Jennifer, the women carefully aimed their weapons as they corralled an entire waiting room of old and infirm patients, including caretakers and several young children, forcing them into a corner. To everyone's amazement one of the ladies in black picked up a chair, broke a window facing Mt. Auburn Street, and hurled two demented patients to their deaths. Following this, they spray-painted Stickman X on the wall and exited.

The entire operation took less than eight minutes.

Five minutes later, the telephone call to the secretary of the hospital's CEO, Seymour Branhill, was brief and to the point: "Wire $1,000,000 by the end of the day to the following bank account number—6578234213—or we do it again."

Afterwards, driving in their rented car, the women were pumped with excitement and thrill. They were finally going after those they disliked most—the medical establishment. The deaths caused them no concern. The women had earlier convinced themselves that demented people have no idea what is going on anyway and their lives are at a dead end. As for those who delivered meaningless health care to them, the Lupus Ladies of London had no remorse.

None had remorse. "Are we not supposed to feel bad?" Violet inquired to Jennifer.

"Yeah, I find it strange that I don't *feel* when we do this," inserted Marilyn.

"I'll tell you why," answered Jennifer. "We're doing the right thing, and although it may go against some of society's norms, we know in our hearts it's right. Besides, we're accomplishing more for the sick in a few days or weeks than most people, certainly physicians, accomplish in a lifetime."

"I agree," answered Violet, Marilyn nodding her head, and the two returned to their manuals on weapons.

Over the next several weeks, the same scenario was duplicated at Barnes Hospital, the University of Vermont, Cornell, University of Chicago, University of Iowa, Duke, University of California at San Francisco, and several others. Many hospitals and medical schools ignored the demands, but twelve gave in. Still, the attacks continued at other institutions. Medical institutions were totally unprepared to deal with such a horror. No large medical facility was safe.

Hospital administrators blamed the medical schools for lack of security, and the medical schools blamed the hospitals. In institutions where they were the same, individuals blamed each other. The physicians, in most cases, had no authority to administer or manage the facilities where they worked, despite their providing the medical care. Operating rooms were shut down, medical libraries and cafeterias were closed, and patients became afraid to visit their doctors.

Patients in dialysis units were killed, elevators servicing Intensive Care Units were destroyed, and magnetic imaging machines, which netted hospitals millions of dollars, were blown apart. Hospitals and medical schools suffered enormous financial losses in patient revenue and equipment damage. Authorities had no idea who was behind these heinous acts, and a price of one million dollars was small for these institutions. Increasingly, they paid it.

The violence did not abate and soon encompassed individual physician's offices. It was easy for two people to enter a medical office, in some cases that of a solo practitioner, or storm procedure rooms where physicians performed colonoscopies. The physicians and their medical staff could not readily abandon their patients, certainly not in the middle of a procedure, which could lead to disfigurement or even death.

The only clue to the identity of these savage attacks was the same clue in each attack: Stickman X. And always, after each attack, there was the phone call and demand to send money to a specified numbered account.

Many institutions let it be known they would pay up front, before the attacks. These comments were made in interviews to the media, but the Lupus Ladies of London paid them no heed. Their requests were made only after they struck. To date, neither those who paid nor those who refused were harmed again. But the fear was there, and so was the increasing mayhem in the medical community.

Finally, there was possible closure to these attacks. One week following the latest deaths, letters were sent to newspapers throughout the United States. Pictures of dead bodies were attached, so the papers knew the correspondence was genuine.

> We shall no longer wait. We want action now. All hospitals and medical schools will send one million dollars to the numbered account, below. We no longer wait for governments to place one-tenth of their budgets into medical research. We want the money now. We shall do it ourselves. If you do not follow our instructions, no operating room is safe, no patient secure, and no doctor or hospital administrator can count on going home alive. Send the money now and help the sick, or become one of them

The letter was signed with Stickman X.

* * *

There are over one hundred medical schools in the United States. Full cooperation would yield one hundred million dollars. Even a small response meant big money. The price was cheap for large institutions, and the consequences grave. Attorneys could sue hospitals and medical schools for not providing safety for patients and non-patients. Revenues plummeted and health care costs increased, not only as a result of the cleanup after the attacks but also because of additional security measures.

Unlike banks and jewelry stores, hospitals, medical schools, and physicians' offices provide minimal security, and access is not difficult. They all recognized they had a problem, a real problem. For medical schools and the hospitals, one million dollars was a drop in the bucket, given that most (especially the hospitals) had reserves in the hundreds of millions. Most members of boards governing these facilities, or the CEOs or presidents directing them, did not want bad publicity concerning lack of security, let alone publicity keeping patients away.

As for the account to where the money was deposited, which was in an overseas bank in Switzerland, medical schools and hospitals notoriously, especially when one included members of their respective boards, made frequent large deposits and withdrawals in several Swiss accounts, so the pattern of deposit was not new, at least not at this early stage of extortion.

* * *

Jennifer Pettigrew could not believe how easy this was. The money did not come in as a trickle. It came in as a downpour. The fact that Gantemirov checked his account balance frequently through his computer and honestly told Jennifer how financially successful were her group's endeavors reinforced her secure feelings about the Chechen.

* * *

Chapter Thirty-one

GHOST FROM THE DEAD

After several weeks of intense panic in the medical community, affecting patients, medical staff, and administrators, the attacks in the United States finally ended. A few poorly coordinated attacks persisted elsewhere, in Europe and Asia, but the majority, which had been in the United States, came to a halt.

* * *

In London, Jennifer met with Jokhar Gantemirov.

* * *

The police had no idea who was responsible for the killings and destruction. The United States government enlisted the services of the FBI, Homeland Security, and, most important, the Financial Action Branch of the CIA to trace the money that had been wired.

* * *

The CIA no longer has difficulty tracking money processed through mainstream financial institutions. Most of their attention focuses on unregulated systems, such as *hawalas*, a popular method for transferring money in the Persian Gulf and much of South Asia, which leaves no paper trail. *Hawalas* are the most commonly used method today for transferring large sums of money through terrorist organizations.

Someone who wants to transfer money can go to a *hawala* broker, hand over the money in cash, and the broker places a telephone call to the recipient's nearest *hawala* dealer, who then pays the recipient out of his own account. Everything is done on trust. The records are handwritten, but the money never moves through any banking system.

Most of the CIA's efforts to follow money trails pertaining to terrorist activities are directed toward *hawala* dealers. The CIA was poorly equipped to work on short notice on something similar to Gantemirov's arrangement with Jennifer Pettigrew. The entire period of attacks was over in several weeks. Governments are unable to respond to a new problem that rapidly.

* * *

After holding each other for the night, Jennifer discussed with Gantemirov her activities. "It's sort of addicting, the rush, the excitement, and the fact that it's all for a good cause. And you know, you would think killing someone would bother me. It didn't bother me at all. The fact these people were in doctors' offices even gave me sort of a rush."

“It is exciting. And it shouldn’t bother you. Everyone dies. It happens to us all.”

“That’s the way I look at it. Besides, we’re helping people.”

“Did you have any problems?”

“No. It wasn’t even difficult. All I did was make the call, give the number, and tell them to wire the money. You called me on my cell phone and told me when money came in. All we talked about were numbers, so I hope no authorities understood our conversation, in case they listened in.”

“Maybe they did, maybe not. But be careful, my love. Interpol and governments across the world will try to trace the money. It may take them a while, but they won’t give up. As I told you, I have it. All you have to do is come in with me and we can take it out. Or if you want, we can wire it to any charity you choose.”

“I don’t want it. I want to send it to charities. Besides, who would care if we transfer one million dollars to the United Way, Easter Seals, the March of Dimes, Queens Square Hospital, Newcastle Upon Tyne, the Salpetriere in Paris, or other charitable institutions? It doesn’t look suspicious, does it? And even if it does, I can’t imagine the authorities prosecuting us for such a good cause.”

“Don’t think that. Prosecutors make a living out of prosecuting, and they aren’t committed to helping anyone except themselves.”

“Well, tell them to get ready because we haven’t even begun. Now,” with a mischievous look in her eye, “let me begin my own cause, on you." Jennifer reached behind her neck, thrusting out her chest, her beautiful white Egyptian cotton shirt sinking to the floor.

* * *

Major Cervantes anxiously awaited Dick Swept. "This whole thing is not simple. We have a bunch of crazies out there, blowing up medical schools, hospitals, national monuments, killing people in Aspen, and who knows what else they're responsible for? This is a movement, a blasted movement. And I think Gantemirov is behind it."

Swept listened attentively. The fact that Gantemirov appeared at the International Speech Forum meeting was suspicious for something, but Swept was not certain what. Also, was Allendorf's death linked to the terrorist movement? Was his own attack linked to such a movement?

"Richard, you're more familiar with medical schools and hospitals than probably anyone here at the agency. We need your help in figuring out what the hell is going on. Any ideas?"

"I tried to see Jennifer Pettigrew in London, but she was gone. She disappeared before the attacks began. I didn't pay it much attention until recently. I checked the airline registry and passport control. Ms. Pettigrew flew to the United States a few days before the attacks and left a few days after. I have plans to fly to London, tonight."

"Good. See her and report to me."

Swept was leaving Major Cervantes's office. He smiled cordially at Lenora, the new secretary, who never took her eyes off the handsome neurologist as he exited. She made a mental note to try to run into Swept in the cafeteria and invite him to her place for a drink.

* * *

Dick Swept flew British Airways to England, arrived at Gatwick, twenty-seven miles south of London, took the Gatwick Express to Victoria Station, and then hailed a taxi to Claridge's Hotel. Only slightly fatigued, he enjoyed tea in the foyer lounge, confirmed his dinner reservation at Gordon Ramsay's restaurant, and decided to enjoy a brief nap before setting out to find Jennifer.

Jennifer lived near Knightsbridge, which is east of Belgravia and north of Chelsea, and boasts elite residential streets and ultra-shopping venues. Swept originally planned to go to her apartment, ring the doorbell, and take it from there. Who knew? Perhaps his charm would sway her into telling the truth, whatever that truth might be. If she weren't there, then he would call MI6 and Interpol and break down the door.

It seemed Jennifer Pettigrew was involved in the attacks in the United States, but why? And how did Gantemirov fit into this?

At the last moment, Swept decided not to drive out to see Jennifer. Instead, he telephoned. Swept always felt confident winging things this way—put a lot of variables out there and then play things by ear.

Swept reached Jennifer on his first call. He said he happened to be in town and invited her to join him for dinner at Gordon Ramsay's that evening. Few women would turn down such a delicious offer at this famous restaurant, and Jennifer was no exception.

Swept was happy to take a taxi to Jennifer's and escort her to Ramsay's, but she insisted on meeting him at his hotel, professing it was foolish for Swept to take a cab, pick her up, and then return to Claridge's. They met that evening in the hotel lobby and departed to the restaurant.

Jennifer was stunning. She seemed so alive, so filled with energy. Her tight lace dress hugged every inch of her beautiful figure, and her hair flowed freely down her shoulders. True, her face was badly scarred, but Swept always appreciated the more alluring part of a woman: her inner warmth and kindness, her passion, and her knowledge. Swept truly appreciated Jennifer as a very sexy woman.

"Well," announced Jennifer, her British accent arousing the American neurologist. "You are looking good. Just happen to be in town, huh?"

"I never miss a chance to go to London. I needed to meet with some investigators at the National Hospital about my research in Alzheimer's disease. I thought I'd take a chance and call you. It came up suddenly, so I apologize for the short notice. I'm glad you could make it."

"I changed my plans to see you."

"Really? I hope you're not missing something too exciting."

"We'll see if it's worth it." Jennifer Pettigrew took Swept's arm and walked him into the restaurant. "Now, Dr. Swept, let us have some good food. And you can tell me about your life."

"My life isn't that exciting. I'm a physician-scientist, trying to figure out Alzheimer's disease."

"Really? And you're not here to try to figure me out?"

"It depends," chided Swept.

"On what?"

"On how much there is to figure out."

The captain at Gordon Ramsay's helped the couple arrange themselves at the table. Over a 1961 Puillac Bordeaux, followed by an excellent 1996 Chassagne Montrachet, Jennifer enjoyed her Dover Sole while Swept dined on steak with béarnaise sauce.

"Do you often order a red wine, especially one from a wonderful vintage year, followed by a white?" Jennifer inquired.

"No, but I do if one of us has meat, the other fish. If you must know," Swept said, reaching out to fondle her charm bracelet, "you can have whatever you want."

"I'll keep that in mind," Jennifer coyly responded. "You might regret it later."

Swept snickered, but a tingle ran through his veins.

"So, Dr. Swept—," as Jennifer slowly ate her fish, talking between bites, "why did you call me? Love at first sight?"

"Possibly, but I'm not impetuous. I called because I happened to be in town, as I said, and I also want some information. Maybe you can help."

"How is that?"

"Well, first things first. You said you knew Jokhar Gantemirov. I find that strange, since he only recently escaped from jail, and I presume the people he hangs out with are probably not nice people. Yet you seem okay." Swept had still not discussed with Jennifer the attempt on his own life.

"Go on," responded Jennifer, placing her fork down and chewing her fish with a near-sexual overtone.

"Then, we have these terrorist attacks in the United States, in medical schools and hospitals. I'm a researcher, but my research laboratory is with the government, the CIA, if you must know. The medical people there asked me about the attacks."

"So, you thought you'd ask me?" Jennifer's eyes fixated on Dick Swept. Swept continued.

"The agency told me you left England shortly before the rash of attacks and returned soon after. Since I had to return here for my research, I decided to talk to you and see what's up. So, what's up?"

"You think I'm involved with the attacks we read about? You think I'm a terrorist?" Swept could not tell whether Jennifer's tone was indignant or self-righteous.

"I don't know. Are you?"

Picking up her napkin, tapping her mouth, Jennifer replied, "First, I am not a terrorist. I have a disease, lupus, and rely upon doctors and medical facilities. Second, let us have some crème brûlée for dessert and then go to your room for a drink, where you can ask me whatever you want. How's that for an answer?"

"I don't know. We'll need to see."

"Then, 'see' you will."

Swept ordered crème brûlée and Italian espresso coffee. Jennifer excused herself, implying she needed to go the bathroom. Swept wondered whether she had other motivation but believed he had to rely on his instincts.

Ten minutes later, Jennifer reappeared at the table, shortly before the dessert arrived. Swept was delighted to enjoy a properly made delicacy, recognizing that too many restaurants offer an alleged crème brûlée that is merely custard instead of being what is supposed to be—custard that has been spooned into individual serving pots, a good layer of granulated sugar sprinkled on top, and the pots placed under a hot broiler until the sugar melts and darkens into a caramel. The pots are then chilled, the caramel sets hard, and the consumer of this wonderful treat then shatters the caramel with a spoon, relishing the custard beneath.

Following the dessert and excellent espresso, the couple decided to forego dessert wine and go upstairs to Swept's room.

Soon, the two people, a neurologist with the CIA and a lupus-stricken terrorist working with a Chechen underground criminal, lay naked in bed. Swept's passion was genuine and firm, while Jennifer proved herself confident, sensitive, and carefree.

"So, Dr. Swept. Now that you have made love to me, do you still think I'm a terrorist? Do you make love to terrorists? Is that your job at the CIA? Or do they teach you that in medical school? Or possibly, are you just wrong?"

Swept placed his right hand gently under Jennifer's chin. "Are you?"

"No."

"Why were you in the States?"

"I went to see my dermatologist. She's in New York, if you must know. She placed me on a new steroid cream and then sent me to Boston, to see another doctor. I heard about the attacks in the hospitals and medical schools and decided it was risky to stay in America, since I was visiting some of them, for my own medical condition—remember, my lupus. I decided to come home, but before I did, I toured a few museums. Does that meet with your approval?"

Swept studied Jennifer. In the dark, it was difficult to see her lesions. The outline of her torso was splendid. Swept could not feel an ounce of fat, except for a small area on her hips and mons pubis. The woman was truly something.

Before Swept could answer, there was a knock at the door. "Who's there?" inquired Swept.

"A surprise for you," said Jennifer. "I took the liberty of ordering a bottle of champagne when I went to the bathroom. They're late." Without waiting for Swept to respond, Jennifer wrapped a sheet around her and began to walk toward the door.

"Wait," said Swept, putting on his robe. "What kind of champagne did you order?"

"I didn't tell them what kind. Just 'the best.'"

Swept knew something was amiss. If a woman was concerned about mixing red and white wine and wanted champagne sent to the room, why would she not select the vintage and vineyard? Why would she say only "the best"?

Swept approached the door, stepping in front of Jennifer. He wondered whether he should have grabbed his gun, just as he turned the knob, but was ready to strike with his fist. After opening the door, he just stared.

Aleksander Kostokov stood there, but Swept knew Aleksander Kostokov was dead. Swept killed him over eighteen months ago.

"Surprised, Dr. Swept? I just thought I would give you a little 'hello' from the dead. Now," motioning with his gun, the ghost of Kostokov instructed Swept to sit in the chair, "sit over there."

Swept stared at what he knew could not be Aleksander Kostokov. "Don't worry," said the man. "I am not Aleksander Kostokov, and I won't do to you what you did to him."

"Who are you?"

"None of your business. Although, maybe it is." At that moment, Jennifer struck Dick Swept on the head with a fax machine still connected to long wires. Swept dropped to the floor. Jennifer's sheet fell to the ground, leaving her stark naked. She smirked over Swept's body and proudly looked at Stoli, seeming to tempt him. Stoli knew better, since Gantemirov would kill him.

Jennifer dressed and left the room with Stoli.

* * *

Chapter Thirty-two

MONEY IN THE BANK

Major Cervantes spoke to Swept on a secure line. "Let me get this straight. You made contact with Pettigrew, had dinner with her, met a Kostokov look-alike, and then someone smashed your head. And now, you have no idea where either one is?"

"That's about it."

"How could this happen?"

Swept was silent. He never liked people who alibi but was not convinced it was his fault. "I'll take care of it," Swept explained.

"See that you do. Find Gantemirov and figure out what he's doing."

"Don't you think I need to find Pettigrew too?"

"I don't care about her. Gantemirov is the key."

"What do I do when I find him?"

"I'm not sure. Somehow, he's tied into these terrorist acts. Figure out how. Try not to get smashed on the head again. What were you doing when all this happened?"

"You don't want to know."

"I can guess. Keep your pants on and find Gantemirov."

Before Swept could say goodbye, Cervantes hung up the phone. Nursing his still throbbing head, Swept decided to relax with a Fontpinot Brandy in Ramsey's bar, as well as a Cuban Cohiba cigar.

While Swept enjoyed the fine brandy and the taste and draw of a good cigar, he thought about his carelessness with Jennifer. If he was going to work undercover for the CIA and be as excellent in CIA operations as he was in his scientific endeavors, he had to be more careful. Swept realized he had been careless. He should never be without his gun. He was aware as he approached the door that the way Jennifer ordered the champagne made little sense. He had been careless in France, careless in London, and recognized he might not get another chance. Swept was thankful that his injury was slight and there was no permanent damage.

Swept realized Jennifer and the Kostokov look-alike could have killed him had they wanted. For some reason, they did not. Perhaps, Jennifer liked him and did not want him harmed. The moment Swept thought about that possibility, he recognized he was being self-serving and, again, careless. No, they did not kill him because they saw no benefit in so doing or had been told by someone not to kill him.

Gantemirov! The answer had to lie with Jokhar Gantemirov. Swept had to find the Chechen.

* * *

Jokhar Gantemirov sat in the red leather chair, viewing London's Kensington Gardens through a lead-glass window. He turned to Stoli. "Not bad. You have your brother's character. You're a good man."

Stoli seemed unimpressed, surprisingly so, given his earlier need for approval and definition from the Chechen. "What do we do now?"

"Leave that to me. Tell Jennifer she can come in. Wait for further instructions on this phone," handing Stoli a cell phone Gantemirov recently purchased using fake identification and address. Stoli left the room, went outside to the street, and walked through the gardens.

A few minutes later, Jennifer Pettigrew was in the room. She seemed aloof, somewhat cold, but incredibly confident. Gantemirov encircled his arms around her and kissed her.

Jennifer spoke first. "Are you happy with the way things turned out with Dick Swept?"

"Very, my love."

Jennifer displayed little emotion. "How are things going with the payments?"

"We have over twenty-five million dollars in the account. You can start distributing it to charities. It would go in anonymously, but who cares?"

Gantemirov continued, "Jennifer, listen to me. Why don't you wait until you have two or three hundred million dollars? That way, even if we're caught, the authorities will see that so much money went to charities that most people may not be that upset. You brought up that idea before. Maybe you're right. It could help you—and me—if we are ever tried in court."

"I don't know. Right now, we have about twenty-five million dollars, but I think we do need more."

"Well, twenty-five million, whether you want to give it to charities or not, is what we have. Here, let me show you." Gantemirov displayed for Jennifer sheets with numbers, highlighting the deposits and balance. Jennifer studied the form, pleased that her group had raised this revenue.

"Jokhar, I told you before. You would think killing people should bother me. It doesn't. You would think hitting Dick Swept on the head would bother me. It didn't. Actually, it excites me and even makes me hungry." Jennifer's mood began to change, and she began to remove her clothes, unhooking her brassiere.

Gantemirov had not expected this. He expected Jennifer to be needy, frail, clinging to him. It was in this domain he thought he could control her. "Be careful," he said. "You might become dangerous."

"I am dangerous, sweetheart." Grabbing the Chechen's hand, she placed it on her breast. "Now, tell me. When are we going to get married?"

"Tell me!" Gantemirov smiled. "When are we going to have the two hundred million dollars?"

"Are you marrying me for my money? Remember, I don't plan to keep it. Rest assured, it's not going to any Chechen freedom fighter relief fund."

"I never thought it would," and Gantemirov removed his trousers.

*   *   *

Chapter Thirty-three

DEATH IN A TUB

Major Cervantes was a very unhappy man. When he had married a beautiful, intelligent woman from a locally prominent family, he expected great things. Patricia Chaucer came from a well-respected Virginia family, her father was a successful corporate attorney, and Patricia was Phi Beta Kappa, Homecoming Queen in high school and college, and president of every organization to which she belonged. Patricia provided Major with two beautiful children, May and Paul, was a great cook, and was extremely attractive.

Patricia drove Major crazy. His wife had no interest in hearing about his tortured days, how he had to interact and survive the bureaucratic government nincompoops, how he had been repeatedly passed over for promotion, all because he failed to suck up to the right people.

This lack of interest was made worse by his wife's constant complaining about everything, ranging from his shirts and ties to the books he read, the newspaper articles he enjoyed, and his friends. Cervantes hated low-cut loafers, but Patricia kept buying them for him, in brown, black, cordovan, and light tan. Cervantes preferred oxford shirts with button-down collars, but Patricia insisted on Egyptian cotton without the button downs. Major liked Brooks Brothers ties. Patricia bought him Hermès.

Patricia Chaucer had no interest in hearing her husband's thoughts about Op-Ed pieces in the newspaper. She refused to attend office parties, a necessity for advancement in a government career or in most careers. To make matters worse, Patricia also refused to attend religious services with her husband or with their children. Major Cervantes had married the perfect woman on the outside, given her charm, beauty, and intelligence, but was imprisoned with a cold, uncaring woman on the inside, whose interactions were emotionless.

The truth of the matter was that Patricia Chaucer did love her husband, but love without kindness means nothing. Patricia Chaucer could not have cared less about her behavior or lack of understanding and had no intention of changing anything.

Major Cervantes was so miserable that he sought emotional sustenance elsewhere. And as so often happens, Cervantes found it in another lover.

Major Cervantes's extramarital affair had not been orchestrated. It just happened. It happened because Cervantes, desperately alone and lacking meaningful companionship in his house, often found himself talking to

Carol Bernsen, an administrator down the hall. Tall, dark-skinned, slightly heavy but with a lusty full-bodied figure, the two CIA employees often joked over lunch.

Carol was divorced, without children, and always pleasant. Cervantes was married, had children, and was always angry. In short time, the two found themselves in each other's arms. Carol made Cervantes happy. When he was with Carol Bernson, Cervantes felt loved, and he liked that feeling very much.

No one in the agency knew about this illicit affair. No one suspected this interaction, except for Lenora, Cervantes's secretary. It seemed pretty obvious to Lenora that something was going on between the two, considering they were often together and, when they were, laughed considerably. It did not bother or offend Lenora. Her dream lover was someone else—Dick Swept.

* * *

Swept, who was still at Claridge's Hotel in London, telephoned Jennifer, but no one answered. The agency secured assistance from the London police to enter her apartment. Jennifer and all her personal items were gone. Swept asked the agency to check airports and train stations. They determined that several weeks ago, Jennifer had taken train rides to the outskirts of London, but she was currently not to be found.

Then, it hit him. Jennifer, given her feelings about lupus, was probably a member of one or more local lupus self-help groups. Swept needed to ascertain whether any people in these groups had been in the United States the same time as Jennifer. If so, perhaps they were involved in the terrorist attacks in the US. If he could find them, perhaps he could find Jennifer.

It proved simpler than Swept imagined. The London Self-Help Group for Women Afflicted with Lupus had eighty-four members. Six had left London the same time as Jennifer. Further, the clincher, they returned to London when Jennifer returned. And hard as it was to believe, they were on the same flight.

Swept contacted the agency, which, in turn, contacted MI6. This well-known branch of British intelligence planned to question all the women. Unfortunately, the women had all moved. They were gone.

* * *

Over the next several weeks, acts of terror against national monuments increased dramatically throughout Europe. A bomb in a briefcase was placed adjacent to the obelisk in the Place de la Concorde, the garden outside the Notre Dame Cathedral, and in Monet's home in Giverny. The Coliseum in Rome, the Trevi Fountain, a tourist boat in Venice, the mermaid in Copenhagen, as well as a golf course in Spain's Costa del Sol, all were vandalized. Tourists felt unsafe, governments complained, and always, there was the stickman with an *X* for a mouth and a snake in each hand. Although this was minimal compared to the damage perpetrated in American medical schools and hospitals, the actions signified one thing: Stickman X was still an active, expanding terrorist movement.

Throughout Europe, as well as Australia, Japan, even Lebanon, acts of terror occurred against hospitals and medical schools. It was simple: people went into clinics where patients were infirm, such as Alzheimer's disease clinics, multiple sclerosis clinics, and clinics for people with psychiatric disorders. In some situations, intruders marched into examination rooms and fired wildly. In other scenarios, they carried diesel fuel into the waiting rooms, spilled the contents, and set the area ablaze, panicking patients and personnel and causing mayhem.

Medical clinics throughout the world became increasingly concerned. Usually, the attacks were carried out by a small group of women. However, in some attacks, such as in Japan and Lebanon, a single person, a man, entered the clinic, surreptitiously poured twenty gallons of diesel fuel onto the floor while paying his bill, only to complain about the smell, leave, and then throw a lighted newspaper, creating a large fire. Dozens of people were injured.

Victimized institutions soon included Saint George's Hospital in Beirut, the Institute of Neurology in Belgrade, the Hospital De La Salpetriere in Paris, the University of Adelaide in South Australia, the London School of Hygiene and Tropical Medicine, the Medical School at the University of Essen, the Max Planck Institute of Psychiatry in Munich, and Osaka University.

The attacks then recurred in the United States. Incidents at Rush-Presbyterian-St. Luke's Hospital, in Chicago; the Beth Israel Deaconess Medical Center in Boston; the University of Colorado Medical Center; and M.D. Anderson Hospital in Houston, Texas—all were attacked.

In each of the attacks, multiple flyers of Stickman X littered the area, with demands for money for medical research. In each case, a caller had notified the institution, asking for the main administrative office, providing a code word and announcing the forthcoming attack. Five minutes following the attack, they called the same institution, told the operator the code word, and instructed them to tell the administrators to send one million dollars to a particularly numbered account in Zurich.

In most cases, the administrators received the message. Sometimes, whether due to being unavailable or simply to incompetence, they did not. Usually, the money came in. The new policy was that if the money was not supplied, for whatever reason, more attacks usually followed. The United States was becoming a quagmire of terror within the medical establishment.

* * *

Gantemirov, still in his hotel room overlooking Kensington Gardens, turned to Jennifer. Gantemirov was impressed. Jennifer had amassed a large sum of money, almost two hundred million dollars. What amazed Jennifer was not only that she and the Lupus Ladies had accumulated this large sum but also that some actions taken against hospitals and medical institutions were not orchestrated by her group.

Many of the attacks were copycat crimes. She did not know whether they had demanded money or where it was sent. Regardless, the events proved to the woman personally afflicted with lupus that her cause was just and her actions correct.

"Sort of like al-Qaeda, don't you think?" said Gantemirov.

Jennifer was becoming harder and tougher. "We have enough money to begin distributing it. I'm going to send money to the International AIDS Foundation, the March of Dimes, and the International Lupus Society of the World."

"I think you should wait."

"It's not up to you. It's up to me."

"I guess so. Do your lady friends want to support the same organizations?"

"I think so. We're going to meet tonight. We can decide then."

Jennifer had been staying at the hotel with Gantemirov, not leaving the room except at night. "Can we meet here?"

"Sure. Bring them all."

Later that night, the women were in the Abbey Court Hotel. Gantemirov liked this elegant small hotel, situated in a gracious white Victorian Mansion, located on a quiet street off Notting Hill Gate. Abbey Court is a beautiful place to relax. The deep red wallpapers, Murano glass, gilt-framed mirrors, framed prints, the gray Italian marble baths, and the superb twenty-four-hour room service pampered Gantemirov to his liking.

Gantemirov excused himself and went into the bedroom when the six women entered the suite. They discussed where to send their money, marveling at the ease with which their just cause was rocking the world. In the midst of their discussion about where to direct their financial support, someone knocked at the door.

It was Stoli. Jennifer smiled coyly at the Romanian, who joined Gantemirov in the bedroom, leaving the ladies to discuss privately their plans. When the women were finished, Jennifer announced to Gantemirov and Stoli that they had agreed to make donations to Queen Square Hospital in London, the Stop Lupus Now organization in America, Easter Seals, and one of the international AIDS organizations. The visitors then exited, while Jennifer remained in the suite.

Stoli accompanied the ladies down the stairs and, while in the elevator, announced, "Jennifer has a surprise for everyone. Follow me to her van. There is a special gift for each of you."

Having seen Stoli upstairs in the room with Jennifer and not knowing whether Jennifer recently bought a new vehicle or not, the group walked outside. Stoli made light conversation. Then, he pointed to the Toyota van several blocks down the road.

As the group approached the Toyota, laughing and feeling proud of themselves, the doors of the van suddenly slid open. Two masked men appeared and fired Uzi submachine guns, spraying the women with Teflon-coated bullets, killing all of them. The van drove away while Stoli remained behind, screaming for help.

In the commotion that followed, Stoli slipped away, leaving behind the dead women and a dead old man in a wheelchair, who happened to be nearby.

Stoli called the Abbey Court Hotel and requested Mr. Gantemirov's room.

Jennifer, sitting with Gantemirov in the sitting room, answered.

"I need to speak to Jokhar."

Jennifer put Gantemirov on the line. "It went great."

"Good," replied Gantemirov, and poured a glass of champagne for himself and his lover.

"What was that about?" inquired Jennifer.

"Our cars are ready, we have new personnel, and all is well." Gantemirov silently toasted Jennifer and the two drank heavily, Jennifer becoming sleepy and more docile as they imbibed.

Jokhar Gantemirov, who had always been able to hold his liquor, took the staggering woman to the bedroom, helped her remove her clothes, and, with gentleness and kindness in his voice and gestures, suggested they fill the tub with bubble bath.

The whirlpool baths in Abbey Court are wonderful. The soothing water decreases muscle spasms and stimulates blood flow. Gantemirov assisted the smiling Jennifer Pettigrew into the tub, feigned checking the water temperature with his immersed right hand, and then, without much difficulty, held her face under the water, smiling as he studied her bulging eyes, until the woman stopped struggling.

Holding Jennifer's glass of champagne with tissue paper, the Chechen placed the drink on the side of the tub. He put the champagne bottle in the water, noting that it floated with some champagne still inside, exhibiting a seemingly joyous bounce on the water that contained the dead woman. Gantemirov wiped clean his glass, gathered his few belongings, and went downstairs, outside, to meet Stoli.

Stoli drove Gantemirov to a local copying establishment, where the Chechen made several copies of correspondence. He sent these to various hospitals and medical schools, providing the account number to which monies were to be sent. Gantemirov demanded five million dollars from each of these organizations. They had forty-eight hours to send the money. After that, problems he would cause would make patients forever afraid to go there and damage the institution's reputation for safety, leading to enormous financial losses due to the death and destruction he would cause. Stickman X was on the bottom of each letter.

* * *

After the authorities learned that Jennifer was dead, it took little time for the information to reach Dick Swept. He also quickly learned about the women who had been gunned down. All were members of the lupus self-help group that Swept had investigated. All had traveled to the United States with Jennifer, and all returned with her. Swept found it ironic that they all died within the same hour.

* * *

Within several days, explosions rocked Europe, the United States, Lebanon, Japan, and Australia. Medical schools and hospitals could not protect themselves. It was too simple for someone to enter an elevator, pour fuel on the elevator floor, and then light it on the way out. Bombs in motor vehicles exploded in hospital parking lots, disconnected water pipes in bathrooms flooded halls and stairwells, and fuse boxes serving Intensive Care Units were destroyed. No patient or medical facility was safe.

More money rolled in. Jokhar Gantemirov soon had two hundred fifty million dollars in his Zurich account and was empowered to withdraw it at his leisure.

* * *

Chapter Thirty-four

DEATH OF A CLAN

For the past several days, possibly weeks, Jeremiah MacGregor was neither happy nor sad. He was dumbfounded. People were committing acts of terrorism across the globe, all in the name of Stickman X, his Stickman X. He had no idea who they were, but he knew one thing: Much of the attention was not focused on stuttering, and if money was coming in, as far as he knew, none of it was helping people who stuttered. And he realized, none of it was coming to him.

MacGregor was not against damaging property or killing people, as long as he believed in the cause. Now, here he was, having designed the "Figure of Terror," as so many newspapers described Stickman X, writing the manifestos, and yet had no input where the money from the victims was going and certainly no money for his beloved cause. He had not heretofore wanted money for himself but, recognizing the huge sums involved, saw no reason why he should not be rewarded for an idea that was purely his.

Jeremiah correctly reasoned that the press knew about some of the attacks, but not about others. Calling from different phones throughout Scotland, trying to stay on the line less than thirty seconds but willing to say on longer if it felt right, he called the top twenty hospitals listed in an article in *Newsweek* about excellent medical institutions. Jeremiah had rehearsed his speech several times, which helped decrease some of his dysfluencies.

Each time, he requested the administration offices. Each time, after reaching someone in a senior position, he produced the same speech: "You have not made the deposit. We have not received the money. You will pay for this."

Some of the administrators hung up. Others became angry, and Jeremiah ended the call. However, during one of the conversations, the respondent on the other end of the call became nervous.

"Look. We made the deposit, just like you said, to account 6578234213."

That was the luck Jeremiah needed. Jeremiah wrote down the account number. While doing so, he continued his plan. "Th-That's the wrong number. There's no '6'," and Jeremiah closed the receiver, leaving a worried and perplexed administrator to ponder his alleged mistake.

Following relinquishing the account number, a ruse on which Jeremiah prided himself, he sent a check for one pound British sterling for deposit in that particular account at over one hundred forty-three Swiss banks. One hundred forty-two checks were returned, except the one he sent to Zurich International Bank of Switzerland.

Subsequently, Jeremiah sent a check for one pound British sterling every day to that account at the Zurich

International Bank of Switzerland. Jeremiah's name, address, and telephone number were on his checks. He knew that in a short time, the owner of the account would see the checks and contact him.

Within two weeks, Stoli was at Jeremiah's home.

Jeremiah answered the knocking at his door. One look at Stoli and his two companions told Jeremiah he had found the correct account number and bank.

Stoli spoke first, "Are you the jerk sending the checks?"

"I-I-I am he," Jeremiah said, cursing his stutter. Stoli did not laugh at the dysfluency. "You have thirty seconds to explain who you are and what you're doing."

"S-Simple. I-I-I invented the Stickman, and we need money."

"Who is 'we'?" inquired Stoli menacingly.

Jeremiah proudly stood his ground. "St-St-Stutterers, and me too. We want our share. I started this."

"You're probably right," smiled Stoli. "People like you are hard to find."

Stoli reached out his right hand, seemingly offering a handshake, but, instead, grabbed MacGregor's right arm and pulled it to Stoli's right side as Stoli's left arm thundered across Jeremiah's chest. Simultaneously, Stoli pivoted clockwise on his right foot, sweeping his left leg under MacGregor's legs, causing the Scotsman to fall to the ground. As Jeremiah gasped, trying to talk, Stoli fell upon Jeremiah, his right knee cracking the Scotsman's chest, breaking his sternum. As Jeremiah continued to gasp, stuttering and stumbling as he spoke, Stoli grabbed the man's neck with his right hand and squeezed away life, while his two companions stood motionless, viewing the performance of their trained companion with approval.

Stoli then drew Stickman X with lipstick on the dead man's forehead.

"Let him stutter or stumble on that," Stoli said as he walked away with his two companions.

* * *

Later, Stoli telephoned Ganetemirov. The Chechen knew most hospitals and medical schools would call their local police regarding the terrorist threats and activities. He also realized Interpol and Swiss authorities were probably watching his numbered account. If so, they might already know about Jeremiah's deposit to the Zurich International Bank of Switzerland, although Swiss banks still were sticklers regarding confidentiality of accounts unless criminal activity was definitely established. The fact that Stoli had killed Jeremiah without police intervening suggested the authorities did not know about Jeremiah. Had they known, they might have been watching Jeremiah's activities and Stoli would have been caught, a danger Gantemirov had not shared with his Romanian-raised colleague.

Without waiting for the police to ponder Jeremiah's death, which sooner or later would lead to the account number at the Zurich International Bank, Gantemirov flew from London to Zurich that day and entered the bank. Then, using his fake passport and real code, WOCSOM, Moscow in reverse, he employed his plan to withdraw two hundred fifty million dollars, all in Swiss francs.

* * *

Major Cervantes possessed considerable information about the hospital and medical-school bombings. Due to recent legislation endorsed by the Department of Homeland Security, the FBI, CIA, and multiple local law-enforcement offices were now permitted to share information. Cervantes learned to what account the recent ransom monies had been sent. The agency placed agents near the Zurich International Bank of Switzerland, waiting for something to happen.

Something did. Today, there was a series of explosions two blocks from the bank, necessitating multiple fire trucks and police vehicles, which descended on the area, trying to save lives and property. Passersby were killed, several human beings were literally burned alive, and multiple buildings were ablaze. During this melee, Gantemirov and his coterie of thugs entered the bank and procured, without difficulty, their ill-gotten fortune.

* * *

The withdrawal was accomplished without rancor on the part of the Swiss. The bankers, courteous and efficient, escorted Gantemirov through more elevators and sliding doors he had gone through in his life.

In short time, with the help of Stoli and several other men, Gantemirov had in his possession fifteen satchels filled with the equivalent of two hundred fifty million U.S. dollars. Gantemirov thanked his companions for their adjacent timed explosions, everyone being unperturbed by the loss of innocent life. Now, they were off to Chechnya, where they would purchase the weapons of mass destruction.

* * *

The CIA, struggling to overcome inadequacies forced upon them during past government administrations, botched things again.

Too late, the agency understood that Jeremiah had flown to and from the United States during the initial promulgation of Stickman X, attended the International Speech Forum meeting near Paris, and that Jennifer Pettigrew also attended this meeting. This information, coupled with Swept's data about Jennifer Pettigrew and Gantemirov, connected some of the dots. The dots were further connected when the agency realized that MacGregor had wired money to the account that was the recipient of the terrorists' demands.

Now, the authorities had the necessary information to force the Swiss to release the name of the holder of the account, which turned out to be bogus and led nowhere. Further, there was another problem: The money was gone.

Cervantes firmly believed, as did Dick Swept, that no good was going to come about from this two hundred fifty million dollars. The question was, what did Jokhar Gantemirov plan to do?

* * *

Jokhar Gantemirov was a careful man. He planned his days with care and cogitated tactics for all his strategies. However, he was now infuriated at himself, and he had no one else to blame. Gantemirov realized, possibly too late, that he had allowed the microchip for the GPS system to remain within Jennifer Pettigrew.

The man hoped the coroner's investigation would not discover the chip. Most medical examiners are overworked and usually not as thorough as the public suspects. The chip was not radiopaque, so it would not reveal itself if the coroner's office X-rayed the dead woman's body. However, a thorough autopsy would reveal the GPS chip.

Although Gantemirov hoped the authorities would believe Jennifer was inebriated and fell asleep in the bath, they would surely check to see whether she had been sexually violated, and that investigation required a vaginal examination. That examination would reveal the microchip.

Always having a backup plan, Gantemirov reasoned that, were he caught, he could contend Jennifer drowned because she consumed too much alcohol before going into the tub. He would not be able to deny that they were lovers—too many witnesses, ranging from restaurant employees to people who knew Jennifer, who would confirm that they were romantically involved. Besides, he probably had some of his DNA within her. Gantemirov's main concern was that if the authorities discovered the microchip, they could retroactively trace Jennifer's whereabouts and possibly link her and him to the terrorist attacks. If foul play was suspected, and it related to him, Swiss authorities would cooperate fully with Interpol and the CIA, let alone the FSB and other law-enforcement agencies.

What all this meant to the veteran killer was that he had to act fast. Jokhar Gantemirov wanted the weapons of mass destruction, and he wanted them now. The Chechen purchased a new cellular phone, providing false identification, and made his call.

* * *

Chapter Thirty-five

"TO LIVE OUTSIDE THE LAW YOU MUST BE HONEST"

"Akhmad, this is Jokhar."

"Jokhar, you old son of a pig-headed farmer. How's your back?"

"My back? Nothing's wrong with my back."

"Well then, your front."

"My front is fine too. Are you satisfied I am who I say and all is well?"

"Not really, but it is good enough, at least for now. I hope all is well with you. I periodically read about you. If you have problems, drink vodka. The homemade brew is still best."

“I have a problem, and I don’t need more vodka. I need your help.”

“That is what friends are for.”

“You must know I earlier spoke with your brother.”

“Dzhabrail?”

“Your brother’s name is Taus.”

“So it is.”

“Are you satisfied now?”

“I hope so.”

“Did your brother tell you we spoke a short time ago?”

“Perhaps. How can I help you? My vodka and Angelina, an American college girl, are waiting for me. I taught Angelina how to speak Russian, she has confirmed my excellent usage of English, and we love each other. Now, speak what is on your mind.”

“I have the two-fifty for you. I want the package.”

“You have the two-fifty? It is a good price, I am sure you know.”

“I have it. I want the package.”

“Well, presuming I have this package, how do we arrange this?”

“Can the Chemist drive it to me?”

"If he can stay away from his powder," referring to the Chemist's cocaine addiction, an inference Jokhar Gantemirov well understood.

"I don't want him if he's risky."

"All my people are risky."

"You are not. I am not. How do I get it?"

"How do I get the two-fifty?"

"I have a plan. It involves a jerk who appeared out of nowhere two years ago."

"Does he work for me?"

"No. He is an American."

"I have Americans who work for me. I am international."

"He does not work for you."

"Who is he?"

"Leave that to me."

"How do we do this?"

"You will have the two-fifty before the week is over. Someone will deliver half to you, wherever you choose. Then, my people will take the package. After that, you receive the other half, wherever you choose. Do we trust each other?"

Smiling at the other end of the line as he looked at Angelina, a refugee from the money and effulgence of West

Palm Beach, Akhmad gently touched her beautiful face and kissed her lightly on the lips. His conversation and simultaneous sexual overtures reminded him of what he had read about a former United States president. Then he thought about something else. “Have you ever heard of that American singer Bob Dylan?”

“What about him?”

“He once said, ‘To live outside the law, you must be honest.’” Angelina smiled, querying whether the quotation from an American singer-songwriter was mentioned for her sake. “Do you agree with that, my friend?”

“No. I do not. To live outside the law, you must be strong. You are strong, and I respect your interactions with me as well as your strength. You have known me since we were children. I helped pull you from the rock, taught you to fish.”

“And we killed our first rabbit together.”

“It wasn’t a rabbit. It was a soldier. Will you do it?”

“You have my word. I shall wait seven days. After that, other offers, which are few but real—not many know about the package—have to be considered.”

“We’ve been on the phone too long.”

“You’re the one who mentioned the soldier.”

“I was kidding. There are no soldiers.”

“I was kidding—there are no rabbits. My friend, we are all soldiers,” and Akhmad closed his cell phone. Angelina, who approached Akhmad Edilkhanov and who could not have avoided hearing the conversation, seemed tense. "Do you know something else Bob Dylan said?"

Akhmad smiled back, placing his arms around this young American beauty, with blond hair, sparkling blue eyes, firm small breasts, teeth too small for her lips, and replied, "No."

"Sometimes I think this whole world is just a prison yard. Some of us are prisoners, the rest of us are guards." Akhmad smiled again, poured some vodka from a bottle he kept in an ice-filled Styrofoam cooler and felt sad that, after he was done with this distraught Florida girl, he would make her disappear.

In Chechnya, murder was simple. Fighting was everywhere, between rival Chechen groups and between the Russians and all the Chechen groups. There was no law and there was no order. But there were weapons of mass destruction, and Akhmad Edilkhanov had them.

Soon, Akhmad would have 250 million dollars. With that money, he could buy off opponents he could not kill and become the next president of Chechnya.

"Ah," Akhmad thought to himself. "Life is good." Edilkhanov reached out for Angelina, who was more than happy to comply with all of his desires.

* * *

Many individuals think well but slowly. Jokhar Gantemirov had always been able to quickly muster his intellectual acumen. The Chechen could think on his feet extremely quickly. Years of fighting among Chechens, as well as fighting

Russians, had taught him to think well and fast. Within this milieu, Jokhar Gantemirov had a plan.

Gantemirov needed to take the WMD out of Chechnya. That would not be easy. To bring the WMD into Chechnya, before the American-led invasion of Iraq began, was difficult but proved not impossible. Now that the Americans and the whole world wondered whether weapons of mass destruction even existed, it was becoming increasingly important for the president of the United States and his diminishing group of allies to find them. Moving the WMD out of Chechnya would be difficult and dangerous. Certainly, it would not be simple.

Gantemirov reasoned what better way to move them out of Chechnya than to have the U.S. move them! He not only needed the 250 million for his purchase of the WMD, he also needed money to arrange the transportation and for his own purposes as well.

Jokhar Gantemirov decided to obtain assistance from the CIA, specifically from Dick Swept. Surely, he reasoned, Swept wanted to find him. Swept's appetite must have been whetted by seeing Stoli, who appeared identical to Aleksander Kostokov. Also, Swept had to be inquisitive over the deaths of Jennifer Pettigrew and her band of "sisters," as well as want information about the attack on him at the International Speech Forum meeting.

Gantemirov did not care about Swept's motives or his feelings. What he wanted were the weapons of mass destruction and a lot of money.

* * *

Chapter Thirty-six

SWEPT DOES IT HIS WAY

Reaching a particular operative in the CIA is not easy. The Central Intelligence Agency is a complex, large government agency, and its efficiency, at times, is no better than that of the Internal Revenue Service, the Social Security Administration, or the United States Post Office. These organizations are necessary for the day-to-day activities of the government, but they are run by employees who, in general, are waiting out their time to retirement or enjoying their sinecure. A handful of government workers are focused on competency and, hopefully, alter the milieu and accomplishments of their respective offices. United States citizens who call any of these entities are often at the mercy of whoever answers the telephone.

The best way to reach someone at the CIA and to reach that person in a hurry is to have him find you.

* * *

Gantemirov explained to Stoli exactly what to do. Stoli had always followed instructions very well. Stoli somehow felt whole, knowing he was doing what his dead twin brother had done, feeling solidarity with his brother's DNA, realizing purpose and excitement, and being well paid. In addition, working with Gantemirov was a welcome respite from the loquacious tourists, everyone asking about the former Romanian President Cousceau, what it was like to live under the communists, and all the other vacuous inquiries. Stoli was happy and felt purpose.

Stoli knew that death lurked near. He had earlier seen the former president of Romania slaughter bears, many partially tranquilized prior to the hunt, without the president knowing it, all to satisfy Cousceau's ego, his need to be a great hunter. What was the difference between killing a beautiful bear versus some slob of a bartending waitress or a terrorist like Jennifer Pettigrew? All had lost life, and all lost life was the same. Stoli had never placed a premium on the human condition and saw no reason to begin now.

*   *   *

Following instructions from Gantemirov, Stoli telephoned the Edinburgh police and asked to speak to the investigating officer in the MacGregor murder. As soon as the officer was on the phone, Stoli said that he knew who killed Jeremiah MacGregor. Interrupting anything the officer tried to say, Stoli explained that he was speaking from one of several cell phones, driving one hundred miles outside Edinburgh, would speak for just a brief period of time, and that the police would have difficulty tracing his call. "Listen carefully to me and take notes, in case this is not being recorded." Stoli had the police officer's full attention.

After Stoli briefly delineated the surroundings at the time of MacGregror's death, the officer knew he was not listening to a crackpot. Stoli announced that the killer was Jokhar Gantemirov. He provided the police the account number at the Zurich bank from which Gantemirov had withdrawn funds.

Most important was something else: Jokhar Gantemirov, whom Stoli knew the police were now looking up on their computer screen, had the Iraqi weapons of mass destruction. The officer on the phone half-chuckled. Stoli responded in a matter-of-fact tone, "Jokhar Gantemirov has the the WMDs. They are in Chechnya. Gantemirov was with the KGB, FSB, Pi-Two, all of them. Do what I tell you and listen well.

"Gantemirov will be at Trafalgar Square, in London, tomorrow, six o'clock in the evening, London time, on the north side of Nelson's Column. He wants to make a deal for his freedom and will release the weapons of mass destruction for five hundred million dollars. Gantemirov will speak to only one man, a man he will recognize. That man is Dick Swept, a neurologist at the CIA."

The investigator found this compendium of information a bit more than he expected and far more than he had ever digested in his twenty-year career. He explained that doing all this in so short a time would be difficult. Stoli told the investigator that the CIA was probably already on the case, probably knew about the withdrawal, and he would not be surprised if the CIA were in Edinburgh right now. "Gantemirov is desperate and needs to see Dick Swept."

"If we can do this, how will Dick Swept recognize this fellow, Gantemirov?"

"Don't worry about that. They know each other."

“How so?”

“Dick Swept helped put him in jail.”

“I’ll do what I can. Where do I reach you if there’s a problem?”

“You don’t reach me. There should be no problem. One more thing.”

“What?”

“Tell Dr. Swept I shall be there. He killed my twin brother.” Stoli placed the receiver in the cradle.

Never had working in the Romanian orphanage or the tourist company been so exhilarating. To taste danger at the edge was to taste life.

* * *

Inspector Jamie Blacklok turned to the man sitting on his desk. “Do you believe this? You heard it on your receiver. Think it’s real?”

“I don’t know. I have to make a call,” and the CIA underling working in Edinburgh, Scotland, took an orange cell phone from his coat pocket, pushed three buttons, and asked to be put through to Major Cervantes.

“Sir, this is Rednik. I’m in Edinburgh, and we just received a call about Gantemirov and Kostokov’s twin brother.” Hyman Rednik reiterated the message from Stoli.

Cervantes listened carefully. “Swept is near there. I think he’s in London, at Claridge’s, for Christ sake. After all, why not spend as much taxpayer's money as possible! I'll tell him to be at Trafalgar Square."

"Do you want me to arrange backup? Do we let him go alone?"

"Of course, we let him go alone! You think these people are stupid? They'll spot us in a second if we do anything funny."

"We aren't going to do anything? Why not a hidden mike or a homing device?"

"He won't need it. Do it my way," and the receiver clicked.

* * *

Moments later, Cervantes was on the phone with Swept. "Be at Trafalgar Square, on the north side of Nelson's Column, tomorrow, at 1800. Gantemirov and someone who says he is Kostokov's twin brother want to deal with us for the weapons of mass destruction, the killings of MacGregror, Pettigrew, and who knows what else. You have no back up, unless you want it."

"Wow! Nothing is simple. Why do they want me?"

"I don't know. I'm not certain why they're calling us. You're a smart man and a decent agent. Use your own judgment for whatever comes along. Do you want backup?"

Swept had begun to like living on the edge. For some people, the idea of excitement is eating red meat. For Swept, since he had killed Kostokov, other ex-KGB agents at the National Institutes of Health, and the two assailants at the International Speech Forum meeting, and joined the CIA, a progressive cynicism of life continued to grow, and all these events together made him feel he was living life to the fullest. This experience, however, was not without immense danger, and he did not want to be reckless. "You tell me."

"I'm afraid if we put a bug on you or a homing device, they'll find it and we lose. They contacted us. They must want us or need us or need something. I think you should go in clean."

"This remains a far cry from what you once told me. 'Dr. Swept, you will want for nothing. You can join us and do whatever research you want. Price and lab space are no problem. Just join us, and do whatever you want.'"

"Do we have to go through this again? What we told you was before increased terrorism, increased conflict in Iraq, and a lot else. Besides, is this not what you want? You trained for this and trained well. You aren't obligated."

"I know I'm not obligated. It just doesn't seem like I'm ensconced in scientific quests."

"Dr. Swept, if you want to go back to the lab, back to those glutamate receptors or whatever you're working on, then do that. If you want to help us in other ways, in particular your country, do this."

"I just want you to realize I'm not doing what either you or I thought I would be doing."

"That's your point? Just that—that you aren't doing what you and I thought you would be doing?"

"Yes."

"Well, get a grip. No one does what they thought they'd be doing. Certainly, not me or anyone else. Otherwise, we'd all be bored to death."

"This isn't getting us anywhere," Swept responded. "Regardless, I need to do this my way. If I authorize something, it goes. When I want backup, I have it, and anything I want to do is approved by the agency. Is that square with you?"

"Done."

"Oh—and one more thing."

"What's that?"

"I continue to stay at whatever hotel I want, eat wherever I want, drive what I want, and get no grief from anyone. And I still have the option of returning to my research whenever I want."

"What if I say 'no'?"

"Then I'm back in the lab now. Look," Swept explained, "I can't negotiate with these people or anyone else if I don't have approval from the top. People need to know I mean what I say and that my word is golden. If I'm going to be some type of a conduit for getting things done, certainly something as important as obtaining the weapons of mass destruction, I need validity for anything I promise—or threaten."

"Deal! You do what you want. Just don't get yourself killed."

"With arrangements like this, why would I want to be killed?" Swept hung up the receiver and felt incredibly alive and electrified, as he thought about meeting with killers tomorrow evening.

On the other end of the telephone connection, Major Cervantes thought about the implications of what he had said: that no one anticipates what life holds in store. He thought about the unhappiness in his marriage and walked down the hallway to see Carol Bernsen.

* * *

Chapter Thirty-seven

CURRENCY BREEDS CREATIVITY

Trafalgar Square is the center of London, substantiated by a plaque on the nearby corner of Strand and Charing Cross Road, from which all distances in the United Kingdom are measured. The square is the home of the National Gallery and one of London's most distinguished landmarks—Nelson's Column.

Many people refer to Trafalgar Square as London's "living room," since it teems with Londoners and tourists and hosts New Year's Eve celebrations, as well as many weddings, elections, and sporting triumphs.

At 6:00 in the evening, on the north side of Nelson's Column, Dick Swept emerged from the crowd. His external insouciance belied his intense inner focus. Swept methodically scanned the square, detected no one of obvious importance, and decided to wait five minutes.

Within thirty seconds, a man carrying a satchel approached him. The man removed his sunglasses and fake beard for all to see. It was Stoli.

"We meet again, Dr. Swept."

"Anyone going to hit me on the head this time? I promise you, that was a big mistake."

"So was killing my brother, Dr. Swept. Let's get to the point. There's a bomb in this bag, and we all die if anything funny happens."

"You're an idiot. I'm here alone. Where's Gantemirov?"

Swept felt a hand on his left shoulder, from behind. Without turning, the neurologist responded, "I presume *you* aren't stupid enough to hit me on the back of my head. Correct?"

"No, Dr. Swept, fortunately for you, I am not," as the Chechen came into full view. Gantemirov was smiling, his face clean-shaven and his appearance well rested. Swept recognized him in an instant but had forgotten how huge a frame the man possessed. Jokhar Gantemirov was a large man, powerful, ruthless, and, as far as Dick Swept knew, extremely intelligent.

The Chechen spoke. "This is like a family reunion, is it not?"

"What can I do for you? What do you want?" said Swept, looking around the square cautiously.

"I presume you are not armed or bugged, Doctor? Correct?"

"Correct. They offered it, but I figured, 'Hey! If I can't trust you guys, whom can I trust?'"

"'Well put,' as you Americans say." Gantemirov openly frisked Swept, in full view of the tourists, and moved some type of wand across him.

"Satisfied?" said Swept.

"Maybe," replied the Chechen. "Now," placing his arm around Swept's shoulders, "we must talk." The two men walked toward Northumberland Avenue, with Stoli several paces behind.

"I see you've met my colleague, Stoli."

"Great name! I met him more than once," Swept said, transiently turning to face Kostokov's twin brother. "I have a question."

"Fire away. What is there if not honor among thieves?"

"Did you try to kill me in France?"

Gantemirov stopped walking. Still smiling, he directly faced the neurologist. "Indeed I did, but you are a hard man to kill. Very difficult."

"Did you kill the man whose leg I broke?"

"Yes, I did. I could see that you were questioning him. I didn't want him to talk."

"You could have killed me, sparing him."

"I could have, but then we would have one dead assailant, one dead CIA cop or neurologist or whatever you call yourself, and a very wounded man. It was easier to kill him. Besides, I had a better view, a better shot of my colleague. Regardless, you're alive, which is now fortunate for us both."

"Why did you want me dead?"

"Because I saw no good from you being alive. I was afraid you were sent to capture me. But now, I know different. The CIA is as stupid as the FSB. Again, I'm glad you're not dead—I need you."

"You're lying, aren't you?"

"Perhaps."

"We can discuss all this later. What about Allendorf? Did your brilliant thinking decide he had to die too?"

"No. I had nothing to do with that. Probably some local criminals, not highbrows like us." Gantemirov continued to smile.

"This is all a game to you, isn't it?" Swept responded.

"I can assure you that it is not a game. And if it were, the first rule of the game would be that it is *not* a game." Gantemirov resumed walking, coaxing Swept along with him. "I am very serious. And let me promise you one thing."

"Which is?" asked Swept.

"I only play games I win."

"Good for you." Swept looked at the trained killer and did not smile.

"Here's the problem," continued Gantemirov, still smiling. "I can get you Americans the weapons of mass destruction. It will cost five hundred million dollars. You give me the money, I give you the WMDs. Plain and simple."

Swept was nonplussed. "You don't expect me to believe that, do you?"

"Actually, I do. Why else would I be here? I even admit to killing that girl Pettigrew. Perhaps you know about my microchip. My friends and I killed MacGregor. And I am certain your government now knows about my withdrawing money from Zurich International. I'm not hiding anything."

"Except the weapons, allegedly."

"No, that is not 'allegedly.' I do have the weapons, and I am prepared to sell them to you."

"Let me get this straight," said Swept, raising his right eyebrow and focusing his stare at Gantemirov. "You have the weapons of mass destruction and all the United States has to do is give you a check for five hundred million dollars, and bingo, you'll turn around and give them to us? Pretty simple. Gee, why didn't I think of a stunt like that earlier?"

"Because you don't have the weapons and I do."

Swept smirked and began to walk away. Gantemirov reached for him.

"Listen to me, you fool. Why would I be here if I didn't need to be here? I can't get to the weapons without you. Actually, I can get to them, but I can't get them out. They're in Chechnya, and I figure the CIA can do this without a problem. You give me the money and you get your WMDs."

Gantemirov recognized that he now had Swept's attention. "You don't have to pay anything until you see the weapons. You can see them for yourself. Then, give me two hundred fifty million dollars and we all take the weapons out of Chechnya, to wherever you want. After the WMDs are secured in your hands, you give me the other two hundred fifty million dollars."

"Just like that, huh?"

"How would you do it? Look, I don't give a damn about you or your government. All I care about is the money. I know where the weapons are, and I can't conceive your president doesn't want to prove to the world that he was right—Saddam Hussein had weapons of mass destruction. I know where they are, and I can deliver them to you."

"How did you get them? The American forces, the Brits, the UN, for whatever they're worth, none of them could find the WMDs. How did you find them?"

"That's not a matter of your direct concern. I can tell you that it wasn't on purpose, but I found them. I escaped from jail, an escape made too easy for my sensibilities, and then met with some friends."

Chechnya? Swept stared at Gantemirov. "Chechnya?"

"Chechnya. Members of the Baath Party, loyal to Hussein, moved them in a caravan of trucks a few weeks before the American invasion."

"Other countries participated in the invasion too, you know."

"I'm not here to argue about the Iraqi war. You do or think what you want. My only point is that leaders in Britain and America talked about how dangerous Saddam was, in part because of his weapons of mass destruction. Now, no one knows where they are or if they even exist, except me."

Gantemirov continued, detecting cynicism in Swept, "Saddam loyalists moved them to Chechnya before the *American* invasion." He was stressing "American" to see whether he could still rile Swept. He could not.

"Tell me more."

"The man behind the biological weapons is a cokehead, called 'the Chemist,' a real jerk. But if you want to know, I don't care about him either. I just want the money."

"How did you find the weapons?" Swept asked.

"I didn't. They found me. I had some contacts in Chechnya. Remember, I am Chechen, despite living in Moscow for so many years. One of the freedom fighters in Chechnya came into contact with the Chemist. One thing led to another—the Iraqis had to have some place to live, eat, and find women. Most Chechens are Sunni Muslims. We're on pretty good terms with the Sunnis in Iraq, so my friend became involved."

"I don't suppose you'd give me his name."

"You don't suppose right, but you'll probably meet him."

Swept stared at Gantemirov, digesting Stoli's presence in the background as Londoners and tourists brushed past.

Gantemirov continued, "Dr. Swept, the problem is simple. We have the WMDs in Chechnya and can use them against the Russians, the Israelis, Shiite Muslims, the rich, the sick—hell, I don't even care if we use them against the dead. But I can assure you, if we decimate the Russians, we'll still have to deal with them, even if we destroy Moscow. Maybe yes, maybe no. However, we want the money. I want the money. You do whatever you want to convince yourselves that we have the weapons of mass destruction, and I'll go along. We do have them. After you give me the initial two hundred fifty million dollars, you can have them, and then give me the additional money. Frankly, after that, I don't care if all of you go to hell, Allah, heaven, Jerusalem, or Miami Beach. I don't care. I just want the money."

"What are you going to do with five hundred million dollars? Do you keep it all?"

"That part is none of your business. Do we have a deal?"

"Why do you want the money? Are we going to have more problems after you have that kind of money, even though we supposedly have the weapons?"

"You're a scientist. You should understand: Currency leads to creativity. Don't you agree? Currency will make me more creative—that's why I want the money, so I can be creative, like you, in your chemical research of people with memory disorders. Now, do we have a deal?"

"I need to make some calls."

"Bullshit! I bet you're authorized to do what you want."

"You don't understand how democracies function."

"Wrong. I understand exactly how democracies function. That's why I know you'll give me the money. I'll see you here in exactly twenty-four hours." Jokhar Gantemirov walked away, and Stoli followed.

"One more thing," interjected Swept. Gantemirov turned around.

"Which is?"

"What *are* the weapons of mass destruction? Are they nuclear weapons, biological weapons? We need to know if we're going to transport them."

"All you need to know right now is that they'll fit in one large cargo plane."

"And then we all die from radioactivity?"

"I'm not stupid. You check all this out, any way you want. You pay me, and you will have the weapons of mass destruction. Until I have the money, this part of the conversation goes on hold."

Swept studied Gantemirov's face and glanced occasionally at Stoli. "This better be right."

"Don't worry, Dr. Swept. This is the real thing."

Gantemirov now walked away quickly, Stoli at his side.

* * *

Chapter Thirty-eight

TREATY AT TRAFALGAR

Dick Swept discussed with Major Cervantes his conversation with Gantemirov. Cervantes put Swept on hold and returned thirty minutes later. "I just spoke to the director. It's a 'go'. You contact me when you need the money. And"—Cervantes's voice took on a menacing tone—"you tell that piece of garbage Chechen that if he screws with Uncle Sam, the director of Central Intelligence and I shall personally suture his testicles to his chin. Tell him that, exactly!"

"Sure," replied Swept. "I'll be sure to tell him. I'm certain he's very much afraid of tough guys like us." The two men made the necessary arrangements.

* * *

Twenty-four hours later, Dick Swept stood near Nelson's Column, mesmerized by the bustle of people around

Trafalgar Square. A man from India, probably a tourist, judging from the assortment of maps he was trying to manage, kept dropping some of his recent purchase of candies while his young child refused to stay in one place, gathering the dropped delicacies, all the while his mother admonishing him about germs. Swept readily recognized Gantemirov, who seemed to flaunt his being conspicuous.

Gantemirov approached Swept. "Well? What's the plan? Did you get approval from your *democratic* government?"

"Yes, I did."

"Good."

"I was told to tell you something. I'm supposed to threaten you, if you try to screw us."

"Tell your government not to worry. No one needs to threaten anyone. This is a business deal, not a wrestling match. I have what you want and you have what I want. What could be simpler?"

"A lot! Spare me the polemics. Here's what we want to do: You and I go to the weapons. You show me what you have. If I think they're legitimate, fine. If you can't convince me they're legitimate, I call in some specialists, who we may need because I lack particular expertise in weapons designed to blow mankind off the face of the earth. If these assistants agree everything is on the level, we call in the CIA and move the weapons where we want. We give you two hundred fifty million dollars when we load them up and two hundred fifty after we arrive at a place of our choosing."

Gantemirov listened carefully as the two walked slowly amidst the pigeons and tourists. "And, Mr. Gantemirov, if neither I nor my assistants are satisfied that the weapons are real . . ." Swept smiled and looked at Gantemirov with a mixture of amusement and disdain.

"Then, what?" asked the Chechen.

"Then," replied Swept, "I personally shall sew your balls to your chin."

The burly Chechen laughed. Putting his arm around Swept, feeling the neurologist tense as he did so, knowing the American could strike, he said, "Dr. Swept. We are going to get along fine."

"I don't think so. Remember," said Swept, "it's a business."

"That's why we'll get along. Now, let's have some coffee and none of that American crap."

* * *

Chapter Thirty-nine

I HAVE THE MONEY

Dr. Regina Bruxton's physical therapist was pleased with her progress. Regina's gait was less spastic, her fine motor control continued to improve, and, most of all, her spirits were good. Her self-confident air was returning, and it was apparent that the plastic surgeon would have no permanent damage to her intellect. What was not yet clear was whether Regina would have compromise in fine motor skills necessary to perform surgery.

"Having a better day today, Dr. Bruxton?" inquired Mona, the petite therapist from Lake Charles, Louisiana. "You seem much better. Your walking, even without the walker, keeps improving. Good for you."

"Thanks, Mona," replied Dr. Bruxton, her face betraying considerable discomfort as she negotiated the turn around the corner of the Skilled Nursing Facilities Unit. Suddenly, a smile appeared on the face of the physically damaged but still beautiful plastic surgeon.

"Well, look who the cows brought home on this huge Texas ranch," Regina exclaimed.

"None other than me, the great rancher from the East," laughed Harold Ranger, offering daisies, making his way toward the patient. "How are we doing today?" Ranger lightly shook Regina's hand and politely acknowledged Mona.

"Dr. Bruxton is doing fine, Dr. Ranger. We're going to try a four-post cane soon. She is really doing well." Mona took the daisies and put them on an adjacent table.

"Tell you what, Mona. I can take over from here," and Ranger pressured Mona to the side, making certain Regina's walker was steady.

"Do you have time to be here?" asked Regina.

"Sure, that's why I'm here. I'm so important I had to get away. It's good practice."

"What's good practice?"

"To get away."

Regina looked at Harold Ranger and laughed. "Good to see you," and the two made it down the hall together, back to Regina's room. The plastic surgeon sat on her bed, facing Harold Ranger, who was now slouched in a chair, ringing the nurses for coffee.

"Regina, I am very happy you are getting around and feeling better."

"That makes two of us."

Ranger smiled and buried himself in some scientific papers.

* * *

Back in London, Dick Swept sat at the bar at Gordon Ramsay's, in Claridge's Hotel, smoking a Cuban Cohiba cigar. Swept had long appreciated good cigars, especially with his Ketel One. Swept momentarily contemplated that if the United States eases the Cuban embargo, then college kids, with their copies of the *New York Times* and *Playboy,* would flood into Cuba and probably indirectly lead to the toppling of Castro.

As Swept thought about the mess Castro had made of Cuba, enjoying his Cohiba and Ketel One, he pondered British loyalty to the United States in the Iraq war. Britain was loyal to America yet refused to join the American embargo against Cuba. This emphasized to Swept that the two countries were democracies, not two gangs in cahoots with each other.

No matter, thought the neurologist. His job was not to dissect political decisions. Rather, his job, aside from glutamate receptor research in Alzheimer's disease, was to assess the veracity of the alleged weapons of mass destruction and take them home.

Tomorrow, Swept left for Chechnya, and hopefully, sooner than later, the United States government would know whether Gantemirov and Dick Swept could deliver the WMD.

* * *

Jokhar Gantemirov spoke to his friend Akhmad. "I have the money. Tell me where you want me to wire or send it and it's yours."

"I want cash."

"What currency?"

"American dollars or Swiss francs."

"I have the francs. How do we do this?"

"Be outside the Fortnum and Mason department store in London tomorrow, at two o'clock in the afternoon, your time. A man will come by, eating a sandwich. He will tell you where to deliver the money. Anything else?"

Gantemirov felt uneasy. The exchange could not be that simple. "What is he going to tell me? Where I deliver my packages or where to wire them or what? What about what you're delivering to me?"

"We want the hard product—cash. Nothing wired. Be ready to deliver within a few hours after meeting him. I trust him with my life, so you can trust him with yours. We'll take care of the rest. You and I go back a long way. You can trust me."

"What's his name?"

"Joseph. His name is Joseph. After you give him what will be mine, come and meet me in Grozny, at our usual place, where we played as children."

"It's all bombed out there."

"I know. That's why I like it. Are we done?"

"Okay. Say hello to Angelina."

Without losing pace in the tempo of the conversation, the voice at the other end of the secured line said, "I can't."

"Why not?"

"Because she's dead," and Akhmad Edilkhanov closed his cell phone.

* * *

In the early afternoon, at the appointed time, Gantemirov met with Joseph, who followed Jokhar to his apartment, made a telephone call, and five men showed up to cart away 250 million dollars in Swiss francs. They had a dolly, several suitcases, and were dressed as furniture movers. The men loaded the bags into their furniture truck and sped away.

Gantemirov did not know whether to be impressed or worried at the seemingly lax security, but he knew better than to ask. Akhmad could have agents throughout the building, on the corner, or wherever he wanted, so Gantemirov presumed that everything was safe, secure, and on target.

* * *

Akhmad Edilkhanov, one of the most powerful men in Chechnya, was rumored to be the future president of Chechnya, regardless whether the Russians were still there. It was no problem for Edilkhanov to ensure security in London for a bunch of guys moving satchels into a furniture van. Akhmad Edilkhanov was well connected and had contacts throughout Europe, Asia, and the United States.

* * *

Swept and Gantemirov flew from London to Azeerbaijan as guests on a Cessna Citation jet, courtesy of the CIA, where they refueled and left for Grozny, Chechnya. As the jet approached the airport, Swept took in the late twilight aerial view of the city. Gantemirov interrupted him.

"I presume your country spoke to the Russians, so they won't shoot down our plane."

"So they tell me."

Shortly, the Citation landed in what Swept realized must have once been a beautiful city. The tarmac was peppered with bombed-out potholes, and the pilot had to negotiate these built-in hazards on the runway.

The two men went through Customs without much difficulty and hailed a taxi for downtown Grozny's Minutka Square. This square, where the proud Dudayev Palace once stood, had been dynamited and leveled by the Russians. There was a half-buried missile silhouetting the sunset, and Swept became immersed in thought as he studied the grounded projectile.

"Pretty amazing, don't you think, Dr. Swept? This is my country. Look what Moscow did to us! They ruined a nation and continue to try to ruin our culture. But they cannot destroy our people, the Chechen people. Do you know about us? Do you know who and what we are?"

Swept grimaced, only slightly. “Actually, I do. I have always been interested in history and have done considerable reading about your country.”

“Really? Tell me about us.”

“If you like.” Swept began to present the history of the Chechen people, hoping to build trust in Gantemirov and to preempt any long soliloquies from Gantemirov about how great were the Chechens or evil the Russians.

* * *

Chapter Forty

CHECHNYA

Gantemirov allowed his gaze to fall on Dick Swept, as the neurologist began to present the history of Chechnya, trying to instill confidence in the Chechen murderer.

"Chechens were originally aboriginals from the north slope of the Caucasus Mountains, where they built fortresses to withstand attacks from adjacent nomadic tribes. At one time, many Chechens were Christians, but Sunni missionaries converted most of them to Islam between the sixteenth and nineteenth centuries. Since then, Islam has served as a basis for Chechen nationalism, which carries somewhat of a xenophobic flavor."

Gantemirov nodded.

Swept continued, "Over recent centuries, Chechens have had to resist, often unsuccessfully, Russian advances, which produced several fanatic secret societies, well suited to clan-based, underground warfare against an occupying power. Many of those societies still exist, as they did during the eighteenth century, when Russia fought the Ottoman and Persian empires. At that time, Ossetians, a local Christian people, welcomed Russia as a protector against the neighboring Chechen Muslims, and this provided Russia a base of operation.

"The Chechens fiercely resisted the Russians. Later, during fighting from 1817 to 1864, Russia brutally subjugated the Caucasian peoples. This conflict entrenched within the Chechens as well as the Russians vile beliefs about the other, and that has persisted to this day."

"Go on," said Gantemirov, now stone-faced.

"Russia then constructed several powerful forts from the Black Sea to the Caspian Sea, to protect their national territory. One of these, Grozny, became a focal point from which Russia would send punitive expeditions to destroy Chechen villages, burn crops, and kill civilians."

"Nice people, don't you think?" smiled Gantemirov.

"I'm reciting information, not passing judgement. Do you want me to continue?"

"Go ahead."

"In retaliation, Imam Shamil led resistance against Russia, a resistance that formally lasted until 1858, when the Russian empire formally absorbed Chechnya. However, fighting persisted. A few years later, Russia discovered oil near Grozny. That's when they built a railroad to Baku, laid through Chechnya. That railroad carried Russian settlers into the lowlands and cities of Chechnya, and they displaced many Chechens from their employment in farms and industries.

That made the relations between the Chechen people and Russia worse.

"During revolutionary times in Russia, from 1917 to 1920, Chechens again tried to drive out the Russians and almost succeeded. However, beginning in 1920, the Bolsheviks reasserted Russian power over Chechnya. The Chechens still maintained their fierce nationalism and hated the communist Soviet Union. Later, during World War II, when Nazi Germany neared the Caucasian oilfields, Chechens were found on both sides of the war. Because of this lack of loyalty and support for the Soviets, after the war ended, the Soviet Union deported the Chechens to Siberia."

"I had family members who died there," interrupted Gantemirov.

"I'm sure you did, and I'm sorry. But remember, many Chechens supported the Nazis."

"So what! They promised us our own country."

"Well," quipped Swept, "the Nazis lost and—"

"So will the Russians," interjected Gantemirov. "So will the Russians."

"Regardless, you wanted to know if I am well-versed in your area. In 1957, under Kruschev, the Soviet government considered Chechens 'rehabilitated' and formally reestablished the Chechen territory. This resettlement produced tension with neighboring peoples, who had moved into Chechen villages and now had to be expelled. Later, to make matters more complicated. Chechens refused to follow the Soviet antireligious bias and clung to Islam. So, by 1975, half of the Chechen population belonged to Sufi brotherhoods that were secret societies, nationalistic, anti-

Russia, and tied to Islam. Trying to keep tensions low, Moscow officially reopened the mosques in 1978.

"Later, during glasnost years, the Chechens' desire for independence increased. In 1991, Chechen leaders declared an independent Chechen republic. A retired bomber pilot, General Dzhokhar Dudayev, seized control and was elected president in October 1991, the year the Soviet Union disintegrated. In 1992, Russia sent troops to the region to quell fighting between local ethnic groups, and President Dudayev called for a holy war against Russia."

"Good for Duduyev," snarled Gantemirov.

"Hooray for everyone," responded Swept. Continuing, "In December 1994, Russia officially launched a strong offensive against Chechen rebels, which was a military disaster for Russia. Consequently, two years later, Moscow signed a peace agreement with Chechnya.

"But as we know, there is no peace in Chechnya. Chechen 'freedom fighters' continue to strike Russia, often at the heart of Moscow, in an attempt to rid themselves of what they perceive to be Russian dogs. At the same time, Russians perceive Chechens as dishonest and ruthless thieves."

Raising his right eyebrow and loosening his shoulders, Swept looked at Gantemirov and said, "And that's that." With a half-smile, Swept inquired, "How did I do?"

"Well, Dr. Swept. You did very well." Gantemirov was obviously impressed with Swept's knowledge about the Chechen people. "You've done your homework. Do you realize we are a great people?"

"Perhaps. All races view themselves as 'great people.' That wouldn't be so bad if the perception didn't often mandate that other people were not great people and, therefore, inferior."

"I'm not here to lecture you on our culture, Dr. Swept, nor you on mine. Chechens have a culture, a land, and are loyal to one another. Whatever anyone thinks about us as a culture or a 'people,' Russia has no business being here. But why should that bother you? Your country is all over the Middle East, and you don't belong there."

"I don't make policy for my country, but I support it."

"Blindly? Do you follow orders blindly?"

"No, I just follow orders. Now, why do the 'great people' of Chechnya need weapons of mass destruction?"

"We don't. What we need is money. As fate would have it, we have the weapons. Now, we want the money. I want the money. Don't forget—currency breeds creativity."

"But you're not going to have the money, are you? at least not all of it? Aren't you going to have to pay someone for the weapons?"

"It becomes complex, Doctor. All you need worry about is how to get them out of Chechnya. That shouldn't be too difficult for the CIA. Then, what I do is my business."

"Why were they sent to Chechnya? If you were going to use them against Russians or anyone else, why give them up? Are you and your terrorist friends that broke?"

"Hardly. Right now, I intend to give the weapons to you, you give me the money, and I become powerful in Chechnya. Now, before we talk ourselves to death, let's walk down the road to the house near that corner," Gantemirov said, pointing down to the missile-damaged road. "Sasha is there, with coffee, food and vodka."

Swept walked with Gantemirov. He was actually beginning to like him.

* * *

"So," Regina asked coquettishly, "are we going to become lovers?" Harold Ranger stared at Regina Bruxton, a blush almost appearing on his face.

"Could be. Although, I have to tell you, I haven't held a woman in my arms for years."

"Don't worry," responded the healing plastic surgeon, her stiffened arms supporting her leaning backwards in bed, while the drooping hospital gown revealed too much of her breasts. "With a body like mine, injuries and all, I probably can't hold anyone."

Harold Ranger, who had yet to kiss Regina Bruxton anywhere other than her cheek, stood and smiled. "This might actually work out," he said as he exited the hospital room, stopping at the nursing station, where he requested another cup of coffee, and walked to the elevators.

Regina Bruxton felt a smile appearing on her face.

* * *

Chapter Forty-one

A DEAL IS A DEAL

Jokhar Gantemirov made certain Dick Swept had his mask on tightly before entering the old warehouse halfway between Grozny and the city to its east, Argun. He then escorted Swept to an old black Ford pickup, out of which stepped Akhmad and the Chemist. After cursory introductions, the latter two put on their respective masks, Akhmad checking twice that his was airtight.

Gantemirov supplied everyone with thin polyester gowns fitting over their entire bodies, including the gas masks. Gantemirov also provided each man with gloves and shoe coverings, not unlike operating room shoe coverings with which Swept was familiar. Swept was pleased that he could clearly understand the men when they spoke to him. When they spoke among themselves, they spoke Russian.

Gantemirov opened an old door, removed a padlock on another, and showed Swept the large number of cases containing botulinum toxin-Q, twenty-eight canisters to a box, sixty-nine boxes in all. Gantemirov instructed Swept to choose any one of the canisters and hand it to him.

"These are some of the weapons. Watch what I am about to do. Gantemirov opened another door, this one having a brass chain wrapped through several padlocks, and entered a dark room, stinking from human excrement.

Gantemirov lit two small lanterns, which provided enough light to view the contents of the room. There were twenty or so men, each tied with duct tape and baling wire to a chair. The men were gagged, and some appeared near starvation.

After adjusting their eyes to the light, the bound and gagged men were obviously terror stricken at seeing the four men in gowns and gas masks.

"Gentlemen," announced Gantemirov, speaking in English and turning to the prisoners. "This is Dr. Richard Michael Swept. He is a physician, a neurologist to be exact. Neurologists treat brain and nerve disease.

"However, do not be elated. Dr. Swept is not from the Red Cross, members of whom you bombed and killed. No, Dr. Swept is here for a singular purpose: to watch you die."

The men focused on Gantemirov and his small contingent of gown—and mask-clad companions. Their eyes revealed terror. Some muffled faint protests, prompting Gantemirov to kick over the chair on which the loudest protestor bemoaned his fate.

"Realize, Dr. Swept, not one of these men speaks English. My prose is for your ears. Now, my American friend, watch the potency of this chemical," and the Chechen poured from the thermos ten drops of fluid on the floor and stood back. The men began to gasp, their muffled screams receiving no response from Gantemirov or his colleagues, as the captured men's eyes stared, bulged, and seemed to want to produce some statement, some message, to say or do something. However, their struggles soon ceased, and within ten minutes, they were dead.

Swept was numb. He had never witnessed such cold, wanton killing.

Gantemirov was the first to speak. "Don't tell me this bothers you, Dr. Swept. Death is easy to digest when you drop a bomb from the sky. This is the real thing, the hard stuff, like what you did to Aleksander Kostokov. This is real killing, the true process of removing that which unites us all—life!"

Swept, Gantemrov, and the other two men were still in the room with the dead prisoners. Swept spoke, "You didn't have to do this."

"Oh, yes I did. Believe me, I had to. Otherwise, you would have never been convinced. So, are you now satisfied? If this is what a few drops will do, imagine what gallons can do. The chemical paralyzes all muscle tissue. You're probably familiar with it. It's a form of botulinum toxin. Pretty effective, don't you think?"

Akhmad and the Chemist were silent. They stared at Swept. The men showed neither joy nor sorrow at the murders. It was business.

Swept turned to the victims, looking at each broken life individually. "I want to check them."

"Satisfy yourself. Believe me, they're dead. But suit yourself. When you're done, my friends will destroy everything, including the gas masks."

Swept felt nauseated from the killing, accentuated by the powerful smell of human excrement that his mask could only partially filter. Swept wondered what these men had done to deserve such a fate. He examined a few of the dead, but his exam was cursory. The men were certainly out of life's cycle.

Later, outside the building, having discarded his protective clothing and mask into a special receptacle, standing near Akhmad and the Chemist, Swept turned to Gantemirov. "This is your proof?"

"Do you want us to kill more people, people in a restaurant, movie theater, school, try an airport? This is the real stuff. These are the weapons of mass destruction. We can knock out a city with this. Now, what about your end of the promise?"

Swept, as did many Americans and others pursuing the WMD, falsely supposed a large cache of dangerous weapons. The reality was sixty-nine crates, each containing twenty-eight canisters. The chemical was mobile and surely lethal. What Swept did not know was that there were an additional twelve canisters of this lethal toxin, not included in these sixty-nine crates.

Swept and Gantemirov climbed into a Ford pickup different from the one in which they arrived. Somehow, the vehicle materialized, signifying Gantemirov had more men in the area. Akhmad and the Chemist returned to the previous vehicle and headed toward the center of Grozny.

Gantemirov drove Swept along the potholed road to Argun, not far from Grozny. Turning toward Gantemirov, Swept said, "Why are you doing this?"

"You keep asking me that."

"Do you want to help your people, the Chechen people?"

"Dr. Swept, I care about my people. And I care most about me. My people can't help me if I'm in trouble."

"Speaking about trouble," said Swept with a sardonic look on his face. "Why did you kill those men?"

"Why? Well, I had to do something to convince you we have the WMDs. Those men were all Saddam loyalists, loyal to the former president of Iraq and members of his now-outlawed Baath Party. They were Sunni Muslims, as am I and my friends here. However, these Saddam loyalists were also thieves. They moved the WMDs here to Chechnya and spoke with my friend Akhmad. My friend knew that Saddam wanted him to safeguard the weapons, but unfortunately for Saddam, he no longer has power in Iraq, no longer has access to money, and, more important, has no base of operation. These men, the men he personally entrusted to take the weapons you Americans talk so much about, wanted to sell them to Akhmad. They wanted to sell the weapons their supposed great leader, the man who trusted them, gave them to guard! There were also some other interactions, interactions I don't know a lot about. Anyway, my friend made them a deal, a phony deal, telling them he would pay them for the weapons."

"Did he?"

"Yes, but after he took the weapons, he took the money back. The money was hard cash, American dollars. After physically persuading a few to talk, he discovered the whereabouts of the money."

"No honor among thieves, I take it."

"I don't know about that, but these Iraqi men had no honor. We cannot trust such scum."

"So, you killed them?"

"What would you have done? Let them wander around the world with their money and possibly provide information harmful to my friends, one of whom, I might add, will one day be president of Chechnya?"

"How do I know you won't try to kill me? You tried before."

"Good question, but lacking merit. First, I don't want grief with the CIA."

"You already have grief with the CIA. Have you forgotten Pi-Two and the other atrocities you and Kostokov committed?"

"No, I have not. But I don't want more trouble. Besides, I don't think your government views me as a threat. And even if they do, now that I am supplying them the WMDs, they might even like me."

Swept looked at Jokhar Gantemirov, amazed. This man murdered so many people and was not the least perturbed by his actions. Swept knew if Gantemirov thought it suited his interests, he would kill Swept in a moment.

"One more thing, Dr. Swept."

"What's that?"

"I don't think you would let your government kill or harm me. You are a man of substance."

"Don't be so sure."

"I didn't say I was sure, only what I thought."

As the two rode in the pickup, Swept occasionally experienced searing back pain as they coursed along the shell-pitted road. Swept had another question. "What about your two friends? What happens to them?"

"Only one of them is my friend. Akhmad Edilkhanov is a true friend, whom I have known all my life. We were friends as children, belonged to the same 'secret societies,' as you call them, and we killed Russians together. I owe my life to him and he to me. The other man, the one they call 'the Chemist,' is the Iraqi cokehead I told you about. He is bizarre, but a brilliant chemist. He's the one who developed botulinum toxin-Q."

"You didn't answer my question. What happens to them?"

"You pay me, I pay Akhmad and he has enough money to become even more politically powerful in Chechnya. As for the Chemist, I don't know. He knew about the forthcoming fate of his comrades and didn't care. He needs money, lots of it, for his cocaine. We pay him and he's happy. Also, he's useful to us, given his extensive chemical knowledge."

"Where did he train, since he's so brilliant?"

"You have too many questions, but to prove I'm your man, I shall do my best to answer. The Chemist dropped out of Brandeis University, where he majored in physical and organic chemistry. He had a scholarship there, but was more interested in girls. Somehow, he wound up at Stanford, then UCLA, and, later, managed to get his PhD from Princeton. He worked for some hot shot pharmaceutical company, became addicted to cocaine, and was fired."

"Is he Iraqi? How did he wind up working for Hussein?"

"He is Iraqi, but different from most. His parents, both Iraqis, fled the country and were educated in London. Later, the family moved to America. After the Chemist was fired from the pharmaceutical company, he traveled to Iraq, not only because of his ethnic roots but also because he hates Jews. He blames them for his being fired."

Swept shook his head slightly. "Was he really fired because of Jews?"

"I doubt it. Jews don't run the company he worked for. Now, Dr. Swept, given that I have been honest with you, answered all your questions, when do I get my money?"

"We can wire the two hundred fifty million dollars to any account you want, or do this any way you want."

"I want it now, in hard currency, in Swiss francs."

"I'll have it flown in tomorrow. When we have the weapons where we want them, you'll get the rest of the money."

"You give me my two hundred fifty million dollars in Swiss francs tomorrow, you get the weapons, and then I receive the rest. Am I correct?"

"Yes. You give them to us and the money is yours."

"Fine. See how simple the world can be?" Gantemirov smiled and continued driving, struggling to avoid the bomb-made potholes.

Jokhar Gantemirov, avoiding a large crater on his right, turned to Swept. "Now, I have a question: where do you intend to sleep? This is a dangerous place."

"I'll leave that to you. I'm sure you want to keep me alive, at least until tomorrow."

"My friend," laughed the Chechen. "you really do not understand me. I do want you to stay alive. I have been very honest and frank with you. Besides, a deal is a deal."

"Tell that to Saddam's men, the ones you killed."

"I did tell them. Evidently, they didn't digest that philosophy, so I had to kill them. There is no one who has worked for me who would not say that I am a man of my word. Those men were dishonest and not to be trusted. That is why they are dead."

Swept looked at Gantemirov, trying to figure out whether the man was a blatant sociopath or had some inner matrix of worth. Regardless, he was certainly dangerous.

That night, Dick Swept and Jokhar Gantemirov slept in tents outside Gudermes, a city east of Gorzny.

* * *

Chapter Forty-two

AN EXCHANGE IS BEING MADE

Regina Bruxton was delighted that she was ready for discharge, after several weeks in the hospital. She believed her thinking was good, her mind clear, and her fine motor skills continued to improve every day. She could walk fairly well, although she still required her four-point cane. Harold Ranger offered to drive her home, and Regina accepted his kind offer.

In Ranger's car, a beat-up BMW, the surgeon gratefully said, "Dr. Ranger, thank you very much. You have been a good friend."

"I try. And don't forget, please call me 'Harold,'" the neurology department chairman replied with a halfhearted, exasperated voice.

Within a short time, Regina was home. "Now," cooed the plastic surgeon, "you can be an even better friend. Spend the night." Regina smiled at the chairman with her alluring, coquettish smile, a smile her attackers could not erase.

After the two were upstairs, not an insignificant feat given Regina's weak legs, but one with which the chairman gladly assisted, Ranger sat near Regina's bed. Ranger ordered some pizza, and the two devoured the meal upstairs, in Regina's bedroom. The plastic surgeon went to the bathroom and returned in a terry-cloth robe.

Ranger looked at Regina, somewhat nervously. "As I told you before, it has been a long time for me."

Limping to the bed, now lying supine on top of her bedspread, Regina softly responded. "Harold, you talk too much. I'm the one with the physical problems. You'll do fine. Now, if you don't mind, given my infirmities, turn off the lights. It's hard for me to get around."

Regina smiled at Harold Ranger. Her smile remained a long time.

With expertise and tenderness, Regina Bruxton, heretofore cold and tough-minded, called on all of her female tricks to see to it that Harold Ranger did fine. And he did.

When morning arrived, Regina Bruxton, ensconced in the neurology chairman's arms, gently kissed him. "Well, Mister, you sure are something."

Ranger looked at Regina, somewhat dumbfounded. "Well, whatever I am or did, I owe to you."

Regina replied, "Does this mean we're an item?"

"It means whatever you want it to mean," he replied and rolled toward her.

*   *   *

The Special Citation X, constructed especially for the Central Intelligence Agency, capable of speeds approaching three-quarters the speed of sound, made a steep landing at one of the many landing strips west of Grozny but one of the few that remain safe and smooth. Two stiff-backed men, dressed in black and loaded with AK-47s, Glock 17Ts, and grenades, stepped down to the tarmac and approached Swept, who turned toward Gantemirov. "Everything is set. Let's see what you have. We'll check it out, and then you get the money."

"How do we do this?" inquired the Chechen. "What keeps you from taking the canisters and leaving me without my money or my life or both?"

Gantemirov, well trained and certainly experienced, had anticipated a larger aircraft. This Citation was seemingly a fancy businessman's jet and did not have cargo room for the botulinum toxin-Q canisters. Gantemirov was sure that Swept knew about the lack of cargo room, so the Chechen anticipated more air power to appear.

Swept, noting a look of consternation on Gantemirov's face, replied to the question. "The same thing that keeps you from giving us bogus weapons and shooting us after we pay you."

"Don't you love this?" answered Gantemirov. "Here we are, within the wheels of history, and no one trusts anyone. You might be interested to know I trust you."

"Bullshit! We're going to the crates."

Swept signaled to the men, still silent, and they returned to the cabin of the jet. Several minutes later, they had gas masks, gowns, gloves and shoe coverings, as well as radioactive protective gear."

"Don't you think this is overkill?" asked the Chechen.

"We have our rules."

"Democracies always do."

The men approached the boxes allegedly containing the botulinum toxin-Q and placed several devices with large red and yellow wires in random locations within several boxes. They gently lowered a meter and a stainless-steel well. The process took close to one hour.

Swept removed a cell phone, talked to someone, then nodded to the men. They returned to the jet and reappeared seconds later, each man holding a suitcase. The men approached the boxes, opened their respective suitcase, and removed a small aliquot from each of several thermos containers, placing one drop at a time on the machine inside the suitcase.

Gantemirov broke the silence. "What are they doing?"

"They're using a spectrographic analyzer. They can read the vapors in an instant."

"Don't let the vapors blow this way or we're all in the wheels of history."

"They're careful."

"So am I." Turning to the men, Gantemirov yelled, "Careful. You can kill us all." The men did not look up.

Swept turned to Gantemirov. "If it happens to me, it happens to you. You be careful. Besides, as you so surely realize, we all have to die sometime."

"True, but not now. That stuff is really dangerous. Are you sure those Rambos know what they're doing? I presume you know, and they know, the boxes can't all fit in that plane."

"I'm careful too. Don't worry about it. What about life not being that precious?"

"I don't need you to explain value systems to me," and with that, Gantemirov walked toward the two men.

Two hours later, which seemed too long for Swept and Gantemirov, one of the men signaled a thumbs-up sign to Swept. Swept turned to Gantemirov. "Okay. The deal is on and met. Here's your money."

With that, the two men returned to the plane and disembarked with dozens of bags containing Swiss francs and placed them in front of Gantemirov. "Want to count it?" asked Swept.

"I wouldn't have, but you checked the boxes." Gantemirov held up his right arm and circled it clockwise. Two pickups appeared shortly, with several men in the bed of each, each one brandishing a Kalishnokov rifle. Gantemirov opened each of the bags, looked inside, and turned to Swept.

"You won't understand this, but I do. You haven't been in this business long enough to be a bastard. You still believe in all the nonsense—patriotism, goodness, God, love, country. That's why I trust you."

Swept looked at his colleague-in-arms, not saying a word. Gantemirov continued, "But you should understand something as well as you understood anything in your life. I know a lot about you. I know about Ricki Hardson, Regina Bruxton, Dr. Harold Ranger, all of them. If you ever try to steal from me—and understand, this is *my* money—I shall cut you into little pieces, and as for these people dear to you, you have no idea what I am capable of."

"I have every idea what you are capable of. I have seen you in action. Count your money. We're leaving."

With that, Dick Swept walked toward the jet and, as he climbed the stairs to the cabin, turned to Gantemirov. "It's all there. You make certain before I leave. For all I know, one of your men will steal from you and you'll blame me."

Swept picked up an electronic device that looked like a small banana and spoke into it. "What the hell is that?" screamed Gantemirov, trying to make his voice heard over the sound of the Citation's engine, which had just been engaged.

"Part of my patriotism," yelled Swept. Within sixty seconds, they heard the loud noise of a C-130 turbo-prop transport plane, just as it came into view

The C-130 planes are based at Florida's Hurlburt Field, and they belong to the Sixteenth Special Operations Wing, part of the U.S. Special Operations Command, consisting of approximately seven thousand highly trained military professionals, ready to conduct special operations missions at a moment's notice. The Sixteenth Special Operations

Wing specializes in unconventional warfare. At the direction of the National Command Authorities, the SOW can place these seven thousand soldiers anywhere in the world on short notice. Usually, their objectives relate to national security. Their motto is "Any Time, Any Place," and they mean it.

Swept, through Major Cervantes, had secured the Sixteenth SOW's assistance. Swept stood on the steps of the Citation as he watched the C-130 land, and, with swift precision, a team of forty men exited the cargo area and loaded the crates onto the plane.

Gantemirov stood there, watching. He briefly checked the contents of the satchels holding his money and motioned to his team to load them onto the trucks. He smiled at Swept and walked away, Swept nodding his approval.

Twenty minutes later, the C-130 was in the sky, the Citation circling above them. Swept could see jet fighters in the distance, on both sides.

As Swept sat in the Citation, he was certain that none of the men aboard the C-130 had any idea their cargo was 1,944 canisters of botulinum toxin-Q, the weapons of mass destruction. However, Cervantes certainly did, and Swept decided it was time to call him.

* * *

Chapter Forty-three

VALERIE IN THE SKY

"I have the packages. We're okay, and our friend has the first installment."

"Good. Any problems?"

"No, smooth as can be."

"Never think that. Nothing is vanilla."

Swept decided against saying he said "smooth," not "vanilla." "We're going to Langley, as directed. Then, what do we do?"

"You'll see when you get here. Meet me in my office day after tomorrow, at 0800. That should give you enough time to get some sleep."

Swept said goodbye and closed his eyes. He was delighted to see the plane was stocked with Ketel One vodka. The only scotch available was Dewar's, but that would suffice. Swept added a half drop to the glass, poured in what must have been three jiggers of vodka, and closed his eyes, trying to relax. Then, to his surprise, Swept heard a familiar voice.

"Well, look here. You still can't stay away from me, can you?"

Valerie VanDance had just left the cockpit and approached Swept. "Here we are again, you without anyone but me, and me without anyone but you. Pretty compelling, don't you think?"

Swept was more than surprised. "I thought you were in Kenya." Valerie, a CIA mole who had worked as a nurse for Harold Ranger in the past, had returned to the agency full time after her cover was blown during the Pi-Two affair. She was still as beautiful as ever, with straight blonde hair, a twinkle in her smile, and a longtime half jocose innuendo at wanting to spend more than platonic moments with Swept.

Valerie laughed. "I keep hearing great things about you." She kneeled on the floor and rested both arms on Swept's thighs. "You know, Bob One and Bob Two, the guys in black, are in the cabin with the pilot. It was real cramped there, so I decided to come back here. I outrank them and said we don't want to be disturbed."

Swept, exhausted and tired, looked at Valerie. "Will you knock it off? I am dead tired."

"Not a chance, cowboy," and with that, Valerie stood, turned off the lights, pulled down the shades of the windows, and unbuttoned Swept's trousers.

* * *

Harold Ranger spent every night with Regina. Downstairs, in her home on Friar Tuck Lane in the posh Memorial section of Houston, there was a huge kitchen, full bathroom, game room, and a giant family room with a large plasma television screen. Upstairs were the bedrooms.

Ranger had forsaken the façade of going to Regina's home as an overture to help with household chores. No, he went there because he liked to go there. Bit by bit, the once soured man was increasingly feeling better, increasingly so, about himself and the world.

* * *

At 0800, two days later, Dick Swept was in Major Cervantes's office. "You did a good job, Richard."

"Thank you."

"I do have one question."

"Yes, sir?"

"Did you enjoy seeing Valerie VanDance?"

Swept could not conceive that Cervantes knew about his sexual interlude with Valerie. Cervantes certainly could know that Valerie had been on the flight, but there wasn't a chance Valerie discussed their dalliance.

"It was nice to see her."

"I'm sure," said Cervantes, thinking about his marriage and lack of joy going home this and every other evening.

What kept Cervantes emotionally well anchored in most days were his splendid afternoons with Carol Bernson. He wondered whether Swept had such comfort in his life. Cervantes decided not to pursue the topic.

* * *

Carol, a full-bodied woman with a tired look on her face and little makeup, was a good listener and intelligent. Carol always had something worthwhile to add to any conversation. Although her hair was obviously dyed black and her glasses too thick, Carol Bernson's sense of humor, enthusiasm, and curiosity, and especially her kindness, were exemplary. As an administrator, she was reliable and highly efficient. As a woman, Carol was a delight.

Unlike Cervantes's wife, Carol Bernson smiled every time she saw Cervantes, and that made his hormones surge. Cervantes fully intended to leave his wife for Carol, and Carol believed, 100 percent, that Major Cervantes intended to divorce his wife.

Cervantes had initially loved his wife, when they courted, but Patricia's continuous badgering, constant complaining, and her interfering with his maintaining any friendship with men or women served both mates poorly. Cervantes hated being home, except for his three children, whom he dearly loved. If there ever was a man who stayed in his marriage because he believed it was good for the children, it was Major Cervantes.

Each time Cervantes entered his house, it was like being doused with cold water. He could not stand discussing anything with Patricia. She killed all joy for him. His only pleasures in life were playing with his children, reading to them, and holding Carol Bernson in his arms.

* * *

Cervantes, trying not to think about his afternoon plans with his administrator, asked Swept to sit in one of the chairs facing his mahogany desk. Swept obliged, looking at the pictures of presidents behind the desk, and watched Cervantes step around, sitting in the chair facing Swept, a small Persian throw rug between them.

"You really did well, *Richard.* We now have the weapons of mass destruction. This is good for the agency, and it can help us both get promoted. After the president decides what to do with this information, he and the British prime minister, both of whom bet that these weapons existed, will probably soar in the polls."

"Thanks. As for a promotion, I don't need it. All I want to do is return to my lab."

"Ah, yes, your lab. The great scientist, the great researcher. Are you still working on those glutic receptors?"

"Glutamate receptors. Yes, I am. As you and I have discussed several times, I'm a physician-scientist, not a field agent. I'm happy I could help, and now I want to get back to the lab."

"I thank you, Dr. Swept—er, Richard. One more thing."

"Sure."

"The president of the United.States wants to see you."

"The president wants to see me? Why?"

"I don't know. I think he thinks you're a hero."

"I'm not."

"I know that. Actually, if anyone deserves the credit, it's me. It was my thinking that unfolded all this."

Swept looked puzzled. "Never mind," Cervantes chided. "Never mind."

"By the way, Richard. We have rules we're supposed to follow. Screwing a field agent on a plane isn't one of them."

Cervantes stood and walked to his chair behind the desk. Swept, slightly puzzled, still believed that Valerie was not the kind of woman to kiss and tell, and that Cervantes was just fishing.

Dick Swept, with focused pitch, said, "My personal realm is my personal realm. You think what you want. I am always a professional. Speaking of which, I promised Gantemirov the remaining two hundred fifty million dollars. Did we send it to him, as planned?"

"You don't need to worry about that—that's taken care of. And for your information, I am also a professional and a damn good one." Cervantes straightened the corner of his desk and sat down. Swept left the office thinking of a Bob Dylan quote: "If you got something to say, speak or hold your peace. If it's information you want, get it from the police."

* * *

Chapter Forty-four

ALL WOMAN

"I never told anyone," Valerie insisted. "My sex life is my business. Cervantes might have known I was on the plane because I had to clear that through the agency. I never, never discuss my private life. Now, let's get in the shower."

Valerie VanDance began to unbutton Swept's shirt. Swept gently pushed her away.

"This isn't a good idea."

"I don't believe that, not for a second."

"It isn't. I have an important meeting tomorrow, and Cervantes told me things other than about you and me, which I don't like."

"Such as?"

"I don't want to say, but I think there are problems. Valerie, let me take you home. I need to get a good night's sleep. I have a very important meeting tomorrow and I don't want fatigue to be an excuse for any errors I make."

"Suit yourself, my friend," and Valerie left, without displaying or feeling any anger, Swept not unaware that this was much different from Ricki Hardson's earlier behavior.

"I'll call you tomorrow, Valerie, after my meeting. How about dinner?"

"You know my number," and Valerie VanDance left the room with a bounce in her step.

Dick Swept poured himself some club soda and sat down. He had a lot to think about. Swept sat in his favorite old green leather chair, a bona fide antique from the French empire period.

Swept had never been very interested in furniture, but years ago, an interior designer friend introduced him to the French empire period, and he liked that type of furniture ever since. Swept especially appreciated Louis XIV chairs and very much liked this one. He had the cushions overstuffed, making the chair incredibly comfortable. Swept turned on the Golf Channel, using Tivo, and sipped his club soda.

Swept wondered what Cervantes meant by his implication that the success of the mission to Chechnya for the WMDs was his idea. And why would the president of the United States want to see Swept?

As Swept thought about these issues, trying to consider all the possibilities and variables, his phone rang.

It was Louise.

* * *

Regina Bruxton felt increasingly close to Harold Ranger. Her personal challenges following the attack—struggling to regain muscle dexterity and strength, trying to obtain reimbursement from insurance companies, and internally feeling for the first time that one's financial prowess has little to do with the quality of interpersonal relations or one's health—led her to discuss with Harold Ranger a very personal health issue.

"Harold, I have something to tell you, a problem."

"Shoot. What is it?"

"It's rather personal."

"We're rather personal. Maybe I can help."

Taking a deep breath, Regina nervously announced, "I have what is known as an ovarian streak. I can't become pregnant. I'm not normal. My ovaries aren't normal. There, now you know and that's that! You can leave, stay or do what you want." Regina drew another breath and waited for her lover's response.

Ranger was surprised, this burst of information coming out of the blue, not related to anything. "That's it? That's the problem? Why would I leave? There are people with worse problems. Besides, your body doesn't appear vestigial to me," he said with a smile and a tone of kindness.

"I can't have children."

"Well, I don't know enough about ovarian streaks, or a lot about children. Why are you telling me this?"

"I don't know, but I am."

"Have you seen physicians about this, about this ovarian streak? There's a lot of recent research in fertility. When were you examined?"

"Years ago, when I was a child. My cycle isn't always normal and—look, I don't need to discuss this in any greater detail. For whatever reason, I've never told anyone. My parents had me evaluated years ago. The doctors wanted to ascertain whether I have Turner's syndrome, you know, the one where you only have only one X chromosome. I've never been analyzed for it, but ninety-seven percent of women with ovarian streaks have Turner's. I probably do too. My parents never wanted that confirmed, and I didn't either. Once I knew I wanted to be a physician, I never wanted to find out . . . you know . . . whether I'm less than full woman."

"This is ridiculous! Regina, you are all woman. If this bothers you, for God's sake, get another opinion. Get evaluated."

Regina buried her head in Harold Ranger's chest, something no woman had ever done. Ranger was not used to a woman confiding in him. Patients sometimes did, but that was done out of blind trust in a physician. Given that Harold Ranger had never heretofore liked the human condition, identifying with Bertrand Russell's love of mankind but hatred of people, Ranger had felt over the past few weeks that he was coming out of a shell, a cocoon.

Tenderly, Harold Ranger picked up Regina's chin, looking into her eyes. "Tomorrow, you call Ken Morrison or

Evan Hartwig, both experts in fertility at the college. I don't know much about this, but unless someone looks directly at your ovaries, they can't say a damn thing."

Ranger continued, "Did your gynecologist tell you to have a laparoscopy?"

Regina inhaled deeply. "No."

"Who's your gynecologist?"

."I don't have one. After I was told about this, I never returned to see a gynecologist."

"So you don't even know if this is accurate?"

"I know I don't menstruate regularly."

"But you do menstruate. For crying out loud, you're an intelligent woman, a physician. You don't have a gynecologist? Regina, check this out!"

"I have. I told you, my parents did."

"Regina, see one of these two doctors, Morrison or Hartwig. Get this answered. And don't think for a second that this alters how I feel about you."

"We'll see," said Regina, and she put her arms around her new lover and her best friend.

* * *

The following day, Ranger called Regina, interrupting her seeing patients. She had returned to work, part time. "Did you call Morrison or Hartwig?"

"You'll be proud of me. I did, but they're both away at the International Fertility Association meeting in Aspen. They'll be back in one week, but that week, I attend the American Plastic Surgery Federation meeting. The following week, I see Ken Morrison. Thanks for your interest."

"My pleasure. Listen, I'm free during your meeting. What do you say we go together?"

"Sure. What do you say we eat at my place tonight?"

"I say yes."

* * *

Regina and Harold slept with each other every night for the next two weeks. Regina confided that she used no contraceptive device since she was certain she could not become pregnant, holding back tears as she discussed her infertility.

Ranger said more than once, "A woman is a woman, with or without children."

"I'm not. It's not the children. I bet I have Turner's syndrome. The anxiety is killing me."

"Even if you do, so what? You are who you are, period—no pun intended! This is a ridiculous concern. You certainly made a man out of me, and if that doesn't make you a woman, then what does, or who cares? If there was ever anyone missing a chromosome, it's me, not you."

Regina smiled and almost laughed. She enjoyed being with Harold Ranger, more so every day. Not only was she increasingly happy in her new relationship, but her walking was improving daily, as were her surgical skills.

"I have a question for you," Ranger inquired.

"What?"

"You never discuss the rape, the attack. Is it because it was so terrifying?"

"Harold, I don't remember anything about it. He, or they, beat me so severely I don't recall most of that entire day. Thank goodness my other memory functions have gradually returned. I'm glad the police captured them. They admitted to the attack. As I understand it, they are two paraplegics and are both in jail."

"Well, sweet lady, I'm glad it's behind you and that it doesn't bother you. I just want you to know I think about you all the time." Harold Ranger kissed Regina passionately. He cupped her face with his hands and smiled. "Regina, there is something else I want to say."

"What's that?"

"I love you."

Regina smiled ear to ear. "I love you too, Harold," and the two embraced as neither had embraced before.

* * *

Chapter Forty-five

ALL MAN

Two weeks later, Regina Bruxton was concerned her menstruation was even more erratic than usual. She had not menstruated for ten weeks, three weeks longer than her previous record. She decided to test herself. She was pregnant.

Regina Bruxton's genes were fine. Now, she had to decide what to tell Harold Ranger. Regina did not support abortion, but she did not want to have a baby out of wedlock.

* * *

"Richard, good to talk to you."

Swept was amazed. Here she was again: Louise Konos. Louise was always in and out of his life, but whatever this woman's position in Swept's life was, it was always changing.

"I received your message the other day," Swept said. "Are you married?"

"I was engaged. I didn't know whether it was a good idea to share that with you, but I decided I wanted to."

"Sure, why not? Feel free to tell me whatever you need to."

"Are you upset I called?"

"No, and I'm not upset you're calling now. So, are you married?"

"No. His name was Jake and it didn't work out."

"This is a pretty short time we're talking about. You were engaged a few weeks ago and now you're not? I'm sorry."

"I'm not."

"Where are you now?"

"Billings. Billings, Montana."

"Billings, Montana? I don't recall your being an outdoor aficionado."

"I'm not an aficionado of any sort. You're the one who was perfect. Me, I was just passing through. I was never good enough."

Swept thought to himself, true, Louise was not good enough. Not because she wasn't attractive, bright, or kind. She was. But Louise never tried to understand his feelings about things, why he liked what he liked, why he enjoyed the art he did, or his core values. Louise and he both held high standards, but somehow, Louise never made him feel whole.

Swept looked down at his copy of *Harper's* and picked it up. "Louise, it's good to hear from you. Are we going to discuss quests for perfection or what? Are you all right?"

"I am, Richard. I really am. I just wanted you to know I'm not engaged, I'm not married, and if you want to see me sometime, I am here."

"Okay. Right now, I'm kind of busy."

"With what? Why don't you come out here?"

"When?"

"Tomorrow."

"Tomorrow? It would be nice to see you, but tomorrow is out."

"Why?"

"Well, if you must know, I have to meet with the president."

"The president of what?"

"The president of the United States, hard as it is to believe."

"Wow!" said a not-so-believing Louise. "Then, why don't I come out there? Maybe I can meet the president too."

"Be my guest. Everything else in my life is changing. Louise, honestly, it would be nice to see you, but I can't make it tomorrow. Maybe in the next few days. I'll call and let you know."

"Sure," and Louise hung up.

Swept poured himself a Ketel One, with a dash of scotch.

* * *

"Regina, this is great news. You're pregnant! What could be better?"

"Well, for one thing, we could be married, which we are not. For two . . ."

"All right, then, let's get married."

"You don't know if you want to get married. You—"

"I sure as hell do. This would be the best decision of my life and certainly the most spontaneous. Let's get married tomorrow."

"Harold, you need to think about this. I need to think about this. We—"

"We don't need to think about anything. I love you and you love me. And guess what? You're normal, just like I said. And guess what again? We're going to have a baby, at least you are. Let's get married and get married now."

"Are you sure you want to do this?"

"I have never been so certain of anything in my life."

"Are you ready to be a father?"

"Probably not. I'm not certain I was such a good one before. But I am certain of a couple of things."

Regina waited for Harold Ranger to continue.

"One, you are all woman. Two, I love you very much, and, three I want to marry you. That's pretty simple, at least it is to me."

"Harold, I love you too." Regina decided to cancel tomorrow's outpatient surgery, and Harold Ranger went to the closest nursing station for another cup of coffee.

* * *

Chapter Forty-six

MEET THE PRESIDENT

Swept had long understood that all men and women are created equal, some more successful than others, some more intelligent, and some more fortunate. But as a physician, a God-fearing man, and a loyal patriot, Dick Swept believed that all human beings share a common bond and a common unity.

Swept did not feel intimidated at meeting the president of the United States.

Despite living in the D.C. area and having made at least half a dozen trips there prior to his move from Houston, Swept had never been to the White House. He soon learned that the White House is really just a huge office, busy with multiple guards and scores of people scurrying around. After Swept entered the building, wearing his CIA identification badge, he noted little resemblance to depictions on the *West Wing* television program. Silly as it was, he actually felt disappointed.

Ms. Candice Roper, an officious woman in her thirties, ushered Swept through a maze of security channels. Ms. Roper had thin lips, wore her hair in a tight bun, and seemed a walking caricature of a spinster, were it not for her also being beautiful, well proportioned, and self-assured.

Ms. Roper continually moved her hands as she and Swept walked down multiple corridors, while she authoritatively barked orders at passersby. As the two approached the president's private study, Swept noticed the guards were now wearing different badges. Swept, still wearing his CIA badge, had been given a small laminated placard on a chain to place around his neck. Ms. Roper opened a drawer in the hallway and gave him two more badges, one purple with a yellow stripe, the other yellow with a purple stripe, both on plastic chains. Ms. Roper placed them around his neck, making certain they swiped both passes against a series of electronic devices as the two continued down the hall.

Suddenly, Candice Roper stopped walking and pointed Swept to the right. "Down that hall, Dr. Swept. The president is expecting you. Just knock on the door," and she disappeared.

Swept followed her directions and knocked on the door. After hearing no answer, he knocked again. "Come on in," said the voice with an accent he recognized. Within a few seconds, Dick Swept stood before the president of the United States of America.

* * *

Jokhar Gantemirov sat with Akhmad. "I thank you for the weapons. You have your money. I hope you do well with it, my friend."

"And you?" inquired Akhmad. "What about you? What

are you going to do? Are you going to use the weapons or are you going to sell them, if you haven't done so yet?"

"I don't know."

"I don't believe that, not for one second. Don't forget, I know everything that goes on here."

"Akhmad. You want to be president of Chechnya. You would be a good president. You understand our people. You can work with a wide variety of people, with different needs and different values. You can even work with the Russians. You have a purpose and have always had a purpose. Me, I have some money and may just hang out for a while. Besides, I have to be careful. I escaped from a Russian jail, and they are probably looking for me right now."

"They're incompetent blunder heads."

"Not always. I'll be in touch." Jokhar Gantemirov hugged his friend and walked toward his Ford pickup. His own money was safely hidden, and he wondered what he was going to do with his 500 million dollars, once the United States government fulfilled its promise and paid him the remaining 250 million dollars.

As Gantemirov walked away, he turned toward his friend. "Akhmad, are there more canisters?"

"What if there are? They are still mine."

Gantemirov nodded his head and thought about his money.

* * *

Chapter Forty-seven

A CONVERSATION WITH THE PRESIDENT

Dick Swept was alone with the president of the United States. He studied the president's face as the two talked. Swept had never seen the president in person, but it was striking how much he seemed to have aged while in office. After initial small talk about his home state, the president became very serious. "Dr. Swept, let me be frank. We have known for some time about botulinum toxin-Q. The American people and the media know nothing about this because the dangers are so substantial; we are afraid panic would ensue. Botulinum toxin-Q is extremely potent. A few drops can kill hundreds, possibly thousands. A quart can kill millions."

"Mr. President," Swept was trying to be formal and polite. "Am I the only one in the agency, aside from Major Cervantes, who knows about B-Q?'

"I and a few others have known for some time. Now, you and Major Cervantes know."

"With all respect, sir, why am I here? I'm relatively new to the CIA and Major Cervantes is my superior. I report to him. What is it I can do for you?"

"Major Cervantes is being arrested as we speak."

"Arrested? Why?"

"We knew exactly how many canisters there were of botulinum toxin-Q. There were 1,944 canisters, packed twenty-eight to a box, totaling 1,932. That leaves twelve. Major Cervantes tried to buy some canisters, at least one, several weeks ago. He did not succeed. My concern, our nation's concern, is that we find the other twelve canisters as soon as possible. Now that we have the sixty-nine boxes and someone active in the field who knows the players, we can get rid of Cervantes."

Swept was trying to process the information about Cervantes, wondering if it had any bearing on Cervantes's comments to Swept about his relationship with Valerie. "There are other canisters?"

"Twelve of them. Major Cervantes knew this and tried to buy them."

"Why would he do that?"

"We can think of a number of reasons, ranging from financial gain to showing off what a great agent he is. I have no idea. But he never told anyone else in the agency, including you, so we think something is sordid."

"I never knew about them. I presume, but I could be wrong, that Jokhar Gantemirov, the Chechen I worked with, didn't know either. May I ask how you know Major Cervantes never told me?"

"It would have been in your reports. It would have been in his reports that he told you. Also, we bugged his office."

"You bugged his office?"

"You bet. And in case you're wondering if it was legal, it was. We had permission from Justice. The man was a threat to our nation's security."

"What happens now? What are you going to do with him?"

"We're taking him to Guantánamo, in Cuba. He'll cooperate. We've been listening to him in his office and know about what he has done and his personal life, including an affair with an administrator, whose personal life we don't want to disrupt. She loves him, for whatever reason, and thinks he'll marry her. He isn't marrying anyone. He's going to prison."

"Do the people who bugged his conversations also know about the canisters?"

"The people who made the recordings from Cervantes's office did not listen to them. The people who know about these canisters, aside from you and Major Cervantes and some trusted agents interrogating him, are the director of the CIA, secretary of defense, secretary of state, national security adviser, and the vice president. And British prime minister Tony Blair and Russian president Vladimir Putin"

"The prime minister and President Putin? You are kidding."

"No."

"But the press is all over you and Prime Minister Blair for not finding the weapons of mass destruction. You could end that in a moment by telling them."

"Not a chance. I might plummet in the polls over this WMD issue, but I have to do what is good for the country. If people know you can fill a soda can or a soda bottle with botulinum toxin-Q and wipe out one million people, panic would set in at every school, bus station, airport, sports arena, church, synagogue, whatever.

"There are other issues too," the president continued. "President Putin is certain that if the Russian army knew the Chechen rebels have access to botulinum toxin-Q, they would insist on an even stronger response in Chechnya. More than that, since many of the Russian military senior officers believe Putin is a weakling, and I can assure you he is not, they might try to take over the country, insisting President Putin is inadequate to protect it. That would be devastating for Russia and our relationship with them and possibly send us back to the cold war. If the armed forces took over in Russia, and President Putin believes this will happen were it known that the Chechen rebels have the weapons of mass destruction, it would be good for no one. The bottom line is President Putin wants us to keep this quiet, and we all agree."

Dick Swept was glued to the president's words, as he continued, "Russia is increasingly a good ally, and we need Russian support in foreign affairs. We cannot let it be known that the weapons of mass destruction exist, and although we have most of the canisters, some are still in Chechen rebels' hands."

Swept was listening, trying to follow the logic.

Swept was silent, the president astute and polite enough to allow Dick Swept to let this information seep into his brain. Swept inquired, "May I ask, how did you find out about Major Cervantes and the extra canisters?"

"Our man in Baghdad. Everyone thinks they know him, but they do not."

"Who is he?"

"They call him 'the Chemist.'"

Swept, aghast, looked at the president. "I met him. He's the guy? He was there when Gantemirov ruthlessly killed several Sunni Muslims."

"He is the guy. Major Cervantes was able to make contact, through some CIA source, with the Chemist, not knowing the Chemist was our man. Cervantes tried to buy some canisters from him. The Chemist told us. Dr. Swept, we have a lot to discuss. The country needs your help.

"Our undercover agent, the Chemist, tells us there are no other weapons of mass destruction aside from the extra canisters. For all we know, he's wrong and there are more than he knows. I don't want Congress to decrease our budget for the ongoing search for the weapons of mass destruction. There are several in Congress who would say, 'We found the WMDs. Now, let's stop searching for more.'

"I was elected president of this great nation to do a job. I intend to do that job. The American people placed their trust in me, and I have no intention of letting them down. I can't release information that we not only know what are the weapons of mass destruction but know who has them. We don't know where they are. Well, that's it, in a nutshell."

"One more question, Mr. President."

The president nodded, inviting Swept to ask. "Why didn't we capture Gantemirov, interrogate him, and try to find out about the extra canisters from him?"

"That would have been appropriate, perhaps. Major Cervantes elected to do nothing. Regardless, we don't know whether Gantemirov or Cervantes knew about the canisters at the time you interacted with Gantemirov. This is all moving very fast, too fast. I'm concerned that the Chechen rebels, now that they have money, will initiate major attacks against Russia. Then, we'll have a real problem, especially given that we know about the weapons. Moscow is working as hard as they can on this, as we speak."

"Mr. President, I'm happy to help in any way I can, but I'm not certain what I can do."

"Dr. Swept, we have a lot to discuss."

* * *

Chapter Forty-eight

A REAL FLAKE

"Regina," Harold Ranger exclaimed, "I have never been happier in my life. Actually, 'happy' is the wrong word. I have never felt so whole, so complete. Let's get married now. You're normal, ovarian streak and all, which is something I could have told you. I never doubted for a second that you were complete, normal as can be. Let's do it. Let's get married."

Regina Bruxton gazed steadfastly at what formerly had been a face that never engendered any feelings within her. Here he was, Harold Ranger, M.D., a world-famous scientist whose main focus heretofore had been the study of mitochondria, the small organelles that provide energy inside cells.

Ranger, also a superb clinician, had previously not had much interest in treating patients. From a clinical standpoint, he had never been empathetic, caring only about his science and not people. It had been easier for Harold Ranger to interact with test tubes and agar plates than with humans. Now that he was in love with Regina Bruxton, everything had changed.

Ranger expanded his clinic hours, eagerly scheduled more patients, and even took weekend call when he was in town. Ranger also established a myoadenylate deaminase clinic, focusing on the role this chemical has in muscle disease. Many patients with muscle disease enthusiastically welcomed this clinic, the acronym of which is MAD. The *Houston Chronicle* published several articles on the MAD Clinic, lauding Dr. Ranger's valuable scientific insights.

Ranger had become a different man. Regina made him a different man. He loved her, and Regina loved him. "Well," Regina said jokingly, "what do I do about the initials on my silver? Your name begins with an *R*, mine with a *B*. And I don't want the name 'Bruxton-Ranger.' It sounds like a cereal or an SUV."

"I don't care about that. And I don't have any silver, so this way, we keep yours and save the money." The two chuckled and made arrangements to marry later that week in the local courthouse.

* * *

The Chemist turned to Akhmad, "What are we going to do with the twelve canisters? We used some toxin from one of them, but that canister is still nine-tenths full. I suggest we open it in synagogues in Russia."

"My friend," said Akhmad, "I don't understand your hatred of Jews. I despise Russians far more than Jews. Besides, your telling me that your dislike of Jews resulted in your being fired from the pharmaceutical company was inaccurate. I checked into that company and only two or three Jews work there, and they work in the shipping department. You were fired because of cocaine addiction."

Akhmad continued, "Also, there are hardly any Jews in Iraq, and you constantly complain about Jews in Baghdad. We all hate Israel, I guess, but you never stop complaining about Israel. And now, you want to kill Jews in Russia? Cocaine is making you paranoid."

With that, Akhmad Edilkhanov leaned over to the mirror from which the Chemist was beginning to snort his lines of coke. Akhmad became astonished and angry. He looked carefully at the powder, squinting his eyes. Then he put some on his index finger and tasted it. "This isn't cocaine! This is flour! Why are you doing this? Who are you?"

"Must be a bad batch," the Chemist said, nonchalantly.

"I do not believe that!" said Akhmad, eyes bulging with anger. Within seconds, two huge thugs were holding the questionably fake addict.

Akhmed bellowed, "Who are you?"

"Who do you think I am? Are you crazy? I'm the one who developed botulinum toxin-Q. I'm the one who refused to be bribed about the toxin. I told you when Major Cervantes contacted me. I don't know about *this* cocaine," looking at the powder sitting on the tarnished mirror, realizing it did look more like flour than coke. "I don't know what the stuff is like until I take a hit. I thought this was Peruvian flake."

Akhmad Edilkhanov studied the Chemist with care. "The only flake here is you. I don't need you now and I don't know whether I'll need you later. You may very well be dispensable. Now, why are you asking about the canisters?"

"First, because I developed what's in them, namely the toxin. It is mine, my product. Next, I need to know what my own plans are going to be. If you stay in Chechnya, where do I fit in? Do I go back to Iraq or what?"

"Where do you fit in?" asked Akhmad, as he motioned to his thugs to loosen their grip on the Chemist. "How do I know you didn't turn and spy for the Americans or the Russians?"

"Spare me. Why would I do that?"

"I don't know. Maybe for money, power, more so-called Peruvian or because you are one of the most screwed-up people I know. I'm going to be watching you, and if I suspect anything, you're dead."

With that, the Chemist opened another packet of cocaine, showed it to Akhmad and said, "You want to check this? Maybe this is flour too."

This cocaine certainly looked different. Akhmad felt and then tasted the powder. It was real.

The Chemist was glad he always carried a packet of real cocaine.

* * *

Chapter Forty-nine

FIND THE WEAPONS

"Here is the problem, Dr. Swept," the president confided, fatigue exacerbating his southern drawl. "We made contact with a man in Iraq who was a little bizarre but brilliant. He had developed a biological program of incredibly lethal chemicals, capable of mass destruction. However, he became frustrated at the ineptitude of the Iraqi regime and very upset when Saddam's men tortured and murdered a local Baghdad woman whom he hoped to marry. We don't know why Saddam's men killed her. We also don't know why Saddam also killed the parents of one of his friends. In the midst of poverty and anger, this man, known simply as 'the Chemist,' joined our side. He told us about the weapons of mass destruction and Saddam Hussein's intention to wreak havoc across the planet with his chemicals.

"The problem," the president continued, "and there are many problems, is that we can't always maintain contact with the Chemist."

"What's his real name?"

"You would think we would know, but we don't. Regardless, we don't always have solid contact with him. Our people had no idea Saddam was going to move the botulinum when he did, three weeks before our invasion. We found out when the Chemist contacted us, somewhere from the Russian Republic of Georgia. None of us, including him, knew they were going to Chechnya."

"We also had a mole in Grozny, a young woman named Angelina, who became Akhmad Edilkhanov's lover. As you may know, Akhmad is a prominent Chechen terrorist who is also politically active. Through Akhmad, Angelina was able to touch base with the Chemist. For some reason, Akhmad had her killed. The long and short of this is, we found out about the 1,944 canisters. Our plan was to storm Grozny and capture everything. However, our plan hit the skids."

"Because? . . ."

"Because of Jokhar Gantemirov. He escaped jail, we're not sure how, and became involved in this crazy Stickman X movement and somehow wound up in Grozny. Evidently, he's a friend of Akhmad's. We didn't know whether Gantemirov was going to take some of the canisters or what we should do. When he contacted us, asking to speak to you, we figured, 'What the heck?' We took what we could get our hands on. The problem now is that we don't have all the canisters and don't know what Akhmad is going to do with the ones, supposedly twelve, that he has."

The president continued, "We have a real problem. I am terrified of leaks from this office, the CIA, and across the board. I'm sure you read the papers. We have leaks and can't stop them all. The secretary of defense, the CIA director, and our National Security Agency advisor are people I am positive we can trust. But I can't vouch for anyone else."

"So, why am I here?" asked Swept.

"Why are you here? Because there is nobody else. Once Cervantes became involved, we bugged his office and home. He tried to buy some of the canisters himself through the Chemist. After Gantemirov messed things up by entering the picture, and we're still not certain how he fits in, and you became involved with Gantemirov, we had to tell Cervantes about the weapons of mass destruction and what we were doing. However, we never told him about our man inside. He never knew, and still doesn't, that the Chemist works for us."

"I want to be certain I understand this. The Chemist, whose real name we don't know, is the person from whom Cervantes tried to purchase extra canisters of botulinum toxin-Q?"

"It seems that way."

"How do you . . . or 'we' . . . know that Cervantes was not just trying to get some of the chemical for his own analysis?"

"We don't, but that wouldn't make a lot of sense. The CIA has procedures, and he is not authorized to make decisions like that. We're going to question him until we have the truth."

"Mr. President, again, what do you want me to do?"

"Find the canisters."

"How?"

"I don't know, but find them. You have full authority from this office to do anything you need to do to find them. This office will help you in any way you need—men, money, equipment, anything—just find the canisters!"

"And I presume you don't want the media to know about this? If they did, that would certainly halt an awful lot of criticism about your inability to find the weapons of mass destruction."

"I'm certain it would. But people would go crazy all over the world if they knew about the extra canisters. And again, President Putin keeps asking me, personally, to refrain from announcing that these weapons exist. We had to tell him, once we knew that Chechens had weapons of mass destruction. If we announce that we have the weapons, people will want to know where they are and how we know all this. The issue of the Chechens having them would certainly come up, and the Russian army would probably take over. It's better that we keep it quiet. Besides, as I said before, how do we know there aren't pockets of other potent weapons elsewhere? No, I can take the heat. I may not always be popular, but that's okay. At the risk of sounding self-serving, or grandiose, the nation's interests remain more important than mine."

"You are a great man."

"Not really. I'm just doing my job. Now, Dr. Swept, you do yours. Find those canisters and find them fast."

"And if I do? Then what? Do we destroy them, bury them, or what?"

"We'll cross that bridge later. First, let us find the canisters. I thank you for your time, but I have some other appointments. You are a good man, Dr. Swept. Our country is counting on you."

The president returned to his desk and touched an ivory button. Within a few moments, the secretary of defense entered the Oval Office. "Dr. Swept?" said the secretary, extending his hand.

"A pleasure to meet you, sir," and the two men left the office, the secretary motioning Swept down the second corridor on the left, and then into a large room on the right.

*   *   *

Chapter Fifty

BAD COFFEE

Cervantes was livid. He had never been arrested in his life. "You bastards bugged my office? My home? I never bribed anyone. If it weren't for me, you wouldn't have a thing."

"Well," said one of the CIA agents, "you tried to bribe someone for a canister. You never told anyone at the Company about it. Why not? You tried to get a canister and we want to know why."

Major Cervantes was trying to think fast. True, he tried to bribe one of the Chechen thieves, the one who called himself "the Chemist," but how could the CIA know this unless the Chemist was a plant, a mole? But were he a mole, someone certainly would have told Cervantes, since he was running the operation.

All Cervantes wanted was one canister. He could have set up a go-between and sold the damn thing to his own government, to any government, for millions. Then, he would have enough money for himself, Carol Bernson, and his children to leave his wife. Any thought of his wife continued to sicken him.

Cervantes decided to cut to the chase and show his loyalty. "Gentlemen, I don't know why you think what you do or everything that's going on, but let me share something with you."

The men listened attentively. "As I said, were it not for me, you would have had no idea about the WMDs. This goes beyond anything you know."

The agents were listening.

"Because of me, because I went outside protocol, we now know about the weapons of mass destruction. And just as I went out of protocol to engage in something that netted us the WMDs, which I shall explain in a minute, I also tried to obtain a canister for ourselves, to analyze it, and develop antidotes. True, I did not go through channels. We've had too many leaks, and I didn't want to take chances."

"Go on," said one of the men, the shorter one, with a faint scar across his right forehead that crossed into his adjacent cheek. "What did you do outside protocol that led to the WMDs?"

"I arranged, indirectly, for Jokhar Gantemirov to escape." The men continued to look at Cervantes, without expression, as he explained how easy it was to bribe the Moldovan guards to be lax, leave doors open, all in the name of *glasnost.* The reason, Cervantes explained, was because he was convinced that Gantemirov had underground terrorist ties in Chechnya and Russia and, if he escaped, would touch base with these terrorists.

"Did you have anyone follow him?'

"I didn't have to. I knew, sooner or later, the Company would become involved in tracking him down, and then we'd know more about his terrorist links. And that's exactly what happened."

After further questioning, the agents left the interrogation room and reported directly to the director of the Central Intelligence Agency, as instructed, who then telephoned the White House.

Within a few minutes, the president was on the phone with Swept, who was meeting with the secretary of defense. "Here's where we stand: Gantemirov's escape was arranged by Cervantes, who bribed guards at Gantemirov's jail. He had this birdbrain idea to let him escape and then see what Gantemirov did."

Swept, wondering if he were out of turn, responded nonetheless, "His idea resulted in the death of two tourists, Jennifer Pettigrew, probably a barmaid, and who knows who else? I'll say you've got a problem in the CIA. How did that happen?"

"I don't know, but because of Gantemirov, our plans fell through in Chechnya. At least, we think so. The Chemist was supposed to tell us where the canisters were, the good guys were supposed to come in, take them, and we were all supposed to live happily ever after. Instead, this guy, Akhmad Edilkhanov, still has twelve canisters and, from what we understand, a lot of money. We don't know how much money Gantemirov gave him, but it was probably in the hundreds of millions. Gantemirov, somehow, got his hands on everything, ranging from the weapons of mass destruction to Ms. Pettigrew, the Allistons, and probably a lot more."

"Including, I suspect, Stickman X events."

"Probably true, Dr. Swept. Well, Cervantes isn't going anywhere. He still doesn't know that the Chemist is our man, and we need everything played close to the chest. Are you able to find the canisters?"

"I don't know, but I can try."

"Trying isn't enough. You've got to find them. All hell is going to break loose, and soon, if you don't." The president hung up the telephone, and Swept returned to his conversation with the secretary of defense.

* * *

Swept spent considerable time in numerous meetings, being briefed by the secretary and the director of the CIA. Swept's mind teemed with information, as well as rules, regulations, and procedures that the two men stressed. At the closure of his most recent meeting, Swept left the Pentagon, briefly stopped at his laboratory, checked on some of the intracellular recording paradigms, especially the paroxysmal depolarization shifts, and returned to his apartment. He needed to finalize his plan.

Despite it being late in the day, Swept decided to go for a jog. Jogging was always good in situations like this, helping him to relax and focus his energies. In a short time, Swept was in Rock Creek Park. Here, again, was Larry Leventine, still scowling and staring. Swept passed him, perspiration dripping into his eyes, having forgotten his headband, and remembered when he formerly jogged in Houston, always listening to Dylan. Bob Dylan's music still filled Swept with energy, but Swept did not want to be distracted by the singer-songwriter's words. Rather, he wanted to think. Swept had enough energy inside him.

When Swept returned to his apartment, there was another message from Louise. She was coming into town, tomorrow.

* * *

Akhmad Edilkhanov had survived multiple dangerous exchanges with Russians as well as with various Chechen factions, all because he was a cautious man. Being exceedingly cautious, Akhmad no longer felt comfortable with the Chemist. He decided to test him.

"We are going to need one of the canisters. It is time to kill Russians."

"Good," said the man under suspicion. "Just tell me what to do."

"I will." The two men and a handful of others climbed into the pickup truck, Akhmad and the Chemist sat with the driver in the front, while the remainder sat in the bed of the vehicle. They went through several concrete and barbed wire checkpoints, often sticking money out the window as they passed, encountering only little difficulty. They carried no major weapons, only small firearms, except for a canister that looked like a coffee thermos. No guard at any checkpoint found it necessary to look inside the coffee thermos.

The Chemist nervously inquired, "What if someone looks inside the thermos? It will kill us all,"

"Mr. Chemist, do not worry. If that happens, we'll say it's stuck or bribe the guard with money or vodka or shoot him. No one inspects a thermos."

After they arrived at the hospital, Akhmad turned to the Chemist. "Walk in with the thermos, tell them you're bringing some hot coffee for the nurses, make up whatever you have to, and leave. At a minimum, someone will open it."

"Isn't this a waste of the chemical? There's enough in there to take out the entire city."

"That is no longer accurate. I poured out most of the contents into the other eleven canisters. There are only a few drops in there. I filled the rest with coffee."

"Then it won't work."

"Why not?"

"Caffeine destroys the lethal part of the toxin. It's a phosphodiesterase inhibitor and destroys the 'Q' portion of the toxin."

Akhmad nodded. "All right then, let's call it quits," and threw the canister, which he knew to be empty, onto the street.

"I still don't trust you," said Akhmad.

"I guess not," responded the Chemist.

* * *

Chapter Fifty-one

DEATH AND THE CANISTERS

As promised, the United States government wired the remaining 250 million dollars to Jokhar Gantemirov 's Zurich account. In addition, Swept left a message he hoped Gantemirov would receive. "Call Dick Swept." The bank delivered the message. Even the Swiss will deliver a message for a depositor who delivers that much money, especially when the message seemed as innocuous as this.

"Well, Dr. Swept," said Jokhar Gantemirov wondering whether he should keep Swept's telephone number that the bank had provided. "The bank left a message to call you. You're not going to tell me this is counterfeit, are you?"

"No, I'm not. I have a problem and need your help."

"Why would you think your problems are mine?"

"I don't. But I still need your help. There are twelve more canisters. Did you know that?"

"No. I had no idea whether there were more canisters. Besides, I wouldn't have told you if I did, but I didn't. Regardless, I kept my part of the bargain. I gave you the canisters. You gave me the money. That's that."

"We are still keeping our side of the bargain. You have your money. But we have a problem. My government says there are other canisters and we're concerned they will fall into the wrong hands."

"They probably will. So what?"

"If they fall into the hands of Chechen rebels and they kill Russians, a lot of them, Russia will probably demolish your so-called republic forever."

"I see. And if nothing happens to the Russians, they will leave us alone, like they haven't done for half a millennium, and we shall live happily ever after, like your oppressed people in Puerto Rico?"

"Look, let's not get into politics, yours or mine. Understand something: If you or your colleagues kill a large number of Russians, everyone you know will probably get killed. Aside from a major war, the Russians have never lost the number of people one canister can kill. I need to know about the other canisters. Can you help me?"

"The stinking Russians lost over twenty million to the Germans during World War II, and as far as I'm concerned, that wasn't enough. However, for all I know or you know or anyone knows, if there are more canisters, they can also be used against the United States, France or Chad or Sierra Leone for all I care. Look, I delivered what I said I would. I now have my money. You find someone else to play the good guy."

There was a pause. The Chechen continued, "Swept, there are no good guys. There are no bad guys. These things don't make a difference. We are what we are and that's it. You're a Christian, I presume. I'm a Muslim, a Sunni Muslim. I could have been born you, or you me, but I wasn't. Hell, I could have been born Chinese or Japanese, black, brown, or purple. We are what we are. There is no inherent value in any of it. What matters is money, and I have it. So, as your governor of California says, 'Hasta la vista, baby.'" The line went dead.

* * *

Four days later, a frustrated Dick Swept heard the news, directly from the national security adviser. Over seven thousand Russian commuters had been killed. They were in the subway. All died from respiratory paralysis. The media said it was due to a severe strain of SARS, the deadly flu-like disease that originated in the People's Republic of China. However, even the media could not swallow another lie when, two days later, everyone in the Bolshoi Theater, the Maly Theater, the Musical Operetta Theater, and the Young Spectators' Theater, all in the heart of Moscow, dropped dead during the performance.

The following day, the same scourge of death occurred in the Museum of Contemporary Russian History, the Andrei Sakharov Museum, the Pushkin Literary Museum, and the Tolstoy Museum. Moscow was under attack. People were dying by the tens of thousands

* * *

A photocopy of a letter sent to the president of Russia arrived at the American embassy in Moscow, making demands and consequences very clear. "We intend to kill Russians, millions of them, and destroy all civil life in your putrid Russia unless Russia leaves Chechnya. In one week, we kill millions." There was a picture of an empty canister, with Stickman X painted on it in bold red.

The embassy contacted the Russian authorities, who had their own copy of the letter, as well as the State Department in the United States. The State Department relayed a copy to the secretary of defense. The president asked the secretaries of defense and state, as well as the directors of the FBI, CIA, and National Security Agency whether anyone, especially Dick Swept, had made progress.

The secretary of defense spoke first, "Not that I know of. Swept is somewhere in Europe, trying to do something, but I'm not sure what. He is aware that the toxin caused the Moscow deaths."

"Any ideas, people?"

Responses were negative.

The director of the CIA responded next, "We'll have to see what our neurologist friend does."

The president was perturbed. "He'd better do something. This is more than a brain tumor," and the president walked out of the office.

* * *

Dick Swept left another message at the bank for Gantemirov, but this time, he did not hear from him. He learned through the CIA that the account had been closed.

Swept had an idea and telephoned the president of the United States. "Mr. President, I have a plan. I need help from President Putin, that is if he is still president of Russia."

"I guess he is, if the military hasn't killed him. What do you want?"

Dick Swept told the president his plan. The president telephoned his Russian counterpart, Vladimir Putin. Within a few hours, the FSB, under direct orders from President Putin, faxed certain documents to Dr. Richard Michael Swept, who was staying at the Crillon Hotel in Paris.

* * *

Swept arrived in Grozny on a fairly pleasant Citation X flight, exchanging innuendos with the attractive female pilot. A driver met him at the airstrip and took Swept to his rendezvous with a Russian agent, Andrei, who seemed to know his way around Grozny.

"I arranged the meeting with Akhmad," said Andrei. "It was difficult, but not impossible. He and his men now continually change locations, and their whereabouts is never the same. However, I did establish contact and followed your instructions. I said someone from the CIA wanted to talk to him on behalf of Russian business. You can guess what he probably thinks."

A short time later, Dick Swept was in the room with Akhmad Edilkhanov. Akhmad's men poured Swept some tea, and the two sat at a small table, facing each other, Akhmad's men standing behind them. Swept was pleased to see the Chemist there. Neither man acknowledged the other.

"You wanted to see me?"

"Yes. I have some information for Jokhar Gantemirov. I don't know where he is, but I figured you did." Before Akhmad could say anything, Swept handed him some documents obtained from the Russian Ministry of Education.

The Russian Ministry of Education maintains all information pertaining to Russian citizens' education records and all information concerning adoption. "As you can see," Swept said, "Martin Heidegger, the famous German philosopher who supported Hitler, had a love affair with several students, many of them young Jewish women. One of them was Hannah Arendt, a bright young Jewish girl, nineteen years old, who subsequently escaped the Nazis and lived in America, where she became famous in her own right."

Swept continued, "The history books are filled with stories about Heidegger's love affairs. Although he was a Nazi, he truly had a thing for young Jewish women, and Hannah Arendt was only one of them. Arendt discussed her relationship with Heidegger in her later years, when she was an accomplished philosopher."

Akhmad Edilkhanov interrupted, "This is why you wanted to see me? To give me a lecture on German history and the Nazis?"

"Bear with me. These papers show that one of these women, we don't know who"—showing Akhmad the document—"mothered a child with this famous Nazi. Heidegger's wife knew about the affair and went crazy after she learned about the baby, a baby girl. His wife wanted him to kill the baby. Heidegger refused and shipped the baby to Austria. Later, after the war, the young girl was sent to Moscow, where she was raised in a foster home by a married couple, both Muslims. The husband was a government worker, someone tied into the postal system, and who was later transferred to Chechnya. After he was in Chechnya for a few years, it seems he left his job and joined one of the secret societies. The child was Jokhar Gantemirov's maternal grandmother. Do you know what that means?"

"No, I don't, and I'm not sure I care. You are wasting my time." Akhmad Edilkhanov put down his teacup and started to rise from his chair.

Swept held up his right hand, palm extended. "I am not wasting anyone's time. You may not care, but Jokhar Gantemirov will. This means that Jokhar Gantemirov is Jewish."

"Hardly," said Akhmad, firmly placing down his tea and rising from the chair. "I've known Jokhar Gantemirov all my life. We've worshipped in mosques together. He is a Sunni Muslim As for you, you can get out."

"That may be, but in the eyes of Judaism, the religion is passed down through the mother. His maternal grandmother was Jewish. Her children, including her daughter, were Jewish. That daughter's child, Jokhar Gantemirov, is Jewish."

"So what?" Akhmad was ushering Swept to the door. "Why are you boring me with this? Why would Gantemirov care?"

"You tell him. See whether he does."

"This is why you came to see me? So I can tell my friend he's a Jew?"

"You tell Gantemirov I want to talk to him. You tell him if he doesn't call me at this number"—and Swept gave Akhmad a series of digits—"every jerk in the Middle East with a gun will know his ancestry."

"Do you think Gantemirov will care? Do you think people who know him will care about his background which, for all I know, you forged?"

"Actually," said Swept, "I do think he will care. And it's not forged. Everyone else on this planet cares about people's backgrounds, so why should Jokhar Gantemirov be different? I need to talk to him. Also, tell him one more thing."

"Don't tell me. Let me guess."

"Tell him we are taking our money back."

"What money?"

"Tell him. He will understand."

Swept left the room, fairly confident that no one was going to blow his head off and fairly certain Akhmad had no idea that the real reason Swept sought him out was to deliver the old parched documents, which secretly contained a small embedded microchip. The CIA's sophisticated GPS satellite tracking system could easily follow the whereabouts of the document, which Swept thought would stay, at least for a short while, with Akhmad.

* * *

Jokhar Gantemirov telephoned Swept within a few hours. "The money is mine, you prick! I already have it. It stays with me. And if you did anything to make it self-destruct or whatever bullshit the CIA does, those people I told you about, the ones you hold dear, will be dead."

Swept remembered that Louise was coming in to see him in Washington, D.C., and he had inadvertently stood her up.

"We don't want the money. The money is yours. I said what I said because I wanted you to call me. We need your help. You must help us. Where are the canisters? They're slaughtering people in Moscow!"

"I don't know, and I don't give a damn about the people in Moscow. I also don't care who my grandmother was. And I am not Jewish. Besides, even if I were, my maternal grandfather was a Nazi."

"You won't help us?"

"I won't help you, and I wouldn't if I could. Besides, I don't know anything."

"Fair enough." Swept replaced the receiver.

Swept telephoned the White House and spoke to the president. Shortly, five C-130s, all part of the Sixteenth Special Operations Wing, arrived in Grozny, negotiating potholes and debris on the tarmac. American high technology, especially the GPS microchip embedded in the documents, provided the exact coordinates of Akhmad Edilkhanov's whereabouts.

Five special-ops teams, totaling fifty men, each wearing Point Blank armor, Kevlar helmets, CQC tactical goggles, Bates boots, and carrying weapons ranging from SOF .308-caliber carbines by ArmaLite to Kimber Tactical Custom II .45-caliber pistols, as well as M16s, AR-15s, and the new Lewis

Machine and Tool Carbine/CQB MRP, descended upon an ill-prepared Edilkhanov and his contingent. Akhmad had never expected such an attack, and despite valiant efforts, he and his men were soon dead, most of them burned alive as the Americans conflagrated the compound, including the stored petrol. Fortunately, there were no U.S. casualties, which was an unanticipated surprise.

During the struggle, the Chemist made it to the periphery, waving a white rag and making it clear he wished to surrender. The U.S. soldiers had been briefed on who he was and had even been provided his picture.

The Chemist, gasping for breath in the midst of the smell of cordite, burning fuel, and burnt flesh, explained, "They poured the contents of one of the twelve canisters into the remaining eleven. Then they used one of the eleven, using much more than they had to, on the subways, theaters, and museums, leaving ten. The toxin is far more lethal than they realized. They could have used only a fraction. Anyway, they're all here, buried and beneath the blast wall in the southern part of the compound."

Amidst the rubble and the smell of carnage, eight feet below the ground was a trunk. A giant Stickman X, painted with blue, white, and red colors, parodying the colors of the Russian Federation flag, was on top of the trunk. Inside the container were ten canisters, each sealed with duct tape and each boasting another Stickman X.

Dick Swept notified the president who, in turn, called Russian president Putin. "Mr. President, we have the canisters. It's over."

* * *

Chapter Fifty-two

THE PRESIDENT'S MAN

When Dick Swept returned to Washington, he listened to an irate message from Louise, an invitation to dinner from Valerie VanDance, and a message from Michael Drake, informing him that Regina Bruxton had married Harold Ranger and was going to have a baby. Ranger had announced this proudly to the entire medical community.

Swept initially felt strange. At one time, he had held such strong feelings for Regina Bruxton. They had laughed together, embraced each other, yet they never shared true intimacy. Swept had attributed Regina's seemingly lack of emotion to her lust for money, but he did not know to what he might attribute his own current feelings of emotional nonchalance.

Swept had no idea, Harold Ranger now being informed otherwise, that Regina carried a burden of wondering about her genetic load, an issue fueled by her clinical history but distorted by her own thinking. And now, here she was, Regina Bruxton, marrying Swept's former chairman, a man whom Swept had always thought held no feelings for anyone or anything, short of his scientific queries. And to further complicate matters, Swept still remained alone, thinking about a woman he truly loved—so he believed—but whom he absolutely did not want to marry. Swept was not against just marrying Ricki. He was against marrying anyone. In this midst, he still felt strong, secure, and at ease with himself. But on some level, it bothered him to be alone.

This loneliness, if one could call it that, was becoming a part of Dick Swept's life, as was cynicism, a quiet arrogance, and killing.

Swept poured himself a vodka but then decided not to drink it. Instead, he went outside to run, trying to focus on the meeting he had in a few hours with the president of the United States.

Again, there was the scowling, sour-faced Larry Leventine. The paraplegic sat in his wheelchair, holding a copy of the *Washington Post,* the headline discussing the capture of Chechen rebels responsible for the deaths in Moscow.

* * *

"Dr. Swept, we cannot express how thankful we are for your help. You found the canisters and saved the day. The people in this room"—the president looked at the secretary of defense, the CIA director, the national security adviser and, a recent addition, the secretary of homeland security—"are the only people, aside from President Putin and the British prime minister, who know about the weapons of mass destruction. We are not mentioning this to the public."

Swept was silent.

"Do you understand why?"

"You believe the Russian people will be too upset and the armed forces will take over the government."

"More than 'too upset,'" said the secretary of homeland security. The secretary of defense chimed in, "We have a problem. We do not know whether there are other weapons of mass destruction. We believe that Iraq is filled with weapons. The place is a living munitions dump. Also, President Putin believes if it comes out that we knew about the canisters, which we did, people will ask whether we all could have done more sooner, so that so many Russians wouldn't have died."

The secretary of defense continued, "What could we have done? I guess we could have attacked Akhmad and his gang when you were there with Gantemirov, but we never would have been able to test anything or know what was really going on. For all we knew, the B-Q was a hoax. We had to test the chemical ourselves."

The national security adviser, an intelligent outspoken woman in her midforties, spoke next, "None of this would have happened if Major Cervantes had kept his nose clean. His arranging the escape of Gantemirov—"

"Which would also make the Russians angry," added the voice from the secretary of state.

The woman from National Security Agency continued, "Cervantes arranging Gantemirov's escape makes us look like a bunch of idiots, which in some ways we are. However, we did obtain the WMDs and arrested the culprits responsible for the Moscow deaths. There were several metal boxes in the rubble after our attack, and we obtained several names. Those whom we captured were, shall we say, 'encouraged' to tell us about their comrades."

"How do you know Akhmad and his group killed the Muscovites?" inquired Swept.

"The Chemist told us," the CIA director added. "He was also helpful supplying names of other coconspirators."

"What is the Chemist's real name?" asked Swept.

Everyone shook their head. No one knew. "You know," the CIA director said, "under Presidents Clinton and Carter, the CIA was essentially dismantled. We were forbidden to work with known criminals. Over half the people we normally work with are known criminals—that's why they know about the things we need to learn. Now, after September 11, we're more sensible. I don't know his name, and I don't need to know, but he surely helped us."

"Gentlemen," Swept interjected, "is there anything else you want me to do, or may I go? I do have a lab investigating Alzheimer's disease and memory research, if I can ever get there."

The president stood, prompting everyone else to stand. "Dr. Swept, I need to talk to you." Everyone, except Swept, left the room. The president walked over to Swept.

"I would appreciate your being a special envoy, a special liaison, to the Oval Office. You are among the few who know about the weapons of mass destruction. Everyone in this room, as well as the president of Russia, respects you, and we still don't know whether similar weapons exist. I am offering you a special position, working with the Office of the President, working with me. I need to be able to pick up the phone, go directly to someone in the field, and get answers."

"The people in this room are tied to the laws of the nation, as they should be. We have made a decision we think best for the country, not to mention our finally possessing the WMDs. You asked whether that issue might harm me in the polls. Maybe, but as I told you, the nation comes first. It has to. Will you do it?"

"Mr. President, I am honored to be considered for such a position and honored that you respect me. However, I am a neurologist, a physician-scientist. I have training for the field, but I am not a field agent. Besides, what about my lab? What about my being a neurologist, seeing patients?"

"Your being a neurologist will help you and therefore us a great deal. You're familiar with biological agents used in terrorism. Look at this botulinum toxin-Q. You understand how that chemical works."

"May I still do research? What if I want to continue to see patients at the National Institutes of Health? I may decide I want to see more patients or maybe less."

"You decide what you want and call me in a few days. Anything you need, we can try to accomplish."

"Thank you, Mr. President. I am honored and pleased to be of service to my country. On another note, as I said earlier, you are truly a great man, a man of substance. I'm not sure how many Americans know how much you place our country first, above your own political career."

"Tell that to the voters in Florida," and the president laughed. Swept had heard the man had a fine sense of humor, and he did.

* * *

Chapter Fifty-three

A CHANGE IN HERITAGE

The *Houston Chronicle* article on Regina Bruxton highlighted how well patients can do in good rehabilitation medicine programs. Fortunately, Regina had no recall of the brutal attack. This loss of memory due to brain injury was a blessing. Also, fortunately, her skills as a surgeon and physician had been spared. What was more than a blessing was her newly found lover, Harold Ranger.

* * *

The Chemist threw away his cocaine paraphernalia. He had learned a great deal over the past several months, especially over the past several weeks. He was glad to get out alive and looked forward to returning to Baghdad. Maybe, he could do some good there, now that there was a new regime.

Since it was Friday evening, the beginning of the Jewish Sabbath, the Chemist lit two candles to thank God. Even though he considered himself a nonobservant Orthodox Jew, he welcomed the opportunity to return to Baghdad, the seat of ancient Mesopotamia. He had lived a lie for too long.

The Chemist no longer felt it necessary to put on any airs of ethnic prejudice. He wanted to live in Baghdad, the birthplace of his parents, and hoped for improvement in his native country. He was glad that no one knew his name.

* * *

Jokhar Gantemirov decided to call Dick Swept. He still had the number. "Remember me?"

"How could I forget? You refused to help us."

"I didn't refuse. I had no idea where the canisters were. I told you that, and I meant it."

"What are you doing with the money?"

"Why did you kill Akhmad?"

"Take a guess. Now, what are you going to do with the money?"

"I decided I'm only going to keep one hundred million. You tell me how I send the rest back."

"Are you having a change of heart? A conscience?"

"Maybe. But if there ever was a man who cared about Chechnya, it was Akhmad. Yet killing all those innocent Russians was a disaster. It was uncalled for. And now, Akhmad is dead. You killed him. Anyway, I figure that if I give you back four hundred million dollars, leaving one hundred for me, that should keep your so-called democratic government happy, so they won't kill me, like they did Akhmad."

"How is it different from the Allistons, the tourists you killed? Or you trying to kill me?"

"I never said I don't kill. And I can't say it bothers me, because most of the time, it doesn't. I killed the Allistons because I had to. You killed Kostokov because you had to. We do what we have to do. One more thing."

"I can guess what it is. Fire away."

"Am I really Jewish?"

"According to the Russians, you are. We wondered about this before, back in your glory days of Pi-Two. I can't be certain President Putin didn't forge the documents, but I think it's for real."

"What a place, this planet."

"It's okay, I won't tell anyone if you don't. But it sure puts things in perspective, doesn't it? One day you're in one group, the next day another."

"It's enough to make a man pensive. You still want the money?"

"Sure. Maybe I can use it to study glutamate receptors."

"What?"

"It's a joke. Gantemirov, one more thing, from me."

"Fire away."

"Let me know how I can reach you. We may work together in the future."

"It would be a pleasure." Gantemirov provided his telephone number and gave his goodbye.

* * *.

The president of the United States was delighted with Dick Swept. "I am pleased you decided to join us. You can do your work with your chemical receptors and see patients at the NIH. Also, we are keeping the four hundred million dollars in a special account for you. The money is at your disposal for any missions that require your participation. I don't anticipate calling you often, but I can't promise. You are a good man, and we need good people on our team."

"Thank you, sir. I appreciate your confidence." Swept said goodbye and then went to Rock Creek Park.

Again, there he was, Larry Leventine. Swept approached him, scowling, himself.

"You, in the wheelchair. You're a jerk, a real jerk," said Swept, out of breath, his hands on his hips.

Leventine stared at Swept. "Stare all you want," continued Swept. "You have this stupid scowl, sitting here, doing nothing, acting as though the world owes you a lot. The world owes you nothing. You sit here reading every day, so you must have some kind of brain that's functioning. Your arms work and you can get around. Get a job and cut the self-indulgence!"

"What do you know about people like me?" said the surprised Leventine.

"Wrong question. It should be, 'What do you know about people like you?' The answer, I am sure, is 'nothing.' I don't feel bad running while you sit, moping. Your sitting here doesn't disenfranchise anyone from their normality. You act like some bullshit intellect, reading all the time. I'm a neurologist, a brain doctor, and I've seen scores of patients sicker than you who walk circles around you. That's all I want to say," and Swept jogged away, leaving a mystified Larry Leventine sitting in his wheelchair, feeling he had lost ammunition.

Two weeks later, when Larry was able to get himself worked into the neurology clinic at the NIH, he was surprised to see Swept. Swept looked at him twice, checking the medical chart.

"Mr. Leventine, glad you could make it. I'm Dr. Dick Swept. Welcome."

Larry Leventine smiled, for the first time as far as Dick Swept could tell.

* * *

Chapter Fifty-four

NOT ENOUGH NAMES

For years, Dick Swept had thoroughly enjoyed reading Lewis Lapham's editorials in *Harper's* magazine. On one occasion, Swept had the honor of meeting Lapham. Swept had anticipated a snickering, snobbish member of the New York intelligentsia but, instead, met a polite, erudite gentleman who was open, friendly, and incredibly knowledgeable.

Lapham reminded Swept of good scientists, men and women not polluted by the top-down thinking of others but, rather, asking questions that sought answers to mechanisms of systems, not just their descriptions.

Swept picked up his *Harper's,* placed his Ketel One on the table, and began to read. The doorman phoned, saying a man, "Stoli," was downstairs, requesting to see him. Swept had no idea why Stoli was there or how he had found him.

Swept, now fervently intent on being cautious following his earlier errors, told the doorman he would meet Stoli downstairs and pocketed his Glock semiautomatic. On his way down to the lobby, in the elevator, he had a subtle feeling he might not have the opportunity to read Lapham's column that evening.

Swept met Stoli in the lobby. It still amazed him how much Stoli looked like his brother, Aleksander Kostokov. The only difference between the twins was that Kostokov always appeared tired, carrying strong lines of strain on his face. Also, Stoli's facial features appeared younger than his dead brother's. Swept shook Stoli's hand, ready to pull out his new Glock 20, 10-mm semiautomatic at any moment. The two walked outside the building.

"What can I do for you?" inquired Swept.

"Tell me about my brother."

"Gantemirov never told you?"

"He told me that he was a great man, a loyal man, dedicated to his work. He was my twin brother. You're the one who killed him. I want to know what you think."

"Truthfully, I don't and didn't think a lot about it, one way or the other. Your brother killed a lot of people. He worked for the KGB. After *glasnost,* when the KGB became the FSB, he joined a splinter group. He saw me once as a patient, using a fake complaint and a fake name. The next time I saw him, he killed my dog and tried to kill me. That's all I can say. Had he killed me instead of my killing him, you might be asking your brother what I was like."

"I don't think so."

"If there are no more questions and you are done, I would like to go back to my reading."

"You think it's as simple as that?"

Swept again recognized, within himself, a growing cynicism, almost wanting to tempt death to come his way. The sensation was exciting, electrifying, even somewhat addicting, but not without risk.

Swept was not pleasant. "Get something straight! Your brother was a murderer. He killed people. I've killed people. Some do it for money, some out of loyalty to their country, others because they probably don't have anything else to do. Do I think your brother was evil? No. Do I think he was a bad man? No! Do I think he's dead? Yes. His side, a bunch of guys and one woman wanting to take over the world, lost. Plain and simple, they lost. The good guys won. And I don't think the good guys always win. But lucky for the world, the good guys did win this time. If you've got a problem with that, you work it out."

Swept continued, Stoli listening almost too politely, "There's a man who sits in a wheelchair all day long in the park. For years, maybe decades, he hasn't worked his life out, but recently, he's trying to. Talk to him, if you want. Me, I'm going upstairs for a drink and to read my magazine."

With that, Swept turned and went back to the elevator, prepared at any second to turn around and empty his semiautomatic into Stoli's head, should Stoli menace him.

Stoli said nothing and walked away.

Swept thought about having too many people in his life whose names he did not know. There was "the Chemist,"

"Stoli," and no one ever called the president of the United States by his name, always "Mr. President," except for the media, which referred to him by last name only, often without respect. Life was becoming too confusing.

Swept went back to his apartment, pleased he could return to his reading and his drink. When he entered the apartment, his answering machine beeped, indicating someone had called.

"Richard, Valerie. I hate talking into these things. I've been assigned to, of all places, Chechnya. Figure that out. I just want to be certain we're friends. Anytime you want to pick up the phone, you can find me. You're a wonderful man, and I hope we see each other again. Right now, I'm packing for Grozny and have a lot of work to do. Goodbye"

* * *

The following day, Swept used his contacts in the government to obtain information. He spoke to the CIA director and soon had data from the Russian Ministry of Education. It was not difficult for the agency, especially with their improved cooperation with Putin, to obtain more sealed packets of records on Aleksander Kostokov and his brother's adoption.

During the year Kostokov was born, a bad year for Russian crops, necessitating an alteration of another infamous five-year plan, Russia imported more wheat from Canada. Money was scarce, winters were cold and without heat, and many families were unable to provide for their children. A family named Kostokov had triplets and could not afford to raise them. The hardworking father was unable to make ends meet in the Soviet economic system. After one of the triplets died from pneumonia, the impoverished Kostokov parents, terrified they could not provide food, shelter, and health care for their remaining two sons, offered one of their children for adoption.

There was a scandal, known among very few, involving members of the Adoption Section at the Ministry of Education who transferred babies to orphanages in Romania. Romanian orphanages frequently had babies available for adoption. Many people from the West adopted these children, at a high price.

Stoli, whose real name was Yuri Kostokov, was sold with other babies on the black market to an orphanage in Romania. The Kostokovs now had money and were able to get their child, Aleksander, into the best schools. Later, Aleksander qualified for the KGB, a conduit for advancement in communist Soviet Union. Aleksander Kostokov was very bright and advanced rapidly in the KGB.

Swept thanked the agency for their help and decided, if Stoli ever contacted him again, he would share this information. Meanwhile, who knew what Stoli was doing now, or even how he got into the United States? Swept would check that out tomorrow, but he doubted Stoli was a danger. If he were, the Company could pull him in.

* * *

Chapter Fifty-five

AGENTS OF THE DIALECTIC

Jokhar Gantemirov decided to visit Israel, the land of his genetic code. He found himself increasingly more interested in history than politics and landed a job as a guide in the Museum of the Diaspora in Tel Aviv. At least for a while, this would prove interesting. Gantemirov had enough money to last a long time and was not oblivious to the fact that one day he could prove useful to the United States or the Israelis or the Palestinians. Gantemirov had a lot of thinking to do.

* * *

Swept flew to Houston to see his friends at the Houston Medical Complex. It was especially nice to see Michael Drake, who was still practicing superb internal medicine but contemplating hospital administrative work due to the hassles of dealing with insurance companies, PPOs, HMOs, and bureaucratic grief.

Swept and Drake dined that evening at Fleming's. Drake discussed some interesting cases. The medical school had recently affiliated with the Duluth Foundation for Improved Mental Health, a national organization treating psychiatric problems of the ultrarich, and asked Drake to see a patient.

"Richard, this is truly amazing. The man is a paranoid schizophrenic who complained of headaches for years, had severe clubfoot, and hated physicians. He kept saying, 'No one helps me with my headaches. You're all against me, trying to destroy me.' On several occasions, in the midst of his incessant complaining about his long-standing headaches, mixed with his paranoid schizophrenic aberrations, he said he killed the president of the American Medical Association. The Texas College of Medicine's famous academic psychiatrists were unable to mollify his complaints. In an effort to quiet him, and probably make the nurses stop complaining, the psychiatrists decided to consult me. Guess what I found?"

"I shudder to consider it."

"I, a lowly practitioner, figured how do we know what's paranoia and what isn't? I found abnormalities on his neurological examination. The psychiatrists must not have looked in his eyes. There it was papilledema, swelling of his optic nerve. I ordered an MRI of his head, and you guessed it—he had a giant brain tumor, benign, a meningioma. He's probably had it for years."

Drake continued, "Then guess what I did? I called the police, who brought in the FBI because of the Stickman X events surrounding the AMA assassination, and sure enough, he's the guy who murdered the AMA president in Aspen. No one ever listened to him. That's why the medical school doctors need people like us practitioners: at least we know how to examine patients! Who cares if we don't do research, we're good doctors."

"I didn't fly to Houston to argue about the Texas College of Medicine and the hospital. And I never doubted you're a good physician. Did the psychiatrists consult neurology?"

"Of course not. That way, in case they missed something, they wouldn't have to be embarrassed. You would think they'd be embarrassed that an internist made the diagnosis. Pretty amazing, don't you think?"

"Yes, I do. Can I change the subject?"

"Sure."

"How's Regina?"

"Better than you or I. Now, that was a true tragedy. It's good that Regina has no recall of the attack. And here she is, happy as ever, with that jerk of a former chairman of yours. And here we are, dining alone, at Fleming's. Go figure!"

Swept decided not to make futher comment on Regina. "You know what else amazes me, Michael?"

Drake looked inquisitively at Swept.

"The Stickman X movement dried up. For a while, the media talked about stuttering and Stickman X. Now, no one says anything. One day a disease is popular, or a movement is popular. The next day, it's history. No one cared about stuttering before, and they don't care about it now. Whatever publicity Stickman X achieved for stuttering or research in healthcare, it's gone."

"Richard," Drake inquired, "did the government find out who was responsible for the attacks on hospitals and medical schools?"

"Yes. It turns out that a group of women from London were responsible, at least for most of them. After they were caught, the movement lost its energy and dried up. There was also a person in Scotland, Edinburgh, involved in some property damage and, probably, the killing of the pandas."

Swept thought about how decentralized and independent the Stickman X movement had become. Yet, when the nucleus behind the movement, namely, Jeremiah MacGregor and Jennifer Pettigrew, disappeared, the movement seemed to lose energy and its alleged splendor.

Swept also kept to himself that the government knew in which attacks Jennifer Pettigrew had directly participated, since an alert medical coroner had found the DM 3382 GPS microchip in the dead woman's vagina, enabling the CIA to back trace her whereabouts through the data saved in the satellite tracking system.

Michael Drake thought for a moment. "Everything is unstable. Nothing lasts. All systems, health, education, everything, are internally unstable. That's why the health-care system is falling apart. That's why nothing works and these things happen"

"How's that?" inquired Swept.

"How's that? One group or force or sector or whatever you want to call it wants health care at a low price. The other force wants to deliver it at a large profit. One force despises the clinicians, low-lives like me. The opposing force salutes research and brilliant scientists like you. One force wants us to die at home, inexpensively. Another says being alive is a blessing and we should do everything possible to maintain life. Everything is a conflict, sort of like a dialectic."

"Well, here's to dialectics," and Swept saluted his friend with his vodka, thinking about conflicts in which he had recently engaged and their internal dialectics.

* * *

Harold Ranger was another matter. The man had undergone a metamorphosis. He was actually pleasant and had no qualms about marrying a woman who had been Swept's former lover. Nor was he embarrassed that Regina became pregnant prior to marriage, a fact any observer could deduce, since the couple married on little notice and the plastic surgeon soon had the physiognomy of carrying a child.

Ranger was happy for Regina and her full complement of chromosomes. Regina was happy with Harold Ranger and that she was going to be a mother.

Regina Bruxton, M.D., soon found herself taking time off from her busy practice to look for baby clothes and come home early to be with her husband. Swept telephoned to congratulate her.

"Regina, I offer my warmest congratulations. Harold Ranger is a wonderful man."

"You have no idea how wonderful."

"Perhaps not, but I respect him, and you. I wish you two nothing but the best."

"Thank you. How's everything in your life?"

"Personal or professional?"

"Both."

Swept could have told Regina about Valerie, Ricki, Louise, even Genevieve. He could have mentioned glutamate research, directly working with the president of the United States, and his personally delivering the weapons of mass destruction. But Swept did none of these things. "Actually, Regina, I'm just kicking along, just kicking along."

"Well, don't kick too hard, you'll become unstable."

"Like a dialectic?"

"I'm not that highbrow, Richard. You be well. Goodbye."

I'm not that highbrow? "Fair enough. Goodbye."

* * *

Swept called Harold Ranger and made arrangements to meet with him to extend best wishes.

"Richard," said Ranger, "you should see the work we're doing in the MAD clinic. There are several patients with neuromuscular disease who have chemical abnormalities in their neuromuscular system, and we're going to unravel all of them. Years ago, people looked at MAD, but so many patients and commercially driven doctors jumped on the bandwagon that little progress was made. We even recently discovered a family of patients with amyotrophic lateral sclerosis who have MAD deficiencies and also lost half their cytochrome C enzyme. There may be a group of patients whose ALS is triggered by this enzyme. It's amazing!"

Swept had never seen Harold Ranger so excited about patients. He was happy for Ranger and wondered whether his former chairman would be happy for him, were he to know all that Swept had recently accomplished. Swept looked at the man, under whom he had trained, knowing now he would be working for another leader, the president of the United States.

Swept said goodbye to Ranger and his friends in Houston and flew back to Washington. He felt excited but still did not feel whole. When he arrived at his address, there she was, waiting outside the building: Ricki Hardson.

"Richard, I called the lab. They said you were out of town and would be back today. Things didn't work out for me."

"Ricki, I . . ."

"Richard, don't say anything. I've given this a lot of thought. I love you. You love me. We can talk about marriage later. Let's go upstairs."

"Ricki, I'm not really against marriage—"

"Yes, you are. It's okay. Other things, other men, didn't work out for me. Let's talk."

Ricki, do you know what a dialectic is?"

"I haven't a clue."

"Good. Let's go upstairs."

* * *

LaVergne, TN USA
30 December 2009

168525LV00003B/2/A